A SUDDEN SEDUCTION

Travis encircled her waist with his hands and pulled her closer. "So what were you looking for in my bureau, Suzanne?"

She laughed softly and tossed her head back, sending a cascading wave of dark curls spreading across her shoulders. "Why, a shirt to use as a nightgown, silly. But you came up too soon."

Travis decided to see just how far she'd go with her little charade before she panicked. Then he'd find out the truth. He pulled her hard up against him, crushing her body to the length of his. His arms wrapped her in an embrace that nearly stole the air from her lungs. "Umm, what an enticing image that invokes," he whispered. "You, in nothing more than my shirt, and in my bed. Absolutely irresistible." Travis lowered his head and pressed his lips to the tantalizing swell of bosom revealed above the low-cut décolletage of her gown.

He felt a shudder wrack her body at the intimate touch and smiled to himself. "But if you had told me you were coming up here, Suzanne, I would have come sooner," he said, his voice growing husky with the passion that her nearness was instilling within him.

Suzanne fought the swirl of desire that suddenly swept over her at the feel of Travis's lips on her breast. "I wanted to surprise you," she whispered, afraid that if she spoke aloud he would notice the quavering she was certain was evident in her tone.

He pressed against her, crushing her skirts and crinolines. His lips covered hers hungrily, ravishing her senses, demanding her surrender . . .

* * *

HEARTS DENIED

"A keeper! Superb action-packed story with many exciting twists and turns. An outstanding saga from a master of her genre."

—*Rendezvous*

". . . a refreshingly original and delightfully intriguing western romance."

—*Affaire de Coeur*

CHERYL
BIGGS

Hearts Denied

[handwritten inscription: I hope you enjoy reading your two ... like he did mine. Thanks! Cheryl Biggs]

ZEBRA BOOKS
KENSINGTON PUBLISHING CORP.

ZEBRA BOOKS are published by

Kensington Publishing Corp.
850 Third Avenue
New York, NY 10022

First Printing: December, 1994

Printed in the United States of America

Chapter One

Virginia City, Nevada
Spring 1862

"I told you, Charlie, I'm not a joiner," Travis said. He pulled a gold watch from the pocket of his silver-threaded black vest, flipped its cover open with a flick of his thumb and glanced down at the roman numerals painted on the face of the timepiece.

"Judge Terry's not too happy that you keep . . ." Charles Mellroy glanced over both shoulders to make sure they weren't being overheard, and downed the last of the whiskey in his shot glass before banging it down on the bar and continuing, ". . . that you keep turning down his invitations to attend the Knights meetings, Travis."

"Then maybe he should stop asking." Travis snapped the lid of the watch closed and returned it to the pocket of his vest. He tugged on the silk lapels of the black broadcloth cutaway jacket that stretched taut over his broad shoulders and tapered inward to end at his waist, straightened the cuffs of his white shirt, and glanced into

the huge gilt-framed mirror over the bar to straighten
the black string tie at his throat and run a hand over the
dark waves of his hair. He was ready. "The South has
my support, Charlie, and David knows that. I just don't
give it the same way he does. Now, if you'll excuse me,
I have to meet a stage."

Travis pushed through the swinging doors of the
Mountain Queen and walked out onto the raised and
shaded boardwalk that fronted the saloon. "Where the
hell is that stage?" He stepped to the edge of the walk
and stared down C Street, second of the two "official"
main streets of Virginia City. It was a sea of activity as
some miners coming off their shifts flooded into the
more than dozen saloons that dotted the narrow thoroughfare, while others going on shift were just leaving
breakfast houses, hotels, and boardinghouses and trudg-
ing down to the mines whose tunnels bore directly beneath the streets they lived on. Heavy ore-laden drays,
buckboards, carriages, and saddle horses were tied up to
hitching racks, pillars, and water troughs while still others moved along the street.

A flicker of green on the boardwalk directly across the
street caught Travis's attention. A smile drew his lips upward as he watched the woman move from the shadows
of the overhanging roof, the brilliant emerald threads of
her satin gown and its black lace trim intensifying as she
stepped into the sunlight. The long strands of her chest-
nut mane had been piled high on her head, green-and-
black ribbons entwined within the curls, and then both
hair and ribbons allowed to cascade loosely down her
back and over her shoulders, drawing the spectator's
gaze to the daringly low-cut neckline of her gown and

the generous swell of golden bosom that dwelt there. But then, that was Magnolia's intent.

She blew him a kiss and laughed. The rough, almost bawdy sound drifted to him above the din of noise made by the daily routine of the city's inhabitants.

Travis chuckled and waved back. Magnolia Rochelle's saloon, the Silver Lady, was located directly across the street from his own Mountain Queen and had proven one of his fiercest competitors, yet Magnolia and Travis had managed to remain friends ... good friends. He smiled. *Very* good friends. It helped that they were both from New Orleans, that their sympathies concerning the war that was tearing the country apart were in alliance, and that, in spite of the fact she was at least four or five years older than Travis, she had one of the most delicious bodies in Virginia City.

"So, *mon cher,*" Magnolia called out, "where is this little songbird you are importing to put my Silver Lady out of business?"

Travis shrugged. "The stage is late." He glanced down C Street again. A cloud of dust could be seen in the distance, rising from the curve of the mountain road that led into the city. Travis's smile widened and he added, "But I think it's about to arrive."

Magnolia followed his gaze. "Well, *mon cher*, if you find that your little canary has changed her mind and flown elsewhere, perhaps you will still consider my offer, yes?" Her lips curved in a seductive smile.

Travis laughed. "We're both too headstrong and stubborn to ever be partners, Magnolia."

"Ah, a pity," Magnolia said, "but then one never knows what the future may bring, yes, *mon cher?*"

The stagecoach from Sacramento came into view at the end of C Street.

"I'll wager my future is bringing Georgette Lindsay to the Mountain Queen right this minute, Magnolia, and I'll have all the customers tonight."

Magnolia feigned a pout. "Then I will be all alone."

"You're never alone, Maggie," Travis said. "But if you do get lonely tonight," he winked, "or any night, you know where my room is."

She threw him a saucy grin, then both turned toward the approaching stagecoach as the pounding of hooves, rattling of leather straps, harnesses, wood and chain rigging, and creaking wheels filled the air.

The stage driver, a grizzled old man in buckskins, sat in his seat high above the coach, the thick leather reins held securely wrapped around his gnarled fingers. He slammed a moccasin-encased foot down on the brake pedal and pulled back hard on the reins. "Whoa there, you bone-headed, good-for-nothin' beasts!" he yelled gruffly. His foot pressed harder on the brake pedal as his body stiffened and he leaned back over the top of the coach, drawing up the reins. "Whoa, damn it! Whoa!"

Six well-muscled horses, their brown bodies sleek with perspiration, tossed their heads about in protest causing their long black manes to whip at the air. The driver threw his full weight against the coach, reaching down to draw the reins even tighter, his foot pressing even harder on the pedal. The huge wheels of the stage creaked loudly in response. The horses looked about wildly, their brown eyes wide and staring. They snorted and finally pranced to a halt. The coach rocked on its leather shocks as the wheels ground to a standstill in the dirt street.

An agent ran from the express office that occupied the building next to the Mountain Queen and shouted a greeting to the driver. The man wrapped the reins quickly around the handle of the brake pedal, jumped down from his seat, and reached to open the passenger door.

Travis ambled forward, a wide smile on his face. Several months ago he had contracted for Georgette Lindsay to play at the Mountain Queen. Though he had never met her, or even *seen* her in person, he felt confident in the decision. She had come highly recommended from acquaintances who had witnessed her performance in San Francisco and Denver. When her manager had contacted him and said she was interested in playing Virginia City on her way north, he had been more than happy to oblige. Travis had lofty hopes that she would bring in a good portion of the kind of money his brother, Trace, had written that the Confederacy needed.

"Good luck, *mon cher,*" Magnolia called out.

Travis waved to her, but his attention, and his eyes, were on the door of the stagecoach, which was just swinging open. The driver's hand held the knob, but just above it, resting lightly on the bottom frame of the door's glassless window, was a delicately graceful hand encased in a glovelette of dark-brown lace which allowed her slim fingers to remain bare.

Months ago, when in San Francisco, Travis had seen a poster of Georgette Lindsay and had found her not only beautiful, but hauntingly familiar. But he knew those announcement posters never were quite accurate, and had shrugged off the feeling that he'd seen her somewhere before.

The coach swayed slightly as she placed a dainty foot, only momentarily visible beneath a mound of ruffled crinolines and the percale hem of her cocoa-colored traveling suit, onto the boarding step and emerged. Beneath a closely narrow-brimmed straw hat adorned with a trail of yellow and brown feathers and ribbon, her dark-brown hair had been pulled up and a fall of sausage curls allowed to drape one shoulder. As the sunlight touched them, the darkness of the curls suddenly shone with red-gold highlights.

Travis caught a glimpse of her profile and knew instantly the poster he had seen of her had indeed not done her justice. Her cheekbones were exquisitely carved curves of grace, her nose pert yet aristocratic, and the creamy richness of her skin, accentuated by earth-rich darkness of the swirls of hair beneath the feathered bonnet, reminded him of a day-old gardenia, magnificent in its whiteness, yet touched by just the softest hint of gold.

Travis paused on the boardwalk directly in front and slightly above her and bent to offer his hand. Thickly ruched brown lashes fluttered heavenward as she raised her head to look up at him.

"Why, thank you, Travis," she said.

Travis froze. He felt her fingers come to rest lightly upon his hand, heard the soft, almost musical quality of her voice, and was faintly aware of the fragrance of jasmine that seemed to surround her and reach out to him. His voice was caught somewhere deep in his throat, paralyzed by shock and disbelief, while his eyes met hers, midnight gray fusing with winter's morning blue, melding, bringing back a rush of memories he had thought long forgotten.

It had been seven years since he'd seen Suzanne Forteaux, since he had refused to marry her and left New Orleans.

He felt his body stiffen, every muscle, every cell filled with tension. He stared deeper into her blue eyes. She smiled and Travis jerked from his musings and chided himself. This was not Suzanne. Something about this woman reminded him of Suzanne, that was all. Her eyes. That was it, her eyes. Such a clear, brilliant blue. He smiled at the beautiful creature climbing from the stagecoach . . . at Georgette Lindsay.

Lifting the velvet corded skirt of her traveling suit with her free hand while leaving the other encased within his, she stepped beside him onto the boardwalk. "Travis?" she said again, when he failed to speak. Her eyes sparkled in rivalry of the afternoon sky.

He drew on the strong self-reserve that was such a part of him, forcing a composure that he was truly far from feeling. "I'm sorry. I thought for a moment you were someone el—I mean . . ." He shook his head and bowed slightly, lifting her hand and pressing his lips to the gentle curve of her fingers. "I'm sorry. Let me start over. Welcome to Virginia City, Miss Lindsay."

A hint of amusement and satisfaction twinkled in her eyes and, as if she knew what he'd been thinking, she said, "You *were* right, Travis."

He frowned as his mind swirled in confusion. She kept calling him Travis. She knew who he was and yet how could she know? They had never met before. His mind searched for an answer and found none other than she had assumed, because she was going to sing at his saloon, that he would meet her stage. Yet she seemed so sure. His eyes shadowed with further puzzlement. And her words about him being right . . . She couldn't be inferring what he thought.

She smiled.

Travis stared down at her for a long moment, a moment that brought with it a bustle of activity around them, punctuated by a series of grumbled curses from the stage driver as he unloaded her luggage, as well as that of the other passengers in the coach.

It couldn't be. No. It was impossible. And yet she was standing before him, her hand still settled intimately within his. And finally, he knew, as she had said, his first impression had been right. "Suzanne?"

She nodded. "Yes, Travis. Suzanne."

"Suzanne Forteaux? From New Orleans?"

She smiled and nodded again. "Yes. Suzanne Forteaux from New Orleans." She gave an exaggerated sigh and held a hand over her heart. "The girl you left behind so long ago." A merry chuckle escaped her lips.

He shook his head. "No. I don't believe it. What? I mean, how . . . ?" He steeled himself against the surge of conflicting emotions that had erupted within him at the first sight of her. She was one of the most beautiful women he had ever seen . . . and, in spite of her smiles and laughter, she must thoroughly despise him. He couldn't blame her. She had good reason. Excellent reason. "What are you doing here, Suzanne?" Travis forced himself to say. "I mean, here in Virginia City? What are you doing here?"

Chapter Two

Suzanne smiled sweetly and fluttered her dark lashes up at him. "Why, Travis, you contracted with my manager for me to play your saloon, the Mountain Queen. Remember?"

Her words hit him like a cannon ball dropping on his head. He stared at her in disbelief. "Contracted you?" He shook his head. "No, I'm sorry, Suzanne. I mean, there must be some misunderstanding, some mistake. I contracted for Georgette Lindsay to play the Mountain Queen."

Suzanne laughed lightly, the sound wafting from her lips like the sweet, golden song of a spring sunrise. "But Travis, I *am* Georgette Lindsay."

He felt his mouth drop open in surprise. He hadn't seen her in seven years, yet now he realized why her poster had seemed so familiar, even though she was no longer the shy sixteen-year-old girl he had last seen. Suzanne Forteaux had grown up, and she'd become breathtakingly beautiful in the process.

For only a moment, Travis allowed his mind to hurtle back in time to the summer of 1855. His father, Thomas

Braggette, had seen to it that a rumor circulated through town, a vicious rumor claiming Travis had seduced Suzanne Forteaux, and as a result, she was carrying his child. Travis had been outraged when'd he heard the gossip. He'd damned his father, who had merely laughed and then blustered that he expected Travis to do the only honorable thing and marry the girl. Suzanne, it just so happened, was the only daughter of Landon Forteaux, one of the wealthiest men in New Orleans, and someone who could have lent considerable support to Thomas Braggette's political ambitions. It came as no surprise that the woman Travis had been in love with then and planned to marry had promptly rejected him. Travis defied his father and refused to marry Suzanne, knowing that if she *was* with child, it was not his. But Thomas Braggette was a stubborn and determined man, and went on with his plans.

So, on the very day of the wedding, Travis had done the only thing he could think of: he'd run away. He'd left Shadows Noir Plantation, left his family, and left Suzanne standing at the altar.

"Travis, for heaven's sake," Suzanne said, pulling her hand free and slipping her arm through the crook of his bent one. She chuckled softly as her eyes sparkled with amusement. "Close your mouth before you catch a fly."

The stage driver tipped his hat to her. "That there's all your bags, ma'am."

"Thank you."

Travis flipped the driver a coin.

As the old driver nodded and walked into the express office, Suzanne turned to look back at Travis. "Well, are you going to show me to the hotel, or do I have to find it on my own?"

"Suzzzzzzanne."

The voice, which sounded more like the whining drone of a lovesick coyote, drew the attention of both of them. Travis looked back at the stagecoach. A small, wiry man with a protruding stomach, and feet and hands that looked smaller than any woman's, emerged from the coach. His gray pinstriped suit was slightly rumpled, though the stiffly starched collar of his shirt looked as if it were strangling him. A black bowler hat sat somewhat askew on his head, and a pair of tiny spectacles perched on the end of his thin, pointed nose were covered with dust.

"Oh, Clarence." She looked back at Travis sheepishly. "Travis, I'm sorry. In the excitement of seeing you again, I . . ." She shrugged. ". . . forgot my manners. Travis, this is Clarence Lonchet, my manager."

Travis held out his hand. "Glad to make your acquaintance, Mr. Lonchet. I'm Travis Braggette."

"Clarence," Suzanne interrupted hurriedly. "Help Addie before she falls."

The tiny man frowned at the request but turned back to the stagecoach and grabbed at the arm of a woman who was trying to step from the coach to the boardwalk.

"Oh, Mr. Lonchet, I can't seem to get my . . ." The heel of her shoe slipped off of the edge of the coach and caught in a ruffle of her bunched-up crinolines. She grabbed for the doorframe.

"Addie, for heaven's sake!" Lonchet squealed. He threw up one hand and began to flail the air in an effort to keep her billowing cape from draping over his head.

Travis stepped forward to help just as the woman's weight, and a jerk on her hand from the flailing manager, pulled her forward. As her free hand clawed the air in a search for something to grab to prevent her fall, a look of panic flashed across her face and a shriek escaped her lips.

"Addie!" Suzanne gasped.

Travis caught Addie's arm, grabbed a handful of gray muslin skirt and yanked her upward. Clarence found himself suddenly in the way of a flying female. Sputtering obscenities, he received a faceful of swelling muslin and a foot smashed against his shoulder. His bowler went flying as, thrown off balance, he landed on his rear end in the dirt street.

"Oh, Addie," Suzanne asked. "Are you all right?"

The petite woman brushed her skirts into place, tugged at her long bell sleeves, and reached up to tuck in a brown curl that had fallen out of place from beneath her prim charcoal-gray bonnet. She smiled widely and answered Suzanne, but kept her gaze pinned to Travis. "Yes, Miss Suzanne, I'm fine, thanks to this gentleman."

"Of all the clumsy . . ." Clarence climbed onto the boardwalk, his face a contortion of fury.

"Travis, this is my maid and personal assistant, Adelina Hays," Suzanne said. "Addie, this is Mr. Travis Braggette, the gentlemen who owns the Mountain Queen."

Everyone ignored Clarence.

"Pleased to meet you, Miss Hays."

"Oh," Addie gushed. "Call me Addie, Mr. Braggette. Everyone does." She thrust her hand out at Travis.

Travis took Addie's hand in his, lifted it, and pressed his lips to her fingers. "My pleasure, Addie."

"Ohhh!" She batted her eyelashes and looked as if she were going to swoon right into his arms.

"Pleasure? Hah!" Clarence said. He slapped at his clothes, creating a small cloud of dust, and glowered up at Travis. "You didn't happen to mention in your wires that Virginia City sat on top of a mountain peak, Mr. Braggette. Or that this area was knee deep in snow at this time of the year despite the fact that it's almost spring. Or that it was such a harrowing ride up the mountain. *Or* that your stage line is so . . . so antiquated."

"Clarence!" Suzanne admonished. "It wasn't that bad."

"Oh, honestly, Suzanne, the coach didn't even have leather awnings, for heaven's sake." He removed his spectacles and pulled a handkerchief from his vest pocket, flapped it in the air dramatically, and then began to clean the dusty lenses. "We couldn't even keep out the wind. I guess we can only thank the Lord that it didn't snow or we'd be drenched." He gave an exaggerated shudder. "The seats! Why, the padding was almost nonexistent. And that driver, all the way here he kept cursing horribly and snapping the reins to try to get the horses to go faster and—"

"I was under the assumption, Mr. Lonchet, that Georgette, uh, I mean, Suzanne, had played quite a number of theaters in the West," Travis interrupted.

"She has, but nothing as . . ." Clarence waved a hand in the air, indicating the town, "out of the way as this. I mean, it's as if you're out in the middle of nowhere and . . ."

"Clarence!" Suzanne interjected.

Travis was struggling to keep a lid on his temper. After all, it was Lonchet who had contacted him about Georgette playing Virginia City, not the other way around. "Virginia City is only fifteen miles from Carson City, Mr. Lonchet. Not that far really."

"Well, it certainly seemed farther. That mountain road up here is ghastly. Simply ghastly. I thought we were going to plunge off the road and plummet to the depths of hell any min—"

"Clarence!" Suzanne said again, her tone a bit harsher.

"We've played California. And Texas. And even in the Arizona Territory, but we've never had to . . ." He whipped the bowler from his head, revealing a pate as bald and pink as a newborn baby's rear end and framed with a circle of wispy-stranded light brown hair, screwed up his lips in dismay, and began to wipe at the hat with his handkerchief. "Oh, look at this. It's positively ruined. Ruined!"

"Clarence!" Suzanne cautioned one last time.

But he continued on, ignoring her admonishment. "And I feel as if I've been wallowing in dirt myself. Just look at my clothes. Look at them. All that mud and slush the wheels threw up, and dust, and no awnings, and . . ."

"I'm sure the hotel will be happy to draw you a bath," Suzanne said.

"As they should be, for the price they charge for a room." Clarence sniffed. "I should have insisted that the hotel bill be covered in your contract, Mr. Braggette." He snapped the bowler back onto his head.

Addie rolled her eyes.

Travis felt his simmering temper begin to boil like a cauldron of soup left ignored. He had formed an immediate opinion of Suzanne's manager, and it wasn't a favorable one. The man's voice was more like an annoying snivel echoing from an empty nasal tunnel, and his attitude left quite a lot to be desired.

"If Suzanne's performance is as good as I've been led to believe, Mr. Lonchet," Travis said stiffly, "and brings in the profits I expect, I'd be glad to pay for *her* room at the hotel. And that of Miss Hays, of course. *You* are welcome to stay in one of the rooms above the saloon."

Clarence glared at Travis. "Above the saloon?" His thin brows soared skyward. "Stay in a room above a saloon? I should say not."

Travis shrugged. "Suit yourself." He turned to Suzanne and offered his arm. "I'll send someone back for your bags. Can I show you to the hotel now?"

"Please."

He offered an arm to Addie. "Miss Hays?"

"Oh, Mr. Braggette, how gracious," she gushed, and threw a superior look at Clarence Lonchet.

The quartet proceeded toward the Union Belle, Travis walking between Suzanne and Addie, Clarence scurrying along behind them and mumbling a string of pithy oaths which Travis ignored and the women pretended not to hear.

Travis threw a furtive glimpse at Suzanne. It had been a shock coming face-to-face with her after all these years. An even greater shock to find out she was the woman he'd hired to sing at the Mountain Queen. He glanced past Addie and into the window of the general store they were passing. Suzanne's reflection met his eyes. He marveled at the change in her. She bore no resemblance to the sixteen-year-old girl he remembered and had left standing at the altar of the St. Louis Cathedral on that long-ago spring day. A surge of the old guilt washed over him and he fought to ignore it.

Suzanne Forteaux had definitely grown up. Where once, as best his memory served him, there had been only straight lines, there were now subtle curves, and where her limbs had been gangly, she was now a picture of grace and litheness. His eyes raked over her, moving from the high collar of her gown, a sheer covering of lace that stretched from just above her breasts to her throat and was gathered in an array of ruffles secured by a brown velvet ribbon and a cameo brooch, to the curve of her breasts, to the narrow breadth of her waist. And since he couldn't see beneath the folds of her traveling skirt and petticoats, his imagination supplied the picture of well-turned hips and slender, long legs.

The window suddenly turned to wooden wall. Travis looked back and found himself ready to plunge off the boardwalk as the end of it loomed forth only a step away. He said a quick and silent prayer of thanks, helped Suzanne and Addie descend, and guided the two women across the busy and dusty street to the Union Belle Hotel.

"Land almighty, Travis, where'd you get such pretty young things?" Mavis Beale called out.

Travis smiled at the hotel owner's wife, all three hundred pounds of her. "Mrs. Beale, this is . . ." he looked quickly at Suzanne, "Miss Georgette Lindsay. She's come to sing in the Mountain Queen."

Mavis's eyes narrowed slightly. "Sing, huh?"

"And this is her maid, Addie Hays."

Mavis grabbed two keys from behind the desk and, taking hold of Suzanne's arm with one hand and Addie's with the other, began to usher the women upstairs. "Where's their satchels, Travis?" she called back over her shoulder.

"Hank will bring them over."

"Freddie, fetch me up some hot water for these ladies so's they can bathe."

"Yes, Ma," a young male voice hollered out from a doorway behind the desk.

"And hurry it up."

"Yes, Ma."

"Mrs. Beale," Travis called after her. "Mr. Lonchet, Miss Lindsay's manager, also needs a room."

"Well then, give him a key," Mavis called down, never missing a step.

Travis chuckled and walked around behind the desk.

"But I want a bath drawn, too," Clarence wailed, his gaze pinned to the wide girth of Mavis Beale's back as she mounted the stairs.

Travis tossed him the key. "I'm sure she'll get around to you, Lonchet, in good time."

Clarence scrambled to catch the key, losing his bowler again as he did. The hat rolled across the floor on its rim, bounced into the iron fender before the lobby's fireplace, and settled onto the rough-planked floor. "Now look what you've done," he snapped, and hurried to pick it up. He brushed off a few ashes from the crown as he gave Travis a scathing look. "Does that . . . that cow of a woman call this service?"

Travis's amusement with the situation disappeared instantly. His eyes narrowed and his jaw tightened in anger. "Mavis Beale is a good woman, Lonchet, and well liked around here. You'd do best to remember that, and pay some mind to who you're calling names. Of course, if you don't like the service around here, you can always stay at the Queen and serve yourself."

Clarence slapped the bowler back onto his head and

turned to stalk off, then suddenly stopped and looked back at Travis. His face was a mask of apology. "I'm sorry, Mr. Braggette," he said, surprising Travis with his abrupt change of mood. "You're right. I *have* been rude. Terribly rude."

Travis merely glared, having no urge to readily forgive the man.

"It was my idea for Georgette to play here, I admit, so I have no excuse to complain. Please accept my apologies." He smiled sheepishly. "I guess that ride up here just frightened me beyond reason."

Just beyond the open door of the hotel, standing in the shadows of the boardwalk's overhanging roof, Magnolia Rochelle watched Suzanne Forteaux as she ascended the narrow staircase. A slight frown pulled at Magnolia's brow and one hand, hidden within the voluminous folds of her green satin skirt, clenched into a fist. "Now, my little songbird," she whispered, "it remains to be seen if your brother is indeed more important to you than Travis Braggette."

Chapter Three

Suzanne settled into a brocade-covered ladies' chair before the fireplace. After nearly shivering herself silly on the ride over the mountain from Carson City and clenching her teeth together to keep them from clattering, the heat from the fire felt like a godsend. She quickly unlaced her shoes and slipped them off, then placed her feet close to the grate's brass fender, stretched out her hands, wiggled her toes, and smiled patiently as she endured Mavis Beale's incessant chatter. The woman bustled around the room drawing back curtains, fluffing pillows and opening the doors of a tall armoire she called a wardrobe.

"Oh, you'll have a full house every night at the Mountain Queen, Miss Lindsay, yes, you will," Mavis said. She pulled the bed's white cotton coverlet back and tucked it beneath the pillows. "There ain't a whole lotta ladies here in Virginia City, I can tell you that. One for every couple hundred men, I figure. And every one of them will want to get an eyeful of you and hear that sweet voice of yours. Yes, ma'am." She turned and smiled. "The men, I mean."

Sunlight streamed in through the tall window beside Mavis Beale and settled on her gray-streaked carrot-red hair, turning the wild mound to an explosion of fire and ice about her round face. Mavis pushed several way-ward locks away from her cheeks with a pudgy hand and attempted to tuck them into the chignon high on her crown, but they immediately slipped back out, their color accentuating the generous sprinkling of freckles covering her face. Hazel eyes danced with interest and curiosity.

Suzanne smiled but didn't respond. She was too tired, and still too cold.

"You grow up in the theater, Miss Lindsay?" Mavis waved a dismissing hand at herself the moment the words left her mouth. "Oh, never mind me, being nosy and all. Ain't none of my business where you grew up." She started for the door, then paused as her son entered with two steaming buckets of water. "Oh, Freddie, you're back. Good." Mavis watched as her son poured the water into the green slipper tub that stood on a small wooden pedestal in one corner of the room.

Suzanne thanked the woman, hoping that was the end of it and the two of them would leave. She was road-weary and wanted nothing more than to relax in the hot water and then lie down.

"Well, with the first two buckets of water, and now these two, I guess you've got enough for your bath," Mavis said. "We'll just run along now and attend to that gentleman fella who came with you." She turned to her son. "What room did Travis put him in, Freddie?"

"Thank you, Mrs. Beale," Suzanne said again.

Mavis waved a hand at her as she began to close the door. "Oh, just call me Mavis, honey. Everybody around here does. Mrs. Beale makes me think my William's mother is hovering over my shoulder." She chuckled. "And believe me, that ain't a sight I want to see again."

Mavis Beale's laughter echoed down the long hallway.

Suzanne sighed, removed the jacket of her traveling suit, and tossed it carelessly over the back of the ladies' chair. She was exhausted, and tired of smiling when all she wanted to do was cry, tired of being nice when she wanted to scream in frustration and rage. Every bone in her body ached, every cell in her brain wanted to close down and allow her to just hide from the world in a void of warm blackness. She didn't want to be here; not in Nevada Territory, not in Virginia City, and certainly not in the company of Travis Braggette. But she didn't have any choice. If she wanted to find out what had happened to Brett, where he was, she had to go through with this.

Digging into one of her satchels, Suzanne pulled out a small jar and, walking to stand beside the ugly green bathtub that looked more like a washtub with one side stretched out and up to form a backrest, poured a small portion of bath salts into the steaming water. She capped the jar, then leaned over and swirled the water with one hand. Snowy white bubbles immediately appeared atop the water's surface.

A knock sounded on her door.

"Oh, now what?" Suzanne snapped to herself. She walked to the door and opened it. "Oh, Addie, come in."

"I thought I'd unpack your things," Addie said, and made straight for the satchels on the bed that Travis's saloonkeeper, Hank Davis, had brought over and placed there. "Unless you'd rather I help you with your bath."

"No, I'm fine, Addie. Thanks." Suzanne walked to the window, pulled back the sheer panels and looked down on the street below. It appeared much the same as the other mining towns she'd been in lately. Maybe a little cruder, a little less finished, less refined, but much the same: mostly wooden clapboard buildings, a few of brick and mortar, and in the distance a sprawling vista of dingy white tents. They dotted the rolling hills behind the town, which led up the side of Sun Mountain, and in the opposite direction were sprinkled over the valley floor, which she couldn't see from her window but had viewed from the coach upon approaching the town.

She looked to her right, back down the block toward Travis's saloon. Above the boardwalk, attached to the overhanging roof, was a large white sign. The words Mountain Queen Saloon were painted on it in bright red letters. Her gaze dropped to the boardwalk.

Travis Braggette stood leaning against one of the roof's support columns. Suzanne felt a small knot of emotion catch in her throat. He was even more attractive than she remembered. His black hair was ruffled, a bit shaggy around the edges, nudging the tops of his ears and the back of his collar, the dark strands a stark contrast to the white of his shirt. One lock fell rebelliously onto his forehead. Suzanne smiled. Some things never changed.

"You want anything special laid out after your bath?" Addie asked, breaking into Suzanne's reflections. "Maybe one of your silk gowns?"

She glanced over her shoulder at the maid. "No, Addie, just a daygown. Whichever you choose is fine. I don't care." She turned back to the window. He was still there. She watched him reach into an inside pocket of his jacket and pull out a cheroot. He snipped off one end of the thin cigar, scraped a lucifer against the wooden column at his side, and cupping his hands about the flame, held it to the end of the cheroot. White smoke curled up from between his hands.

The black cutaway jacket he wore was a striking compliment to his wide shoulders. Its contour followed the line of his body and ended at his waist, accentuating its narrow breadth. The somber color served to emphasize his coal-black hair. His trousers, held taut by *sous pieds* looped beneath the instep of each boot, displayed with near indecent clarity the long length of his well-muscled legs. Travis was taller than she remembered him to be, broader, handsomer, darker. His skin, always a golden reflection of the Creole blood he'd inherited from his mother, was now a burnished bronze, and his face was a bit leaner than her memory recalled.

But he was still Travis, still the man who had haunted her dreams for the past seven years. Suzanne's heart fluttered slightly. Though from this distance she couldn't really make out his features, they had been imprinted indelibly on her mind long ago, and then again upon her arrival in the mining town. His eyes, those beautiful gray eyes that she had once thought she could lose herself within, held a new maturity, the near aquiline nose still bespoke of pride and aristocracy, the square cut of jaw professed the streak of defiance that had always caused him problems, and the lips . . . Suzanne suddenly remembered the one and only time Travis Braggette had kissed her. She'd been sixteen, and her father had arranged for her to marry Travis. The arrangement had been a wonderful and welcome surprise to her, but she discovered later, to her heartbreak, that it had been neither wonderful nor welcome to Travis. For the first few weeks after the announcement he hadn't come near her. When he finally did, he walked her out into her family's garden, pulled her into his arms and kissed her. After the initial shock wore off, Suzanne had found herself not only enjoying his kiss, but thinking she'd died and ascended to paradise.

A short, scoffing laugh escaped unbidden, and Suzanne quickly covered her lips with her hands and feigned a cough so that Addie would not be curious.

Her memories continued. The euphoric feeling Travis's kiss had aroused within her had been short-lived. As abruptly as he'd kissed her, he released her, spun on his heels and stalked away. She'd heard the hoofbeats of his horse echo on the afternoon air as he'd ridden off. That had been the last time Suzanne had ever seen Travis . . . until now.

As if he felt her gaze on him, thoughtful and assessing, Travis turned and looked up at Suzanne's window.

Her heart nearly thudded to a standstill as she felt a moment's panic. He knew why she was here. Her heart began to pound madly and her hands trembled. He couldn't know, her mind screamed. He couldn't. But he does, she argued back.

It seemed as if he nodded to her, though at the distance that separated them she couldn't be certain. Suzanne jumped back from the window, letting the curtains fall back into place. *Calm yourself, Suzanne,* she told herself. *You're just nervous. He doesn't know a thing.*

Travis stared up at the second-story window of the Union Belle for several long moments after Suzanne moved away from the window. Ever since he'd left her at the hotel his mind had been wandering a labyrinth of confusion, first at her arrival in Virginia City, and then at the way she had greeted him. None of it made any sense. After what he'd done seven years ago, he would have expected a flurry of angry words, a slap across the face, hostile coldness, or, at the least, indignant outrage. What he never would have expected was her to be warm, friendly, and flirtatious. Yet that was exactly what she had been, and he found it a puzzling mystery he could not accept at face value.

Why? The question nagged at him, and he knew it would give him no rest until he found an answer for it and several others. Why didn't she hate him? Why had she come to Virginia City? Why was she singing? Why hadn't she let him know she was Georgette Lindsay? Why was her father, one of the most prominent men in Louisiana, allowing his only daughter to traipse all over the country as a performer? Travis inhaled deeply of the whiskey-soaked cheroot and then let the smoke slowly escape his lips and dissipate upon the chilled morning air.

"Travis, I've been looking for you, son," a deep voice suddenly said from behind him. A hand slapped down on his shoulder, forceful and hard.

Irritation flashed in Travis's dark eyes, but he remained silent as he turned toward Judge David Terry.

The judge dropped his voice to just above a whisper. "Charlie tells me you declined my invitation again."

"Charlie told you right, Judge. I'm not interested in attending your meetings. It would probably save us both a lot of grief if you'd just stop asking."

"Yes, yes, it's a beautiful morning," the judge suddenly bellowed loudly for anyone near enough to hear,

then, almost under his breath said, "You're a southerner, Travis, and the South needs your support." Terry,
a stout man of several years Travis's senior, wrapped his
hand around the lapels of his heavy wool greatcoat and
puffed out his chest, which brought his more than ample
stomach along with it. "I know our efforts here failed
before, Travis, but we're working on another plan. You
could be an important man around here, after . . ."

Travis shook his head. "No, Judge, I'm not interested.
The South has my support, you know that, it's just not
through the Knights anymore."

David Terry stroked his gray-streaked black beard
and pinned Travis with a riveting stare. "Travis," he
looked over his shoulder in both directions to assure
himself they were not being overheard, "you've been a
member for a while now, and you know what good
things the KGC has done for the cause, and what it will
keep doing."

"Judge, I don't want to . . ." Travis interjected.

"But," David Terry said, overriding Travis's objection
as he glanced around again, "there's too many Yankee
sympathizers in this town. If we're going to accomplish
anything here, we've got to stick together."

Travis flicked the cheroot into the street and watched
the thin roll of tobacco arc through the crisp morning
air and land with a soft sizzle in a small pile of snow at
the base of one of the hitching racks. "Thanks for your
concern, Judge, really, and the invitation, but my answer is still no."

The smile on Terry's face wavered. "Your father was
a good member, Travis, a very good member. I doubt
he would have approved of your . . ."

Travis turned back to the judge, his eyes hard, every muscle in his face taut with anger. "My father is dead."

"Yes, I'm sorry, I just meant, he was a good man. Loyal to the South, and as a member of the KGC he—"

"He was a rotten son of a bitch, Judge," Travis hissed. "And whoever killed him probably did the world a damned big favor."

Travis stood near the swinging doors that led into the Mountain Queen, one booted foot resting on the polished brass footrail that ran the length of the mahogany bar. He settled his right forearm atop the bar's curved front lip and looked toward the stage at the opposite end of the room. The red velvet curtains with their gold torsage fringe were still drawn closed and Hank, his saloon manager, was lighting the lanterns that were placed several feet apart at the edge of the stage. Just before and below the raised performance area several musicians were tuning their instruments. Travis cringed as the violinist drew his bow across the instrument and a loud, very off-key screech cut through the merry tinkling of the piano music.

"Sounds more like you're stretchin' a chicken's neck than tunin' that there fiddle," someone yelled out.

Travis chuckled and silently agreed. Hopefully the man could play better than he could tune. Not only was Georgette Lindsay new to his stage, but so were the musicians. The last group, except for the piano player, had skedaddled out of Virginia City months ago when the first few flakes of snow began to fall, each vowing they weren't about to get snowed in on Sun Mountain another winter.

"Jed, give me a drink," Travis said to his barkeep.

"Tarantula juice, or the good stuff?" Jed asked. He smiled slyly, his brawny, almost puglike features softening as he looked at Travis.

"Save the tarantula juice for the boys," Travis said. "They seem to like it. Guess it gives them that extra kick of energy they need for the mines." He chuckled. "I'll force myself to make do with the good stuff."

Jed nodded. He grabbed Travis's special bottle of bourbon from a shelf beneath the mirror that covered the wall behind the bar and poured a shot, then slid the glass across the bartop to him.

"You missed a spot when you were polishing your head, Jed," Travis said. He took a sip of the golden bourbon and savored the feel of the rich, smooth liquid as it slid down his throat and warmed his insides.

Jed glanced in the mirror. "Damn, you're right, Boss." He pulled a towel from the waistband of his apron, spit on it and rubbed at the spot of flesh, then turned back to Travis. "How's that, Boss? Better?"

Travis smiled. "A perfect shine, Jed, just like always."

Hank moved up beside Travis. The saloon manager's white shirt stretched taut over a mountain range of shoulder muscle and provided stark contrast to the red mustache and beard that covered the lower half of his equally brawny face. "We've got us a packed house tonight, Boss. Game tables are full and the whiskey's flowin'. Now all we need in here is that little songbird you brought in." He chuckled and turned to watch another group of miners pile through the doorway. "I'd say from the looks of it, Maggie's going to have an empty place tonight, Boss, not to mention half the other saloons in town."

Travis let his gaze roam over the room. Hank was right. The gaming tables were full. There was little more than standing room left in the saloon, and more people kept pushing through the swinging doors. His dealers, bartenders, and waitresses would earn their wages tonight.

The Mountain Queen was one of the most elegantly furnished and decorated saloons on the mountain, and that's exactly how Travis had wanted it. Red velvet curtains, matching those drawn across the stage, framed the street side windows, expensive French silk paper covered the walls, the floor was polished oak plank, the furniture all carved cherrywood, and the chairs' padding was covered in richly colored brocade.

One of the Mountain Queen's waitresses smiled at him. Travis smiled back. Her blue satin gown was low cut, revealing a hint of breast and lot of shoulder, but it was tasteful exposure, not vulgar. Unlike many of the saloons in town, Travis's waitresses were just that, waitresses. If a man wanted a whore, there were plenty of other joints where he could find them. He could saunter on down to Nellie Sayer's place, go to one of the D Street parlors or cribs, or he could just trip across the street to Maggie's Silver Lady. But in the Mountain Queen he'd only find decent whiskey, honest tables, pleasant-looking waitresses—a frown settled on Travis's brow . . . and Georgette Lindsay, also known to a few as Suzanne Forteaux.

That brought his thoughts back to Suzanne.

He noticed the curtains of the stage move as someone behind them brushed against the fabric. An eager hoot went up from the miners in the audience. Travis pulled his watch out and flipped it open. It wasn't quite time for the show yet. He snapped the watch closed and slipped it back into the pocket of his vest.

Why had the daughter of one of New Orleans's richest and most prominent citizens become a singer, traveling from town to town, from camp to camp? Travis lifted his shot glass to his lips and, tossing his head back at the same time, he downed the last of the rich amber bourbon. Suzanne Forteaux. He hadn't given much thought to her over the years, except maybe for a flash of guilt here and there during that first year after he'd left New Orleans. He looked back at the stage, suddenly willing the red curtains to part, needing to see her again.

Maybe he'd made a mistake. But how could he have known Suzanne would blossom into such a beauty? He felt a mild stirring of desire coil deep within him. Travis turned back to the bar and signaled Jed to refill his glass. No, it hadn't been a mistake. He wasn't the marrying kind.

Just then the band struck up and every miner, gambler, businessman, and manjack in the house instantly quieted, the cards, dice, or greenbacks in their hands forgotten as their heads turned and they stared expectantly at the stage.

The red curtains parted in a swirling fold of velvet and Suzanne Forteaux walked out onto the stage.

"Man, she's some beauty, Boss," Jed said from behind him, his tone filled with awe.

Travis nodded, but his eyes remained on Suzanne. She was dressed all in white. Her gown was silk, the skirt full and voluminous, the bodice snug, the neckline plunging daringly low between her breasts. White lace, adorned with tiny seed pearls that reflected the glow of the stage lights and overhead chandeliers in iridescent

radiance and shimmered seductively with each movement she made, dripped from the puffed sleeves that
ended just below her shoulders, edged the low-cut neckline and the flounces of silk gathered at each hip. Her
dark hair was pulled high in a profusion of curls which
were allowed, on one side, to drape down and over her
shoulder. Several white ostrich feathers secured by a diamond brooch surrounded with lace was pinned behind
one ear.

The miners crowded into the Mountain Queen went
wild before she'd even finished her first chorus of song.
They cheered, stomped, and sang along. They thumped
the tables with their fists, clapped their hands continu-
ously, and undressed her with their eyes.

No, Travis thought again. He hadn't made a mistake
seven years ago. Marriage wasn't for him. Not then, and
certainly not now. Hell, maybe he'd even done them
both a favor. But the pleasure of her company in his
bed, now that was a different matter altogether. And he
wasn't too late for that . . . if the lady was willing.

"Hush up, Clarence," Suzanne snapped, more irri-
tated than she'd been since starting this charade. There
had been a time when she would never have used such
harsh words to anyone. She tossed the ostrich-feathered
hair ornament onto the small table that occupied one
wall of her backstage dressing room. It crashed against
the mirror with a loud clink. "I'm doing it the way you
said, aren't I? So, just hush up and stop badgering me."

"But you still care for him, don't you, Suzanne?"
Clarence persisted, his whiny voice scraping against her
already tense nerves. "I can tell. You do, don't you?"

She whirled around to glare at him. "Of course I do. The man left me standing at the altar of the St. Louis cathedral in front of all my friends and family. I was the laughingstock of the city for months. So, of course I still care for him. For cripe's sake, Clarence, I love him. What does it matter that I looked like a fool? Or that no gentleman ever looked twice at me after that?"

Clarence had the decency to look abashed at her outburst. "I'm sorry. It's just that you seemed so glad to see him this afternoon."

"Wasn't that how I was supposed to act?" Suzanne replaced the ostrich pin with a more sedate cluster of white-and-blue ribbons to match the gown she'd changed into, and gave herself an assessing glance in the mirror. She was dining with Travis and wanted to look her best, so she'd chosen to wear a gown of white Caldedonia silk. A hint of blue shadow, created by the unique weaving of blue threads beneath the white, shimmered within the skirt's folds and highly puffed pagoda sleeves each time she moved. A trimming of white Valenciennes lace trimmed the neckline, which was just low enough to tantalize but not to scandal. Lace also adorned the sleeves, the flounces that draped each side of the skirt, and the hemline.

She tried to ignore Clarence, and prayed that he'd believe her little tirade. Reaching into her satchel, Suzanne pulled out a pearl necklace and secured it about her neck, then retrieved the cazenou cape she'd worn going from the hotel to the saloon. She swirled it about her, letting it drape across her shoulders and envelop her gown, then stopped, her hand pausing in midair as she turned toward the door and reached for its knob.

The cazenou would be too light for the crisp nighttime spring air of the mountain town.

"Where are you going now, Suzanne?" Clarence asked. "With him?"

She ignored the question, removed the cape and reached for another that hung from one of the other hooks by the door. The capuchin was heavier, warmer, and had a hood. Thank heavens she'd thought to have Addie bring it to the saloon, too.

"Suzanne!" Clarence said, his tone harsher now.

She looked back at him, animosity shining from her eyes. "We're going for a late supper, Clarence."

"Good. Just don't forget why you're here," he said, as she stepped over the threshold and into the hall.

Chapter Four

Suzanne looked back before closing the dressing-room door. "*I* won't, Clarence. Just make sure *you* don't forget our bargain and your end of it." Anger burned within her very core. The man was an infuriating little creep, and if she didn't need him she'd most likely bash him over the head with a lantern. She closed the door behind her with a snap, spun around to leave, and collided with what felt like a stone wall.

Travis grabbed her forearms to steady her as she wavered and bounced back from the collision with his chest.

"Suzanne?"

"Travis!" Suzanne quickly collected herself, pushed a curl that had sprung loose from her carefully lacquered coiffure from her forehead and smiled up at him. "I'm sorry, you're early. I mean, I thought I was supposed to meet you in the saloon."

"I would never force a lady to hunt me down in the saloon." He smiled and, lifting her hand in his, tucked it within the crook of his arm.

Suzanne glanced up at him. How much had he heard

of her argument with Clarence? Did he know? Did he suspect? Oh, Lord, if he did, then their plan was ruined and she'd never find Brett. Suzanne took a deep breath and forced herself to calm down. He didn't know. He hadn't heard anything. If he had, he'd be asking her questions. If he knew, he'd most likely say something, or walk away from her in stony silence, just like he'd done seven years ago.

Her free hand, hidden within the folds of her cape, clenched into a fist as the old anger, hurt, and humiliation once again filled her mind and her heart. Travis Braggette was no better a man than his father had been. He'd proven that. Everyone had said that after he'd left. Being his wife seemed like the most unconscionable, despicable, most horrifying thing she could imagine, and she could only thank the angels that she wasn't, and never would be, married to him.

At the same time, though she was loath to admit it, she knew some little spark of fire deep within her had reignited itself the moment she'd stepped from the stagecoach and their eyes had met. But she'd fight it. She had to. There was no room in her life for emotional complications.

They weaved through the maze of tables in the saloon, Travis yelling to his barkeep that he was leaving for a while, Suzanne making certain to keep her gaze directed downward so as not to encounter that of Clarence Lonchet. At the moment he was about the last person she wanted to see.

"Where would you like to dine, Suzanne?" Travis asked, breaking into her thoughts. "Or should I call you Georgette?"

She smiled up at him. "Suzanne is fine, Travis. I only

use Georgette Lindsay as a stage name. My father insisted. Heaven forbid anyone important should discover that Suzanne Forteaux is working for a living. And, horror of horrors, on the stage yet." She laughed. "Scandal and all that, you know."

"Of course." It was a lie. He didn't know, and he didn't understand how the Landon Forteaux he'd known could let his only daughter traipse around the country singing in saloons. But then, things change. People, too. Perhaps, especially with the war going on, the Forteauxs were not in the same financial position they'd once been in. Travis decided to write his mother and inquire, to satisfy his curiosity if nothing else. He surely couldn't ask Suzanne.

"I don't know the town very well, Travis," she said. They stepped past the saloon's swinging doors and out into the night. The cold, crisp mountain air was like a touch of ice to her skin. She shivered. "Perhaps you should decide where we'll dine. And please, make it somewhere close."

He smiled. "It does get a bit colder up here than us southerners are used to."

"Just a bit," Suzanne said.

"There are several good places nearby, but I prefer the Diamond House. It's right around the corner actually, and serves some of the best food you can find west of the Mississippi."

She laughed lightly. "Then by all means, the Diamond House it is. I'm famished."

He steered her onto Taylor street. It inclined steeply, and Suzanne was forced to lift the front of her cape and skirt in order to proceed up the hill. The Diamond House sat on the next corner, a two-story brick structure whose windows were ablaze with candlelight. The soft strains of a violin solo filtered out onto the night air to greet them.

"Is this where you bring all of your lady friends, Travis?" Suzanne asked coyly. She hoped her flirtations weren't too brazen. A sigh nearly escaped her lips. She wasn't used to wielding her feminine charms. For a long time after Travis had left her, she'd done nothing but hide and sulk at the Forteaux plantation. Then, when she'd finally gotten up the courage to once again face the world, she had found that both her interest and her trust in men had disappeared. Her brother Brett was the one exception. He had been the only man she cared to have in her life, and she still felt the same way.

Travis took her hand in his as they crossed the street. A tremor of warmth swept up her arm at his touch. Suzanne felt the urge to jerk her hand away but refrained. Why was she reacting to him like that? Why, after what he'd done to her, after she'd spent the last seven years damning him, was she suddenly finding herself attracted to him again?

Light from a lantern which hung on an exterior wall of the restaurant dispersed a golden glow over the boardwalk before the building. Suzanne looked up at Travis. The soft illumination had created tiny pinpoint sparks within the waves of his hair and left his face a momentary landscape of deep, curving shadows.

He turned toward her then, the movement chasing away the shadows, and smiled as he opened the door to the restaurant. "Only the very special ones are permitted to enter," he answered, and stepped back to allow her to precede him inside.

"Oh, so now I'm special?"

He didn't know how to interpret that and the smile that had been on his lips froze nearly into a grimace. Was she referring sarcastically to what had happened between them years before? How he'd treated her? Or was it merely an innocent remark of the moment? A flirtation? He followed her into the reception area of the restaurant and, taking her cape and removing his greatcoat, handed both to the maître d'.

Travis decided not to pursue her comment further. "As you could hear in my saloon tonight, Suzanne, Georgette Lindsay is considered very special by almost ever manjack in the city." He congratulated himself on his reply. It was the truth, it was a compliment, and it was a safe enough answer to her question. He turned to the maître d'. "A quiet table away from the windows, if you have one," he requested.

The man nodded and motioned for them to follow him.

After being seated and ordering for both of them, Travis turned back to Suzanne, who was admiring the elegantly appointed restaurant with its rosewood furnishings, velvet seats and curtains, and gilt-framed mirrors.

"Not bad for a somewhat small mining town perched on the side of a mountain, huh?" he asked.

Suzanne smiled at him. "Not bad at all. I almost feel as if I'm home."

He nodded. "I haven't inquired, but how *are* things back home, Suzanne? Your parents? Your brother?" Travis asked politely. Actually, he didn't really care about Suzanne's parents. Landon Forteaux had been a similar type of man to Thomas Braggette, a braggart and a bullying brute, interested more in himself than anyone or anything else, including his family. As far as Travis was concerned, the fewer of those types there were in the world, the better off they'd all be.

"Oh, everything's fine so far. Mama writes to me often, though sometimes, with me traveling so much and all, her letters are a few weeks old by the time I get them. But in the last letter I received, she said the Yankees had made an attempt to get at the city. They failed, naturally. I mean," Suzanne chuckled lightly, "they'll *never* take New Orleans. Foolish of them to even try. But Mama's fine, and Papa, well, he worries a lot about things. The plantation and all. And about my brother." She watched him closely at the mention of her brother.

"What is Brett doing nowadays?" Travis really hadn't known her brother very well, and he was only asking because the man was part of Suzanne's family. Brett Forteaux had been a few years younger than Travis, and more a friend of his brother Traynor than of his.

"Oh, he's supporting the cause," she answered evasively. "Naturally."

The waiter placed several platters of food between them, but Suzanne continued to watch Travis through partially lowered lashes, intent on catching even the slightest reaction to her brother's name and his situation.

But Travis immediately changed the subject. "So, what brings you to Virginia City, Suzanne?"

The waiter placed two gleaming white china plates before them, and served their food: trout almondine, green beans with onions, roasted potato slices, and cherry tomatoes stuffed with shrimp. After he poured wine into the cut-crystal glasses that had been set in front of each of them, he gracefully disappeared.

Suzanne smiled wickedly. "Why, *you* did, Travis."

He laughed. "No, I mean, this singing. When did you start? And why?" Suddenly, at hearing his own words and watching the smile falter slightly on her lips, he silently cursed himself for asking the question. Maybe she *had* to sing. Maybe the Forteaux fortunes were gone. Maybe this was how she was managing to survive the war.

Suzanne brightened. "I discovered I'm not the homebody type. I want to see the world, all of it, and Papa didn't approve. In fact, he refused to help me, so I had to do it on my own and the only things I knew how to do were sew, knit, play the piano, run a house, and sing." She shrugged, and the smile widened. "I really didn't think sewing or knitting would support me, my piano playing was never quite that good, and being a maid was out of the question. So I'm singing my way around the world."

Travis nodded. He actually had done them both a favor seven years ago. He felt like breathing a sigh of relief, but managed to restrain himself. Now if he could just find a way to get them both to do each other a favor again. The faint hint of a smile touched his lips as a vision of Suzanne Forteaux, lying in his arms, naked and fired with passion formed in his mind. It was definitely a vision he wanted to turn into reality.

After dinner Travis walked Suzanne back to the Union Belle Hotel. He would much rather have prolonged the evening with a midnight ride beneath the stars, but the nights were still too cold, the roads still crusted over with ice in some places, snow in others. Better yet he would have rather taken her back to his suite of rooms over the Mountain Queen, except that there was no way of inviting her there without having to walk through the saloon. That would not have been a very subtle move.

After crossing C Street, Travis helped her ascend the boardwalk, and holding her hand in his, paused beside the hotel's entry door. It was encased within shadows created by the overhanging roof. The shadows were just inky enough to obscure them from the curious glances of anyone else on the opposite side of the street, though not dark enough to veil his view of her.

Suzanne looked up at him, her eyes unreadable, her lips neither smiling nor indignant.

Without another word, Travis pulled her into his arms. Her body did not resist him, yet did not surrender. But Travis was too lost in his own thoughts, his own desires, to notice. His arms slipped around to her back, one hand moving to splay across her back and crush her to him as his head lowered and his lips captured hers. Fire bristled to life within his blood and a knot of gnawing need hungered at his groin. He felt her lips part beneath his and he deepened his kiss, his tongue darting forth to fill her mouth, to explore the hidden cavities of sweetness, to taste the honeyed softness.

He savored her exotic taste, relished the feel of her lithe body within his embrace. Travis had known the pleasures of many women over the years, some innocent, many experienced, but none had ever touched his heart, and none, he vowed, ever would. The memory of giving his heart once, and of the woman, throwing that love back in his face, had forever hardened him to that emotion and convinced him he could do without it— happily. But though his heart might survive without love, his body had no intention of forsaking the pleasure of passion. Suzanne Forteaux was no longer the prim and proper little southern belle. She was a performer now, a songbird in the mining towns and camps, and Travis felt certain she was an experienced woman who knew what it was like to be with a man.

His hands slipped to her waist, pulling her even closer, until there was no space of night air left between their bodies, until she was pressed to his length, the folds of her skirt billowing out to half encircle his legs. He took his time kissing her, cajoling as well as demanding, utilizing all the skills of seduction he had mastered over the years. His lips traced a line of kisses along the curve of her jawline and then down the column of her throat as he moved one hand lightly, teasingly, over her back, his fingers tracing a featherlight trail up her spine.

He felt her shiver with desire, heard the faint moan that echoed from her throat and, bending his head, brushed back the front of her cape and pressed his lips to the soft golden mound of her breast.

Suzanne's hands, lying against his chest, suddenly pushed hard against him as she jerked back and out of his arms. Her breathing was hard and ragged, her breasts rising and falling rapidly as she stared up at him, a glittering hardness in her sky-blue eyes. "No, Travis. You could have had that and more seven years ago," she said breathlessly, tears gleaming in her eyes, "but you chose to turn your back and run." She put a hand on the door.

"Suzanne, wait." Travis reached out to touch her arm. "I shouldn't have done that, I know. But there were other things going on. I was angry. And I was scared. Please, I'm sorry."

She paused and turned back to him. "You're sorry?

You left me to face that scandal alone, Travis. To face not only the humiliation of being jilted on my wedding day, but also to face the horrid, vicious lie that I was already carrying your child. And you *knew* it was a lie, Travis. You knew, and said nothing. Worse, you left."

"I didn't know what else to do."

"Do you know how long it took to live that down, Travis? Before everyone finally figured out that I wasn't carrying *anybody's* child?" All the old anger came rushing back to her as memories filled her mind. "But by then it was too late. Everyone, including all my so-called friends, assumed I'd lost the baby as a result of your rejecting me. No one believed I had never been pregnant, never even been with a man."

He shook his head. "I . . . I thought they'd just realize the rumor had been a lie, Suzanne. I'm sorry."

"Thank you," she said, unable to prevent the sarcasm that laced each word. "That helps a lot. When I get back to New Orleans I'll be certain to tell everyone you apologized."

Travis didn't like the turn their conversation had taken. The past was dead, and he didn't want to relive it, but he owed Suzanne an explanation of his actions. "I was in love with someone else then, Suzanne. It would have been wrong to marry you."

Her dark brows soared skyward. "So, instead of saying that, you just left me? Your father started that lie, Travis. You knew that, and you left me to face it alone."

A deep frown gouged its way into his forehead. He grabbed her arms. "My father?"

"Yes, your father," Suzanne snapped, and twisted away from him. "If you didn't want to marry me, Travis, you should have said so in the beginning." The tears slipped from her eyes and streamed down her cheeks, but she ignored them and continued, "You shouldn't have let my family announce the engagement, plan the wedding, and invite nearly everyone in town. You shouldn't have let me go to the church, Travis, and wait for you, and . . ."

He pulled her back into his arms as a sob wracked her body. "I'm sorry, Suzanne," he whispered, and God knew, he truly meant it. He'd never intended to hurt her. All he'd wanted was to get away from his father, to escape all Thomas Braggette's schemes and machinations and forget that, because of him, the woman he'd loved had turned her back on him.

Suzanne pushed away from Travis again and quickly brushed the tears from her cheeks with her fingertips, then looked back up at him. "Thank you, Travis, but it really doesn't matter anymore. There might have been a time for us once, but no longer. It's too late now. Too many things have happened between us, and there are other things, more important things now, that I must see to."

He reached out for her, but she stepped away from him, avoiding his touch. Travis dropped his hands to his sides. "I'd like to see you while you're here, Suzanne. Take you to dinner. Maybe talk some more."

She shook her head. "I don't think that's such a good idea, Travis. Let's just say good night now, shall we? Before more memories cause either of us to say things we might regret." She held her hand out to him. This wasn't what she was supposed to do. In fact, it was exactly the opposite, but she couldn't help herself. She was afraid of him, afraid of herself. She'd thought she was long over him, thought her bitterness over what he'd done far surpassed any tenderness she'd ever felt for him. She'd thought she could do what Clarence had instructed with no problem, no feelings. And she'd been wrong. "I'm glad you're well, Travis. Good night."

He clasped her fingers in his. Quelling the urge to hold her close again, he pressed his lips to the back of her gloved hand. "Good night, Suzanne," he said softly.

Minutes later, safely locked within her hotel room, Suzanne ripped off her gloves and threw them on the dressing table, followed within seconds by the crash of her necklace and earrings as she angrily tossed them beside the gloves. She began to pace the room, her fingers busily fumbling with the buttons of her gown. "Damn you, Travis Braggette!" she swore beneath her breath. "It wasn't supposed to be like this." She practically ripped her blouse off. *"You* weren't supposed to be like this." She let her crinolines and hoop cage fall to the floor, followed by her skirt. "Damn you, Travis." She glanced at the window. "Damn you, damn you, damn you."

A knock sounded on the door from the hallway.

Chapter Five

Travis stood on the boardwalk in front of the hotel after Suzanne disappeared inside, his mind a jumble of questions without answers. Seven years ago he had kissed her, and felt nothing. Absolutely nothing. A short while ago he had kissed her, and now he was having one devil of a time putting her out of his mind. No woman, even Lisa, the one woman he had thought he truly loved, had ever really affected him like that, and he'd wanted to marry Lisa, to spend the rest of his life with her. He was not in love with Suzanne, though he had to admit she was one of the most beautiful creatures he'd ever seen. And definitely the most attractive—and refined—to ever come to Virginia City.

"So, Travis, what's got you standing out here in the dark? And in such deep thought?"

He turned to see a woman standing next to him, the midnight-blue hue of her taffeta gown melding with the night, her dark hair coiled at her nape in a large chignon. She wasn't a pretty woman, really, but she did have an allure that attracted nearly every man in town. Which was why she was not only one of the most well-paid whores on D Street but one of the most well liked. She'd only been in town a few months, yet there wasn't a man in Virginia City, rich or poor, who didn't care deeply for Julia Bullette.

"Or should I say *who?*" she added when he didn't answer immediately, and with a smile, winked at him.

Travis returned the smile. "Is there anyone in this town who can keep a secret from you, Julia?"

She laughed playfully and pulled her short black pelisse cape tighter around her shoulders in an effort to ward off the cold. "Perhaps a few, sweets, but not many. Now, come on," she slipped her gloved hand around his arm and urged him to walk beside her down the boardwalk, "tell Julia what's troubling you. Maybe I can fix it."

As they crossed the street, he shook his head. "Nothing to fix, gorgeous. Just thinking about my family back home, that's all," he lied. For some reason, he didn't want to tell her, or anyone, about Suzanne.

She shrugged. "Well then, since I can't fix it, and you obviously don't want to talk about it, why don't you buy me a drink instead?"

Travis walked beside her toward the swinging doors of the Mountain Queen. "My pleasure, milady," he said, gallantly sweeping a hand before her.

Suzanne stood behind the sheer bedroom curtains and watched Travis disappear from view, a tall, dark-haired woman clinging to his arm. She spun around and stalked back to the side of the bed. "What do I care what he does?" she mumbled. Her fingers pulled at the pale-blue ribbon that held her camisole secured. Within seconds she had practically ripped her way out of her underclothes, flinging camisole, pantalettes, corset, and gossamer stockings about the room as she paced. She grabbed the batiste nightgown Addie had laid out for her only moments before and pulled it over her head, then flopped down on the bed. "Obviously he has a harem of women in this godforsaken town just waiting to fall into his bed at the snap of his fingers!"

Suzanne rolled onto her side. She should get some sleep, surely needed her rest. She closed her eyes, but her mind wouldn't turn off. The fury that was boiling in her breast, churning about in her mind, and charging her with renewed energy had chased her exhaustion away.

All she was supposed to do was play up to Travis, make certain he was still a Knight and that he wasn't familiar with Clarence. That was all. She didn't know why they wanted her to do that, why they wanted her to make certain he kept his attention on her, and she didn't care. If that's what she had to do to find out about her brother, then fine, that's what she'd do, and everything else be damned.

Anyway, what did she care about Travis Braggette? He was nothing but a scoundrel. A rogue. A damned coward who had run out on her instead of facing her like a man.

She turned and rammed a clenched fist into her pillow several times, then slammed her head back onto it. Travis Braggette was a rake. A no-good, low-dealing, cowardly rake. Just like his father had been.

And it hadn't been any kind of desire or passion she'd felt when he'd kissed her. She was just lonely, that was all. She wasn't experienced when it came to seducing men. She wasn't even experienced when it came to *kiss-*

ing them. She'd only been kissed by two men in her entire life. One was her brother, so that didn't count. The other had been Travis. Once. But it didn't matter. Instinct would get her through this ordeal. Instinct and the driving need to know what had happened to Brett. To find out where her brother was. If he was all right. And if Travis Braggette got hurt in the process, so what? He deserved it . . . didn't he?

Unable to sleep, Suzanne slipped from the tall bed and, lighting a lamp, walked to one of her satchels on the floor. Kneeling beside it, she flipped open its clasp, reached inside and pulled out a small square metal box, then carried it back to the bed.

Slipping back under the coverlet, Suzanne laid the box on her thighs and folded back its top half, revealing that both sides were actually a picture frame. Her own portrait was secured on one side, her brother Brett's on the other. She stared at his image. The portrait had been taken the day he'd left New Orleans to join Forest's cavalry unit. He could have headed his own unit, but Brett admired Forest and wanted to serve under him. She recalled how he'd said the man was one of the most intelligent strategists he'd ever met.

Tears blurred Suzanne's vision, and she blinked them away. Brett had looked so handsome in his new gray uniform with its butternut collar and cord embellishments. He'd carried a sword that had belonged to their grandfather, and their mother had tied a red silk sash around his waist for luck.

A tear dropped onto the glass covering Brett's portrait, and Suzanne wiped it away with the coverlet.

Brett had written home faithfully every week, until a year ago. Then he'd left the Army to join the Knights of the Golden Circle. Her father had been shocked, or so he'd said. Her mother had been astonished and confused. Brett had written, in that last letter, that he had an assignment to travel to San Francisco, though he couldn't say why, and there had been no more letters.

Then, when they'd received no word from Brett for several months, Landon Forteaux had finally admitted that it had been he who had convinced Brett to join the Knights. He'd feared Brett would be killed in battle and felt he'd be safer with the Knights, working behind the lines, secretly, to help the cause. He blamed himself for Brett's disappearance, he could not find out what had happened to his son.

"Where are you, Brett?" Suzanne whispered to the portrait. "What's happened to you?"

A loud rapping suddenly sounded against her door. Startled, Suzanne flinched, and in doing so snapped the framed portraits closed.

"Suzanne? Suzanne, open this door!"

Outrage instantly roiled within her breast. How dare he bang on her door in the middle of the night! Throwing back the covers, Suzanne rammed her arms into her wrapper, knotted it at her waist and marched to the door. "What do you want, Clarence?" she said through the paneled wood.

"Suzanne? Open the door."

"No."

"Suzanne, we need to talk. Now. And I'm not going to stand here in the hallway speaking through a wall."

He began to pound on the door again.

"I'm not dressed!" Suzanne shouted. "And you're going to wake up everyone in the hotel with this ruckus."

"Then put on a wrap and open the door."

He pounded again.

"All right, all right." Suzanne unlatched the lock and swung the door open. "What is so important you had to practically bang down the door, Clarence?"

He strode past her and into the room, immediately settling himself into one of the chairs before the fireplace. A log was still smoldering in the grate.

Suzanne stood at the open door, one hand still on its knob, and glared at him.

"Come and sit down, Suzanne, and tell me what happened tonight." He slowly lit the thin cheroot he pulled from his pocket, then, extinguishing the match with a shake of his wrist, he tossed it into the fireplace.

Suzanne bristled. "Tell you what happened tonight? That's what is so urgent?"

"I need to know."

"It's late, Clarence," she said, holding herself stiffly. "We can talk about this tomorrow."

"We'll talk about it right now," he answered, and met her gaze in a blatant challenge.

Suzanne suddenly crumbled in surrender. She sighed, closed the door, and walked over to the settee opposite where Clarence sat. "What do you want to know, Clarence?" She continued before he could answer. "We went to dinner at a place called the Diamond House, on Taylor and B Street, I think it was. Around the corner from the Mountain Queen. I had trout. So did Travis. Green beans and onions, potatoes, cherry tomatoes with shrimp. I had wine. He had . . ."

"Suzanne."

She smiled sweetly. "Yes, Clarence?"

"I want to know about Travis."

"Well, I was telling you about Travis," she said with feigned innocence.

Clarence threw the cheroot into the fireplace. "I do not want to know what you had for dinner, damn it all. I want to know about the two of you together." Irritation pinched the corners of his mouth. "Did anything happen, Suzanne? Between you? Did you . . ."

"Seduce him?" Suzanne looked at him in a mocking pose of wide-eyed shock.

"Yes." Clarence's pallor began to evidence a purple tinge as his eyes narrowed and his jaw clenched in frustrated anger. He drummed his fingers on the arm of the chair.

"Why, heavens no, Clarence. I *am* a lady, you know."

He jumped up from his seat. "I don't care if you're a fish, Suzanne. You agreed to seduce Travis Braggette. You agreed to—"

"I agreed to find out if he still considered himself a member of the Knights," she said, cutting across his words in a tone now thick with scathing reprimand. Clarence Lonchet was a toad, and she'd gotten to the point she could barely tolerate him. If she didn't need him to lead her to Brett, she would most likely have *killed* him by now. "I agreed to find out what he knew about Judge David Terry and his division of the Knights, and whether or not Travis had transferred his loyalties. And I agreed to attract and keep his attentions while we were here. That's all, Clarence. I did not agree to seduce the man."

Clarence shot her a vicious look, but then his attitude seemed to reverse abruptly. "So," he said casually, flopping back down on the chair, "what did you find out?"

He kept his eyes averted from hers and busied himself taking another cheroot and lucifer from his pocket.

"I'd really rather you didn't smoke that in here, Clarence. I'm not fond of the smell." It was a lie. She had always enjoyed the scent of a good cigar, but denying him the pleasure of smoking in her company always caused him such a jolt of annoyance that she experienced a soothing salve of satisfaction each time she did it.

He shoved the cigar and match back into his pocket. "Fine. Now, what did you find out?"

"Nothing." *Except that his kiss makes me go weak in the knees just like it did seven years ago,* she thought to herself. Her own anger flared at the self-confession. Travis Braggette was a miscreant of the lowest type, and she'd do good to remember that, whether he could kiss like Satan himself or not.

Chapter Six

The next morning over a dozen bouquets of flowers and five boxes of candy were delivered to her room, all from admirers who had been in attendance at the Mountain Queen for her first performance. Suzanne felt a slight wave of disappointment to realize that none of them were from Travis. Then, angry at herself for even the thought, she stormed from her room and marched down to collect Addie. The two women breakfasted together in the little dining room Mavis Beale used to serve her guests their morning meals, and then Suzanne and Addie decided to see a little of the town.

"You two ladies going to be back for noontime dinner?" Mavis Beale called out from the dining room.

"Don't hold it up for us, Mrs. Beale," Suzanne answered. "We'll get a bite wherever we happen to be."

Mavis poked her head around a corner of the wall. "Just be careful out there. Ice is still slippery on the roads, and some of them miners ain't used to having real ladies around, if you know what I mean. Their manners ain't what they should be."

Addie laughed softly, though a blush colored her

cheeks as she fussed with straightening the skirt of her gown. A hand moved subtly to the reticule hanging from her other wrist. She pressed against the figured velvet and felt the solid shape of her little derringer. Her confidence jumped a notch, and she smiled. If she and Suzanne encountered trouble, at least she'd be able to make some of her own.

"We'll be fine, Mrs. Beale," Suzanne called back from the door. "See you later this afternoon."

"And if we get a zephyr, you make sure and get yourselves in off the street right quick!" Mavis added. "Them winds can be real killers. Sweep you right off the walk, out of town, and into the canyons."

Addie and Suzanne stepped out onto the boardwalk, closing the door quickly behind them to keep the cold air from swirling into the hotel. The street was a bustle of activity. Drays pulled by huge workhorses lumbered up and down the streets, some filled to overflowing with various goods, others rattling along empty. Carriages of all shapes and sizes moved amongst the work wagons, or were parked at the hitching rails that lined the streets. The boardwalks were crowded with a flurry of pedestrians, which included well-dressed gentry, scruffy children, and even scruffier miners.

"Let's go over to that general store first," Suzanne said, pointing across the street to a store on the corner. Painted across its flat storefront were the words Hanson's Dry Goods.

It should have taken less than a minute to step from the boardwalk, cross the street, and walk to the entrance of the store. Instead, it took a full five as Suzanne found herself stopped by a half dozen gentlemen who tipped their hats, kissed her hand, and complimented her performance of the night before. Four of the gentlemen asked her to dinner. The fifth asked her to join him in a drink that evening after her performance. The sixth requested her presence in his hotel room. She felt like slapping that one's face, but refrained. Instead, she smiled primly and, acting as if she hadn't the faintest idea what he was inferring, informed him that she would have to decline his generous offer because she already had her own hotel room, thank you very much.

"Well, I never," Addie exclaimed, staring after the man. "The nerve of him, asking you to go to his room like that." She threw Suzanne a furtive glance as they continued on their way. It was a well-known fact that some actresses and singers supplemented their income with a little prostitution on the side, and even though Addie had only been with Suzanne for a few months, she knew that Suzanne Forteaux, or Georgette Lindsay, or whatever she wanted to call herself, wasn't one of them. But then, she would have known that anyway. After the amount of research she'd done on Suzanne before her contacts had gotten her the job as Suzanne's personal maid, she knew just about everything there was to know about the girl, including her past association with Travis Braggette.

Suzanne caught the look. "Is something wrong, Addie?"

Addie swore silently at her carelessness, and smiled at Suzanne. "No, I guess I was just worried that . . . well, you know, about the man's awful comments and all. I mean, they were scandalous, and I don't want you getting yourself all upset."

Suzanne laughed. "Don't worry, Addie. I won't."

Just before reaching the store, Suzanne caught sight

of a woman dressed in brilliant green stepping from the saloon directly across from the Mountain Queen. The woman raised a hand and waved at someone. Suzanne looked to see who the woman was waving to.

Travis Braggette, mounted on a beautiful bay stallion, was just approaching the front of his saloon. He waved back at the woman.

Suzanne jerked her eyes away. He could wave to every woman in the world for all she cared. She purposely turned her attention to the storefronts on the opposite side of the street, and then the panorama behind them.

Sun Mountain, which rose high above the western side of the city, was still half covered in white snow. The morning sun glinted off the pristine patches of ice as well as reflected from several of the store windows fronting the opposite side of the street.

Suzanne shook herself back into composure, or at least a semblance of it. "Come on, Addie," she said, forcing a cheeriness to her voice, "let's find something to buy."

The remainder of the day passed pleasantly enough, as long as Suzanne didn't think about Clarence Lonchet or Travis Braggette. Thoughts of Clarence only got her temper going, and thoughts of Travis got everything else going, including a distinct sense of confusion. Why did she suddenly feel guilty about deceiving him? The man deserved every low-life, scheming trick that anyone thought to pull on him. So why did she feel as if she were suddenly the lowest of the low, and pulling the worst of the worst schemes?

"What do you think of this bonnet?" Suzanne asked, trying to get her mind on something besides Travis. She held up the hat to Addie, who had been looking over several bolts of cloth.

Suzanne didn't hear Addie's answer. Her attention was no longer on the bonnet she held in her hands, or on whatever Addie had to say about it, but on the tall figure who had just appeared at the entrance to the store.

He stopped when he saw Suzanne.

She stared at him, unable to help herself.

The man standing there was a vision of darkness silhouetted against the doorway. The morning light at his back afforded him a bearing of incredible strength, of hidden power and mystery, while the light of the store's lanterns created a labyrinth of shadows upon his face and form, lending him a sinister aura.

Suzanne felt an icy shiver skip its way up her back and spread down each limb, leaving a blanket of goosebumps atop her flesh. Yet even as she felt herself filled with trepidation, she also felt something else, something that was in direct conflict to her thoughts: a desire to feel his lips capture hers again. She pushed the idea away. It was ridiculous, and most likely only born of intrigue and perhaps a bit of fantasy.

His eyes seemed to weave a hypnotic spell upon her as they stared out from beneath winged black brows. He reached up to brush at one shoulder, as if feeling something there that should not be. Startled from her reverie by the movement, Suzanne flinched.

"Why, look, Travis honey, it's your little songbird." Magnolia Rochelle, her bright red hair flowing free across her shoulders and decked out in a flowing capuchin cape of emerald velvet with white ermine trim, pulled her arm from Travis's and walked directly across the room to stand before Suzanne. She smiled down at her.

Suzanne, taken aback, jerked her eyes away from Travis to gawk at the woman who reminded her of a Christmas tree.

Magnolia smiled at Suzanne. "Ah, *chér*, I see by the look on your face that Travis has not mentioned me." She feigned a pout and glanced over her shoulder at Travis. "Naughty, *mon ami*, to forget Magnolia like that."

"Maggie," Travis said, his tone edged with a warning note.

The woman turned back to Suzanne, smiling once again, and taking Suzanne's hand in hers and dropping her voice to a conspiratorial whisper said, "Ah, *chérie*, we must plan a little visit, yes? And talk?"

"Maggie," Travis interrupted, clearly impatient, "pick out your hat, would you?"

She waved off his comment. "Soon, *chérie.*"

Suzanne stared at the woman. Who was she? Obviously not someone of the best breeding, considering her garish attire and speech pattern, but she *had* been with Travis.

"If you should get tired of the pittance Travis pays for your talents in the Queen, *chérie,*" Maggie whispered quickly, "come and see me in the Silver Lady, across the street. I let my girls earn more than just their regular wages."

Suzanne's mouth nearly dropped open. A saloon madame? The woman was a saloon madame? And she was with Travis?

"I don't think so, Maggie," Travis said from directly behind them. "Now, why don't you pick out that hat I owe you and let's go. I have a few things to do today besides accompany you on a shopping trip." His voice again held a warning note, and again Magnolia ignored it.

Suzanne felt a flash of jealousy, and quickly stomped it out. Why in heaven's name should she be jealous over Travis Braggette? She didn't even care for him. Unwittingly she straightened her shoulders beneath her cape. It was just that this could prove a minor setback to her plan, that was all. Anger. She'd felt a twinge of anger, not jealousy. Travis Braggette was a rake. A rake. A rake. She stared into the mirror at herself and kept repeating the words over and over in her mind. A rake.

Magnolia laughed merrily, the throaty sound filling the interior of the small store.

Addie's brow screwed into a frown of disapproval.

Suzanne's eyes darted from Magnolia to Travis and back to Magnolia.

Travis flinched inwardly. Why had he chosen today of all days to pay up his bet with Magnolia? Why hadn't he just come to Hanson's himself, bought the damned hat and taken it over to the Silver Lady and handed it to her? Why had he let her talk him into accompanying her to the store and helping her pick it out? He felt the tension that had coiled into a knot in the pit of his stomach at the first sight of Suzanne in the store tighten further. He clenched one hand into a fist behind his back. Why in the hell did she have that effect on him? A string of oaths danced their way through his head, but he bit down on the inside of his bottom lip to keep them from tripping their way out through his lips. What the hell was it about Suzanne Forteaux that had him so on edge? It wasn't as if she was the only woman in Virginia City. Or that he hadn't had a woman in so long his body was about to burst from need.

He glanced down at Magnolia. She was always more than willing to share his bed, as were half a dozen of the other prostitutes in town, though it had nothing to do with money. Travis looked back at Suzanne. So she was beautiful. So she was a lady. So he still felt guilty about jilting her seven years ago. So what?

A knot of frustration joined the knot of tension. In another minute, he knew, if he didn't get out of that store, away from Maggie's sultry glances and away from the sight of Suzanne, which invoked a memory of the kiss they'd shared and the hidden desires it had promised to reveal, a knot of passion was going to attack him. And, combined with the other two knots already coiled within him, he'd be lucky if he didn't end up a writhing idiot on the floor.

Chapter Seven

"We've got a meeting later tonight at the King place," David Terry said, the words spoken so softly that Travis almost hadn't caught them.

He looked at the burly man standing next to him at the bar, their shoulders touching. His fingers wrapped around a shot glass and he brought it to his lips and downed the whiskey before answering. "I told you, Judge, I'm not a Knight anymore."

"You'll always be a Knight, Travis," David Terry countered. "You joined, and that means for life."

"I was young. I made a mistake in judgment."

"You made a commitment."

Travis glared at the older man. He could see why Terry had as many enemies as he had friends. The man was like a bulldog; stubbornly determined. Those who benefited from this determination admired Terry, but those who got stepped on because of it loathed him. Travis sighed. "So consider me uncommitted," he finally said.

The judge shook his head. "You took an oath, Travis, and you're expected to live up to it."

Travis felt his temper flare and struggled to control it. He didn't want to argue the point. Thomas Braggette had been a high-ranking member of the Knights, and he had coerced each of his sons into joining the organization. But in time each had rebelled.

"Judge, you know I haven't been active in the KGC for a long time."

"We need every man now, Travis. Every one."

Travis felt himself being squeezed into a corner, just like he'd always felt whenever he tried to deal reasonably with his father. But his father was dead, murdered almost two years before, and Travis was no longer that brash young man who had barely survived his father's tyrannical rule. He was stronger now, independent and confident in himself, and no one was going to run his life for him again. No one. "Why, Judge?" he said finally. "Why now?"

The judge looked over both shoulders before answering. " 'Cause we got plans now, that's why."

Travis slammed down his glass on the bar, drawing a curious glance from the bartender and a few nearby patrons. Travis waited to speak until they turned away. "Damn it, David, what the hell are you stirring up? We don't need trouble here on the mountain."

Judge David Terry smiled. "Who said anything about trouble, Travis?"

Two years before, after going to New Orleans and attending both his sister and brothers' weddings—unfortunately at just the same time Beauregard had decided to open fire on Fort Sumter and start the damned war—Travis had returned to Virginia City. He found Judge David Terry in residence there, and the entire mountainside town in complete chaos. A lot of southerners lived in the area, and Judge Terry's arrival and his organization of the Knights of the Golden Circle in Virginia City had ultimately resulted in the soldiers being called in from Fort Churchill to keep the peace.

"Midnight, Travis, at the King place. I'll expect to see you there," the judge said. He downed the last of his whiskey, placed the glass on the bar with a solid *thunk*, and turned to leave.

"Don't hold your breath, Judge," Travis mumbled.

David Terry paused and turned back. "Travis, you're either with us, or you're against us. I hate to say it, but," he shrugged, "there isn't any middle ground here anymore."

Travis stared at the burly judge as the man made his way through the crowd of miners who milled about the gaming tables. He exchanged a word or two with several, and then headed for the door.

Travis whirled around and, leaning both arms on the bar, yelled for Jed. "Give me a damned bottle, man," he ordered in frustration.

Suzanne took her last bow and, throwing a kiss to the cheering miners, gamblers, and businessmen who made up the audience, hurried from the stage. But rather than head for her dressing room as usual, she walked to the corner of the stage and descended the short flight of stairs that led down into the barroom.

"Miss Suzanne!" Addie called in a whisper from behind the stage curtain.

Suzanne paused, looked back, and smiled. "I'm all right, Addie," she said. "I'll be back in a few minutes."

"Hey, sweetheart, you lookin' for a little lovin'?" one of the miners called out. He patted his lap in invitation.

"Yeah, I got some for ya," another snarled. He shot up from his seat at the table Suzanne was passing and grabbed her around the waist with a beefy arm.

The breath was knocked from her lungs as the man crushed her against his chest, and the rough weave of his cheap and shabby jacket scraped against her bare arms and chest. The room spun crazily for a second, during which she felt his whiskered face suddenly bury itself within the cleavage of her breasts.

Suzanne screamed in shock.

"Hey, Skinner, save me some of that!" another man called out.

Finally catching her breath and her wits, Suzanne pushed at the man whose grip was as strong as a bear's, and just as secure. She felt his tongue, hot and wet, suddenly slip between her breasts, and a wave of revulsion swept over her.

"Stop!" she ordered, pushing at him. "Stop."

Suddenly the man spun away from her, his arms ripped from around her so violently that she was thrown to one side and nearly toppled into a table.

"Didn't you hear the lady tell you to stop?" Travis growled. He held Skinner Jones by the back collar of his jacket.

"Ah, c'mon, Trav, I didn't mean no harm. I was just funnin', and, anyways, she was askin' for it. All them whores ask for it, you know that."

"Miss Lindsay is not a whore, Skinner," Travis said, loud enough for all to hear.

"Yeah, that's what they all say," another man chimed in.

Travis released his hold on Skinner Jones and turned an angry eye on the men in the saloon. "You want whores, gentlemen, go on over to Magnolia's. You want good whiskey, a fair game, and a chance to hear a real lady sing, you come here. It's your choice." He reached out and curled steely fingers around Suzanne's bare upper arm, jerking her after him as he began to make his way through the crowd of tables and men. "And frankly, boys, I don't much give a damn what you do."

Suzanne tripped, skipped, hopped, and ran after him. Gratitude to him had immediately disappeared from her thoughts as fury at his nearly yanking her off her feet and hauling her across the room like so much baggage fired her blood. And to think she had been about to saunter over and flirt with him! Well, forget that.

Travis banged through the swinging doors, pulling Suzanne along behind him, and then stopped abruptly once they reached the boardwalk.

Though it was nearing midnight and not much over thirty degrees, the streets were alive with activity; music and the roar of voices and laughing drifted out from every saloon and bawdy house on C and D streets, and miners traipsed from one saloon to the next, or down to the mines to start their shift.

Suzanne jerked her arm from Travis's grip and glowered at him. "Why'd you do that?"

"Because you were about to get your favors shared around the room with every manjack in there, that's why!" he said, nearly snapping her head off with each word.

"I am perfectly capable of taking care of myself, Travis Braggette, and protecting my favors."

"Oh, really? Then maybe I should have just left you to your own devices."

"Well, you did before, why not this time?" she retorted, unable to help seven years worth of hurt, anger, and humiliation from bubbling into and blending with her present indignation at him.

The comment stung, but he angrily brushed it aside with his firm command. "Don't flaunt yourself in front of the men like that again, Suzanne. Next time I might not be around to save you."

Fiery indignation consumed her. "I wasn't flaunting myself."

"Sashaying in front of the men when you're singing is one thing, they expect that. But flaunting your assets in front of them later, that's something else."

"I wasn't flaunting," she said again.

"You were."

Fury seized her in its mind-searing grip. "I'll flaunt whatever I want wherever I want," she snapped back. "And I'll thank you to just nevermind."

"I thought you came here to sing, Suzanne," Travis snarled, "not lay on your backside with every man in town."

"Why you . . ." Her arm swung upward in a wide arc that immediately began to sweep back down again.

Without taking his eyes from hers, Travis reached up and grabbed her wrist, stopping her arm in midstride and preventing her hand from connecting with the side of his face. "No," he growled, every muscle taut with anger, his eyes blazing.

"You're despicable, Travis Braggette," Suzanne whispered. "You're the most horrid son of a—"

His mouth suddenly clamped down atop hers, effectively cutting off the curse that had been about to pass her lips. His arms pulled her close and crushed her against his length as his tongue moved in between her lips and his hands splayed against her back. He was playing with fire, he knew, but for the moment he couldn't help himself. Suzanne Forteaux was all woman. She was stubborn, ornery, and full of fire. Seven years before she'd been a prim and proper little girl. But Suzanne had grown up, and Travis had no doubt that prim and proper had been discarded along the way with the innocence of childhood. She was a woman now, and that's exactly what he wanted in his bed this night. A woman. Not a whore. Not a lady. A woman.

Suzanne looked up at Travis as he kissed her. The blackguard. Who did he think he was . . . She suddenly caught a movement out of the corner of her eye. As Clarence moved into her line of vision, Suzanne groaned.

He nodded his approval and promptly stepped inside the swinging doors to the Mountain Queen, and then turned back to continue watching, though less obviously.

Travis, believing her groan had been a moan of passion, tightened his arms around her and deepened his kiss. His tongue suddenly filled her mouth, his hands caressed her back.

Suzanne slipped her arms around Travis's neck, pressed herself against him, and began to return his kiss. She'd feel nothing, she told herself. She wouldn't. The warm tingling in her hands was merely a result of the cold temperature this night. And that gnawing ache in the pit of her stomach, that was just hunger.

His tongue curved around hers, dueling, teasing.

A stab of desire pierced Suzanne's calm. No, it wasn't

desire. She had a cramp. Probably she'd pulled a muscle while on stage. Too vigorous in her dancing, that was all.

The gnawing ache heated her with a searing intensity. She ripped herself out of Travis's embrace, gulping for air and frantically trying to regain her composure.

Clarence made a slight movement by the doors.

Suzanne forced a teasing smile to her face and turned to Travis. She swallowed hard and closed the space between them, slipped her arms around his neck again, and brushed her lips across his teasingly.

"Travis, darling," she said softly, "I'd love to stand out here all night and continue this but . . ."

A frown creased his brow.

Suzanne laughed softly. "But I think I'm about to freeze to death."

He felt her shiver against him and tightened his arms around her.

At that moment Clarence stepped out onto the boardwalk, Addie holding his arm. "Well, I think I'll call it a night." He smiled, then nodded to Travis. "Do you think you could be good enough, Mr. Braggette, to see Suzanne back to the hotel?"

She threw him a glaring look and, though she wanted nothing more than to throttle him, remained still.

"It would be my pleasure, Mr. Lonchet," Travis answered, placing a proprietary hand on the small of Suzanne's back.

She smiled sweetly.

"Fine, then we'll be on our way. Good night."

Addie flashed Suzanne an apologetic glance and allowed herself to be led off by the diminutive manager.

Travis and Suzanne stepped back into the saloon, but the moment the swinging doors were behind them, and

Clarence out of sight and hearing range, Suzanne pulled away from Travis. "Thank you, Travis," she announced, "but I'm perfectly capable of seeing myself back to the hotel."

Puzzled at her abrupt change of mood, Travis merely stared as she flounced herself past the bar and disappeared through the curtained doorway that led to the rear of the stage and the dressing rooms.

"Jed, give me a drink," Travis shouted suddenly, and sidled up to the bar.

"You okay, Boss?" Jed asked.

"No."

Jed snickered and set a glass in front of Travis. "Didn't think so." He retrieved a bottle from beneath the bar and filled the shot glass with the bourbon Travis ordered especially for himself.

Travis downed the liquor and snapped the glass back onto the bartop. "And just what is that supposed to mean?" he snarled.

Jed shrugged. "You been asking for a shot pretty often lately. That ain't like you, that's all."

"Yeah, well, maybe I'm beginning to understand why some men drink. You know?" He glanced toward the doorway through which Suzanne had disappeared.

"Yeah, sure, Boss. Whatever you say," Jed said. "Whatever you say." He put the bottle back into its place and turned away to serve someone else.

Travis felt a sudden surge of intense temper, and for the briefest flash of a second was forced to stifle the urge to throw the small shotglass at the gilt-framed mirror that covered the wall behind the bar.

"Forget them," he muttered to the reflection that stared back out at him from the silver glass. "Terry's a fool and Suzanne's . . ." He didn't know *what* Suzanne was, except trouble. They were both trouble, which was the last thing he needed. He'd had enough trouble to last him an entire lifetime.

But forgetting about Suzanne was easier said than done, though he couldn't even explain it to himself. It wasn't as if she had been especially nice to him since her arrival, or had gone out of her way to flirt with him, or gain his favor. She'd been polite and friendly enough, at first, but she'd also nearly taken his head off a couple of times. Then again, her kiss had stirred a hunger in him that couldn't be denied.

"Bed her and get her out of your system," he said to the reflection in the mirror.

Turning away from the bar, Travis stalked across the room. He threw back the curtain that covered the doorway to the rear of the stage and walked directly to the door of her dressing room. A cheer filled the air, filtering to him from the saloon. He knocked on the door. "Suzanne?"

No response.

He knocked again. "Suzanne, it's me, Travis."

Still no response.

Travis felt a flash of anger. Damn the woman. Now, what kind of game was she playing? He turned the knob and pushed the door open. "Suzanne?" He stepped into the small room, but she was nowhere in sight. "Suzanne, damn it, where are you?" Travis walked to the dressing screen that stood in the corner and looked behind it. She wasn't there. He turned back and surveyed the room, then swore softly beneath his breath. The Union Belle might only be a block away, but with a town whose population of thirty thousand consisted of at least fifty percent woman-starved miners, it might as well be a mile. A very hazardous mile for a *lady* out alone at night.

"Trouble. Women are nothing but one passel of trouble," Travis grumbled as he stalked out of the dressing room. And if his own problems with Suzanne didn't prove it to him, all he had to do was remember Lisa and how she'd refused to believe him when he'd sworn he'd never been with Suzanne Forteaux.

Or even better, he could remember the jaunty little trail of deceit and intrigue his two sisters-in-law had led his elder brothers on. Granted, in the end it had been rather comical, and they had ended up getting married, but still, Belle and Lin had caused one hell of a lot of trouble. And he had no doubt that they weren't done yet, since they still hadn't located their father or cleared him of the charges of having killed Thomas Braggette.

He swiped at the curtained doorway. The red velvet swathe snapped aside in a tangle. Travis stormed past and into the saloon.

The sound of breaking glass suddenly erupted. The mirror! Travis looked around and suddenly Skinner Jones, arms outstretched, came hurtling across the room, backward, and slammed against Travis, knocking them both back through the curtain and against the wall. The miner slunk to the floor while Travis stood leaning against the wall, gasping for breath and feeling as if he were the inside of a sandwich someone had just stomped on.

The sounds of breaking wood and glass met his ears and caught his attention just as he regained his breath. Fury washed over him at the realization that a fight had broken out in the saloon. "What the hell?" He stormed back past the curtain. "Jed, get the damned shotgun!" he yelled.

Another miner went flying past. A chair careened through the air and crashed against the wall, its legs splintering and sending a shower of slivered wood over the floor.

"Hank!" Travis yelled, spotting his redheaded bull of a saloon manager and friend in the middle of the melée. "What the hell's going on?"

"Gambler was cheatin', Boss," Hank called back, his blue eyes twinkling merrily at the enjoyment of a good fight. "And he got caught." A fist full of knuckle connected with his jaw, and Hank spun around.

But instead of going down, Hank, built like a block of solid granite, which meant he was nearly as wide as he was tall, looked around for the man who had hit him.

A half-empty whiskey bottle flew through the air and crashed against the wall just a foot from Travis's head.

He ducked to one side as shards of glass and a spray of whiskey flew everywhere.

"Jed!" Travis called again. "Stop this damned thing before they break every table and chair in the place."

The barkeep raised a shotgun into the air, pointed it at the ceiling, and pulled back on the trigger. A glass soared toward Travis and crashed against his chest. Whiskey splattered across the front of his white shirt.

An explosion of ear-piercing sound filled the room as shotgun pellets burst from the end of Jed's gun barrel and flew toward the ceiling.

Everyone froze and all heads turned toward the bar. Jed lowered the gun, pointing it at the crowd of tangled arms and legs. "Any more fighting in here," he said, "and we'll be having us a few funerals, too."

The men grumbled, a few cursed loudly, but they broke away from one another and, picking up their chairs and righting their tables, most went back to playing cards. Some left.

Travis looked down at his shirtfront. Wonderful. He smelled like a damned whiskey bottle. He'd have to change before going after Suzanne. If he approached her this way, she'd probably mistake him for a drunk and stab him with her parasol. Or maybe she carried a gun and would just primly blow his head off. He started toward the stairs that led up to his rooms. Now there was a thought. Suzanne with a gun.

He mounted the steps two at a time, feeling a need to get changed and over to the Union Belle to make sure Suzanne was all right. Why he should be concerned about her well-being he wasn't sure. She'd told him, in no uncertain terms, that his company wasn't wanted. " 'Cause I'm paying her a damned fortune to sing here," he mumbled to himself. "And I don't want my star attraction roughed up by some overzealous, love-starved gambler, that's why."

He reached for the doorknob and paused. The hair on the back of his neck suddenly bristled. Instinct warned him to be quiet. He stood still and listened.

A soft rustling came to him from the other side of the door.

Reaching slowly beneath the left front flap of his jacket, Travis's fingers slipped around the polished wooden handle of the derringer he carried there and pulled it out. With his thumb on the hammer, he pulled it back slowly, cocking it, then held the weapon beside his chest, its barrel pointed toward the ceiling. Slowly he wrapped the fingers of his other hand around the knob, turned it, and, kicking the door with his foot, sent it slamming back against the wall with a loud crash, as he lunged into the room.

At his entrance, Suzanne screamed and spun around to face him.

Chapter Eight

Travis stared down the short barrel of his gun, his finger still tightly pressed to the trigger, his thumb poised on the hammer. Suzanne stood across the room, directly centered in the barrel's sight. A violent tremor shook his body as he glared at her in shock, realizing instantly how close he had just come to killing her.

Suzanne's breasts heaved rapidly with her building panic and, in a reflexive move, her trembling fingers twisted the shirt she held in her hands, one of Travis's best. Her gaze was riveted on the gun pointed at her heart and her lips quivered so severely that she had to bite down on the lower one to keep it still. When she was finally able to tear her eyes from the gun and recognized Travis, she sagged back against the bureau she'd been searching through and released a sigh. But her relief was short-lived.

"What the hell are you doing in my rooms?" Travis demanded, fury at himself, at her, at the situation, overwhelming him and blotting out all other emotion.

Suzanne pulled herself up, trying not to look like a thief just caught in the act. But her mind wouldn't come up with a plausible excuse. At least not one she thought he'd accept. Her heart thudded madly against her breast, and she couldn't stop the shaking that had assailed her body. What was she doing in his room? Her mind raced about in search of an answer. What was she doing in his room? What? What? What?

"Suzanne?"

She stared at him blankly. "Huh?"

Travis released the hammer on the gun, and, pulling aside the front flap of his jacket, returned the weapon to its holster. He looked back at her. "What are you doing in my room?" The words were spoken just as harshly as they had been the first time, but at least he hadn't yelled them again.

Her eyes darted toward the floor. She twisted the shirt, then tried to close the bureau drawers by leaning against them. What could she say to him?

Travis took a step forward. "Well?" A frown pulled at his brow and his eyes had narrowed.

Suzanne tried to straighten her shoulders and stand tall, though inwardly she felt herself flinch. "I was . . . uh, I was . . ." And then it came to her. So simple. And she knew he'd believe it. Why wouldn't he? He was a man. Confidence filled her. She smiled, a sultry curving of her lips, seduction suddenly glinting from her blue eyes as she lowered and raised their thick ruche of lashes and threw him what she hoped was a wickedly luring glance. "I was waiting for you," she drawled, her voice low and teasing. She let the shirt she'd been twisting fall to the floor and walked toward Travis, giving a little extra sway to her hips and thrusting her breasts out toward him. "Isn't that what you wanted, Travis?"

She closed the space between them, and then, boldly

pressing her body to his, fitting her curves to the solid, hard planes of his length, slid her hands up and over his chest and wrapped her arms around his neck.

Travis stared down at her in surprise. This was exactly what he'd wanted, but after her performance of a few minutes ago he had been certain he'd never get it. She had more moods than a cat had lives. He started to pull her into his embrace when his gaze caught sight of his bureau. The suspicion he'd felt at first finding her in his room instantly returned, twofold. The drawers of the tall dresser were half open and his clothes were strewn about on the floor, hanging over the edge of the drawers, or lying within them in a crumpled mess. Obviously she had been doing more than waiting for him. She had been searching for something, though he couldn't for the life of him think of what it could be. Unless she was just a thief and after whatever she could find.

Somehow, though, he had a hard time believing Suzanne was a plain thief. Or a plain *anything* for that matter. He inhaled deeply, and the faint scent of her jasmine perfume filled his nostrils. His body began to harden in response to her nearness, and though he would have liked nothing better than to take her up on the veiled offer, something told him it wasn't sincere. It was merely a ploy that she'd thought up on the spur of the moment after being discovered ransaking his things.

But if that's how she wanted to play it, he was certainly more than happy to oblige. Travis circled her waist with his hands and pulled her closer. "So what were you looking for in my bureau, Suzanne?" he whispered, and pressed his lips to the curve of her throat.

She laughed softly and tossed her head back, sending a cascading wave of dark curls spreading across her shoulders. "Why, a shirt to use as a nightgown, silly. But you came up too soon."

He glanced quickly over her shoulder to the floor. Several of his shirts lay before the bureau in rumpled disarray where she had evidently tossed them. Several more hung haphazardly from the open drawers.

Travis decided to see just how far she'd go with her little charade before she panicked. Then he'd find out the truth. He pulled her hard against him, crushing her body to the length of his, her breasts pressed against his chest, her hips melded to his, their lips separated by only a hairsbreadth. His arms wrapped her in an embrace that nearly stole the air from her lungs. "Umm, what an enticing image that invokes," he whispered. "You, in nothing more than my shirt, and in my bed. Absolutely irresistible." Travis lowered his head and pressed his lips to the tantalizing swell of bosom revealed above the low-cut décolletage of her gown.

He felt a shudder wrack her body at the intimate touch and smiled to himself. "But if you had told me you were coming up here, Suzanne, I would have been here sooner," he said, his voice growing husky with the passion that her nearness was instilling within him, "and there would have been no need to look for a shirt—or put anything on to cover yourself from my view, for that matter."

Suzanne fought the swirl of desire that suddenly swept over her at the feel of Travis's lips on her breast. *He's a rogue,* she told herself, over and over, intent on fighting the shocking onslaught of emotion he had incited in her. *A scoundrel,* her mind screamed. *A beast. A knave. A cur.* "I wanted to surprise you," she whispered, afraid that if she spoke aloud he would notice the quavering she was certain was evident in her tone.

He pressed against her, crushing her skirts and crinolines. His lips covered hers hungrily, ravishing her senses, demanding her surrender.

She brazenly allowed his assault, confident that she could withstand it without feeling.

His tongue plunged into her mouth, a burning flame that seared wherever it touched. She caught her breath as the warmth of desire suddenly prickled her skin and stabbed at her center, a fierce, abrupt assault that left her weak with languor and spellbound in his arms.

Travis cupped her breast with one hand. He began a rhythmic massage of the taut nipple, teasing it through the fabric of her gown and camisole.

"Travis, no, please," Suzanne said, her voice ragged as the cold shock of reality, of what she had allowed him to do, of what she had felt, rushed in on her. She pushed against him. "I can't, please . . ." She tried to twist her way out of his embrace, suddenly afraid . . . of him, and of herself.

He released her abruptly and stepped back. One black brow arched haughtily and his gray eyes turned near midnight black. He kept his features rigid, making sure not to let the smile he was feeling show itself on his face. She had panicked sooner than he'd expected. "Isn't that what you came here to offer, Suzanne?"

"No. I mean . . ." She felt her cheeks burn with the heat of a blush. "Yes, but, well, you don't understand. Please, Travis, it's not what you . . . I mean, I didn't intend for this to happen, I only wanted . . ."

Without taking his eyes from her, Travis lifted his foot

and, kicking it back against the still half-open door, slammed it shut.

Suzanne jumped at the loud crash, along with the implication that the slamming of the door provoked. She took several hurried steps sideways as if trying to skirt around him. "Travis, please, I have to go."

He shook his head. "Not until you tell me why you came up here."

"I told you. I wanted to surprise you, but I, well, I've never done this before and . . ."

"What were you looking for, Suzanne? What was it you thought to find in my bureau?"

"Nothing. I told you. Nothing. Really." She felt her hands begin to tremble again and clasped them hastily behind her back. "I was just looking for a shirt to wear. Honestly. To surprise you."

"Fine." He scooped one up off the floor, and, moving to stand before her, held it out. "Then wear this one."

She stared at the shirt as if it were a snake hanging from the tip of his fingers and ready to strike at her if she dared to move.

"Put it on," Travis urged.

"No."

He dropped the garment to the floor and shrugged. "You don't need it anyway." He purposely kept his tone hard, and his eyes as cold as the smile that drew his lips upward. "Just take off your clothes and slip into my bed. I'd rather you were naked."

"What?" She stared at him, aghast. "You don't think I'd . . ." She took a step back. "You can't believe I meant to . . ." Suzanne stammered, wringing her hands. "You don't really expect me to just . . ." She threw a panic-filled glance toward the huge poster bed.

Travis nearly bit off his tongue in an effort to keep from laughing. His bluff had worked. He'd known damned well seduction was not why she was in his room, but acting as if he were going to take her up on it just might garner him the truth. "Oh, I'll pay you, Suzanne. I wouldn't expect a girl like you to do anything without getting paid." He reached inside his jacket and pulled out his billfold. "How much?" He began to pull greenbacks from within the leather sheath. "Ten?" When she didn't answer, he pulled out another greenback. "Twenty?"

Suzanne's hand swung toward his face.

Travis dropped both his billfold and the money. His own hand flashed upward and caught her arm, his fingers wrapping around her delicate wrist like a band of steel.

"You tried that before, remember?"

"Let me go, Travis," she snapped, and tried to yank her arm free. "Let me go or I swear I'll scream."

Travis glared down at her, still holding her wrist secure in his grasp. "Go ahead, scream. It's my saloon. Who do you think is going to help you?"

Her other hand swung toward his face. Travis caught that one, too.

Suzanne writhed and twisted. She jerked away from him, and when that didn't work, she kicked out at him. Her legs became tangled in the ruffled crinolines beneath her gown. The huge hoop cage she wore swayed outward and she lost her balance, falling backward.

Travis, maintaining his grip on her arms, could have held her upright, but he didn't even try.

They tumbled onto the bed. Suzanne lay on her back, Travis coming down on top of her, though he broke his fall with a knee to the mattress. His hands still held her arms stretched taut above her head.

"Now tell me, Suzanne," he said harshly, his face only an inch from hers, his gray eyes ablaze with fury, "What the hell were you searching my room for?"

She squirmed beneath him. "Let me up, you beast."

"Tell me."

She tried to twist away. "You're hurting me."

His lips came down on hers again, momentarily silencing her and commanding she acquiesce to his demands, both verbal and physical. Though his words had been harsh, his posture hard, his body spoke a language of its own, expressing its own needs, its own demands, and imploring her to respond in kind. His tongue flicked about hers like a flame, sparking fire wherever it touched, igniting sparks within her own blood and stilling the tides of anger that had filled her. He kissed her for a long time, a seemingly endless time, in which old memories and long-harbored hurts did not exist, and where the promise of tomorrow loomed bright and radiant.

Suzanne writhed beneath him, trying to break his hold on her, but it was no use. Each time she tore her mouth away from his, he found it again, and when she decided to lay still and merely endure his touch, she found herself again involuntarily surrendering to the passion he awoke within her.

For seven years she had damned him, and for seven years she had dreamed of being held like this, ravished like this . . . by him. She felt a glorious building of pleasure deep inside her, a wave of rapture like none she had ever felt before.

Travis felt the stiffness leave her body, sensed the moment she stopped fighting him and herself, heard the faint moan that escaped her throat and echoed within his, and lifted his head to look down at her.

"Now, tell me," he said, ignoring the firestorm that had erupted within him and threatened to engulf him, his tone threaded with an iron vein of determination, "what the hell were you looking for?"

At his cold words, Suzanne, lost in a haze of passion she had desperately fought to ward off and finally, helplessly, surrendered to, snapped out of it. She stared up at Travis, dismayed and outraged to find him not at all moved by the intimate contact. Humiliation swelled in her breasts and burned on her cheeks. "A *gun*," she said, spitting the words out as if they were vile curses. "I was looking for a gun so I could put a bullet between your eyes."

Travis's laugh was more a sardonic smirk than a true laugh. "Well, then I guess it's a good thing you didn't happen to look at the wall here, isn't it, Suzanne?" He jerked his head to indicate the wall behind him and to one side of the door. "Otherwise I believe you just might have blown my head off. But we both know a gun is not really what you were looking for, don't we?"

Suzanne's eyes darted to the wall. A Navy Colt, settled comfortably into a leather holster, hung from a wooden peg near the doorjamb. She tried to jerk free of him.

"Now come on, Suzanne, tell me the truth." He lowered his head and, sliding his body down hers just a little, closed his mouth over the taut nipple that pressed against the bodice of her gown and nuzzled it with his teeth.

"Stop it!" Suzanne screamed, embarrassment and a

gnawing, aching stab of desire filling her at the intimate gesture. She tried to twist away from him. Tears filled her eyes, but they were not tears of fear, but of frustration at herself, for deep within her an unreasonable, uncontrollable urge begged him to continue.

"Tell me, Suzanne," he said again. He brushed his lips across hers and then they moved to the curve of her throat and, once again, moved downward, toward her breasts in a featherlight, teasing touch, as his hips pushed down atop hers and the hardness of his arousal pressed against her thigh. "Tell me what you were looking for, Suzanne." His lips left a trail of burning flesh behind with each light, caressing kiss. "Tell me, or I swear I'll take you now, whether you truly want me or not."

Suzanne felt hot tears slip from her eyes. She wanted him. She had always wanted him. But she wouldn't give in. Travis Braggette was a blackguard, not the kind of man she wanted to spend her life with. He might be able to arouse her passion, but he could not arouse her love. Closing her eyes, Suzanne purposely drew on the very memory she knew would stoke her fury: his desertion of her. He hadn't even bothered to send her a note of explanation. Or an apology. "I hate you," she whispered vehemently. She tried to twist away from him again.

Travis's head snapped up, and he glared down at her. "You may hate me, Suzanne, but your body desires me as much as mine does you. So, tell me what you're up to or I swear . . ."

She knew he spoke the truth. Her body had betrayed her, and as much as she had tried to fight the passion he stirred within her with just a touch, she couldn't.

"Suzanne."

"I . . . I couldn't fight it any longer, Travis." Her arms curled around his neck tightly. "I've missed you so much," she whispered, giving him at least part of the truth.

Startled at her answer, and thoroughly confused by it, Travis released her and pushed himself up and off the bed. He looked down at her as she jerked to a sitting position and straightened her gown.

"Missed me? We hardly knew each other."

"That didn't matter to me, Travis. I loved you. I always loved you."

He shook his head. This was impossible. He wanted her, yes, more he thought, than he'd ever wanted a woman, but *love?* No. Not now, not then. "Huh-uh, Suzanne. You can't love someone you don't know."

"Fine. I didn't love you," Suzanne snapped. "I never did, and I never will." She lurched from the bed and made for the door.

Travis grabbed her arm and spun her back to face him. "Oh, no you don't. Now what the hell is going on?"

"Nothing. Never mind." She jerked away from him. "Just leave me alone, Travis. Leave me alone."

He moved around her, his tall, muscular frame blocking the door. His fingers curled around her upper arms, holding her in place as he glared down at her through narrowed eyes. "Suzanne, damn it, what are you up to? Why are you in my room? Tell me! What were you looking for?"

Her temper flared. "I was robbing you," Suzanne spat. "I came in here to find your gold, and your silver, and anything else of value I could get my hands on. But you don't have anything in here I want. So let's just forget it." She twisted away from him, desperate to get to the door, to get away before he made her tell the truth, before she started to cry and blurted it out like a whimpering fool and ruined everything.

His grip held her still. She yanked her arm again. Her mind said run. Her body said stay. Run. Stay. Run. Stay. She felt tears sting the back of her eyes and blinked rapidly to stem their tide. She hadn't planned on letting it go this far. Hadn't planned on getting close enough to him to allow old wounds, old feelings, old emotions to resurface. But she hadn't planned on being trapped in his room by him, either. Or finding herself desiring to share his bed like some two-bit trollop.

Travis forced her back across the room.

"I don't want to make love with you, Travis," Suzanne said, realizing he was steering her toward the bed again.

He pushed her down until she sat on the bed, then released her. "Contrary to what you might believe, Suzanne, I don't normally force my attentions on any woman."

"No, you run away."

He ignored the angry jab. "I had that coming. Now, let's stop harping on what happened seven years ago and talk about tonight, shall we?"

"Why don't you want to talk about it, Travis? Still feel guilty?" she persisted. "You left me standing in the damned church, Travis. In front of everyone."

"I said I was sorry, and I am," he growled. "I can't change what I did, and even if I could, I don't know that I would. You're probably better off for what I did anyway. I'm not the marrying kind."

She pressed her lips together, crossed her arms over her breasts, and glowered up at him.

"Damn it, Suzanne, forget that. I want to know what is going on here *now,*" Travis continued.

"I have nothing to say."

"Tell me!" he roared, his patience totally deserting him. His voice reverberated off the thin walls of his room like a crash of thunder caught in a cave.

Suzanne's nerve endings jumped wildly, near startled silly by his outburst.

"Tell me, or so help me God . . ."

"I did tell you," she retorted angrily. "I was in love with you, and you left me. Humiliated me in front of all my friends. All my relatives. The whole damned town."

Travis stared down at her, his eyes hard. "So you waited seven years and finally came here to get revenge?" The words were hard and mocking.

Suzanne jumped to her feet and, settling her hands defiantly on her hips, pushed her face into his. "Yes. You made a fool out of me, Travis. I couldn't face anyone. And then I met Clarence. He had an acting troupe and offered to let me join. I saw my chance to get out of New Orleans, so I took it."

He shook his head, his rage suddenly softened as he realized he believed her. "What happened to the troupe? Why didn't your father come after you and make you go back home?"

"Because he doesn't care."

"And Clarence's troupe?" He almost gagged on the man's name, but forced himself to stay calm.

"It broke up."

"So now he just manages you."

"Yes."

"What's he holding over you, Suzanne?"

"Nothing."

He took her hand in his. "I never meant to hurt you. It was just . . ." He shrugged and looked away.

She pulled her hand from his. "You never thought about me one way or the other, Travis."

"Suzanne, I . . ."

Her eyes glistened hard as they pinioned his. "Don't lie, Travis."

His temper flashed hot again. "Fine. I'm lying. Now *you* do a little lying and tell me why the hell you came into my room and rifled through my bureau."

Suzanne shot up off the bed. "Because I wanted to find a way to ruin you."

"Ruin me?" The shock of her words rocked him.

"Yes, ruin you, like you did me."

His eyes narrowed in suspicion and a smile, wicked and knowing, curved his lips. "Huh-uh, Suzanne. I don't believe you. There's something else going on here."

Suzanne stared up at him. She couldn't tell him the truth. If she did, it could ruin everything. Clarence would find out, and then she might never find Brett.

"Talk, Suzanne," Travis ordered, his words little more than an angry grating of sound.

Panic began to fill her. She couldn't tell him what he wanted to know. She couldn't. It had been foolish to try searching his room. Stupid to think she could circumvent Clarence and the Knights. "There's no more, Travis, honestly." She closed her eyes and willed them to fill with tears. Letting her lashes flutter open then, she nearly sighed in relief to find her vision blurred. "I just didn't know what else to do, Travis. I was lonely." She wiped at the tears that had begun streaming down her cheeks. "I only wanted ..." She hiccuped. "I mean, when you left me, I didn't know what to do ..." hiccup "... I thought maybe you'd come back ..." hiccup "... and my father was so angry ..." she inhaled deeply and let a little sob wrack her frame "... he said it was my fault, that I wasn't pretty enough to interest you ..." hiccup "or anyone else."

She sagged back onto the bed. Travis joined her immediately and drew her into his arms. He tucked her head to his chest and closed his eyes.

Suzanne rested her head against his shoulder, snuggling against the curve of his neck, and suddenly the tears that she had commanded to appear turned real. It had been so long since she'd really cried, so long since anyone had made her feel protected and cared about. And now Travis was here, just like she'd always dreamed he would be, and he was holding her and whispering that everything would be all right.

A knock sounded on the door.

Suzanne didn't hear it.

Travis ignored it, too absorbed in the abrupt realization that, angry as he still was with her, and still suspicious of what she'd told him, holding her suddenly felt so right.

The door opened and Maggie stepped into the room. "Travis, *mon amour,* you didn't come to my room, so I thought I'd come to yours." Her heavily painted eyes widened at the sight of Travis holding Suzanne in his arms, and then a flash of jealousy sparked within her breast. But she merely smiled sweetly. "Oh, is the child hurt, Travis?"

Suzanne, at hearing another woman's voice, jerked

away from Travis. Her cheeks glistened with the moisture of her tears. She stared at Maggie, knowing instantly why the woman had come to Travis's room. If
there had been any doubt in her mind, it was immediately dismissed when, with a flourish, Maggie swept off
her cape and revealed that all she wore underneath was
a very filmy gossamer nightgown which exposed every
inch of her generously endowed body.

Chapter Nine

Suzanne, after managing to surmount her shock and close her gaping mouth, shot up off the bed and rushed from the room, keeping her gaze averted as she hurried past Maggie.

"Well, that was a marvelous performance, Mag," Travis said, irritation dripping from each word. He stalked across the room and slammed shut the door to the balcony that overlooked the saloon. "And just what the hell was that little act all about?"

Magnolia batted her long, thickly painted lashes at Travis and smiled slyly. "Why, Travis, *mon cher,*" she reached out to stroke his chest with her hand and snuggled close to him, "whatever do you mean? I just thought, when you didn't come by tonight, that I'd give you a little surprise."

"A surprise, huh?" He looked down at her. Any other time he would have gladly taken her up on her offer. He would have embraced her voluptuous body, dragged her over to his bed and teased the gossamer gown from her body with a series of provocative caresses. But tonight neither his body nor his mind were in the mood for Magnolia Rochelle.

She nodded and, standing on tiptoe, brushed her lips across his. "It *is* Friday, *mon cher,* and you know we always have a little, um, *tête à tête* on Fridays." Magnolia smiled and pressed her body seductively against his, swaying back and forth, just a little, so that she rubbed against the hard arousal she felt there. "And tonight I am feeling unusually hungry," she purred.

Travis clamped his hands around her upper arms in a secure hold and moved her away from him. "Not tonight, Mag," he said. "Sorry."

Inwardly Magnolia fumed, every cell and fiber within her wanting nothing more than to lash out at him, and at the little songbird who had obviously caught his eye. "Is it her, *chéri?*" she asked, the words, thick with venom, pouring from her lips before she could stop them. "That Suzanne woman you brought here?"

"No," Travis snapped. "I just have things to do, that's all."

Magnolia merely pouted and tried to sidle up against him again. "Ah *mon cher,* you know you always enjoy our time together. Come, we can . . ."

Travis turned away from her and, bending to the floor, retrieved his billfold and greenbacks. "I said, not tonight, Mag. I've got some other things I have to do."

"But, *chéri,* this is *our* night. We always . . ."

"Magnolia," Travis said, using her full name as emphasis of his anger. "We agreed, remember? No promises, no commitments."

Magnolia's eyes burned with the fury that nearly raged out of control within her breast at his words, but she maintained her composure. Only the stiffening of her shoulders and a momentary clenching of her fingers gave evidence of her anger. "Later, then, *chéri?*" she managed to ask in an even tone.

He opened the door and, settling her cape about her shoulders, motioned for her to precede him. "No, Mag, I'm sorry." Travis saw the flash of hurt in her eyes, the angry stiffening of her shoulders, and felt a surge of guilt. He and Magnolia had been seeing each other on Friday nights for the past several months. They had a lot in common—both came from New Orleans, both ran a saloon in Virginia City—but their relationship wasn't a serious thing, both had agreed to that in the beginning. And nothing had changed, at least not in Travis's mind or heart. He'd tried love once, found it bitter, and wasn't about to try it again.

From the top of the stairs Magnolia suddenly spotted Suzanne exiting the curtained doorway from the rear stage area. The saloon woman swung around suddenly to face Travis and threw her arms around his neck. She pressed her body tightly to his. "Ah, *mon cher,* don't be mad at me. I was just a bit lonely tonight."

Taken by surprise at her abrupt movement, and still wracked by a sense of guilt at being so gruff with her moments before, Travis smiled. "I'm not mad at you, Mag, I just have to . . ."

She pressed her hands against the back of his neck and, rising to her tiptoes, forced his head down to meet her kiss. Her lips captured his, effectively cutting off further words and staking her claim upon Travis Braggette for all to see. Especially Miss Suzanne Forteaux.

Suzanne had caught sight of them exiting Travis's room the moment she'd stepped past the curtained doorway. After the first glance, she determined not to

look back. What did she care what they did? But her
eyes seemed to have a will of their own, paying no attention to the commands of her mind. She jerked her
gaze away, took several steps, faltered, and, against her
own will, turned to look at them again.

Something akin to anger stabbed at her as she
watched the saloon woman wrap her arms around
Travis's neck and kiss him. But it was more a sense of
loss that assailed her when she saw Travis's arms slip
down to circle the woman's waist.

Suzanne tossed her head, sending the hood of the cape
she had retrieved from her dressing room after rushing
from Travis's suite slipping back to her shoulders. What
did she care if Travis Braggette kissed every woman in
this godforsaken town? She had come here for one reason and for one reason only, and that was to find out
about her brother. She didn't care about Travis. She
might have to play up to him, to get in his good favor,
and get him talking, but that was all. And she'd keep her
wits about her from now on when she was doing it. She
didn't care about him. She didn't. She was lonely, that
was all.

She glanced back at Travis as she hurried past the
bar on her way to the swinging doors, and the street. He
and the woman were descending the stairs. Suzanne
hastened her pace. Letting him kiss her had been a mistake. Travis was more of a danger to her than she had
anticipated. But then, why should she have thought herself immune to him, even now, after seven years? she
asked herself. Hadn't she measured every man who had
courted her since then against Travis? And hadn't they
all fallen short when compared to the memory of the
man she had been betrothed to marry?

She slammed through the swinging saloon doors, nearly smashing them into the barreled chest of a miner on his way in.

"Hey, pretty lady, what's your hurry?" he roared through the bush of whiskers that covered the bottom half of his craggy face. "Skinner Jones after you again?" He stepped back and let out a belly-deep laugh.

"Oh, hush up," Suzanne said, and made to move past him.

"Whoa, there." One huge, grubby hand reached out and curled around her arm, bringing Suzanne to an abrupt halt, and almost off her feet.

She yanked her arm in an effort to get away from the man. Did every man in this town think they could just paw any woman they wanted? "Let me go."

"Come on, I'll buy you a drink," the miner said, still laughing.

"Let Miss Lindsay go." Both Suzanne and the miner turned at the sound of the soft voice that came from behind them.

"Addie?" Suzanne gasped, both startled and relieved to see her maid.

Addie raised the small derringer she held in her hand and pointed it directly at the miner's head. "I said, let Miss Lindsay go. Now."

The miner's hand snapped away from Suzanne's arm as if it had just turned to searing iron. "Hey, fine, ma'am. I was just looking for a little fun, that's all. Was going to buy her a drink. No harm meant. Geez."

"Then go have your fun," Addie commanded. "In there." She waved the gun toward the interior of the Mountain Queen.

The miner didn't hesitate. Faster than Suzanne could blink, he dived through the doors and out of sight.

Astonished at what had just happened, and momentarily forgetting about Travis and his paramour, a shocked Suzanne turned wide eyes back toward her maid. "Addie, that was incredible."

Addie shrugged and slipped the small derringer into her reticule. "Just glad I was here, or no telling what might have happened."

"Be back in about an hour or so, Hank," Travis suddenly called out.

Suzanne stiffened at the sound of his voice. "Come on," she said, taking the other woman by the arm, "let's go."

As Suzanne practically shoved her down the boardwalk, Addie frowned and looked back over her shoulder at Travis, who had just exited the saloon. Wasn't running away from the man exactly the opposite of what Suzanne was supposed to be doing? "Miss Suzanne," Addie said, "what's the matter? Why are we rushing so?"

"I didn't know you had a gun, Addie," Suzanne said, ignoring the maid's comment. "But I must say I'm certainly glad you do. I thought you went back to the hotel with Clarence, though." She hurried on. "Did you forget something at the saloon?"

"No, but I thought, well, I thought you might need me for changing your gown and all."

Suzanne nodded, but her mind had already deserted Addie and returned to thoughts of Travis, much to her annoyance. The last thing she had expected of herself when she'd made her deal with Clarence was that she'd experience romantic notions about Travis Braggette again. She'd felt safe in agreeing. Confident. And why not? He was the lowest cur she ever had the misfortune to meet. The most arrogant, inconsiderate, snake-bellied rake. And just like the first time he had kissed her, he still had the power to totally devastate her better senses and send them reeling.

Addie looked at Suzanne out of the corner of her eye.

"I've been a fool, Addie," Suzanne grumbled. "An absolutely witless fool."

Travis pulled his horse up in front of the King house. There were already several dozen carriages parked about, and another dozen or so horses tied to the corral fence. A steady curl of smoke billowed upward from the rock chimney at the side of the small clapboard house, and light reflected from behind the muslin curtains that had been drawn across the two narrow front windows. Travis dismounted and, looping Starhawk's reins over a hitching post that stood to one side of the entry path, walked to the front door and rapped his knuckles against the rough wooden surface.

"Who is it?" a voice asked from inside.

"Braggette."

The door swung open instantly to reveal a room crowded with other men. Some were sitting around a table, deep in conversation, while most of the others stood surrounding Judge David Terry, who was expounding on the merits of being a member of the Knights. He noticed Travis and immediately excused himself from the group.

"Travis," he said loudly, thrusting a hand toward him. "Glad you could make it."

"Hello, Judge," Travis said. He shook Terry's hand. "I only came by to warn you that I heard some com-

ments in town about some of the boys intending to
come out here and break up your meeting tonight."

The judge laughed. "Meeting? What meeting?" he
looked around the room, smiling widely. "Hell, we're
just having ourselves a little social get-together. A party.
Ain't that right, boys?"

A rumble of laughter and affirmative comments filled
the room.

"You can see for yourself," the judge said, turning
back to Travis. "Just a group of friends having a good
time." He stepped up beside Travis and, putting an arm
around his shoulders, steered him deeper into the room.

The door closed behind them.

"Now," the judge said, in a lowered tone, "I'm glad
you came, Travis, real glad, because I have an announcement to make tonight, and it wouldn't have been
right without you here."

"Judge, I really can't stay," Travis said. The last thing
he wanted was to attend a meeting of the Knights. It
had been a mistake to join them in the first place, but
he'd been young, idealistic, and rash. He knew better
now.

"Nonsense, this will only take a minute." David Terry
stepped onto the raised hearth of the fireplace and
raised his hands high. "Quiet, everyone. Quiet," he ordered in his best courtroom voice.

A hush fell immediately over the room.

"We can get down to our other business later, boys,
but right now I have an announcement to make," the
judge said. He looked at Travis for a long moment, then
continued. "I'm going to be leaving Virginia City."

A series of grumbling protests broke out from the
crowd.

The judge put up his hands again in a request for silence. "Please, listen to me, boys. It was a hard decision to come to, but I'm afraid I must leave. As you all know, my brothers and their families live in Texas. Family responsibilities, boys, have prevailed on me and demand my presence there."

"But what about our plans?" one of the men called out.

"Yeah," another said. "What do we do?"

The judge smiled slyly.

Travis felt suddenly very uneasy.

The judge held up his hands again. "You will proceed as planned."

"How? Without you here?"

"Travis Braggette will take my place as your leader."

All eyes turned to Travis.

He stared at David Terry in absolute dismay. What the hell was the man trying to pull?

Just then, the entry door of the small house opened quietly and a slightly built figure, hunched over so that hat and cape became nearly one and hid all features, slipped from the house.

"Braggette ain't one of us," a miner bellowed.

"Yeah, he ain't never come to no meetings."

"You gotta stay, Judge."

David Terry stroked his mustache and held up a hand for silence. "Boys, Travis is a good man and has been a member of the KGC for . . ."

"Hold it, Judge," Travis growled. He approached the hearth and glared up at Terry. "I told you earlier I didn't want anything to do with the Knights, and I meant it." He turned to the crowd. "I only came here tonight to warn you that some of the men in town who don't sympathize with your cause were talking about coming out here and starting trouble. And it sounded like they had the sheriff on their side."

"So we'll give 'em a good fight," somebody called out.

"I didn't come here to attend your meeting," Travis said loudly, overriding the mumbles of the crowd. "And I'm not taking over for Judge Terry. Elect yourselves another leader, boys. But if you're smart you'll get out of here now and do it somewhere else." He stepped down and crossed the room to the door, then paused and looked back at them. "Then again, if you're smart, you'll just disband."

"Go crawl back in your hole, Braggette," a miner shouted.

"Yeah. You're either for the cause or you're against it, and it don't sound much like you're for it," another said.

"I'm a southerner," Travis said. "And a loyal one. I'm just not a Knight."

"Yankee lover."

Travis slammed the door behind him. He mounted Starhawk and, jerking the reins, urged the horse into a quiet lope back toward town. The faction of town that remained loyal to the Union already thought of him as a Johnny Reb, suspecting him of everything from spying to smuggling. Now those loyal to the Confederacy had just turned against him and labeled him a Yankee lover. It was just a damned good thing he'd contracted to have Suzanne sing in the Mountain Queen for a few weeks, otherwise he'd probably be looking at an empty saloon every night. But the men would come for Suzanne.

Half an hour later Travis reined up in front of the

Union Belle Hotel. Most of the windows were dark. He leaned forward in his saddle and glanced through the lace-covered glass inserts of the double front doors. An oil lamp at one end of the front desk glowed softly, bathing the lobby in a golden glow of light, but no one was in evidence.

He dismounted and walked into the hotel.

At the sound of the front door closing, Mavis Beale appeared around the corner that led to her family's living quarters.

"Travis, what are you doing here so late?"

"I wanted to talk to Suz— Miss Georgette Lindsay, Mavis, but," he glanced toward the stairs that led up to the second floor where most of the hotel rooms were located, "I guess she's already . . ."

"You guess right," Mavis said. "Every decent body is in their bed and asleep, and that includes Miss Lindsay. She came in more'n an hour ago and I ain't heard a peep out of her or her maid since."

Travis nodded. "Can you put a note in her key box for me, Mavis?"

"Sure, honey." She shoved a piece of paper across the desk toward him. "Use that quill there the guests sign in with."

Travis picked up the feathered quill and began to write.

We need to talk. Please join me for dinner. I'll call for you at seven, before your first show. Travis.

He folded the note and handed it to Mavis, who shoved it into the box reserved for the key to Suzanne's room.

She looked back at Travis and smiled. "Kinda sweet on that little songbird, huh?"

Travis smiled back and, reaching across the desk, chucked a finger under her double chin. "I could never be sweet on anyone but you, darlin'."

Mavis scoffed and pushed his hand away. "Oh, go on with you now."

"I told you, Clarence," Suzanne said, struggling to keep her anger in check, "there wasn't anything in his room." She turned her back on him and moved to stand before the fireplace, staring down into the dancing flames.

"You mean, there wasn't anything that you found."

Suzanne whirled back around. "I mean exactly what I say. There wasn't anything in his room to find."

Clarence Lonchet glared up at Suzanne from the settee. His brown eyes narrowed until they resembled the beady eyes of a ferret. "Or maybe you found something and you just don't want to tell me about it." His brows rose in question. "Something that wouldn't make your lover look so good, maybe?"

"He's not my lover." Her fingers itched to pick up the crystal vase on the small marble-topped table beside her and throw it at Clarence. She glanced at the vase. Travis had sent her a bouquet of roses. Red roses.

As he eyed the roses, his lips curved in a wily smile. "So you say."

Red roses mean passion, Addie had declared upon accepting delivery of the flowers only a few hours before.

Suzanne glowered at the roses. Passion. She'd show him passion. If he was in the room she'd show him how passionate it was to get hit over the head by a five-pound crystal vase filled with water and long-stemmed roses.

"You haven't forgotten about your brother, have you, missy?" Clarence goaded. "About what we agreed?"

Suzanne forget about Travis. She jerked her gaze back to Clarence. "No, I haven't forgotten about Brett. And you'd just better keep your end of the deal."

Clarence laughed, his bald pate picking up the light of a nearby lantern and glowing pink. "I've given you my word of honor, Suzanne. Are you questioning it?"

Yes, her mind screamed. "No," she said. "Of course not."

"Good. Now, we don't have a lot of time left." He inhaled deeply from the thin cheroot he held between his fingers and, leaning his head back until it nearly touched the intricate rosewood carving of the settee on which he sat, blew the smoke toward the ceiling. "Morgan arrives tonight." He flicked the end of his cheroot with his thumb, and ash fell onto the carpeted floor.

"Clarence!" Suzanne said, appalled. She stared at the floor for several seconds to make certain the carpet didn't begin to smolder.

"Braggette was at a meeting of the Knights earlier this evening," Clarence said, ignoring her reprimand.

Suzanne looked at Clarence pointedly, her attention piqued. Obviously Clarence had been at the meeting, too. Otherwise, how would he know that Travis was there. "So?"

"We have to make certain about Braggette, Suzanne, one way or the other. And soon." He pinned her with an assessing glare. "Can you do it?"

"Yes," she answered softly.

* * *

Addie Hayes straightened and stepped cautiously
away from Suzanne's door. Taking care to make no
sound, she hurried down the hall and slipped into her
own room, quietly closing the door behind her.

Chapter Ten

Addie stood beside the open door of the dressing room. She had purposely left the hotel early, writing a note to Suzanne that she was going for a brisk morning walk and would return shortly to help her dress. It had been a lie, of course, but a necessary one.

Only a soft mumble of sound came from the barroom. There weren't that many miners in the Mountain Queen, the hour being just before the mine's morning shift change. A few professional gamblers, independent miners, and freighters had been in the saloon when she'd entered, along with Jed behind the counter, but Addie hadn't seen Hank.

She only hoped that he was about somewhere.

A door closed down the hallway and Addie peeked out. As if in answer to her prayers, she saw Hank exit one of the rooms. Hastily smoothing down the front of her skirt and straightening her sleeves, raising a quick hand to her head to reaffirm that her carefully brushed and arranged hair was still loose and flowing around her shoulders, Addie stepped into the hall just as Hank was about to pass.

"Whoa, there, Miss Hays," Hank said, stopping short as he nearly barreled over her. "I almost ran you down."

"Oh, Mr. Davis, I'm sorry," Addie said, "I didn't realize you were there."

"First time anyone's ever said they didn't see me a'coming," he said, referring to his large bulk. Laughter rumbled from his chest.

Addie chuckled lightly. "Well, I just wish we'd had you around last night," she said saucily, "when that horrid miner tried to assault Miss Lindsay." She let her eyes rake over his muscular frame. "I'm sure there isn't a man in the country who would fool with you."

Hank seemed to puff up at the flirtatious compliment. "You or Miss Lindsay have any trouble with these yokels around here, you just let me know, Miss Hays. I'll see that they don't bother you no more."

"Oh, Hank, that's so kind of you," Addie gushed. She batted her dark lashes at him and smiled. "But please, call me Addie. Miss Hays sounds so formal."

He smiled. "Only if you call me, Hank, Miss Addie."

"Why, I'd be absolutely delighted, *Hank.*" She turned to go and then, as if a thought had just struck her, turned back and smiled. "Hank, I know this isn't a lady's place, but . . . well, I had to retrieve some gloves I left here last night and, since I was out I thought I'd just stop at the Gold Nugget Cafe for a cup of coffee, being as Miss Lindsay isn't up yet, and, well, I thought maybe you'd, well . . ."

"Just what I was about to do," Hank said. "Would you care to join me, Miss Addie."

"Just Addie," she said. "Please."

Hank nodded. "Addie."

She smiled. Things were working out just fine. "I'd love to, Hank, thank you." She moved up beside him and slipped her arm around his.

The crisp morning air and a harrowing wind greeted them as they stepped onto the boardwalk. Addie's cape, which Hank had helped her slip on just before exiting the saloon, whipped about her legs and she had to reach up with her free hand to keep the hood secured in place.

"You all right, Addie?" Hank yelled, bending down to get a glimpse of her face as she hovered beside him.

She nodded. "Ready when you are."

Holding his hat to his head and tucking his elbow tightly into his side to keep her hand in place, Hank descended the boardwalk and, skirting piles of snow and splotches of ice on the road, steered them to the opposite side of the street.

"Where did the wind come from?" Addie asked, as they hurried toward the restaurant. "It wasn't like this earlier."

"Zephyrs come on just like that," Hank yelled, and snapped his fingers.

"Zephyrs?" Addie repeated, and looked at him questioningly.

"Washoe zephyr," Hank said. "That's what we call the winds up here. Can get pretty bad, too. Actually, this one here's kinda mild."

They entered the Golden Nugget, Addie thinking that if this was a "mild zephyr," she didn't want to be around when they had a severe one.

Hank pointed to a table toward the rear of the room and surprised Addie by holding her chair out for her.

Addie was thankful they hadn't secured a table near

the window. She didn't need either Clarence or Suzanne seeing her with Hank if she could help it. She had her story all ready if one or the other *should* see her; she was attracted to him. That was it. Plain and simple. He'd asked her to join him for coffee, she liked him, so she'd said yes.

A waitress brought them coffee the moment they sat at the table. Addie looked down at it. Obviously, coffee was the staple drink of the morning in Virginia City. She herself preferred tea.

Addie took a quick sip, relishing the warmth that immediately spread through her at the feel of the hot liquid sliding down her throat, but forcing herself not to cringe at the strength of the brew.

After a few minutes of small talk, and ordering a couple of doughnuts to go with their coffee, Addie broached the subject foremost on her mind. "Hank, are you . . ." she looked over her shoulder as if to make sure no one was near enough to hear and dropped her voice to a whisper, "are you one of these Knight people?"

"Night people?" Hank echoed, looking thoroughly puzzled. "You mean 'cause I work most of the night?" He laughed. "I ain't no vampire, Addie, if that's what you mean."

Addie shook her head. "No. I mean, Knight, with a K. You know, that organization that's supporting the South. The Knights of the something or other." She shrugged. "I hear it's pretty strong here in Virginia City."

"Nah, not me." Hank shook his head. "I just do my job at the Queen and mind my own business. Why?"

Addie didn't know whether his answer was just an innocent response to her question, or a hint for her not to continue with her questions about the Knights. She chose to believe the former. "Well, I hear Mr. Braggette is a member and, well, I just like to look out for Miss Lindsay."

Hank took a sip of his coffee, but did not reply.

"I overheard someone say at the saloon this morning that they heard Mr. Braggette was taking over as leader of the Knights here."

Hank shook his head. "The boss wouldn't do that."

"No?" Addie tried to look innocently surprised. "Why not? He's from the South, isn't he? Or . . ." she suddenly looked abashed and dropped her voice even lower, "does he sympathize with the North?"

Hank frowned. "The boss ain't a Yankee sympathizer, Addie, I can tell you that, but he ain't in with them Knights, either. No, ma'am. Not the boss."

"Umm. I wonder why that man said he'd heard Mr. Braggette was going to be in charge?"

Hank shrugged. "Folks say lotsa different things around here. Don't make them true."

Addie looked thoughtful. "No, I guess not," she mumbled.

At that moment the door of the cafe opened and Clarence Lonchet walked in. Addie, startled from her musings, nearly dropped her cup of coffee into her lap. Instead, she smiled and waved to Clarence. "Hello there, Mr. Lonchet," she called out merrily, deciding it was better to bring herself innocently to his attention than try to avoid his notice.

Clarence weaved his way through the maze of tables that crowded the small room. "So, Addie. Good morning. It's so early I would have thought you'd still be with Georgette."

Addie set down her cup and hastily dabbed a linen to her lips. "Oh, I guess I really should be getting back. I went for a morning walk and ran into Mr. Davis here . . . Oh, Clarence, I'm sorry, I wasn't thinking. Have you met Mr. Braggette's manager, Mr. Davis?"

Clarence looked at Hank.

"Mr. Lonchet, this is Hank Davis." Addie stood up quickly and retrieved her reticule from the table. "Hank, this is Miss Lindsay's manager, Clarence Lonchet."

The two men shook hands. Hank grumbled an incoherent greeting, and Clarence eyed him with obvious disdain.

"Well, I really must go." She smiled down at Hank. "Thank you so much for the little breakfast, Hank, and for keeping me company."

"My pleasure."

"Bye now," Addie said cheerfully. She hurried from the cafe and down the boardwalk toward the hotel. Drat, now she'd have to act as if she were hopelessly infatuated with Hank Davis whenever that little weasal, Clarence Lonchet, was around. Addie smiled to herself. Then again, it might not be all that hard an act. Hank Davis might look like more bear than man, with all that hair and brawn, but he seemed to be one of the sweetest men she'd ever met.

Yes, her job did have its benefits.

That evening, Travis leaned over the bartop and tried to pretend he wasn't interested in what was going on behind him. But the truth of the matter was, he couldn't have been more interested. He tried not to glance toward the gilt-framed mirror that hung over the bar's backdrop, but he couldn't seem to stop himself. He stared into the silvered glass and watched, unwillingly but intently, as Suzanne talked with Tom Lowry. The man owned one of the biggest mines in Virginia City and threw his money around like there was no tomorrow, and no end to the rich veins of ore that ran through his claim. To make matters worse, the man was a decent sort, and not half bad in appearance.

Lowry suddenly threw back his head and laughed at something Suzanne had said. Travis felt a flash of white-hot anger sweep through him. He hadn't hired her to flirt with the customers. His fingers tightened around the shot glass he held. He hadn't contracted her to come to the Mountain Queen so that she could sashay around the men in search of a rich man to marry, either.

He saw Lowry reach across the table and take Suzanne's hand in his.

"Jed, give me another shot," Travis growled, shoving his glass across the bar.

The bartender looked at him, frowned, and reached under the bar for Travis's special bottle of bourbon. "Sure, Boss."

Travis looked back up at the mirror and felt his anger surge another notch. Bob Fairmount had seated himself at the same table with Lowry and Suzanne. Travis grabbed the glass Jed set in front of him and downed the inch of bourbon that filled it, then looked back at the threesome. In particular, at Bob Fairmount. If the man wasn't drooling over Suzanne, he was damned near to it.

A flash of movement to Travis's right caught his eye, and he turned to see the red swinging doors of the Mountain Queen push forward. A tall figure, solidly built, filled the doorway for the brief flash of a second, and then stepped into the saloon, and the light.

Travis didn't recognize the man. He was new to town. But he wasn't a miner, nor any other kind of laborer. That was obvious from the suit he wore, brown broadcloth and tailored to fit, though it looked as if he had put on a few more muscles or pounds since the garment had been made. The man held a folded newspaper tucked under his arm, along with a sheath of writing paper, and as he stepped into the room, he paused and looked about, as if searching for someone. Travis felt a momentary sense of familiarity, yet at the same time was certain he'd never met him. His eyes narrowed slightly as he tried to place him. Travis practically stared a hole through the man as he watched him walk past the bar and settle at a table near the one where Suzanne still sat with Lowry and Fairmount.

One of the waitresses sauntered up to the table, took his order, and within a few minutes was back at his side, placing a glass of beer next to the stranger's papers, which he'd spread out on the table before him. The waitress flirted with him blatantly, leaning over to whisper in his ear and expose enough cleavage to allow him to drown in. The man merely laughed, gave her a swat on the fanny, and reached for his beer.

Travis pushed away from the bar and started toward the stranger's table, his curiosity getting the better of him. He'd seen him somewhere before, and he wanted to know where.

"My name's Travis Braggette," Travis said, stopping beside the man's table. He thrust out his hand. "Welcome to the Mountain Queen."

The stranger looked up at Travis from beneath thin

light-brown brows for a long second before responding. A wide grin slowly split his face. In spite of the ravages of age and hard living that had left their mark in pits, scars, and hard lines, aristocratic features were still strongly in evidence. He pushed away from the table and stood. "Travis Braggette. Owner of this fine establishment." He took Travis's hand and shook it vigorously. "Glad to meet you, Mr. Braggette. My name's Benjamin Morgan. Care to join me in a drink?"

Travis settled in one of the empty chairs at the table. "Where are you from, Mr. Morgan?"

"Michigan, originally, but I haven't been back there in so long I don't even remember what it looks like." He shook his head and chuckled. "No, sir, I'm a California man now. Been there, oh," he screwed up his face as if in deep thought, then smiled, "hell, I don't rightly remember *how* long it's been. More than thirty years, though, I can tell you that. Came out with my parents when I was just a sprout."

"What brings you to Virginia City?"

"A story, Mr. Braggette, a story. I'm a newspaper man. *San Francisco Bulletin.* Heard you boys were having a spot of trouble up here again with those southern fellows again. Knights of the Golden Circle."

Travis swore silently and shook his head. "Sorry to disappoint you, Mr. Morgan, and ruin your story, but you got your information wrong. That trouble was over a long time ago."

Ben Morgan chuckled and scratched at his whisker-covered chin, but his blue eyes held none of the humor his words or laughter tried to express. "Well, maybe. But I'm here now, so I might as well look around for some kind of story." He laughed again. "If I don't come up with something, I don't get paid."

Travis stood. "Well, enjoy your stay, Mr. Morgan, and good luck with finding a story. I've got a few things to attend to, so if you'll excuse me?"

"Surely," Morgan said. "Surely." He offered Travis his hand. "Nice to meet you, Mr. Braggette. If you hear anything, anything newsworthy, I mean, I'd be much obliged if you'd share it with me."

Travis shook Morgan's hand, nodded, and turned to go.

"Mind if I use this table here as kind of my office while I'm in town, Braggette?"

Travis stopped and looked back at the man.

Blue eyes, as cold as a winter's sea, stared up at him, waiting.

Travis shook his head. "No, that'd be fine, Morgan, as long as you're willing to share it when the place gets crowded."

"My pleasure," Ben Morgan said. "My pleasure." He took a long swallow of his beer and, setting the glass back on the table, let his eyes roam around the room until they came to rest on Suzanne.

As if feeling his gaze on her, she turned and met it.

Travis watched from where he stood at the bar. He saw Ben Morgan smile at Suzanne and tip his head in greeting. She returned the smile, though somewhat stiltedly, it seemed, and then resumed her conversation with Lowry and Fairmount. Travis wasn't sure whether that was good or bad. She was flirting with the two mine owners, and they were lapping it up like a couple of half-starved pups. On the other hand ... His gaze moved back to rest on Morgan, there was still something about the big man that rattled Travis's nerves, and it wasn't only the fact that he had begun to eye Suzanne with a series of suggestive looks. Though that didn't sit too well, either.

"Waitress! Another beer, please!" Ben Morgan called out, holding up his glass.

Travis continued to stare at the man as the waitress sauntered to his table to retrieve the glass, and then it hit him. Ben Morgan claimed he wrote for the *San Francisco Bulletin*. Most likely that's where Travis had heard his name, or maybe even seen his picture. But his accent, slight as it was, that wasn't San Francisco. And it didn't sound Michigan, either. Travis stared hard at Morgan. Michigan. California. Neither would give him that faint hint of a southern drawl that Travis detected. Most people wouldn't even notice it, especially if they weren't already looking for something about the man that bothered them, and if they weren't southern. But Travis was, and he'd noticed.

Jed slid another shot glass full of bourbon to Travis.

"Thanks, Jed," he said absently, not taking his eyes off Morgan. Travis reached for the glass and pulled it toward him. The man was southern, and he had lied about it. Why?

Suzanne rose from her chair and laughed merrily. The sound, like the tinkle of chimes against the wind, carried to Travis and stoked the ire he'd been feeling toward her and the men around her all evening. She turned to make her way through the maze of tables and patrons, evidently on her way back to her dressing room.

"Miss Lindsay?"

Travis felt himself stiffen at hearing Morgan call out to Suzanne.

She paused beside Ben Morgan's table and looked down at him.

He stood. "I'm Ben Morgan, ma'am," he said loudly, "of the *San Francisco Bulletin.* I'd be honored if you would let me have an interview."

Suzanne smiled and, catching a glimpse of Travis watching, cocked a shoulder impudently. "Well, I'd be delighted, Mr. Morgan," she answered, slowly drawing out each word in a drawl that practically dripped sugar.

Morgan held out a chair for her and she slipped into it, batting her long lashes at him and flashing him another dazzling smile.

Travis growled softly deep within his throat and downed the bourbon in one gulp. What the hell did he care if she flirted with every miner, gambler, and drifter that walked into the place? Obviously, that's what she liked to do. And that story she'd sobbed out when he'd caught her rifling through his things, about her being lonely and wanting to be with him, that story was probably just that, a story, to cover up the fact that she was little more than a common, ordinary thief.

"Looks like you've got everyone around here eating out of your hand, Suzanne," Morgan said, keeping his voice low.

She smiled, but her eyes glittered icy, like diamonds.

"Isn't that what I'm supposed to do?" she said, her tone one of sneering sweetness.

"You find out anything about Braggette yet?"

Suzanne felt a shiver of uneasiness trip its way up her spine. She looked away from Morgan, letting her gaze drift over the surrounding crowd. "No."

"Losin' your touch, Suzanne?"

Her anger bristled and her head jerked back around toward him. Indignation etched itself on every feature of her face. "I don't have a *touch*, Mr. Morgan. I'm here because of Brett. Nothing else. Just Brett."

"Just make sure you remember that, Suzanne, and don't try to do anything to jeopardize our plans, or you might not ever see that precious brother of yours again. Understand?"

"Yes." She snapped the word off like the breaking of a brittle tree branch.

"Good. Now, where's Clarence?" Ben Morgan asked, keeping his tone hushed.

Suzanne shrugged. "I don't know." *And I don't care,* she thought. "He's usually here. Maybe he just stepped out for some air."

"Damned long breath of air, if you ask me. I need to talk to him . . ." Morgan's eyes narrowed as he glared pointedly at her, ". . . alone. Tell him to meet me tomorrow morning out on Six Mile Canyon Road. Nine o'clock."

"Six Mile Canyon Road," she repeated softly. "Any particular part of Six Mile Canyon Road?"

"Just tell him to ride, Suzanne. I'll find him."

Chapter Eleven

It didn't hit him until later as he was climbing the stairs toward his room. He had decided to retire for the night. Business had slowed. Most of the miners who had dropped in after getting off their shifts had drifted to their homes, rooms, or cabins to get some sleep before reporting back to work. The saloon had quieted considerably, though it was far from empty. Travis paused at the landing and looked back down into the barroom. A flash of green satin caught his eye. For a second he thought Magnolia had returned and his temper flared abruptly, remembering her intrusion earlier when he'd been with Suzanne. But his ire subsided just as quickly as he realized it wasn't Magnolia he saw but Elsie, one of his own waitresses. He watcher her slip a black cape around her shoulders and head for the door leading to the street. Her shift was over.

But the sight of the green satin, and the thought of Magnolia it had naturally brought to his mind, also brought with it another memory, causing his eyes to darken as his brows pulled together in a deep frown. Maggie had known Suzanne's name. Her real name.

Travis looked back down at the nearly empty barroom, though in his mind's eye it was Magnolia Rochelle he was seeing. How? How had she known who Georgette Lindsay really was?

Travis rolled over in his bed. Grabbing one of his pillows, he rammed it down over his head and held it there. Had he even gotten to sleep? If he had, it sure wasn't very long ago. The pillow didn't do any good. He could still hear the sound of gunshots. He thrust it away and, rolling to lie on his back, stared through the darkness toward the high ceiling above. In the distance, beyond the mountains, the morning sun began its slow ascent into the sky, and the first paltry rays of dawn suddenly penetrated the darkness of his room. He thought about rising and yanking the curtains closed. Judging by the light filtering in through the window, it was approximately five o'clock. The miners would be changing shifts soon. He'd only come upstairs three hours ago.

"Three hours sleep," he grumbled, then closed his eyes and commanded his body to relax.

Another gunshot rent the air. Travis's eyes shot open. Damn those yahoos, he thought angrily. And where was Morrow? How in the hell long did it take the sheriff to round up a couple of drunks and throw them in the hoosegow for a few hours?

Jerking back the sheet that covered the lower half of his body, Travis rose and stalked to the tall armoire that stood against one wall of the room. He swung open one of the closet doors, its hinges squeaking loudly. He yanked his trousers from a hook and stepped into them, then grabbed a clean white shirt.

"Damned cretins," Travis mumbled as another gunshot sounded. He tucked in his shirt, tugged on his boots, and slipped a vest of black broadcloth laced with silver threads and adorned with solid silver buttons over his shirt. It took him less than ten minutes to exit his room.

Pete, the second-shift barkeep looked at him curiously as he stalked down the stairs, across the saloon, and barged through the swinging doors onto the boardwalk without saying a word.

There were only a few people out and about: Millie from the Diamond House was just exiting Palmer's Meat Market with a basket of fresh eggs, Ron Cabor was in the process of sweeping off the boardwalk in front of his restaurant, and a drunk staggered out of the Silver Lady and slunk down to sit on its stoop.

Travis stalked his way down the boardwalk past several stores and saloons, then crossed the street and marched into the jailhouse. "Liam!" he barked at the deputy who sat lounging in a chair before a potbellied stove. "Where's the sheriff?

The deputy, no more than fifteen years old, his face covered with freckles, scrambled from his seat, the piece of wood he'd been whittling falling to the floor. "Art Spinnal come and got him a bit ago, Mr. Braggette."

Remembering the gunshots that had awakened him and brought him to the jailhouse in the first place, and knowing Art Spinnal was day foreman of the Chollar Mine, Travis jumped to a natural assumption. "Trouble at the mine?"

Liam just shrugged his bony shoulders.

Travis whirled about and stalked from the office, slamming the rough plank door behind him. Damn, it wasn't bad enough that they had a sheriff who couldn't seem to keep the drunks from firing off their guns in the middle of the night, but they also had a deputy who was barely out of diapers and didn't seem to want to do more than warm his carcass in front of a stove and cut up a chink of wood.

"Liam! Liam!"

Travis, who had just stepped from the boardwalk to cross the street toward the Mountain Queen, paused to look at the young boy running toward the jailhouse.

"Liam!" the boy called loudly. He shot around the open doorway, grabbing onto the doorjamb to stop himself. "Sheriff wants you, Liam. Down Devil's Gate. Fast!"

Travis ran back to the jailhouse. "What the hell's happening?" he demanded, standing in the doorway, his feet spread wide and clenched hands rammed onto his hips. He glared down at the young boy who leaned against the wall breathing heavily.

Liam, dropping his whittling again, was hurriedly trying to buckle on his holster.

The young messenger sucked in several gulps of air, his chest heaving, and then answered Travis. "Sheriff said to get Liam, sir."

"Why?"

"Wagon's been robbed. Old Duncan was shot."

"Robbed?" Travis echoed. He crouched in front of the boy. "One of the ore wagons was robbed?"

The boy nodded vigorously, his breath still coming in ragged gasps. "Yes, sir. Old Duncan's."

Liam rushed past him and disappeared through the open doorway.

Travis stood and stared after him. Had this been

what the judge had been planning? He felt a moment's panic. If the Knights had decided to start robbing the miners, there'd be more trouble in Virginia City than anyone could imagine. He looked back down at the boy. "Keep this quiet, Son," Travis ordered. "No sense getting everyone in town riled up."

"Yes, sir," the boy mumbled.

Travis hurried back to the Queen.

"Pete!" he yelled as he took the stairs to his rooms two at a time. "Get one of the boys to fetch my horse from the livery. Quick."

Pete nodded and hastened toward Hank's room, just down the hall from the dressing rooms.

Travis grabbed his holster from a hook inside the doorway and strapped it on, securing the silver buckle just below his waist. With deft expertise, he hurriedly tied the holster's leather thongs around his thigh and, straightening to his full height, shifted the belt to allow it to hang low over his right hip. He pulled the Navy Colt from its sheath, held it out before him and, with a flick of his wrist, snapped open the cylinder. He spun the ammunition chamber. The weapon was fully loaded. Travis jammed the Colt back into the holster and grabbed his hat.

Starhawk was tied to the hitching rack in front of the Mountain Queen. He mounted the tall bay stallion and headed the animal toward the southwestern end of town, and Devil's Gate. "Damn you, Judge," he muttered beneath his breath. "If you or your blasted Knights had anything to do with this, I swear I'll see your hide nailed to a damned barn door."

The road that led from the mountain town of Virginia City down to the smaller mining town of Gold Hill was treacherously steep in places and full of dangerous curves. With patchy layers of snow still covering almost everything in sight, only the nearly continuous traffic of miners, freights, and ore wagons kept the road a snaking trail of mud rather than ice.

Travis maneuvered Starhawk down the road with care, though the horse, purchased the year before from one of the Paiute Indians native to the territory, really needed no guidance. He was a very sure-footed beast, but Travis didn't want to lose him because of a misstep into an iced-over hole and a broken leg.

Gold Hill was a bustle of activity by the time Travis passed through. Word of the attack on Duncan Clyde's wagon had already spread through the small community. Several men called out to Travis as he passed by them, asking if he knew of the robbery attempt, and who he suspected of being the perpetrator. He waved them off, not prepared to speculate on an answer.

"Your Knights went too far this time, Braggette," a deep voice shouted from the porch of the Gold Hill Hotel.

Travis looked back over his shoulder.

A tall, skinny man stood at the corner of the porch, the front of his greatcoat pushed back, thumbs stuck into the sleeve holes of his wool vest. Travis met what he could see of his gaze within the wild mane of brown hair that covered the man's head, upper lip, and chin.

"So have you if you keep calling them *my* Knights," Travis growled back. Why in the hell hadn't the Judge left him alone? For the past year David Terry had done nothing but badger Travis about attending his group's clandestine meetings. And now he had tried to appoint Travis as their leader!

A weird suspicion suddenly nagged at Travis. Or *had* the judge *left* town? Could that announcement have been just another of his ploys? Maybe to get at Travis somehow? And avert suspicion from himself?

Starhawk rounded a sharp bend in the road, and Devil's Gate came into view; the huge rock formations that jutted out of nowhere tightly hugged both sides of the road and created the perfect locale for an ambush.

Duncan Clyde's ore wagon had been drawn off to the side of the road to allow others passage through the Gate. A dozen drivers were crowded around the rig, their angry voices buzzing on the chilled morning air as they discussed what had happened, and what was going to be done about it.

A man sat on the wagon seat, in the process of bandaging Duncan Clyde's arm. Travis recognized him as the doctor who lived in Silver City, just down the road.

"Braggette, what the hell are you doing here?" Sheriff Morrow asked, walking up to stand beside Starhawk as Travis dismounted.

"I heard your boy yelling up and down the street about a robbery and Duncan being shot," Travis answered easily. "Figured I'd like to see for myself just what happened."

"Why?" The sheriff pushed back his greatcoat and hung his thumbs on his gun belt, the gesture accentuating both his protruding stomach and the double chin that hung loosely down. "Wanna make sure old Clyde didn't recognize any of your Knights when they attacked him?"

Travis's jaw clenched in anger, and he felt an almost irresistible urge to punch the beefy sheriff. He restrained himself with difficulty. Kurt Morrow didn't have the common sense God had given a rattler, but he'd been elected sheriff because nobody else wanted the job, including Travis. Slugging him would only give Kurt a reason to throw Travis into jail, and he wasn't eager for that experience. Especially since he knew Kurt was enamored of Magnolia Rochelle, who wouldn't give him the time of day but made no secret of her liaisons with Travis. Jealousy was a powerful thing, and he had a sneaking suspicion that the sheriff might just leave him in the jail until his hair turned gray, if he could find a reason to put him there in the first place.

"They're not *my* Knights," Travis said. He walked around the sheriff and approached the wagon.

Kurt Morrow stepped in front of Travis, hefting a boot covered with mud onto one of the wheel's spokes and leaning into his face. Beady eyes glared at him, challenging.

Travis stepped back. He never had liked the smell of stale whiskey and tobacco, and encountering it on the sheriff's breath was just a little more nauseating than he could take at this hour of the morning.

The sheriff pushed his rumpled slouch hat back off his forehead with a shove of his thumb and screwed his fleshy face into a sneer. "Ain't the way I hear it, Braggette."

Travis smiled. "Then I guess you heard it wrong, Sheriff." He looked up at Duncan Clyde, a regular patron of the Mountain Queen. "Hey, Dunc, you all right?" he asked.

The driver nodded. "Yeah. Sons of a bitch tried to rob me. I think I got one of them, though."

"Shot him?" Travis asked.

"Yeah. Bastard. Gonna have himself one hell of a

sore arm, let me tell ya. He got mine. I got his." The old man laughed heartily.

"Good. Maybe it will make it easier for the sheriff here to catch him." Travis turned to Morrow. "I assume you're going to start checking around the neighboring towns to find out if anyone sees a doctor for a gunshot wound in the arm?"

"I know my duties, Braggette," the sheriff growled. "You just stick to pushing drinks and cheating people at cards."

Travis laughed, but there was no amusement in the cold look that he pinned on the sheriff. "Everyone in town knows the Queen is the most honest house around, Morrow, so if I were you, and thank the saints I'm not, I'd be a little more careful what untruths I went around spouting." He turned back to Duncan. "How many were there, Dunc?"

"Ten. Mebbe twelve. Couldn't tell for sure. Surrounded me before I knew what the hell was happening. Some of them stayed up in the rocks, though."

"Recognize anyone?" Travis asked.

"I'll be the one to ask the questions, Braggette," Sheriff Morrow snarled. "Did you recognize any of them, Duncan?" the sheriff asked with a snide look to Travis.

"Nah. They was all bundled up, you know? Big coats, neckerchief pulled half over their faces, hats low. Ceptin' for that one on the hill."

"What one?" Travis urged, ignoring the sheriff's glower.

"Sat up on the hill there." Duncan pointed to the rise behind where they stood. "Proud as you please, kinda prim and proper like. And just watchin'. I didn't get a long look, mind you, but that one there . . ." He shook his head. "Something weird, you know?"

"Like what?" Travis said.

"Well, best I could tell he was small. Real small. Almost woman small, you know?"

An image of Clarence Lonchet immediately formed in Travis's mind.

Chapter Twelve

Clarence tore off his cape and flung it carelessly at the settee before the fireplace in his room. This billowing wool missed the dark-green velvet piece and landed on the floor in a heap of rumples.

"Damn idiots," he grumbled, jabbing a finger into the knot of his tie and jerking it loose. He hadn't liked this plan in the first place. Why he'd listened to Magnolia was a mystery even to himself. Just because she had the judge's ear didn't mean she knew what she was doing. He snapped the tie from around his neck.

A sound came from the hallway and he paused, wondering if Suzanne or Addie were about to knock and give him the news. Obviously the whole town already knew. But the sound of footsteps moved past his door and on down the hall. "Stupid, that's what it was," he cursed. "Stupid!"

Clarence tried to calm himself, but the turmoil enveloping his thoughts would not cease. And then there was Suzanne. Another problem. She couldn't be trusted, in spite of the fact that they held the threat of her brother's life over her head. She had sworn she hated Travis

Braggette. That she regarded him as a no good black-guard. A coward. And from what Clarence had been able to find out about what had transpired between them in the past, he had felt confident she'd spoken the truth. Now he wasn't so certain anymore. She might still be angry with Braggette for jilting her, but Suzanne definitely did not hate him. That was obvious in the way she looked at him, for a start.

Clarence scoffed. He'd have to be a fool not to see the spark of interest that blazed in her eyes whenever they settled on Travis Braggette. He wadded his tie into a ball and tossed it on the unmade bed, then grabbed another from a satchel on the floor. And he wasn't all that sure of Suzanne's insipid maid, Addie, either. The woman just didn't seem like a maid to him. There was something about her. Clarence slipped a silver-gray cravat around the collar of his shirt. Haughty. That was it. Every once in a while she seemed to be looking down her nose at him.

"Arrogant bitch," he snarled, stabbing the cravat with a gold stickpin. Whether his anger was actually directed at Addie, Suzanne, or Magnolia Rochelle, he wasn't sure. But he *was* sure that if this plan didn't work, someone would pay, and pay dearly.

Travis lazed against the bar, leaning one bent arm along its polished mahogany surface. Eli, Magnolia's day bartender, had given him a cup of coffee and he held it before him. He raised the cup to his lips and took a sip.

Just then a door opened at the rear of the bar and quickly closed with a soft click. The rustling sound of satin swaying against ruffled crinolines met his ear and Travis looked up.

Magnolia Rochelle walked toward him, her hips swaying with practiced provocativeness, her green gown cut low enough over her breasts to give the viewer more than a teasing eyeful, and the smile on her full lips wide, inviting, and seductive.

"Mon cher, what brings you here so early?" She feigned a yawn, covering her mouth daintily with the tips of her fingers. "You nearly caught me still in bed." Magnolia laughed then, and winked. "Though now that I think of it, maybe that might not have been so bad, yes?"

Travis smiled. "I guess you haven't heard about Duncan Clyde then?"

Maggie's eyes widened. "Duncan? That old freighter?"

Travis nodded. "He got waylaid this morning. I thought I was hearing some yahoo shooting off a drunk, but it was actually Duncan getting robbed. Or I should say, *almost* robbed."

"Oh, I heard those shots, too. I had a horrid night and couldn't sleep." She touched a finger to the flesh just beneath one of her eyes and brushed a fingertip across the skin. "My eyes are even swollen this morning."

"Maggie, I want to apologize for—"

"And then someone rode past my window," she said, cutting him off. "Normally I wouldn't have heard them, but I wasn't asleep. Then I no sooner started to drift off and those shots began."

Travis's features tightened as he contemplated her words and forgot his apology. "Someone rode past your window, Mag? Just before the shots started?"

"Yes, a while before. And her horse was such a clumsy beast. Either that or," she laughed softly, "half blind. I mean, it stumbled right across my wood pile. Nearly scared the life out of me, for sure."

"Her?"

Magnolia nodded. "I think it was a woman. I mean, when the horse made all that ruckus, I got out of bed and looked out the window. Thought maybe someone was trying to break into the saloon's back door and rob me. That's when I saw her, the rider."

"Who?"

She shrugged. "I don't know, really. She, if it was a she, was in silhouette, and had on a cape. Pulled up partways over her head."

"So why did you think it was a woman?" Travis urged. "Why not a man? Maybe a small man."

"Well," Magnolia frowned as if in deep contemplation, "she just had the set of woman, you know? Slight. Kind of narrow shoulders. And I thought I saw long hair peeking from the hood. Though I can't be sure of that." She moved closer to him. "It was dark, remember, and not a whole lot of moonlight."

He nodded but didn't like the suspicions that were forming in his mind. As far as he knew, there were only two strangers in town who were women: Suzanne and her maid, Addie. Of course, it could be someone who lived in Virginia City, but he didn't think so. There were basically three types of women in the mining town, wives, whores, and businesswomen like Magnolia. None impressed him as the sort to head a gang of robbers. Or worse, Knights.

He thought again of Clarence Lonchet. The man was

slight, had narrow shoulders, and, his form encased beneath a cape could be mistaken for a woman in the dark. Except for the hair. Clarence was bald, and Maggie had said she'd seen long hair.

"Did they get the wagon?"

Travis shook his head. "No. Duncan put up a fight and at the sound of the gunshots, some of the other miners came running down from Gold Hill to find out what was going on. Whoever attacked Duncan took off."

"Oh, poor man," she cooed, sidling up to Travis and pressing close to him. "He wasn't hurt, was he?"

"Shot in the arm, but it's not serious."

She ran her fingers lightly up and down the front of one of Travis's lapels. "Did he know who it was that tried to rob him?"

"No. They evidently wore masks."

"Oh." She played with the buttons on his vest. "Too bad."

"Yeah," Travis extradited himself from her by pressing his lips quickly to her forehead and grasping her hands, forcing them gently away from him. "That's not why I came here this morning."

"Oh?" A sultry gleam sparkled in her eyes. She slid her tongue suggestively over her bottom lip.

"And neither is that," he said, and laughed.

She affected a pout. "You disappoint me, Travis."

"Sorry." He brushed his lips over hers in a featherlight and hurried kiss. "Maybe tonight."

"Hah!" She waved a hand over her shoulder. "Promises, promises. I am sure now that you are the leader of the Knights that you will not have any time for Magnolia."

"Leader of . . . I am not . . ." Travis paused to get a grip on the surge of anger that had erupted within him at her comment. "I'm not the leader of the Knights here, Mag. I'm not even a member, so don't go talking around like that. Understand?"

She shrugged one lily-white shoulder. "Some of the boys were in here last night, *chéri*, and said the judge, before he left town, appointed you the new leader."

"Well, it's not true. Terry *tried* to appoint me the leader. I refused. And that's all there is to it. I'm not a Knight, and I'm not their leader."

"Whatever." She pressed her body to his and looked up at him from beneath half-lowered lids. "But you can be *my* leader, *chéri.*"

Travis was in no mood for her games. His anger at the judge was still too hot in his blood, along with thoughts of the real reason he'd come to Magnolia's. "How did you know Georgette Lindsay's real name was Suzanne, Mag?"

"Why, I guess I heard you say it, *chéri.*" She moved her body back and forth suggestively. "But I don't want to talk about Georgette Lindsay. I'd much rather . . ."

"You heard me call her Suzanne?"

Magnolia stepped back, piqued at his cool disregard of her advances. "Obviously. How else would I know it?"

"Miss Magnolia," the barkeep suddenly said, interrupting their confrontation. "The doctor's here."

Travis looked down at Magnolia and frowned. "Doctor?" he echoed. "Are you sick?"

Magnolia laughed lightly. "Just a little woman thing. Nothing to worry about." She turned back toward the rear of the saloon. "Perhaps I'll see you tonight, *chéri.*"

Her voice turned slightly derisive. "If you can find the time."

Travis felt a flash of guilt. She was angry with him. And hurt. But he couldn't do anything about it at the moment. He had other things to worry about, and figure out. Like stopping the damned rumor that he'd taken over as leader of the Knights of the Golden Circle, like talking to Suzanne Forteaux and figuring out what she was really doing in Virginia City, and looking into the attempted robbery of Duncan Clyde. He had the nagging feeling that somehow, and he was damned if he knew how, each was related to the other.

Hank walked down the hall toward the dressing-room doors. The soft hum of women's chatter came to him through the thin walls. Addie was helping Georgette Lindsay get ready for her first performance of the night. The frown that had carved itself into Hank's forehead early that morning and remained with him throughout the day deepened. He hadn't told anyone he'd seen Addie ride out of town that morning just before sunup, only a short while before the attempt to rob Duncan Clyde, but it had been bothering him ever since. Especially since he'd made it a point to intercept her later during her morning walk and invite her to have a coffee with him again. She'd accepted, but his careful questioning had garnered him nothing but what he knew was a lie.

When he'd asked her if the gunshots from the robbery had awakened her when their blasts had pierced the quiet morning air, Addie had said yes, and Hank had felt his spirits plummet, knowing she'd already been up and about. It wasn't as if he suspected her of the robbery, but then ... He felt his heart weigh heavy.

He knocked on the door.

"Yes?" Addie called out.

"The boss said to tell you the place is pretty well packed, Miss Addie."

"Miss Lindsay will be out in just a few minutes, Hank," Addie said. She ran to the door and opened it just a crack. "And Hank?"

He'd already turned away and taken several steps toward the curtained doorway that led to the saloon. Hank paused and looked back.

"I'd truly appreciate it if you could walk me back to the hotel later." Addie smiled up at him.

Hank nodded. "My pleasure, Miss Addie," he said.

"Addie, Hank. Just plain Addie. Remember?"

He tipped his head toward her and then walked toward the curtain. The door closed softly behind him. Damn but she was a fine-looking woman. And he liked her, too. But she was hiding something. He felt it in his bones. She was hiding something, and he had a real bad itch to know what it was.

Addie pulled at the strings on the back of Suzanne's corset.

"Oh, Addie, if you pull much tighter I not only won't be able to sing," Suzanne said, and laughed, "I won't even be able to breathe."

Addie held out Suzanne's gown, a moiré silk of midnight-blue with a ruche of white Marseilles lace trimming the low-cut décolletage and dripping in a V between her breasts to her waist.

Suzanne slipped into it easily and stood still while Addie fastened the small buttons that ran up the back of the gown. She glanced in the mirror, fluffed up the pagoda-style sleeves and touched an admiring hand to the white gardenia pinned behind her ear holding back one side of her long hair.

"I can't for the life of me imagine where Mr. Braggette got that gardenia," Addie said. "I mean, they don't grow in a place like this, do they?"

Suzanne laughed. "I have no idea, Addie, but it is beautiful, isn't it?" She stared at the flower and felt a flash of guilt at having rejected Travis's invitation to dine with him before the show. But she couldn't trust herself with him, not alone with him.

"Smells good, too. Reminds me of home."

A look of longing came over Suzanne's face. "Yes, it does."

"Well, come on," Addie said cheerily. "Your audience is waiting."

Suzanne smiled and swept from the room in a rustle of silk and lace.

Travis turned from his position at the bar as he heard Hank, standing in the center of the stage, call for everyone to quiet down and then announced Suzanne, in her guise of Georgette Lindsay.

The red curtains parted, she walked out on stage, and the men went wild, clapping, stomping their feet, and cheering. Whatever else she was up to in Virginia City, she had at least brought him one hell of a good week's worth of business. There wasn't an empty chair or space in the house.

The band started to play and Suzanne, moving saucily about the raised dais, began to sing.

Travis watched her. She was beautiful, graceful, and confident. And up to something, he reminded himself. The memory of her in his room searching his bureau invaded his thoughts and pulled them away from her performance. Just what in the hell had she been looking for? The question had been nagging at him ever since he'd caught her there, but he hadn't come up with even one possible answer. What could she have thought he had that was so important?

Movement caught the corner of his eye and he glanced over his shoulder toward the door. Ben Morgan had just entered the saloon. The big man made straight for the table in the corner he'd designated as his, and several miners already seated there shifted position. An empty chair suddenly appeared as he approached.

Travis felt the tiny hairs on the back of his neck rise.

The red entry doors swung forward again. Travis turned in surprise that another person would try to enter the crowded saloon. The Queen was already so packed there was hardly any room to move. Men began to step aside for the new arrival.

"So, sweets," the lovely and affable whore Julia Bullette said, sidling up to stand at the bar beside Travis, "you've finally managed to find a way to get just about everyone in town stuffed into the Mountain Queen." She laughed softly, the sound like the merry tinkling of a piano, and touched a hand to the neatly pinned chignon at her nape.

Jed set a glass of sherry before her.

"Thank you, Jedidiah," Julia said, her deep voice a

seductive drawl. She picked up the glass and held it outward, as if in a toast, and then downed the dark liquid
in one gulp. Setting the glass back on the bartop, she let
out a long breath. "That was good, Jedidiah. Very
good."

"Best in town," he said proudly.

Julia turned her dark gaze to Travis. "Something's
still bothering you, sweets," she said, placing one hand
on a black, silk-covered hip. "Want to talk about it?"

"I wouldn't know where to start," Travis said.

"How about at the beginning?"

He shook his head. "Thanks, Julia, but the beginning
was just too damned long ago."

"I've got all night to listen, sweets, and I won't charge
you a cent. I've made my money for the night." She
glanced pointedly toward Ben Morgan.

Taking her arm, Travis led Julia out of the salon and
onto the boardwalk. "You were with Morgan tonight?"
he asked.

She nodded. "For a while."

"Did he say anything?"

She laughed. "Well, sweets, he said quite a bit, but I
never would have guessed you'd be interested in hearing
that sort of thing."

"Julia," Travis growled, struggling to hold on to his
patience. "There's something about that man I don't
like."

"Like what, Travis?"

He shrugged. "I'm not sure. Something."

"Well, I wasn't really too fond of him, either, but . . ."

"His accent, Julia. He says he's from Michigan and
has been living in San Francisco lately. Working for the
Bulletin."

"Yes?"

"But his accent is Southern."

She moved to stand at the edge of the boardwalk and looked up at the moon. "So maybe he just doesn't like to admit that." She chuckled. "Not everyone is proud to be a Southerner, sweets. I mean, maybe the man was white trash, you know? And doesn't want anyone to find out. I can certainly identify with that."

"You are not trash, Julia."

"Thank you, sweets."

"You may be right, but I don't think so. He's educated, Julia. I've seen his articles. And he does write for the *Bulletin*. Or at least he used to. But why would he lie about his origins? It doesn't make sense."

She turned back to him and smiled. "You mean it doesn't make sense to *you*, sweets. It probably makes perfect sense to him." She slipped an arm around his. "Now, come on. It's cold out here and I'm thirsty. Buy me another drink."

Travis nodded and they returned to the saloon. But no sooner had he stepped across the threshold than he stopped dead. His gaze had automatically veered in the direction of where Ben Morgan sat. Suzanne had finished her first performance and, rather than return to her dressing room for a rest, was seated at Ben Morgan's table.

"You're sure he didn't say anything, Julia?"

"Well, nothing besides all the ordinary chatter a man says when he wants a woman, or is taking her, except . . ." She frowned, trying to remember.

Travis's head jerked around and he stared down at her. "Except what?"

"Except that he had an important meeting tonight

with someone. That's why he was in a hurry." Julia looked toward the table where Ben Morgan and Suzanne sat. "Maybe it was with your singer."

Chapter Thirteen

Two hours later, Suzanne finished her last performance of the evening and bowed her way off the stage to a roar of applause and catcalls.

Travis waited several minutes and then pushed away from the bar and walked through the curtained doorway that led to the backstage rooms. But no sooner had he taken a step toward the door of Suzanne's dressing room than it swung open.

For some reason unknown to himself, Travis quickly stepped into the adjoining room, which was used for storage. He left the door open a crack and stood pressed to its frame, his head cocked slightly to give him a view into the hallway.

Ben Morgan suddenly stepped from Suzanne's dressing room into the hallway, but rather than continue on his way, he paused and looked back.

"You get better each time, Suzanne," Morgan said, and laughed. "Just keep it up and everything will be just fine, I promise. Come on out when you get done primping and I'll buy you a drink."

Better? The word echoed in Travis's mind. Better at

what? He didn't hear Suzanne's reply to Morgan. He was too busy trying to quell the surge of jealousy that had suddenly swept over him like a tidal wave. His fingers itched to throw open the door, reach out, grab Morgan by the lapels of his too-tight coat and demand an explanation.

How did he know Suzanne well enough to warrant a visit to her dressing room? Or *did* he? Maybe Suzanne had changed more than he realized. Travis felt a sickening churn of his stomach. He started to open the door and step back into the hallway as Morgan disappeared past the curtained doorway and into the saloon, then stopped as more voices filtered to him from Suzanne's dressing room.

"Get out, Clarence!" Suzanne demanded, her tone harsh and full of anger.

Travis stepped back and pulled the door toward him again.

"Watch who you're trying to order around, missy," Clarence snarled. "I ain't no lap dog like Morgan or Braggette. Neither your temper or your charms work on me, and you'd do good to remember that. Along with our little deal."

Something, it sounded like a chair, crashed to the floor.

"I said, get out."

"I'll go, Suzanne, but you just remember what you're supposed to do. You follow orders and do what you're told and everything will work out just fine. You don't and, well, you know what will happen then."

Orders? Travis felt a shudder of uneasiness at the word.

"I know that I'll kill you," Suzanne said, her voice calm, cold, and hard.

Clarence laughed. "Save the dramatics for your lover, Suzanne. He's the one you came here to fool, remember?"

"Get out, Clarence," Suzanne said again. "Get out before I forget that I'm a lady."

"Lady?" His laugh was bitter this time, though he did open the door. "Suzanne, you stopped being a lady a long time ago."

Clarence stepped out into the hallway and pulled the door closed behind him, but as he did something crashed against it, and a sprinkle of china flew into the hallway from beneath Suzanne's door.

Travis watched Clarence pass but remained still, though it was a struggle since what he really wanted to do was step out, block the man's path and not only demand answers to the passel of questions crowding about in his head, but bury his fist in the man's face. It took several long, seemingly eternal minutes for Travis to calm down. He stepped into the hall and walked to Suzanne's door, the tiny bits of china crunching beneath his heels. Travis rapped his knuckles lightly against the door.

"Go away, Clarence," Suzanne called out.

"It's Travis."

"Then you go away, too."

"Suzanne, I want to talk with you. Open the door," Travis ordered, though he kept his voice soft.

"No."

His temper flared. Damn it all, how was he supposed to find out what was going on when she acted like a stubborn mule half the time? "Suzanne, damn it, open this door."

"No. I don't want to talk to you, Travis. Not now. Go away."

Travis slipped a ring of keys from his pocket, held them up to the light, selected one, and jabbed it into the small hole beneath the doorknob. He turned first it, then the knob, and pushed the door open.

Suzanne glared at him from across the room. "Oh, well, that's generous. Very generous. You give me a dressing room, but you keep the key. What about the hotel you took me to, Travis? Do you have a key to my room there, too? Did you plan on visiting me in the middle of the night and seducing me?"

Travis frowned.

He stepped into the room and kicked the door closed with the heel of his boot. "What's Clarence holding over you, Suzanne? What orders are you supposed to follow? And what's the 'or else' he threatened you with?"

She stared at him, fury etched in every curve and plane of her face, glistening from her eyes and the straight, hard line of her shoulders. "So you've added eavesdropping to your other talents, Travis? Congratulations."

"Damn it, Suzanne, stop trying to dance circles around me and tell me what's going on. Who's Ben Morgan?"

"A newspaper man from San Francisco."

"And what else?"

She turned away, crossing her arms beneath her breasts. "I haven't the faintest idea. A goat?"

Travis stalked across the room, grabbed her arm and

swung her around to face him. "What is he to you?" he snarled.

"Nothing."

"And Lonchet?"

She tried to pull away from his, but his grip on her arm was like a band of steel, securing her as his prisoner.

"And Lonchet?" he repeated harshly, the words nearly a growl now.

"He's my manager."

"What else?"

She glared up at him, wanting to hurt him like he'd hurt her. "Would it bother you if I said he was my lover, Travis?"

His fingers tightened around her arm, bruising the flesh. He *was* hurting her, but she didn't care. She should hate him. She'd thought she did hate him, but she'd been wrong, had done nothing more than lie to herself for the past seven years. As long as he was near, as long as she knew he cared, it didn't matter what else he did.

"Is he?" The words were spoken low, menacing, and sent a chill of alarm racing up Suzanne's spine.

She looked up at him, into his eyes, and was surprised at the anguish she found there. For seven years she had both hated and loved him, but not once had she thought that he, too, might have been hurt by what happened. Suddenly the desire to lash back at him, to cause him the same kind of pain he'd caused her, deserted her.

"No," she whispered softly. "He's not."

"Who is?" Travis demanded harshly. He was no longer concerned about what she was truly doing in Virginia City, no longer filled with questions about Ben Morgan and Clarence Lonchet. Every thought had suddenly turned to Suzanne, every concern centered around her.

She shook her head. "No one."

With no conscious thought to his action, no plan or moment of hesitation, Travis dragged her into his arms and captured her lips with his. It was a savagely demanding movement. His tongue instantly forced her lips apart and plunged into her mouth, filling it with the fire of his touch, the desperation of his need, and the searing of his passion.

He felt the start of surprise that shook her body and, fearing she meant to resist him, to pull away, his arms slipped around her waist, pulling her to his tall, hard length, crushing her body to his until there was no space between them, nothing separating their bodies but the frail fabric of their clothes.

But resistance was the last thing on Suzanne's mind. For seven years she had dreamed of finding Travis again, of making him pay for what he'd done to her, of humiliating him the way he had humiliated her . . . but even those thoughts were lost to her now. Instead, she found herself melting into him, aching to know more of the passion his touch invoked within her.

His assault on her lips was both a gentle caress of her senses and a fierce demand for her acquiescence. Once he had been her knight in shining armor, then a heartless blackguard. Now he was the embodiment of every fantasy, every dream, and every nightmare come alive. She hated him, and she desired him. She wanted to destroy him, and she wanted to love him.

His hands pressed against her bare back, the heat of

his flesh melding with the heat of hers. His fingers splayed atop her skin, pressing her closer, closer, until her breasts were crushed against the iron wall of his chest, until the breath was caught in her throat and her heart thudded madly, matching the racing beat of his.

A tiny moan of pleasure escaped her throat as, moving slightly, she felt the hardness of his arousal press through her gown, through her crinolines, and against her stomach. An ache of longing, years of pent-up need and passion enveloped her as Travis's mouth continued its sweet torture upon hers. He had kissed her the night before after seeing her back to the hotel, but that kiss had been nothing like this one. It had rocked her, yes. It had touched her, scared her, warned her that she was still vulnerable to him, but it had not awakened the searing passions that had slept within her for the past seven years, waiting to rise up, waiting for just the right touch, just the right caress, to ignite.

Her senses spun with the realization of being held in his arms once again. Nothing else mattered now. Not the war, not Clarence or Ben Morgan, not the real reason she had come to Virginia City, and, God help her, not even Brett. This was what she had wanted, what she *had* longed for, what she had dreamed of for seven long, lonely years—for Travis Braggette to want her, to love her as she had always loved him.

Locking her body against Travis's rock-hard length, Suzanne clung to him. She held on to his strength, wanting never to let go, never to have to leave the sanctity of his arms and face the world again, with its cruelties and lies.

Travis pulled his lips from hers and stared down at her. They were breathing raggedly, the passion that had

erupted between them so fierce and strong that both
had been taken by surprise.

"I need you, Suzanne," Travis said, his voice husky
with emotion.

Suzanne looked up at him, ready to surrender her
will, to abandon everything she believed in, everyone
she loved, when her eye was drawn by the light of the
lamp behind her as it caught on the delicate gold-and-
ruby ring on her finger. Brett had given it to her a few
days after Travis left her standing like a lovestruck fool
at the altar. It had been his way of trying to make her
smile again.

The small ruby stone reflected the lamplight in a dazzling charge of brilliant red, while the gold, designed in
a flourish of leaves that surrounded the ruby and held it
up like a flower, shone softly.

The icy, unfeeling fingers of reality suddenly wrapped
around her heart and snapped her mind from the world
of passion into which she had allowed herself to be en-
ticed. This was exactly what she was supposed to do
with Travis, exactly what she had been ordered to accomplish. To get close to him, get in his confidence.
This was what she'd been ordered to do and it was
working, except for one thing; she wasn't supposed to
feel anything. Not a thing. And she did. Oh, God, she
did. A swelling of emotion filled her: hate, love, fear,
and anger. But she couldn't allow it. Not after what he'd
done to her, and not if she was ever going to find Brett.

Pulling her arms from around Travis's neck, she
placed her hands on his chest and pushed away from
him.

"But I don't need you," she said coldly. They were
the hardest words she'd ever spoken, and, she knew, the

wrong ones. Clarence would be furious if he found out, but she couldn't help it. She would play up to Travis in public, where it was safe, but she couldn't allow herself to get close to him when they were alone. She had to think of Brett. That would get her through this, allow her to do what had to be done. Travis didn't really care for her anyway, he never had. He only wanted her in his bed. Isn't that what he'd just said? *I need you.* Not *I love you.* Tears stung her eyes, but she refused to allow them release, while within her chest her heart felt as if it were shattering into a million pieces. Taking a deep breath, Suzanne cocked her chin upward and glared at him. She had known this was going to be dangerous, being near Travis again, but they had insisted it was the only way.

He stared down at her, gray eyes melding with blue, questioning, demanding, but she wouldn't look away, and she wouldn't, couldn't, give him the answers he wanted. She would play this damned game in front of Clarence and Ben, she had to, they had given her no other choice. But when they weren't around, she would have to be cold, hard, and unforgiving toward him. It was the only way to ward off Travis, keep him at a distance, and she *had* to keep him at a distance, if not for his sake, then for her own. "How does it feel, Travis?" She forced a hard laugh from her throat. "Not too pleasant, hmm?"

With a bleak slant to his mouth, and fury in his eyes, Travis answered, "Touché, Suzanne. Touché. You have evidently learned a lot in the past seven years. Perhaps much more than I'd given you credit for." Spinning on his heels, Travis walked from the room.

"Touché, Suzanne," she murmured to the emptiness

as the tears she had fought to hold back fell from her eyes to create paths of glimmering silver atop her cheeks. "Touché."

"Hey, Boss," Jed called, as Travis stalked his way toward the swinging doors that led to the street.

He needed air. Cold, bone-chilling, soul-biting air. But he turned and walked to the bar. "Yeah, what, Jed?"

"That guy Morgan you been interested in . . ."

Travis glanced over his shoulder to the corner table where Ben Morgan had resumed his seat. He was busily writing on a pad of paper and nursing a bottle of whiskey. Several others sat at his table but they all seemed to be having their own party, in spite of Morgan's silent presence. Travis turned back to Jed. "What about him?"

"Charlie Mellroy came in and slipped him a note about twenty minutes ago."

"Charlie, huh?" Travis immediately remembered Charlie's badgering visits on behalf of Judge Terry to get him to attend the Knights' weekly meetings.

"Yeah. And I was talking to Efrem Sadler awhile ago. He said he heard that Morgan is a member of the Knights in San Francisco. Said one of his friends saw him at a meeting down there a few months back. Pretty high up on the totem pole, too, if you know what I mean."

"An officer," Travis said, the comment more a statement than a question.

"Yeah."

Travis looked back at Morgan. "What about Miss

Lindsay's manager, Clarence Lonchet? Any rumors about him?"

"No, but a few of the boys been talking about how they'd sure like to find a barrel of tar and a sack of feathers and give him a new coat. That pipsqueak is about as friendly as a porcupine . . . And speak of the devil," Jed whispered, nodding toward the door.

Travis turned to look. Clarence saw him, smiled widely, and walked directly toward him. Travis nearly groaned. The last person in the world he wanted to see right now was Lonchet. Morgan was bad enough.

"Mr. Braggette, good evening," Clarence cooed. He pulled off his gloves and slapped them onto the bartop. "Barkeep, a sherry, if you please," he said.

Jed walked away to get the sherry, shaking his head as he did.

Travis turned back to lean on the bar. He picked up his shot glass and took a slow sip.

"Actually, Mr. Braggette, I would like to solicit a favor."

"From me?" Travis growled, not looking at the man. If he did, he was afraid he might be tempted to hit him.

"Yes, sir. You see, I have . . . um, well, found the company of a very nice young lady in town quite to my liking and . . . um, well, it poses quite a problem to leave her and escort Miss Lindsay back to the hotel. I mean . . ."

"Your lady friend gets jealous," Travis supplied.

"Well . . . uh, yes."

"So you're asking me to do you a favor and escort Miss Lindsay to the hotel?"

"Yes, that's it precisely. I know she likes you and . . ."

"She likes me?" Travis growled.

"Well, yes, so she's said, and ..."

"Maybe you'd better get your hearing checked, Lonchet."

"No, no, she *did* say it. She likes you and I know she'd appreciate your walk—"

"Maybe you'd better get Ben Morgan to do it, Lonchet."

Clarence's brows flew skyward. "Oh, no, Mr. Braggette, I would never do that. Mr. Morgan is such a cru— well, I mean, Miss Lindsay doesn't really care for Mr. Morgan. But she's quite fond of you. Please, it would mean a great deal and—"

"No."

"Oh, Mr. Braggette, if only you could—"

"No."

"But, I assure you that it really would be appreciat—"

Travis turned to stare at the smaller man. "Didn't your mother ever teach you what the word *no* meant, Lonchet?"

"Perhaps Mr. Braggette doesn't care for my company, Clarence," Suzanne said from behind them, drawing both men's attention and stares. The words had been said in a sultry, flirtatious tone, and she smiled sadly, as if her feelings had been hurt at Travis's lack of enthusiasm. "But it's all right, gentlemen, really. You don't have to concern yourselves with me. I can walk back to the hotel alone."

"Oh, no," Clarence said, and shook his head. "No, no, no. I can't allow that. No, no, no."

Travis waited for the man's head to whirl off and go flying across the room.

"I wouldn't hear of it. I'll just tell Millie she'll have to accompany us and then I'll walk her ho—"

Travis pushed away from the bar. "Go on, Lonchet. I'll see Miss Lindsay back to the hotel."

Clarence beamed. "Oh, thank you. That's wonderful. Just wonderful." He hurried toward the swinging doors.

The warmth in Suzanne's smile and eyes when Clarence had been present suddenly disappeared, and she glared up at Travis. "You can go back to your drink now," she said, her tone cold enough to freeze even the sun. "I am perfectly capable of getting back to the hotel myself." She tugged on one of her gloves. "You needn't bother."

Travis took her arm and steered her from the saloon. "You know, Suzanne," he grumbled as they walked down the boardwalk toward the hotel, "you've got more damned mood changes than a mockingbird has calls."

She smiled up at him. "Really? Well, don't try and familiarize yourself with them, Travis. In a few more days my engagement here will be over and, if we're both lucky, we'll never have to set eyes on each other again."

Chapter Fourteen

For the next two days Travis found life in Virginia City and the surrounding communities peaceful. He had decided to stay as far away from Suzanne as he could get, and it was proving a nerve-wracking, if not impossible feat. Her two nightly performances brought in double the usual amount of customers, making the Mountain Queen crowded to overflowing, which was a positive for business and his pocketbook and a large negative for both his mind and body.

Finishing her second performance of the night, Suzanne departed the stage and made her way through the crowded tables. She laughed with the miners, accepted a kiss on the cheek from one of the town's resident gamblers and a gallant bow from a clerk at the Nevada Bank.

Travis stood at the bar in his usual place at the end near the doors, and watched her in the mirror as she passed behind him without even glancing in his direction.

From behind the bar, Jed moved to stand before him. He pulled Travis's bottle of bourbon from under the bar and poured a finger's worth in his empty glass. "Everything okay, Boss?"

"Yeah, real okay," Travis growled without taking his eyes from the mirror.

"Sheriff's been making noise again, Boss." Jed bent forward and replaced the bottle in its place under the bar. "About you taking over the Knights."

"I know."

"What're you going to do about it?"

"Not much I can do. I didn't take over the Knights. I'm not their leader. Not even a member. Sooner or later the sheriff, and everyone else, will figure that out."

"Yeah, but till then, everyone keeps saying you are." He nodded and walked down the bar to wait on a customer.

Travis's gaze hadn't veered from the mirror, or Suzanne. He just didn't want to think about the Knights. Suzanne was standing beside Ben Morgan's table. He said something to her and winked. Suzanne laughed and patted his shoulder flirtatiously.

Travis felt his temper ignite.

Clarence Lonchet suddenly appeared at his arm. "Mr. Braggette, attendance at the Mountain Queen has really been staggering. Wouldn't you say?"

Travis threw him a dismissing glance, as if he were no more than an annoying bug. "Staggering," he echoed, his tone definitely surly.

Clarence turned to lean his back against the bar and propped his elbows on it, which meant he had to stand slightly on his tiptoes. He looked about the room deliberately, and finally caught Suzanne's attention. His eyes narrowed and he jerked his head in summons, though so slightly only Suzanne caught the movement.

As she excused herself from Morgan and Lowry, Clarence turned back to Travis. "Well," he chuckled, the sound high and almost squeaky, "just remember one thing, Mr. Braggette," he lowered his voice to a conspiratorial whisper and leaned close to Travis's shoulder, "our Suzanne may be sweet on you, but she has contracts in other towns to fulfill. And a very lucrative career ahead of her. So," he stood back and smiled widely, "have a good time, but don't be getting any ideas of a permanent nature."

Travis frowned at Clarence, then turned away and downed the last of the bourbon in his glass. Sweet on him? Suzanne? He looked back toward the mirror. She was talking with Tom Lowry, another regular at the Mountain Queen since her arrival. She turned back to Ben Morgan when he said something to her, then, with a light laugh, she waved at the men and began to make her way toward the bar.

"Gentlemen," she said, coming up behind Travis and Clarence and striking an enticing pose. "Aren't one of you going to buy me a drink?" She fixed her gaze on Travis, giving him a beguiling look. A teasing smile pulled at the corners of her mouth.

Clarence tipped his hat. "Sorry, but I've got to get to Millie's. I only stopped in to make sure you had an escort back to the hotel tonight."

"Oh, I'm sure Mr. Braggette wouldn't mind escorting me to the Union Belle, Clarence." She flashed Travis an alluring smile. "Would you?"

Travis stared at her. For the past several days she had gone from hot to cold, back to hot and back to cold, with no warning, no seeming provocation, no reason. And he was not only puzzled by her mood swings, but getting damned angry and frustrated. Suddenly he realized something. When Lonchet was around, Suzanne's attitude toward Travis was all smiles and flirtations, but when the man was nowhere to be seen, she was as frigid as an iceberg.

His gaze moved to Lonchet and narrowed in suspicion.

"Well, good. Since that's settled, I'll be on my way." Clarence made for the doors. "Wouldn't want to keep Millie waiting." He smiled back at Travis and Suzanne. "She made apple pie today."

Travis looked back at Suzanne, just in time to see her whirl around and walk back to where Tom Lowry was seated playing cards. He frowned. Hmm. Lonchet was present, Suzanne was flirtatious. Lonchet leaves, and Suzanne turns into the ice queen.

His gaze moved to settle on Ben Morgan, sitting at the corner table he had staked out as his own. Travis hadn't been able to confirm that Morgan was a member of the Knights, but that wasn't unusual, since the organization's members were sworn to secrecy. But what information he had been able to obtain, by sending a hasty telegram to a friend in San Francisco and receiving a quick reply, left him no doubt that the man was indeed a Knight. Now he just needed to know why he was in Virginia City.

He caught Suzanne throwing him a quick and furtive glance, but when he tried to catch her eye and hold it, she jerked her head away with a swirl of her long hair. Travis cursed silently. The woman was infuriating.

He looked back at Morgan. What was he doing in Virginia City? His gaze strayed back to Suzanne. And

what did Ben Morgan have to do with Suzanne
Forteaux?

Addie smiled sweetly across the table at Hank. "You
know," she said, adding a purr to her voice, "I never
knew there was so much responsibility entailed in managing a saloon, Hank. And you do such a wonderful
job."

Abashed, Hank returned the smile and then looked
everywhere else in the small restaurant except across the
table at Addie.

"Mr. Braggette is certainly lucky to have you, Hank."
She glanced out the window at the snow-covered, dark
street. "I'm really going to miss it here. It's so beautiful."

"Then stay," Hank said.

She laughed. "Oh, I can't. I mean, my job with Miss
Lindsay and all, we have to travel. To the theaters, you
know. She has other engagements lined up."

"So, quit your job."

"Oh, Hank, that's just not possible. Well, I mean,
maybe someday, but not . . ." Settling down was something she had never thought of, never even considered.
She loved her job, her *real* job, but now, looking at
Hank, she found herself wondering what it would be
like, to stay with him and live in Virginia City. To live
a normal life.

Out of the corner of his eye Hank caught sight of
Abram Lyle running down the boardwalk. He held one
long, gangly arm over his head, a piece of paper
clutched within his curled fingers and was yelling at the
top of his lungs. He burst through the doors of the

Mountain Queen, abruptly disappearing from Hank's view.

Addie noticed Hank's attention switch to the window and turned to see what he was looking at. "What is it Hank?" she asked.

He shrugged. "I don't know, Addie, but I got a feeling I should. Let's get on over to the Queen. I just saw Abram Lyle, the telegraph operator, go in there."

"They got New Orleans! The Yankees got New Orleans!" Abram yelled, throwing himself through the swinging doors of the Mountain Queen and stumbling into the room. He waved the crumpled paper on which he'd written the message over his head.

Travis whirled around from the bar and stared at him, unable to believe he'd heard the man right.

Reaction was swift throughout the room. The chatter among the men, the laughter of the waitresses, the clink of coins on the gaming tables, and the sound of the piano playing in the background all stopped. Dead silence hung over the room as everyone froze and every eye in the place turned to stare at the young telegraph operator.

"New Orleans fell to the Yankees," he repeated. "They got it, and Major Butler's taken over the city." He looked around nervously, waiting for a reaction, his large eyes and lanky frame tense with apprehension.

The room suddenly erupted in an outroar of protest and disbelief. Ever since the judge had left Virginia City and the rumor spread that Travis had taken over as head of the Knights, his patrons had consisted mainly of those who supported the South.

"That can't be right," someone yelled. "How in the hell could the Yankees get down there to take New Orleans?"

"How in tarnation did they ride through the entire South and get to Louisiana without gettin' stopped?" another gruff voice asked.

"Took her from the river," Abram yelled.

"Shit."

"Just glad I ain't got nobody down there," someone snarled.

"Damned Yankees."

"Why don't they just mind their own business and stay up north where they belong?"

Travis looked around for Suzanne, then remembered she'd already returned to the hotel. He couldn't let her hear this as a shout from some miner in the street. She had family in New Orleans. The thought struck him like a bolt of lightning: So did he.

His little sister, Teresa, and his mother were there, along with his older brothers' wives, Belle and Lin. Travis pushed away from the bar and made his way through the milling crowd to where Abram Lyle stood accepting a drink from one of the miners.

"Abram, are you sure about this?"

The telegraph operator looked at Travis and nodded. "Wire came in an hour ago from San Francisco. I wired St. Louis to confirm."

"And they confirmed?"

"Yep. April twenty-fourth. That was yesterday," he said needlessly, "Yankee ships sailed into New Orleans and General Butler declared martial law over the whole city."

"Martial law," Travis echoed, struggling to stave off

the knot of fear that had begun to develop in his stomach. The people of New Orleans, he knew, would not react well to their city being occupied by Yankees. Nor would they take graciously to their conquerors inflicting martial law over them. He turned and pushed his way through the swinging doors. He'd tell Suzanne first, break the news to her that New Orleans had fallen, then he'd send a wire to his mother and make sure everything at Shadows Noir was all right.

But the moment he stepped out onto the street he knew it was too late to break the news to Suzanne so she wouldn't hear it elsewhere. People were everywhere: miners, gamblers, businessmen, whores and respectable women alike. All shouting, some cheering, others groaning, and both sides snarling and threatening the other.

He hurried across the street and down the boardwalk toward the Union Belle. One of its front doors stood open, cold air swirling into the lobby. He walked through the open doorway just as Mavis Beale rushed around the far corner of the room.

"Damned yahoos," she grumbled. "Can't be satisfied with dancing about in the street like a bunch of half-wits, they gotta shove open my door and let the cold air in."

"You hear the news?" Travis asked.

"Ain't everybody?" Mavis snapped. She slammed the door shut and turned its lock. "That'll keep them out."

"Is Su— Georgette Lindsay in, Mavis?"

"She came in about an hour or so ago, Travis." Mavis looked at him queerly. "Didn't you escort her here?"

He shook his head. "No." Tom Lowry had walked Suzanne back to the hotel.

"Well, she's here, but I can't guarantee she's awake.

Course, how a body could sleep with all the noise these yokels are making," she motioned toward the street, "I wouldn't rightly know."

"I'll go up and knock."

Mavis turned back toward her own quarters. "Just remember, Travis, I run a respectable place here." She glanced back at him as he mounted the stairs. "And I ain't no madam."

He chuckled. "I'll remember that."

She winked. "You do that."

Travis walked down the quiet hallway and, pausing before Suzanne's door, knocked.

Addie pulled the door open and stared at Travis. "Oh, Mr. Braggette, have you heard the news?"

Travis nodded.

"Isn't it awful? I mean, we just never thought. I mean," she glanced at Suzanne, who sat on the edge of the bed, a handkerchief held crushed in one hand, "well, it just can't be true, can it?"

Travis stepped into the room, but before Addie could close the door behind him, he turned to her. "Addie," he said in a deep voice that was little more than a whisper, "I'd like to talk to Miss Lindsay alone for a few minutes."

Addie looked back at Suzanne, uncertain.

Travis took Addie's arm and steered her out into the hallway. "It's okay, Addie. I know her family back in New Orleans." He nodded at her look of surprise. "Why don't you go on downstairs and make yourself a cup of warm milk? Or retire for the night."

"Well, are you sure? I mean, that Miss Lindsay won't be needing me further?"

"I'm sure." He closed the door.

Addie hurried to her room and, stepping into it only long enough to grab her cape and gloves, hurried downstairs and left the Union Belle by the rear door. If the Knights were going to try anything more, there was a good possibility it would be tonight.

Maggie sent one of her girls across the street to the Mountain Queen to fetch Abram Lyle back to the telegraph office. She watched from behind the window of the Silver Lady until she saw the tall, gangly clerk hurry from the saloon toward his office, then, slipping on her wrap, she followed.

"You want to send a telegram, Miss Rochelle?" Abram asked, as she entered.

"Yes." She thrust a folded piece of paper at him. "Send this right away."

He took the paper and began to unfold it.

"And keep it to yourself, Abram," Maggie ordered.

Abram's eyes moved back and forth as he read. " 'David Smith. Rocking T Ranch. Houston, Texas. Dear Brother. Moving forward in spite of things. All's well. Goods should arrive in two weeks. Sister.' " He looked up at Magnolia. "I didn't know you had a brother in Texas, Miss Magnolia."

She smiled. "Well, I guess there are a lot of things you don't know about me, Abram. Maybe you should come visit the Silver Lady a little more often."

Abram blushed. "Ah shucks, Miss Magnolia, you know my Sarah wouldn't take kindly to that."

"Can you send that right away, Abram?"

He nodded. "Sure thing, Miss Magnolia. I'll do it right this minute."

She turned to leave and, as she opened the door the smile that she'd held on her face for Abram Lyle's benefit disappeared. Her eyes turned hard and the fury that roiled within her, unseen, etched itself momentarily upon her features. They would have to move fast, after what had happened in New Orleans. If the South fell now, their plans would be ruined.

Chapter Fifteen

Travis sat on the edge of the bed beside Suzanne. She turned her face away and looked to the window.

"It'll be all right, Suzanne," he said softly.

A sob suddenly broke from her throat and a shudder of emotion wracked her body.

Travis slipped an arm around her shoulders and pulled her toward him. He had half expected her to resist the offered comfort, but instead, at the first touch of his hand on her, she reeled around and threw herself against him, burying her face into his chest, her arms locking around his neck.

"Oh, Travis, they've invaded New Orleans."

"I know," he whispered against the softness of her dark hair. His arms slid to encircle her waist and he pulled her closer, breathing deeply of the jasmine scent that he knew he would forever associate with Suzanne.

"It's so horrible, Travis. They're in our homes." Her words were half broken by another sob. "Just the thought of it, just the thought, is so awful."

"I know," he said again, slipping a hand up to brush the long tendrils of her hair from one side of her face where it had fallen forward. His fingers moved over the curve of her neck and he felt himself fill with desire.

"And martial law, Travis. They declared martial law." She pushed back and stared up at him. Her face was streaked with the damp evidence of her tears. More hovered within her eyes. She blinked then, and they slid down the curving lines of her dark lashes and fell to her cheeks, snaking their way downward in a glistening path of moisture.

Suzanne looked into Travis's eyes, losing herself within their fathomless grayness, and the harshness of the world's realities seemed suddenly to fade from her mind and heart, replaced by only one thought, one concern, one desire. She found herself intensely aware of everything about him, more so than perhaps she had ever been of anything in her life.

She was aware of his breath upon her cheek, warm and sensuous, rifling the wisping curls of hair at her temple, smelled the faint odor of his specially ordered Southern bourbon and the scent of brandy-smoked cigars that emanated from him, and felt, beneath the hand that rested on his arm, the sleek, powerful muscles hidden within the folds of his silk shirt and encasing black broadcloth jacket. Suzanne gently pulled her fingers from his. This was the man who had promised to love her, had promised to marry her and take care of her forever. This was the man who, with the breaking light of each new day, she had hated and cursed for seven years. But he was also the man who, in the dead of night, alone in her room, in the darkness, she had dreamed of.

Part of her hated him, but it was the part that still loved him, the part that knew she belonged to him, would always belong to him, that governed her immediate actions and thoughts.

She placed her hands upon his chest, then slipped them upward, slid her fingers over the muscular contours of his shoulders, wrapped her arms about his neck, and pulled him toward her. At the same time, she lifted herself slightly from the bed and slid onto Travis's thigh, pressing her body close to his and claiming his lips her prisoner.

But it was a prison Travis surrendered to willingly. With a growl of pleasure, his own arms wrapped around her fiercely. He pulled her body closer, the softness of her curves pressed to the hard muscle of his length, until their shadows, silhouetted on the opposite wall by the lamp at their backs, melded into one and their hearts, each pounding madly, matched each other beat for beat.

The intoxication of his touch, the final release of long pent-up yearnings, and the surrender to desires she had thought herself able to deny, robbed Suzanne of her customary propriety. Her arms held him hungrily to her as her hands slipped within the curls of his hair and slid through the silken blackness. Remembering the wave of passion he had stirred within her earlier with the mastery of his kiss, she plunged her tongue within his mouth, imitating the movements that had sent her senses reeling, flicking her tongue quickly, tantalizingly, from one spot to another, letting it curl around his, caress its length, then teasingly flit away.

The shouts and yells from those outside were no longer a reality to Travis. The world, as he knew it, had temporarily tilted on its axis and spun out of control, and he didn't care. All he cared about, all he *wanted* to care about, was the woman sitting astride his lap.

Searing, aching hunger burned within him as passion, deep, hot, and gnawing filled every muscle, every fiber and cell within his body. It erupted within him as a need so strong, so intense, as to be almost painful.

Suzanne, overcome by passions she had only dreamt about, engulfed within a world of unchartered desires and needs, pulled back slightly from him, though her mouth continued to ravage his. Her arms slid from around his neck. He felt her hands at his throat. She tugged at the black string tie at his neck, releasing it, and then her fingers began to fumble with the delicate pearl buttons of his shirt, releasing one and then traveling down to the next to repeat the gesture.

Travis sucked in a sharp breath of surprise and his body lurched slightly in pleasant anticipation as he felt her hands slip beneath the white silk of his shirt to slide over the hot, hard wall of his chest, then move upward, forcing the garments from his shoulders. He shrugged out of the sleeves, then reached for her again, but Suzanne pushed him back on the bed, her lips moving down the column of his neck. He felt her hands at his waist, felt them release the buckle of his holster and the buttons of his trousers.

"Suzanne," he said raggedly. His hands tangled within the long, silken waves of her hair as he reached for her.

Her lips moved down across his chest in a series of featherlight kisses.

A scalding wave of hunger rushed through him. Her lips pressed to the small indentation of flesh at his stomach.

"Suzanne, for God's sake," Travis growled softly. "Do you know what you're doing?"

She moved on instinct, knowing nothing about a man's body, but curious about it all, hungry to experience its touch, and because the body that lay beneath her was Travis's, the exploration was all the more sweeter.

She slid her hand beneath his open trousers.

"Sweet mother of Mary," Travis hissed. His body jerked at her touch as a thousand sparks of fire burst to life within him. He could stand no more. Reaching for her, his fingers curled around her arms and he pulled her upward, covering her lips with his, filling her mouth with the exploring, hungry, fiery length of his tongue. It was a kiss of demand and conquer, of ravaging need and commanding surrender, and Suzanne returned it eagerly, stroke for stroke, caress for caress.

Perhaps it was wrong. Perhaps tomorrow, in the light of day she would be sorry. But tonight nothing else mattered, nothing but the man who held her in his arms, the man whose touch turned her blood to fire and made her forget all the horrors of the world, all the ugliness and pain. She would face tomorrow—but tonight, if only for a few hours, she would revel in this new world, where only she and Travis existed.

With the deftness of a man who had performed the feat a thousand times, Travis's fingers slipped between the thin blue ribbons that held the front of her gown closed at her breasts and released it. He pushed the sheer fabric from her shoulders and, his mouth never leaving hers, slid the fragile material down over her hips.

"Travis ..." Suzanne moaned softly, mouthing his

name against his lips. Her hands moved over his body like silken flames, burning his skin with each touch, leaving paths of searing flesh behind as they slid here and there. Her hips ground into his, her bare breasts crushed against his chest.

He kicked the boots from his feet, pushed the trousers from his legs with a swift movement of each foot, and shoved his gun and holster to the foot of the bed. Travis held on to Suzanne and rolled her beneath him. He looked down at her then, his gaze searching her face, as if memorizing the darkness of the curls that tumbled across the pristine white pillows, the sensuously full, passion-bruised lips, the satiny ruche of lashes that shadowed her cheeks, and the startling brilliance of the china-blue eyes that looked back up at him.

"Make love to me, Travis," Suzanne whispered, her gaze never veering from his.

"I've wanted to do that since the moment you stepped off that stagecoach," Travis said, his voice a rasping drawl of emotion.

"I've wanted it longer," she said softly.

Memory of how he'd hurt her assailed him, and Travis's eyes dropped away from hers as guilt swept over him.

"Make love to me, Travis," Suzanne said again, as if reading his thoughts and wanting him to know that, at least for this moment, the past no longer mattered.

"I can't promise you tomorrow, Suzanne," Travis whispered, knowing he had to say it, had to warn her. He couldn't take her, not even as badly as he wanted to, if he didn't. Seven years ago his father had promised his tomorrows to her, and he had taken them back. It had been cruel, but it had been done. And he hadn't changed. He wasn't in love with Suzanne Forteaux. He wanted her, more than he'd wanted any woman in a long time. But he wasn't in love with her, and he wouldn't pretend that he was. Love was something for other people, but not for him, not for Travis Braggette. He had tried it once, and found it bitterly wanting.

"Love me, Travis," Suzanne said in answer, not understanding his comment and too intoxicated by the feel of him, the nearness, the rapture he aroused within her, to care.

His head lowered with almost tormenting slowness until his lips touched the naked ivory mound of her breast.

A soft moan escaped Suzanne's lips as her body arched upward to meet his touch.

His lips moved lightly over her flesh as he breathed in the sweet, and now familiar, jasmine scent that always clung to her. As his lips neared her nipple, his tongue slipped out to flick across the rosy pebbled peak and taste the sweetness of her flesh.

Suzanne's body shook with shocked pleasure as his mouth covered her nipple, his teeth gently nuzzled its peak and his tongue laved its swell.

He leaned on one elbow, keeping his full weight from pressing down on her, but the hot hardness of his arousal, the very evidence of his urgent need for her, pressed into her thigh as his other hand traveled over her body, caressing each curve, exploring each valley, sliding over each plane.

Suzanne moved instinctively beneath him, each caress, each touch he invoked upon her a new and exhilarating experience, an intoxication to senses already drugged with soul-routing passion. She felt his weight lift from her completely as he moved to lie beside her, but at the moment she would protest, feeling somehow deserted, she felt his hand slide over the flat plane of her stomach and slip to within the soft warmth of her inner thighs.

She clung to him then, as the hunger within her built.

His head rose and his lips recaptured hers, cajoling and teasing, urgently devouring and demanding, and revealing a brief glance of the loneliness he always kept so well hidden.

Down the street, several drunken miners burst from the doors of the Silver Lady and, drawing guns, shot into the air in celebration of the news that had been telegraphed earlier, but neither Travis nor Suzanne heard the sounds.

They were in a world apart from the earthly, in a time and place that existed only for them, that left war, pain, and death behind and glowed only with sunshine.

His hand slid along the inside of her thighs, taunting her senses until she writhed beneath him, the agony of anticipation nearly unbearable.

Her fingers dug into the flesh of his shoulders, kneading and pushing at the muscles there as her legs tightened around his hand, holding him to her, unwilling to release him, to lose the bittersweet torment of his touch.

He brushed his lips across the ridge of her cheekbone, along the line of her jaw, and then recaptured her mouth with his. At the same moment, his fingers slipped within the tender folds of silken flesh that hid her most sensitive, most secret part, the part of her that was the core of her femininity and passion, the part of her that ached for him.

"Oh, Travis!" Suzanne cried, ripping her mouth from his as a jolt of raw, biting desire swept over her.

"Let me love you, Suzanne," Travis whispered hoarsely, nuzzling the curve of her ear. "Let me love you like I should have done long ago."

"Oh, yes," Suzanne cried, pressing herself to him. "Yes, Travis, yes." She had come here because of Brett, but she knew, deep in her heart, she had also come because of Travis. She had wanted to make him pay for what he had done to her, make him want her, desire her, as she did him, and she had wanted to punish him, and, ultimately, destroy him.

But now all she wanted was for him to love her, to continue the exquisitely sweet torture of his hands upon her body. She felt his fingers begin to move within her again, felt his lips travel across her breasts as his mouth caressed first one, and then the other. Wave after wave of gloriously sweet pleasure swept over her, engulfing her within their shuddering tides, and instilling within her an even deeper hunger. Unable to help herself, she moaned at the yearning ache that filled her, intensified, magnified, by the movement of his probing fingers.

Knowing he could hold back no longer lest he spill his seed uselessly upon the sheets, Travis gently urged her legs apart and then, straddling her, covered her body with his.

Suzanne felt the hot tip of his need touch her between the legs, and though some small part of her called out at her that what she was about to do was wrong, that she would regret it, her heart assured her that it was right, that it was what she had been waiting for all her life.

Plunging a finger deep inside her, Travis felt the hot juices of her passion.

A few seconds later, Suzanne felt the first penetration of his rigid length as it pushed between the delicate folds of sensitive flesh and entered her. He thrust forcefully, half mad now with longing and need.

Suzanne stiffened at the sharp stab of pain that his entrance into her body caused as it tore through the delicate veil of her virginity. Her body tensed against it and a tiny shriek of surprise and hurt ripped from her throat, the sound muffled as his lips moved hungrily over hers.

Travis felt the destruction of her virtue and heard the soft cry of pain that left her lips. Shock held him momentarily still atop her. She was twenty-three, long past the age when most women marry. He had assumed, taken for granted, that in the seven years since he had left her there had been others ... and he had been wrong. Travis squeezed his eyes shut and damned himself. Overcome with a wash of guilt, he began to pull away from her.

Suzanne's arms tightened around him. "Travis," she said breathlessly. "Please."

Her words were more than he could bear, and his own need for her more than he could deny. His mouth covered hers, and his hands slipped beneath her hips, lifting them to meet his thrusts.

Deep within Suzanne a shivering, fiery inferno began to rage out of control. With each plunging thrust, her body shuddered in hungry need and her world spun farther and farther out of its axis. She began to move her hips, rising to meet him, descending as he pulled back slightly and prepared to lunge forward, into her, again.

Her fingers kneaded the soft flesh of his buttocks, her

legs entwined around his, and Travis carried them higher, higher into the stars.

Then, just as Suzanne thought she could stand no more, when she thought the hunger building within her, threatening to overtake her, envelop her within its endless, fathomless abyss, would drive her mad with longing, she felt Travis stiffen, felt her own body suddenly rocked with an assault of mind-reeling pleasure, and her world exploded.

Chapter Sixteen

"I said you can't go in there!" Mavis Beale yelled, stomping after Magnolia.

"I know what you said," Magnolia threw over her shoulder as she hurried down the narrow whitewash-walled hallway.

"And I don't want your kind in my establishment."

Magnolia stopped so quickly Mavis nearly barreled over her. Magnolia spun around and, one red brow rising haughtily, her eyes flashing indignation, challenged Mavis. "And just what kind am I, Mrs. Beale?"

Straightening hastily, Mavis rammed work-roughened hands onto her generously rounded hips and glared down her nose at Magnolia. "You know exactly what kind you are, missy, and it ain't a person been picking grapes in the Lord's vineyard, that's for sure."

"Really? Well, then," Magnolia spun around and hurried down the hall again, "I would advise you not to get too close to me, Mrs. Beale, or my lack of holy virtues just might rub off on you."

"Well!"

Magnolia paused before a door and banged her knuckles soundly against its panel.

Travis jerked around and looked over his shoulder at the door. "Who in the hell can that be?" he wondered aloud.

Suzanne, still nestled within his embrace, mumbled incoherently and snuggled closer to him. Whoever was at the door could just go away and come back later.

An act of instinct, or perhaps premonition, caused Travis to reach for the sheet and pull it up over them.

The door slammed open and Travis watched, disbelieving, as Magnolia Rochelle stormed into the room, the green satin of her gown picking up the light of the lamp near the door and glowing brilliantly, her red hair a mane of wild tangles about her face. She glared down at Travis, who practically threw himself off Suzanne and bolted upright, the end of the sheet, twisted around him by his movement, barely draped across one bare thigh.

Suzanne, abruptly yanked from her haze of passion, scooted to one side and slightly behind Travis. She clutched a pillow to her bare breasts as the burning heat of embarrassment stung her cheeks.

"Well!" Magnolia's eyes, dark with fury, darted from Travis to Suzanne and a sneer curved her lips. "I guess you just never can tell about some people now, can you?"

"Maggie . . ." Travis said, his voice heavy with warning.

"I told her she couldn't come in here," Mavis said from the doorway, her own features set with outrage. "I told her, Travis. I tried to stop her, but she just barged on ahead like a damned mule."

Magnolia threw the woman a glance over her shoulder. "Oh, go bake some bread, you old cow."

"Ah!" Mavis clutched at her breasts.

"It's all right, Mavis," Travis said. "Miss Rochelle will be leaving in just a minute."

Mavis's eyes narrowed hatefully toward the back of Magnolia's head. "Well, she'd better, or I just might call the sheriff. I don't want her kind in my place. No, siree." She turned and retreated down the hall, skirts swishing, hands wringing, and the stomp of heavy footsteps echoing loudly.

Travis stared up at Magnolia. "What the hell do you think you're doing, Maggie?"

"Getting an eyeful, obviously. But that's not why I came here."

"So, just why *did* you come here?" he growled. Not missing the succinct movement of her gaze, and feeling the tension in the room growing, Travis slid from the bed and grabbed his trousers from the floor where he'd dropped them hours before.

"I came," Magnolia said contemptuously, ignoring Suzanne and keeping her gaze pinned on Travis, "because I thought you should know that someone shot Hank. Or perhaps," she raised her chin defiantly and threw Suzanne a look of loathing, "perhaps that's not important to you."

Travis's head jerked up at her words. He froze in place, his hands gripped around the waistband of his trousers, which he had been in the process of pulling on. Gray eyes stared incredulously at Magnolia. "Shot Hank?" he echoed stupidly.

"Yes, shot Hank. Some of those northern sympathizers you're so fond of went into the Mountain Queen after you left and started busting up the place real good. They were looking for you, most likely to bust *you* up. Damned idiots were yelling about Duncan getting shot and how it was probably your idea to rob the freighters, since you lead the Knights now. But," she released an exaggerated sigh, "since you were gone, they decided to teach one of your employees a lesson and they picked Hank."

"Bastards," Travis said. He slid his trousers up over his hips, hastily fastened them at his waist, tugged on his boots, and reached for the white shirt that lay crumpled half under the bed.

"Of course it could have been worse."

Travis looked up again.

"I mean, they could have taken their wrath out on Elsie, or one of your other girls."

"Lucky for them they didn't," Travis snarled. "Is Hank all right? He's not . . . ?"

She shrugged one bare shoulder. "Oh, he'll live. They got him in the arm. Jed tried to stop them from breaking up the place and got a good hit on the head for his trouble. I guess he was out cold when they started beating on Hank."

"Who was it?" Travis barked, and grabbed his jacket. "Who led them?"

Magnolia shook her head. "I don't know. Ask Hank. I'd say him and Jed got a really good look at all of them."

Travis started from the room without a backward glance toward Suzanne, who still sat huddled behind the pillow.

Magnolia started to follow but paused on the threshold and reached back to close the door. She looked at

Suzanne, hate blazing from her dark eyes. "Take some advice, my sweet," she said, "make that the last time you share anything with Travis, humm?" A cunning little smile curved her lips upward, but there was no warmth in the gesture, only chilling hostility. "He belongs to me."

Hours later, Suzanne was still thinking about Magnolia Rochelle's parting words, and remembering those Travis had whispered to her before they'd made love: *I can't promise you tomorrow.* She wasn't sure whether she should cry in despair or scream in anger. She'd been a fool to give herself to him, an utter, complete, senseless fool. Closing her eyes, she leaned back against the headboard. But, stupid as it was, it was done and there was no undoing it. At least she knew Travis Braggette hadn't changed. Maybe now she could forget him. Relegate him to the past where he belonged. Banish his memory from her mind and heart. Travis wasn't her long-lost love. He wasn't her prince, or her knight in shining armor. He was still the same selfish, unfeeling, arrogant boy who had left her standing in the church to face all of their friends and relatives alone.

Her face flamed as the sudden memory of what had happened last night assailed her. She had invited his seduction. She'd been the one to entice him to her bed. Suzanne stiffened with resolution. Well, at least she could put all of that silliness behind her now, all of her fantasies and dreams about him.

A long sigh escaped her lips. She couldn't deny that he aroused her desires, stoked a passion within her like none she'd ever felt, made her feel like a real woman.

Suzanne wrapped her arms about herself and hugged them tightly. No, she couldn't deny those feelings, but she could ignore them.

Addie exited the doctor's office where Hank was being bandaged up and hurried down the boardwalk toward the hotel. At least he was all right. She'd nearly keeled over in a faint at receiving word that he'd been shot. Her reaction to the news had surprised her almost as much as the news itself. Hank Davis was not someone she would ordinarily be attracted to. And she hadn't even been aware she was truly attracted to him. Evidently while she'd been busy prodding him for information about Travis and the Knights, he'd grown on her.

As she pondered this, she passed several men congregated on the boardwalk before the Nevada Bank.

"We oughta run 'em out of town," one man snarled.

"Yeah, with a coat of tar and feathers," another said.

They all laughed.

Addie kept her gaze averted and hurried on. Things were getting touchy in the small mining city, and she was getting uncomfortable. Her sixth sense was acting up, but all it was telling her was that something was bound to happen soon . . . not what that something was.

With the recent news that New Orleans had fallen to the Yankees, the War Between the States had come to Virginia City in full force.

Addie entered the hotel and, lifting the front of her brown skirt, dashed up the stairs. She went directly to Suzanne's door and knocked.

There was no answer.

Addie huffed in frustration. If anything was going to

happen, it was going to happen soon, she knew that as sure as she knew her name wasn't Hays. Now she needed to speak with Suzanne. If Travis really had taken over leadership of the Knights in Virginia City, Suzanne might know. And if those same Knights were planning to pull something, she might know that, too. On the other hand, there was Clarence Lonchet and Ben Morgan. They were Knights, too, she was certain, and had some controlling power over Suzanne, though Addie still hadn't figured out what it was. Nor had she been able to determine why Clarence and Ben, rather than just communicating with Travis as one Knight to another, had Suzanne spying on him. Or did they suspect him of being a Union sympathizer. Addie thought that over for a moment. Travis Braggette? Of *the* New Orleans Braggettes, a Union sympathizer?

She hurried back downstairs to the front desk. "Mrs. Beale?" she called out. "Mrs. Beale?"

The hefty woman waddled around the corner. "Yes?"

"Mrs. Beale, do you happen to know where Miss Lindsay has gone?"

Mrs. Beale wiped her flour-covered hands on the muslin apron that wrapped around her wide girth. "Mr. Nathram, that nice young mine supervisor down at Gould and Curry came for her in a buggy awhile back. I heard him mention something about them dining down at the mansion."

"The mansion?" Addie echoed, her face screwing into an expression of puzzlement.

Mrs. Beale nodded. "The Gould and Curry house, over off D Street. Nathram shares the house with the other supervisor and the mining offices."

"Off D Street?" Addie asked. She turned and headed

for the door, her mind already fast at work contemplating scenarios of suspicion. Suzanne was with a mining superintendent. And someone had tried to rob a freighter just that past night. Were the two things connected? Was Suzanne somehow getting information for the Knights for their robberies?

"Yep. Past Washington a couple of blocks," Mavis called to Addie. "Brick place surrounded by white columns. Real pretty place. You can't miss it."

Addie walked down Taylor and, following Mavis Beale's directions, turned right on D Street, passed Washington and kept walking. Two blocks later, she stopped across the street from the Gould & Curry Mining Company's combination superintendent's house and offices. The hotel owner had been right, she couldn't have missed it. But the house wasn't pretty, it was *beautiful.* Set on a mild downslope of land, the mansion's walls were made entirely of brick, and a sloping roof shaded the white-columned veranda that completely encircled it. Green shutters adorned each tall window and white-painted trellis woodwork shaded the windows and enclosed the walkway of the floor beneath the veranda.

The upper portion of each of the double entry doors held a large oval of etched glass which had been curtained with a swath of ivory lace to match that which hung down before each window and between the heavier, tied-back damask drapes.

Addie stared at the house. A horse and buggy stood at the hitching rail to one side of it. She crossed the street, mounted the shallow steps that led up to the veranda and paused before the entry doors. Addie took a deep breath and knocked.

A tiny woman opened the door. Her gray hair was

pulled into a chignon at her nape and her dark-gray chambray dress was covered by a crisp white apron. She had the look and bearing of a housekeeper. "Yes, ma'am?" Her pale-blue eyes looked at Addie questioningly.

"I'd like to see Miss Georgette Lindsay," Addie said. "I believe she's lunching with Mr. Nathram?"

The older woman nodded. "Yes, ma'am." She stepped back to allow Addie entry into the foyer. "If you'll wait, please, I'll fetch Miss Lindsay."

Barely a minute later, a door opened from farther down the entry hall and Suzanne stepped out. She hurried toward Addie. "Addie, what is it? What's the matter?" she asked breathlessly. She stopped before Addie and grabbed her hand. "What's wrong?"

Addie smiled. "Nothing, Suzanne. I just thought I'd come and make certain you were all right. There's a lot of angry talk in town and some of the miners are, well, they're acting up."

Suzanne laughed lightly. "Oh, Addie, you're such a worry wart. I'm fine." She linked an arm through Addie's. "Come on, though, and join us. The food is wonderful."

"No, thank you, really. I wouldn't want to intrude. Anyway, I thought I'd do a little shopping this afternoon, but . . ." Her brow furrowed into a frown.

"What?"

"Well, I wasn't going to say anything. I didn't want to worry you, and all, but . . ."

"What?" Suzanne urged, anxious.

"Well," Addie dropped her voice to a whisper, "I heard talk that Mr. Braggette had taken over as leader of that club, the uh . . ." She screwed up her face as if trying to remember the name.

"The Knights of the Golden Circle?" Suzanne supplied.

Addie nodded. "Yes, that's it. The Knights of the Golden Circle. Anyway, well, I was just thinking that if it was true, maybe you should not finish your engagement here at the Mountain Queen." She fiddled nervously with the silk cord of her beaded black reticule. "I mean, it is his saloon and all, and there could be trouble. Real trouble. Already his manager was shot and . . ."

Suzanne shook her head. "Travis isn't their leader, Addie. At least he said he isn't, and I believe him. I think. Nevertheless, even if there is trouble, it doesn't concern us. Now . . ." she smiled widely, "are you certain you wouldn't like to join us? Mr. Nathram is a very nice man." She winked slyly. "You might like him."

"But even if the Knights aren't being led by Mr. Braggette, Suzanne, what if they try something else? Like another robbery?" Addie tried to look scared. "The miners could get awfully ugly about that. Maybe start tearing up the town. We could be in danger. Don't you think we ought to leave before something like that happens?"

Suzanne patted Addie's hand and shook her head. "I really doubt the Knights will try anything like that again, so don't worry about it. In fact, I'm fairly certain they won't."

Addie smiled. So, Suzanne did know something. "Did you meet Mr. Nathram at the Mountain Queen?" she asked, changing the subject.

"Actually, no. Clarence stopped by my room earlier

and said that Mr. Nathram had seen me perform and wanted to invite me to lunch, and, well, you know Clarence, always looking for investors to start up a new troupe. So I said all right." She shrugged and smiled. "And, here I am."

Addie nodded and turned toward the door. Clarence. Why did she feel that if Clarence had introduced Suzanne to this Nathram fellow there was a lot more behind it than Clarence was willing to admit. "Well, okay," she said, and smiled. "I'll see you back at the hotel."

Travis stood on the boardwalk before the Mountain Queen, one shoulder leaning against a support pillar. His thumbs were hooked within the belt of the holster that rode low over one hip, and the tip of a cheroot he held clasped between two fingers of his right hand burned steadily. The casual pose belied the tension that held his muscles taut and kept his gaze constantly moving, though shaded by the brim of the hat pulled low over his forehead.

If there was going to be any more trouble in Virginia City, it damned sure wasn't going to be in the Mountain Queen if he could help it. He watched Charlie Mellroy pass by on the opposite side of the street. Travis's features hardened. The rumor that he had assumed leadership of the Knights was running rampant in spite of his denials, and he had a good idea who was still stoking that fire. His only question was why? Why in the hell would the judge want everyone to think Travis had accepted the post? What good did it do to stir up the townspeople about that when there were more important things to think about?

A horse-drawn buggy passed into his line of vision and cut off sight of Charlie. Travis shifted his gaze to the buggy and felt a start of surprise, followed instantly by a flash of agitation. Suzanne Forteaux sat on the vehicle's narrow seat, all aglow in a taffeta gown of brilliant yellow. Beside her, looking proud as a peacock, sat the young new day-shift mining supervisor of the Gould & Curry, Eli Nathram.

She had shared her bed with him, and her body, only a few hours before, and now she was riding through the center of town, proud as you please, beside another man! "So what the hell do I care if she lets every buck and jackel around here court her?" Travis grumbled beneath his breath. "Or bed her for that matter." He flicked the cheroot into the street, watching it arc skyward and, as it descended, narrowly miss hitting Nathram's passing buggy.

"What did you say, Boss?" Hank asked, stepping past the swinging doors behind Travis

"Nothing," Travis shot over his shoulder.

Hank shook his head, and, careful to keep his bandaged arm snugly tucked into its sling and out of the way of passersby, turned away.

The remainder of Travis's day passed in a haze of anger and self-recrimination. The Mountain Queen wouldn't have gotten busted up if he'd been there. Jed wouldn't have a lump on his head the size of an orange if Travis had been there. Hank wouldn't have been beat up and shot in the arm if Travis had been there. And Suzanne Forteaux wouldn't have lost her virginity to him if he'd been at the Mountain Queen.

* * *

Travis let his gaze roam over the sea of men who had crowded into the Mountain Queen that evening. At least a dozen, he was sure, were members of the KGC. The others were definitely either Southerners, or Southern sympathizers. Not one, as far as he knew, was a Union man.

"Son of a bitch," he snarled softly to himself, and turned back to the bar.

"Something wrong, Boss?" Hank asked, sidling up to stand beside Travis.

"Damned right something's wrong. Look at this room."

Hank glanced around. He nodded to several men he knew, then looked back at Travis and shrugged. "What's wrong, Boss? We got a full house, whiskey's flowing good, and nobody's cheating at the cards yet. And it'll get even better when Miss Lindsay comes out for her show."

Travis turned back toward the crowd. "Where's Conner Slate, Hank?" he asked. "Or Ben Miller? Or Johnny Dellos?" His gaze continued to roam. "Or those brothers from California who own the Ophir—what's their names, Ken and Stacy Ferguson? And that Italian who's always hanging around, Tony Brassea?"

Hank shrugged again. "They ain't here."

"That's right, damn it. They're all Union men, and they're not here."

Hank looked back out at the crowd, suddenly understanding what Travis was saying. "Oh."

Travis turned back to the bar and motioned for Jed to bring him a drink.

"So you think we got trouble, Boss?" Hank asked.

Travis glanced at Hank's bandaged arm. "You mean more than we've already had?"

Jed slid a drink before Travis. "Shotgun's loaded and ready," he said.

"Good. Keep it handy." He glanced up at the long crack in the center of the mirror behind the bar and another curse left his lips. It had cost a damned fortune getting that piece of glass from San Francisco up to Carson City, and another small fortune to get it freighted up the mountain trails to Virginia City. The whole time he'd held his breath, afraid it would get broken before it arrived. Now some yahoo had put a crack down its center with a flying chair leg, and all because he believed a rumor. a stupid, damned rumor.

A movement at the entry doors caught Travis's attention. He turned his gaze in that direction and saw Charlie Mellroy entering the saloon.

"Have either of you heard anybody talking me up as leader of the Knights?" Travis asked.

Both Hank and Jed shook their heads.

"Well, keep your ears open. I'd like to have myself a nice little chat with whoever's spreading that rumor."

At that moment the piano player broke into a merry chorus, the curtains on the stage parted, and Suzanne, in the guise of Georgette Lindsay, walked onto the stage. She was dressed in a gown of red satin trimmed with black lace, its puffed sleeves draped off the shoulder. The gown's neckline, dripping with more black lace and curls of black torsage fringe, plunged daringly between her breasts. She snapped open a beaded and feathered black fan and smiled at the crowd. Her hair had been pulled up loosely, pinned, and allowed to cascade down

her back in a fall of dark waves, the strands of red highlights deepened and accentuated by the hue of her
gown. A collage of black-and-red ostrich feathers was
pinned to one side of her coiffure, just behind her ear.

As had happened every night since her arrival, the
men broke out in wild cheers the moment Suzanne appeared and quieted instantly when she began to sing.

Travis watched her, a gnawing ache burgeoning
within him as his eyes followed her sashaying little body
from one end of the stage to the other. When a melding
of desire and anger threatened to overwhelm him, he
turned back to the bar.

The audience cheered her song.

Travis downed his drink. He hadn't spoken with her
since earlier that morning when Maggie had burst into
Suzanne's hotel room to tell him Hank had been shot.
It hadn't occurred to him until much later that he'd left
her without so much as a good-bye. Once he'd thought
of it, after he made certain Hank and Jed were all right
and the Mountain Queen hadn't been thoroughly destroyed, several hours had passed. He'd gone back to
the hotel, but found her gone. Then he'd seen her riding in that damned buggy beside Eli Nathram. Travis
felt a wave of self-disgust wash over him. Whether
Travis said hello, goodbye, or would you marry me, it
didn't mean a damned thing to Suzanne Forteaux. She
had a plethora of other suitors to concern herself with.

The crowd cheered again.

Suzanne's voice drifted to him and interrupted his
thoughts.

" 'The soldier is a lad for me, a brave heart I
adore . . .' "

The miners roared their approval of her words.

" 'And when the sunny South is free, and fighting is no more . . .' "

The audience cheered again.

" 'I'll choose me then a lover brave, from out that gallant band . . .' "

Travis cringed as the crowd behind him went wild.

" 'The soldier lad I love the best shall have my heart and hand.' "

The men were on their feet now, stomping and clapping.

" 'Hurrah, Hurrah, for the sunny South so dear.' " Suzanne waved her hands. "Come on, boys. 'Hurrah, Hurrah, for the sunny South so dear!' "

The crowd broke into loud hurrahs.

Travis clutched the shot glass, and his knuckles turned white from the pressure of his grip. What the hell was she trying to do, incite a riot? He felt himself shake with rage and turned slightly so that he could keep an eye on the swinging doors. Any minute now he expected the other half of the town, the Northern loyalists and sympathizers, to come bashing through the entry to the Queen. He pushed back the lapels of his jacket and lay the heel of his hand on the butt of his gun.

The song ended and Suzanne immediately began a slow ballad. The men resumed their seats, the swinging doors remained still, and Travis breathed a sigh of relief.

" 'Somebody's darling was borne one day, somebody's darling so young and brave . . .' " Suzanne's voice filled the room. She descended the steps of the stage as she sang and moved to stand before one of the men seated at a front table.

Travis strained to identify the man.

Suzanne finally moved on, and the man's head turned so that his gaze could follow her.

Tom Lowry. Travis felt a rumble of disdain resound deep in his throat. What was she doing? Had the Forteauxs truly lost their fortune? Was she trying to find herself a husband? A rich husband? But if that was true, why her interest in Eli Nathram? He was only a mining superintendent. Travis's gaze moved back to Suzanne and his eyes narrowed as suspicion loomed heavy again. He never had gotten a satisfactory answer from her about why she'd been searching his room.

Fifteen minutes later, after several more songs and having moved about the room flirting with at least one man at each table and several at the bar, with the exception of Travis, Suzanne finished her last song of the evening's first show.

She descended the stage and started to make her way across the room to where Bob Fairmount sat at a table near the wall. She had passed only a few tables when Clarence Lonchet entered the room. Travis watched as Suzanne paused abruptly, and met the gaze of her diminutive manager. For only the briefest flash of a second her features hardened and a shadow passed over her eyes, then she changed direction, smiled, and moved toward Travis.

"I waited for you to come back to the hotel this morning," she said, her tone slightly pouting as she moved to stand beside Travis at the bar.

"Not too long, from what I saw," he snapped back.

Suzanne's smile faltered for just a moment, but she quickly caught it. She snuggled up to Travis and slipped an arm around his. "Oh, you mean Eli?" Suzanne waved a dismissing hand before her. "That was just business."

Travis's brows rose in surprise. "Business?" he echoed. "*You* have business with a mine superintendent?" The words were heavily laced with sarcastic disbelief. "What are you going to do, Suzanne, change your profession? Somehow I can't picture you as a mining superintendent. Or are you planning on putting on a private show for the Gould & Curry?"

Suzanne's features tightened with the fury that erupted within her at his insulting words, but she forced the smile to remain on her face and kept her voice calm. "Actually, I've been looking around for some investments, and Eli volunteered to explain the workings of the mines to me."

"*You're* going to invest in a mine?"

"Well, no. Not really. I mean, I was thinking about it, but I've decided not to."

"Right," Travis drawled. He was trying desperately to ignore her arm around his, her body pressed to his, the scent of jasmine that emanated from her, and the fact that his body was on fire with want of her. Every muscle, every cell and fiber within him ached to reach out and touch her, urged him to wrap her within his embrace and pull her up against him. It was only an almost inhuman strength of will that kept him from obeying.

In the mirror over the bar Travis saw Clarence Lonchet behind him say something to Ben Morgan, then both men quickly left the saloon. Travis turned his attention back to Suzanne and was certain she, too, had noticed her manager and Ben Morgan's departure.

She immediately pulled her arm from Travis's and stepped back.

"But you needn't bother yourself wondering about my business affairs, Travis," she said coolly. "I've been managing quite well on my own now for a number of years now, no thanks to you, and I fully intend to keep doing just that."

With a toss of her long dark hair, Suzanne whirled around and flounced her way toward Tom Lowry's table.

Travis stared after her, his eyes darkening with suspicion as an idea suddenly came to mind. Could it be true? At first he felt an urge to scoff at his own imaginings, but the more he thought about it, the more sense it all made. Whenever Lonchet was around, Suzanne was as warm as a long swallow of rich bourbon, but whenever he was absent, her attitude was cold enough to rival the winter zephyrs that blew through Virginia City. Yes, thinking back over it he knew he was right. But why was she like that? What was she up to? Or better yet, what were *they* up to?

Travis watched Suzanne bend low beside Lowry and say something in the man's ear. They both laughed. Travis swore softly and forced his concentration to remain on his growing suspicions. What the hell had Lonchet meant the other night when Travis had overheard him in Suzanne's dressing room ordering her to follow orders or else? It hadn't sounded like anything to do with her singing performances.

He turned back to the bar and picked up the shot glass filled with his special bourbon that Jed had poured and left for him. Travis stared down into the golden liquor and cursed silently. He had a head full of damned questions and no answers.

Suddenly the swinging doors behind him burst open

and crashed back against the inside walls with reverberating force. A tall, gangly miner stood in the doorway. "Somebody robbed and murdered Duncan Clyde!"

Chapter Seventeen

Travis stared at the dead body of Duncan Clyde. The man had survived one earlier attempted robbery of his ore wagon. This time he hadn't been so lucky. But something nagged at the back of Travis's mind, a question he just couldn't seem to shake . . . or answer. Why Clyde? Why had the outlaws picked him to rob again? Why not one of the other ore wagons? Hell, so many of them passed down through the pass on a given day, and night, they could have picked anyone. Why hadn't they chosen to rob one of the other drivers? Maybe one who wouldn't have fought back? Or hadn't already been alerted and half expecting another attack? Why Clyde? It didn't make any sense, but it was just too damned coincidental to be a happenstance.

Duncan Clyde's body lay in a twist of the road just before Devil's Gate. Obviously, the bandits, whoever they were, had hidden in the craggy, shadowed walls of the pass and waited for their quarry. Travis looked back up toward the pass, trying to visualize in his mind what could have happened. On their first attempt the bandits had shot at him, and he'd shot back. But this time

Clyde's assailants hadn't used guns. Travis's eyes narrowed. This time the old freighter hadn't even been warned. A knife protruded from his chest, but there seemed no signs of a struggle, or that Clyde had even attempted to reach under his seat for his rifle. Whoever had killed Duncan Clyde had merely stepped up before and slightly to the side of his wagon, took aim, and thrown the knife. Or maybe, if Clyde's assailant was an expert marksman, he had thrown the knife from a hiding place in the rocks. Regardless, the knife had hit its mark and the old man had toppled from his high seat atop the ore wagon to the ground, most likely dead instantly.

But again, the question. Why Clyde? To silence him? Had Clyde recognized something about his first attackers that would identify them, and perhaps hadn't realized it? Travis's eyes narrowed slightly as he mulled over the questions and possibilities in his head. Had those same assailants realized this and, afraid Clyde would eventually figure out or remember what he'd seen, and might then know who they were, decided to silence him forever rather than take that risk? And of course they could steal the ore at the same time, thereby killing two birds with one stone. Is that why they'd used a knife to kill him? So that this time their robbery would be silent? So that no one would hear their attack? So that their victim would have no warning, and no chance to call for help? No time to draw his own gun and fire back?

Travis crouched beside the man's body and looked around. There was no evidence of footprints nearby. Evidently whoever had thrown the knife had been confident they struck a deadly blow. They hadn't bothered to come near Clyde to make sure. Travis rose to his full height and walked to Clyde's ore wagon, which had been moved several yards away to the side of the road. The bed of his wagon was empty.

Travis's brow furrowed. The whole thing didn't make sense. Clyde worked for the Chollar Mining Company. His wagon had obviously been full when he'd left the mine. So how did the robbers get the ore away? Had they brought their own wagon and, after killing Duncan, transferred the ore? Travis frowned. In the middle of the road?

The sheriff walked up to Travis. "Your boys have any kind of hand in this, Braggette, and I'll see all you rot in jail for the next fifty years."

Travis looked down at the overweight, shorter and older man. At one time the sheriff might have made an impressive figure, maybe even threating, but no more. "My boys?" Travis said, a cutting tone to his voice. He knew exactly what the man meant, but decided to force him to say it.

"Yeah, you know, them Knights."

"The Knights are not boys, Sheriff, and certainly not mine. I know it's hard for you, but I wish you'd get that straight." He moved one hand to rest on the butt of the gun that hung low on his hip. "Let me explain it once more, Sheriff. Slowly, so you'll understand," Travis said, his voice little more than a harsh, grating growl. "I used to belong to the Knights of the Golden Circle, I admit, but I no longer consider myself a member, and certainly not their leader." His fingers slipped into place around the gun. "Did I explain that simply enough so that you understand now, Sheriff? Or would you like me to do it again? Maybe a little slower?"

"Don't push me, Braggette," the sheriff blustered as

the other men who'd accompanied him down the hill moved up to stand behind him. Travis recognized most of them. Of keen interest was the presence of Eli Nathram. "You filthy rebs oughta be smart enough to mind your place," the sheriff said, drawing Travis's attention. He threw out his chest and raised his chin defiantly. "Either that, or get outta out of town and go back to where you all belong."

"Filthy rebs?" Travis repeated. Out of the corners of his eyes he saw the others move slightly, but knew he had nothing to worry about. Rather than swaggering forward to help the sheriff, most were shuffling nervously, staring down at their boots, or just plain refusing to meet Travis's eyes. They might be Northern sympathizers, but they weren't killers. They were miners, townsfolk, or freighters. Travis looked back at the sheriff. "Could you repeat that remark, Sheriff? I'm not quite sure I heard you correctly."

"You heard me just fine," the sheriff sneered. "Filthy rebs. Traitors, that's what you are. Traitors. That's your kind, Braggette, and your kind ain't wanted around here no more. Got it?"

Travis's hand snaked out faster than a rattler's strike. His fingers clutched the collar of the sheriff's shirt and he pulled the man toward him. "Watch what you're flapping off that tongue, Sheriff, or I might just find it necessary to show you how us *filthy rebs* slice off fat little ol' Yankee tongues and use them for bootstraps."

The sheriff's face paled instantly and his brown, drooping eyes grew so large beneath his bushy brows they looked ready to pop from his head. He pushed frantically at Travis's hands with his pudgy fingers and squirmed about, trying to free himself.

"Hey, Travis, stop fiddlin' with that ninny and come look over here," Hank called. He was hunkered down to the ground a few yards away, studying the muddy earth.

Travis pushed the sheriff away from him, releasing his shirt with a snap, and without even a dismissing glance at the man, turned to Hank. "Yeah, what?"

"This horseprint in the mud over here."

Travis bent down beside Hank, who was holding a lantern just above the ground.

"Horse's shoe has a chip in it," Travis said.

"Yep." Hank nodded and moved around from one side to the other the unlit stub of cheroot that usually protruded from his mouth. "None of the boys here have had their horses over this way. Find that there horse that made these prints and I'd becha a hundred greenbacks you've done found one of ol' Duncan Clyde's killers, Boss."

Travis looked up at the sheriff. "You hear that, Morrow?"

"I know how to do my job, Braggette," the sheriff groused. "Why don't you just go on back to town and do yours?"

By the time Travis got back to the Mountain Queen, things had returned to as close to normal as was possible after a robbery and murder. The piano player was tinkling out a tune, the gamblers were fleecing the miners and local businessmen, a few strangers were busy drinking, laughing, losing their money and flirting with Suzanne and the waitresses, Jed was pouring drinks, and the general flow of conversation between the miners who weren't gambling was on who robbed Duncan Clyde's wagon, why they'd killed him, and who could be next. And of course, everyone wanted to know what was going to be done about the situation.

To his surprise, Travis found that both Clarence Lonchet and Ben Morgan were in the saloon and participating in a game of cards at Morgan's table. They hadn't been there before word came of the robbery. He stared long and hard at each man, his gaze assessing, scrutinizing and hard. If they'd been involved there was no way they could have gotten back here that fast. Unless all they'd done was supervise the robbery. Travis looked at the other three people who sat at the table with Lonchet and Morgan. One was a gambler Travis had seen down in Gold Hill the week before. He'd watched the man take several miners for a full week's wages in about fifteen minutes. It was obvious from both the man's cut of attire, his manner, and the faint drawl Travis detected when he called out for one of the waitresses to bring him a drink, that he was a Southerner. Most likely he'd made his living on the riverboats before the war broke out.

The war. The words echoed in his mind like the bell of the St. Louis Cathedral in the Vieux Carré, mourning the dead after the city had been struck by yet another surge of yellow fever. The war. A deadly scourge, just like the fever. Travis turned his attention back to the men at Lonchet and Morgan's table. A miner, Jesse Slaw, sat next to the gambler. Travis wondered what Jesse was doing there. He wasn't a rich man with a lot of money to be throwing around, and gamblers didn't play for small stakes. The last man at the table was Olmer Smith, who owned a general store down near

South Street. Travis knew Olmer was an avowed, if not fanatical, enthusiast of the Southern cause.

Suspicion grew within Travis at the odd assortment of personalities. Clarence Lonchet pushed away from the table, rose and, squaring a bowler on his bald pate, nodded to the other men and left the saloon.

Travis looked back at the remainder of the group. Morgan had dealt a new hand of cards and the men seemed settled in to stay. Travis pushed away from the bar and followed Lonchet through the swinging doors to the street. The little man might be doing nothing but going to the hotel to call it a night, but Travis had a hunch that something else was up. Once out on the boardwalk he looked both ways, but Lonchet was out of sight. "What the hell?" Travis mumbled softly. The moon was high and nearly full in a black sky sprinkled with thousands of glittering stars. A chill hung in the air, and a wind, swift and biting, swept down the street from the direction of the cemeteries at the northern end of town. As he had a hundred times before, Travis momentarily cursed himself for not situating the Mountain Queen on B Street rather than C Street. The other business street was farther up the mountain and seemed to miss the direct onslaught of the zephyrs as they passed, unlike C Street.

A movement across the street and near the far corner caught his eye and brought his attention back to the matter at hand and off the weather. A man, short in stature and wearing a pale-gray jacket and trousers, and what appeared to be a bowler on his head, disappeared around the corner. Travis tensed. Lonchet!

He hurried after the man, taking care to remain in the shadows and out of the moonlight or reflections of light that emanated from the windows of the other buildings he passed. Sidestepping a small mound of snow, Travis crossed the street and cursed silently as he felt his boot heel slide atop a path of slick mud. Only a flailing of his arms and a bit of luck saved him from falling. A second later, nearing the corner around which Lonchet had disappeared, Travis swore again as snow crunched softly beneath his step and, in trying to get away from the sound, he veered too far toward the building's wall and had to slam a hand against its white-washed boards to keep from losing his balance altogether. The sound seemed to echo loudly on the still night air.

Taking a deep breath and praying he hadn't spooked Lonchet, Travis pushed away from the building and continued on after the man. He rounded the corner of Taylor Street and hurried after Suzanne's manager, making sure to stay close to the buildings, off the snow and mud, and out of sight.

Lonchet paused at the corner of D Street.

Travis pulled up short, hastily stepped into a darkened doorway, and watched him. Was the man merely going to one of the cribs for a prostitute? Had he gotten mud all over his good boots, splinters in the heel of his hand, and froze his backside off, all to follow the shrimp to a whore's cottage?

Lonchet moved on down Taylor.

Travis frowned and watched for several seconds before following. He wasn't going to visit a whore, that was pretty certain. There weren't many cathouses below D Street, and none a man like Lonchet would consider patronizing. Travis followed him. So where in the hell *was* he going? At the corner of F Street, the smaller man stepped into a narrow, dark alley and disappeared.

"Damn it all to hell," Travis swore softly, and stared at the alley. There was no way he could follow Lonchet in there. It was a dead end and so narrow his presence would be detected immediately if Lonchet was standing in there talking with someone. A private home bordered one side of the alley, an apothecary shop the other. If Lonchet wasn't standing in the darkness, which building had he gone into? Travis tried to remember who lived in the house, and couldn't. Lon Burrows owned and ran the apothecary shop, and Lon was a member of the KGC. Had Lonchet gone to meet with Lon Burrows? Or was he in the house, possibly with a whore? Travis backed himself into a nearby doorway and watched the alley. It was all he could do. He didn't dare cross the street and try to chance a look into the passageway, or approach either of the houses bordering it for fear someone would see him through their windows.

Ten minutes passed. A very silent, very cold, very long ten minutes. Travis shivered, wishing he'd had time to grab his greatcoat from his room. He rubbed his hands together and blew into them, then tucked them under his arms. Another five minutes passed. He was just about to give up and return to the Mountain Queen, convinced Lonchet had most likely gone into the house to meet a whore, when his attention was drawn to someone approaching on his side of the street. Instinct drove Travis farther back into the blackness of the shadowed doorway. He flattened himself against the cold wood panel and hardly dared to breathe.

A woman walked by hurriedly, her arms clasped

tightly to her bosom, her head, half covered by the hood of her black capucine cape, bent low to her chest.

Travis couldn't see her face, couldn't distinguish the exact color of the curl of hair that blew from around the hood and lay over her shoulder, but something told him he knew exactly who it was. He watched her hasten across F Street and continue down Taylor, the cape billowing out behind her. A slip of red satin showed briefly beneath the flapping cape's hem. As she neared St. Paul's Episcopal Church, she paused and looked both ways up the street, as if checking for traffic.

Travis silently snorted. There was very little traffic out at this time of night. Most likely she was looking to see if anyone was following her.

She dashed across the narrow thoroughfare. The tall wooden structure of the church left that side of the street nearly in pitch blackness, except for the closest corner where light reflected out from one of the building's front windows. It cast a pale-yellow glow on a small, square portion of the street, turning the mound of snow that lay there to a mountain of glistening gold.

If she continued on down the street Travis would have a decision to make: follow her, or remain where he was and wait to see if he could determine what Lonchet was up to.

She paused on the corner and looked about, as if confused or scared. Suddenly, seeming to hear or sense something behind her, she jerked around to her left and stared into the inky blackness at the side of the church. The light from the window momentarily fell on her face and Travis found all of his earlier suspicions of Suzanne returning.

He watched her move hesitantly toward whatever

sound had startled her but stop just before entering the darkness that was like a stygian void.

Another figure suddenly emerged from that fathomless abyss to stand before her, yet still within the shadows. He looked around quickly, stealthily, as if, he, too, wanted to make sure no one else was about to see or hear.

Suzanne pulled a large envelope from beneath her cape and handed it to the man.

"Step into the light, damn it," Travis whispered, ordering the man forward. "Step into the damned light so I can see who you are."

The man grabbed the envelope and, fumbling, looked inside it. Suzanne whirled and took a step away from him. He reached out and grabbed her arm.

Travis tensed, ready to go to her defense if it became necessary.

Suzanne turned back around and said something, then jerked away again. The man, failing to release Suzanne's arm immediately, was yanked forward. Realizing he was in the light, he stepped quickly back into the shadows.

But those few seconds had been enough. Travis stared unbelievingly at the two figures across the street and found himself left with yet another question to add to the profusion of those already crowding his mind. Why had Suzanne walked down to St. Paul's church to meet Hanson Jones, night foreman of the Savage Mining Company? And just as important what had she handed him in that envelope?

Suzanne turned away from Jones then and, drawing her cape tightly about her body to protect her from the wind, started to make her way up the hill toward the center of town.

Travis waited, unsure what to do. Should he wait and follow Hanson Jones? Confront Suzanne here on the street and demand that she explain her actions? Follow her back to the Mountain Queen and say nothing yet? Or wait for Lonchet to reappear and follow him?

He watched Suzanne cross the street and Hanson Jones turn to disappear again into the inky darkness. If he tried to follow Jones, and was successful, what then? The man most likely was returning to the mine. He couldn't very well just walk up to him and demand he explain why he had met with "Georgette Lindsay" in the darkness beside St. Paul's Church and show him what was in the envelope she'd handed him.

His gaze moved to Suzanne. What would he accomplish by confronting her? Rather than answer any of his questions, she'd most likely just coolly tell him to drop dead. And she'd be completely within her rights. Suzanne Forteaux could go out at any hour she wanted, and meet with whomever she wanted, to do whatever she wanted, and it truly wasn't any of his business. Except that he couldn't help but feel that it was.

A curtain in one of the dark upstairs windows of the apothecary shop moved slightly. From behind the plain muslin draping Magnolia Rochelle watched Suzanne Forteaux and Hanson Jones. As she saw the envelope pass from Suzanne's hand to Jones's, a smile curved Magnolia's lips.

Chapter Eighteen

Travis remained still and watched Suzanne begin to make her way back up Taylor Street in the direction she had come, her shoulders held hunched and stiff, her steps hurried. The wind had picked up, and both the furls of her heavy cape and the skirt of her gown and crinolines slapped viciously about her legs. But she didn't cross back over to the side of the street on which Travis stood hidden. He breathed a sigh of relief for that and looked past her. Hanson Jones had disappeared into the blackness of the night beyond the church. Travis swore to himself. He'd wanted to follow the mining superintendent and at least try to find out what Suzanne had given to him in the envelope, but he couldn't budge from his hiding spot without her seeing him until she passed. By then, Jones would be long gone. Travis switched his gaze back to Suzanne.

She started to pass the alley Clarence Lonchet had disappeared into earlier. Suddenly a shriek escaped her lips and she was jerked backward. Her arms flew out to flail at nothing. She disappeared into the darkness of the narrow passageway.

Travis, his heart in his throat, bolted away from the door, ready to run across the street, but something stopped him, some little voice, some warning instinct that had kept him alive through more than one scape in the past. It commanded him to remain still and quiet. He stood at the edge of the shadows, hands clenched tightly, nerves on edge, and squinted his eyelids in an effort to pierce the darkness, but found it unnecessary as Suzanne abruptly appeared in the moonlight again. Her voice, still squeaky with fear but also tinged with indignant anger, traveled across to him on the still night air.

"Clarence! What do you think you're doing, for heaven's sake? You scared me half to death."

Clarence Lonchet reached for her again, grumbling something that Travis couldn't make out, but Suzanne jerked away from him and began to straighten her cape about her with a series of angry, jerking brushes of her hand. The hood had fallen completely away from her head now and her dark hair glistened in the moonlight.

"We need to talk, Suzanne," the manager said, his tone harsh and authoritive. "Privately. And I don't want to do it at the Mountain Queen."

She glared at him. "So you jump out at me from a dark alley in the middle of the night and nearly cause my heart to stop beating?"

Clarence thumped his bowler against his thigh. "What was I supposed to do? Stand in the middle of the street and holler at you so the entire town could hear?"

"A civilized person would have just come to me at the saloon and said they needed to talk. Or sent a note to my dressing room, or the hotel. But I suppose that kind of courtesy would have been out of the question."

"You're right. I didn't want anyone else around to

hear us talking, or see a note. And lately there always seems to be someone else around."

"Well, whatever you have to say is just going to have to wait, Clarence. I have to get back to the saloon. This wind has caused havoc with my hair, it's stung my eyes and made them water, so I'll have to redo my face paint, and I stepped in a puddle and got my shoes wet."

"Suzanne, will you—"

"And," she said, overriding his interruption, "I'm freezing and need to get warm. I don't know why I agreed to play this stupid charade with you in the first place."

"Do I have to remind you," Clarence snarled nastily, "about your dear brother?"

Suzanne jerked her cape about herself. "No, you don't have to remind me about Brett," she snipped back just as nastily. She started to turn away, but Lonchet reached out and grabbed her arm.

"I said, we need to talk."

Suzanne pulled away from him again. "I have another performance to give in a little while, Clarence. Or have you forgotten that's supposed to be the reason I'm here? I sing at the Mountain Queen, remember?"

"I haven't forgotten anything, but we need to discuss what's going on, and I want to do it now. Between Braggette and that maid of yours, I can hardly ever get to talk to you without a damned audience."

"You told me to get close to Travis."

"Yes, well, I'm not so sure you haven't gotten a little too close." He took hold of Suzanne's arm and, jerking her around brusquely, walked hastily up the hill toward C Street, his grip on her arm forcing her to accompany him.

"Clarence, where are we going?" Suzanne demanded. He ignored her and kept walking.

Travis had been unable to hear their conversation, and now he followed them, making sure to remain out of sight. He watched them enter Cabor's Restaurant. The local eatery remained open most of the night, serving dinner to the miners who got off their shift at midnight, and breakfast to those just going on for their midnight-to-eight A.M shift. The place was always crowded, night and day.

Travis edged toward the window as inconspicuously as he could and, remaining close to its edge, peered through. He saw Lonchet steer Suzanne toward a table situated well away from the entry door and against one wall. She sat down and Lonchet took a chair across from her.

A group of miners approached the cafe's door. Travis moved to enter on their heels and, keeping his hat low, his head bent down, the collar of his jacket turned up, and his shoulders hunched, took a seat at another table only a few feet from Suzanne's. He sat with his back to her and Lonchet, far enough away not to attract their notice but close enough, he hoped, to overhear their conversation over the hum of the other chatter filling the room.

"Clarence, you promised me that information," Suzanne said in a frantic whisper. "And you have to give it to me now. I need it."

"You're not done yet."

Travis heard something pound atop the table.

"Yes, I am." Suzanne snapped. "You said this was it, Clarence. You promised that Virginia City was the end. That you'd tell me when we were through here."

Clarence's tone dropped to an ugly mutter. "There's been a change of plans. And anyway, we're not through."

"Damn it, Clarence, you gave me your word and I want you to keep it. This is it. The last job."

"We're through when I say we're through, Suzanne, and not before. And you'd do well to remember that. Unless you don't care about our deal anymore. If that's the case . . ."

There was a long moment of silence before Suzanne answered. Her tone had softened and held almost a pleading note. "Clarence, please, I've done everything you wanted. Everything. I've traveled the entire countryside spying, stealing, and passing information for you and the others."

Travis leaned back in his chair to hear better. He only wished he could see her. It was much easier to judge a person's sincerity when he could see their features. Especially their eyes.

Suzanne's voice began to harden as she continued, the contempt, frustration, and anger she obviously felt making their way into each word. "I've arranged for the shipments to be transported, passed your damned instructions, played liaison, and confirmed that Travis Braggette is indeed a member of the Knights."

"That's all fine and good," Clarence said.

Travis itched to rearrange the man's face with his fist.

"And I've kept him off guard and . . . and in need of a whore, just like you ordered. Now tell me what you know."

Travis started at Suzanne's words. In need of a whore? He nearly laughed, then realized it wasn't really that funny. In fact, it wasn't funny at all. His temper began to do a slow, steady burn. So, all of her attentions to him had just been some kind of ploy. She hated him that much.

"Braggette's still suspicious about things," Clarence answered. "And still dangerous to us, Suzanne. He might have joined the Knights years ago and been loyal to them then, but he's not loyal now, and evidently hasn't been for quite a while. But then, that's what I've been saying all along, isn't it? Like father like son."

Travis's attention shot up at the mention of his father. Could Clarence Lonchet know something about the murder of Thomas Braggette? Travis pulled the hat lower onto his forehead and leaned back in his chair. Two years before, Thomas Braggette had been murdered in his office in New Orleans. Henri Sorbonte, a Mississippi planter and a general in the Knights of the Golden Circle, had been accused, arrested and had been awaiting trial when Beauregard had fired on Fort Sumter and started the war. New Orleans had erupted into celebration, and in the chaos Henri Sorbonte escaped.

Of course neither Travis nor any of the other members of his family had really cared that much, especially since his brothers Trace and Traxton had just asked Belle and Lin Sorbonte, Henri's twin daughters, to marry them.

Clarence and Suzanne's conversation ebbed from his mind as it filled with memories of his father. Thomas Braggette had thought of only one thing in his life: himself. And because of that he had managed to nearly destroy not only his wife, but each of his children. As a result Travis, Traxton, and Traynor had left home. Only Trace had remained, mostly because as the eldest he'd felt responsible for protecting their mother and little sister, Teresa, from Thomas.

Travis took a deep breath and exhaled it slowly. Was Clarence Lonchet involved with the Knights? And if so, did he know something about Thomas Braggette's murder? Why he'd been killed? And by whom? Travis started at his next thought. Had the Knights ordered Thomas Braggette killed?

"You've got to keep after him and find out if he knows anything else, Suzanne," Clarence said, his voice pulling Travis from his contemplations. "We can't afford for things to go wrong now. Our mission here is too important. Terry didn't trust Braggette, and, frankly, neither do I."

"So? Is trusting Travis so important?"

Mission. Travis picked up on the word. The Knights had organized themselves in a manner similar to the military, even going so far as to use ranks and codes, and they always used the word mission to describe their individual tasks and assignments.

"And frankly, I'm beginning to wonder about you," Clarence said, ignoring her question. "Your father said you could be trusted, Suzanne. Was he wrong?"

Her father? Landon Forteaux had gotten his daughter involved with the Knights? With this weasly little toad who called himself her manager? With singing in saloons across the country? Travis waited for her answer, the fingers of his right hand clutched tightly about the fork he held over a piece of untouched apple pie. He wanted her to say yes so that he'd know she wasn't truly a part of whatever it was Clarence Lonchet was involved in. At the same time, he prayed she'd say no. Otherwise, if Lonchet was a Knight and on a mission,

and became convinced he couldn't trust Suzanne, her
life would most certainly be in grave danger. From his
association with the Knights in the past, he knew that
for a fact. It was only due to sheer luck, and his known
skill with a gun, that they hadn't tried to come after him
when he denounced his membership. And that was still
a possibility. Travis nearly held his breath until she answered.

"No, my father wasn't wrong."

"Good. I'm glad to hear it."

Travis wasn't glad to hear any of this, yet for the moment, at least, she was safe. At the same time that he felt
a sense of relief, anger and frustration caused him to
bend the fork he held in his hand in half. Was she lying,
or telling the truth? Whatever Clarence Lonchet was up
to, Travis had a feeling it wasn't good, and Suzanne was
evidently involved all the way up to her pretty neck.

"But I've noticed something, Suzanne," Lonchet continued. "Or perhaps I should say Morgan's noticed
something and brought it to my attention."

So, Travis thought, as Lonchet confirmed his suspicions, Ben Morgan was also in on Lonchet's mission,
whatever it was.

"Oh?" Suzanne said. "Really, Clarence? I find that
most interesting. I didn't think Ben Morgan had the ca-
pability of noticing anything more than a glass of whiskey, unless it was a pretty leg."

Travis smiled.

Clarence waved a dismissing hand at Suzanne. "It
doesn't really matter who noticed, Suzanne, but it's
come to my attention, my dear, that you've only been
playing up to Braggette when I am around. When I'm
not within your sight, well, it's been said that you're,

shall we say, very cold to our Mr. Braggette. In fact, Morgan says you not only don't flirt with Braggette, but you seem to take great pleasure in being coolly aloof toward him. *Antagonizing* is, I think, the word Morgan used."

"Antagonizing?" She laughed. "I think Mr. Morgan is confusing my attitude toward him with what I show Travis Braggette. I believe our Mr. Morgan is merely jealous, Clarence, because he tried to seduce me the other night in my dressing room and I slapped his face for it and then ordered him to leave."

"I don't really care what Morgan did, Suzanne, or what his motives are for telling me you're not fulfilling your end of our bargain. If you don't want to allow him into your bed, that's not my concern," Lonchet said. "What *is*, however, is that if he is telling the truth and you are trying to warn Braggette away by your actions, or protect him from us, well . . ." his tone turned to one of sneering threat, "we both know what will happen. Don't we, Suzanne?"

"No, Clarence," Suzanne snapped angrily. "*We* don't. What will happen? What are you supposedly wonderful, patriotic Southern Knights prepared to do to protect yourselves and get what you want?"

Lonchet laughed. "Well, my dear, let's just say that if Mr. Braggette met with some misfortune, say, a *deadly* misfortune, and you just happened to be with him and met the same fate . . ." he laughed again "Well, I doubt the world, in particular at least half of the good citizens of Virginia City, would mourn the loss of either one of you too deeply."

Travis turned slightly, making sure to keep his hat pulled low and shading his face. Out of the corner of his eye he saw Lonchet lean across the table toward Suzanne.

"And it could happen, my dear. Never doubt that. It could happen very easily."

"I think you forget, Clarence, that both the Braggettes and the Forteauxs are still important members of society in New Orleans. I doubt *they* would take kindly to our demise."

Clarence laughed. "Oh, I'm sure they wouldn't, Suzanne. But you're so far away from home, and you in particular, my dear, are involved in, shall we say, a bit of espionage. Oh, I'm certain everyone back in New Orleans would grieve and rail about your death, but under the circumstances I'm sure it would be looked at as merely a casualty of the war. Quite understandable, even by your father, my dear, if something untoward should happen to you."

"And Travis?" Suzanne persisted.

"A mine accident, a riding accident. There are any number of things that can happen to a person in one of these godforsaken little mining towns, you know. Especially one situated on the side of a mountain."

"Any number of things that would not lead back to a connection with you," Suzanne said. "Or to the Knights. Isn't that what you mean, Clarence?"

"Precisely, my dear. Precisely."

"Did you have anything to do with that miner getting robbed and murdered, Clarence?" Suzanne suddenly asked in a hard voice. "Is that what this is all about? Why we came here to Virginia City?"

Travis stiffened, waiting anxiously for the man's answer.

Clarence laughed. "Of course not, Suzanne. We don't

operate in such a crude manner. That was most likely just a plain robbery that ended unfortunately . . . for the driver. Although it is a shame. The South could have used the ore that freighter was carrying."

"I don't believe you, Clarence. You did have something to do with it."

A derisive chuckle rolled from his lips. "I really don't care if you believe me or not, Suzanne. All I care about is that you do what you're told, what you agreed to do, and remember what could happen if you don't."

"I hate you, Clarence Lonchet," Suzanne said, her tone laced with venom. "I really do hate you."

"Too bad, *ma chère,* since in our own way we are both on the same side. We might have been quite good together, don't you think?"

"Never!" Suzanne spat. "And I hope that wasn't another scheme you've been contemplating in that nasty little mind of yours, Clarence." Pushing abruptly away from the table, she rose. "Because that is one thing that will never happen. No matter what! I'd rather lie down with a rattlesnake." She turned and, holding her cape and skirts up from the floor, raging fury blinding her to everyone and everything else in the room, stalked past Travis and out of the restaurant.

Travis clenched his hands into fists beneath the table. If he could have gotten near Lonchet at that moment, the man would be dead, the breath squeezed from his throat in a second. Except that wouldn't get Travis answers to the multitude of questions buzzing around in his head. And damn it all to hell, he didn't know *how* to get those answers. All he seemed to do was accumulate more questions, and Suzanne obviously wasn't going to give him the answers. It was evident now that she was working under some sort of threat from Lonchet and had been for some time.

And Lonchet wasn't going to just confess because Travis confronted him and demanded to know what he was up to. He searched his mind for a different approach to the problem and remembered Ben Morgan. The man was built like a grizzly who'd just eaten his way through the summer. Travis immediately discarded the idea of confronting the journalist. It would take a lot more physical brawn than Travis possessed to beat a few answers out of that man. He jabbed the tines of his fork into the generous slice of apple pie on the plate before him and rammed a piece of the flaky-crusted pastry into his mouth. No, fisticuffs and guns wouldn't solve this.

Think, Travis, think, he ordered himself. He chanced a peek back at Lonchet. The man was casually sipping on a cup of coffee and enjoying a slice of berry pie. Travis stared for as long as he dared without inviting the risk of drawing Lonchet's attention. Could Clarence Lonchet have been the one sitting on the hill during that first attack on Duncan Clyde? He thought about how Clyde had described the lone rider situated halfway up the hill, away from the other assailants, as if he was their leader. Wearing a dark cape. Poised kind of haughtily. Arrogantly. And physically small. Almost like a small woman.

On the surface it sounded like a woman, but that was ridiculous. He jabbed the pie with his fork again. On the other hand, the description could very possibly fit Clarence Lonchet. The man was certainly small enough so that, beneath a cape and on horseback, and a goodly distance away, he could be described as Clyde had said.

Travis felt like slamming a fist on the table. Duncan's depiction could have fit anyone, man or woman. Hell, it could even have been Suzanne.

Chapter Nineteen

Suzanne finished the final chorus of her last song of the evening and breathed a sigh of relief as she bowed before the cheering miners. It seemed an eternity ago since she'd started the performance, and each tinkle of the piano, each word she spoke, each line she sung, had seemed to go on forever. Her body was exhausted, her emotions were in a frazzle, and her mind was weary. She had done everything they'd requested of her, and yet they still refused to give her any information about Brett. Over the past few months, as they'd traveled from town to town, being ordered to do this and that, she'd nearly worried herself to death. But they kept promising, and issuing veiled threats of what would happen to her brother, and to her, if she didn't cooperate with them, if she didn't continue to do their bidding. And now there was Travis. He was in danger because of her.

Her heart nearly skipped a beat.

She should never have agreed to come here, to see him again. She should have told them she couldn't, that the memories were too painful, that she was still vulnerable to him. Suzanne inhaled deeply in an effort to slow her racing heart. But she hadn't *thought* she was still vulnerable to him. She'd believed she could hate him, that she did hate him. But she'd been wrong . . . dead wrong.

Her gaze roamed over the crowd as she forced the smile on her face to remain there, pressed her fingers to her lips and blew the cheering men a kiss. All she truly wanted was to go back to the hotel, submerge herself in a hot bath and crawl into bed and try to forget the horrors of the day.

But that obviously wasn't going to be. At least not for a while. Her eyes moved again to the table in the far right corner of the bar. Clarence and Ben Morgan met her gaze, both men looking arrogant and haughty. She knew what they expected her to do, and she'd do it. She had to, for Brett. She only hoped that Clarence was telling the truth and could lead her to her brother, and not to his grave.

Tears filled her eyes and she fought them back, replacing them with a swell of anger at the thought that something might have happened to Brett because of his affiliation with the Knights, and that they had been deceiving her and her parents so they could use them for their own purposes. If that turned out to be the case, she would . . . she would . . . She didn't know what she would do, but Clarence Lonchet would pay for this deceit and treachery, that was for certain. He would pay for whatever had happened to Brett, for what he had forced her to do, and for the anguish he had caused her parents.

She stepped from the stage and made her way toward Travis, just as Clarence and Ben expected, demanded, that she do.

But Travis had anticipated her approach. She saw that in the flash of his dark eyes as she paused before him. Suzanne steeled herself against the feelings he aroused within her, against thinking about her actions. When Clarence had explained to her what had to be done in exchange for him breaking his vow of silence with the Knights and revealing to her the whereabouts of her brother, she had agreed, convinced that she could do it, that she could play up to Travis, kiss him, entice him, tease him and let him hold her, and she wouldn't feel a thing. Logic and reasoning had been on her side then. Hadn't she silently damned Travis Braggette for seven years? Hadn't she wished upon him every bad thing she could think of? But that had been then, and even though she knew better now, there was no turning back, no changing what had to be done. She cocked a bare shoulder toward him flirtatiously and forced a smile to her lips.

"Aren't you going to offer to walk a lady back to her hotel, Travis?" She inched closer. "And maybe buy her a cup of coffee along the way?" she asked sassily, putting enough suggestive sultriness into her voice to lure even the hardest of bandits into a jail cell.

But Travis didn't move. Instead, he settled a flinty gaze upon her and continued to laze against the bar. He lifted the glass of bourbon to his lips, never taking his eyes away from her, sipped at it slowly, and then set it deliberately back on the bartop.

She saw no warmth in his features, and her heart nearly plummeted to the bottoms of her feet. It was exactly what she wanted from him, yet it wasn't. She didn't want him to care, then maybe he'd be safe, and yet she *did* want him to care about her, with all of his heart.

"I didn't think you wanted my company anymore, Suzanne," he drawled. "Or did I misunderstand something the other night?" He straightened and looked down at her.

"Oh, that," Suzanne said, and laughed. "I just had a little headache, that's all. Really, Travis," she fluttered her dark lashes, "I wasn't fit company for anyone." She sidled closer to him and slipped her arms around his waist. "Especially you, Travis."

"Especially me, huh?" His insides felt suddenly as if they were consumed by a raging inferno, a voracious and out-of-control fire that threatened to overwhelm and consume him. His body was rigid with need, and at her nearness and the suggestive tone of her voice, an ache of desire hit him so hard, he almost doubled over. One hand clenched tightly at his side, the other remained wrapped around the small shot glass that held his bourbon. He forced himself to remain still, to appear calm, cool, and poised, even though every inch of him was taut with tension and the need to assuage the gnawing hunger inside of him. He wanted to pull her up against his length and wrap her in his embrace. He wanted to bury himself within her arms, taste the honeyed sweetness of her lips, let the unforgettable scent of her surround him, and feel her body, naked, hot, and wet with need, pressed to his.

Many women had shared his bed and his passion, but none stirred the desperate hunger in him that Suzanne had. At first, upon her arrival in Virginia City, he had believed bedding her once would assuage the gnawing ache her presence had caused to rave within him, but he'd been wrong. He wanted her again, now, even more than he'd wanted her the first time.

His eyes narrowed slightly. But Suzanne didn't want him. Not really. She had only been following orders. The cold thought, breaking through his consciousness like the heartless stab of a cold steel rapier instantly cooled his ardor and turned his thoughts.

She was using him, just as Lonchet was using her. It was obvious he was not going to find out what was going on from Lonchet or Morgan. And he knew Suzanne wouldn't willingly tell him. But she might let something slip in a moment of passion. Yes, Travis thought, and smiled down at her insolently, a moment of passion. Two could definitely play this game.

"Yes," Suzanne cooed. She looked up at him, long dark lashes framing rich blue eyes, and he was reminded of how badly he still wanted her, and why he would not take her again. "Especially you, Travis."

He brazenly slipped an arm around her waist and jerked her toward him, crushing her violently against his length, her hips pressed tightly to his, her breasts pushing into his chest. If she wanted to play this game, then he would oblige, at least partially, and for all the world to see. "Then why are we wasting time here?" he growled softly, suggestively. He moved ever so slightly, just enough so that she could feel the hardness of his arousal through the silk folds of her skirt and make no mistake what he was inferring. "And why bother with coffee?" He bent toward her and pressed his lips to her neck. "I want you now, Suzanne," he rasped. "I need you."

Suzanne felt a shiver of desire snake up her spine. She closed her eyes and willed herself to remain calm.

She squeezed her eyelids tighter together and tried to ignore the burning sensation his lips created upon her flesh, the aching hunger that sprang to life within her whenever he touched her. He could arouse her desires, that was true, but passion was all he wanted. Hadn't he said he couldn't promise her tomorrow? She had to keep telling herself that. To share her bed for a night, to use her body for his own pleasures, that was all Travis had wanted from her. All he still wanted. And even though she couldn't deny that her silly heart had once again fallen for him, she couldn't let herself forget that he didn't truly want her.

Out of the corner of her eye she saw Clarence Lonchet nod toward her in approval, a smug, satisfied smile plastered across his face as he rose from the table he'd shared with Morgan and left the saloon. Suzanne immediately pushed away from Travis. She didn't care that Ben Morgan was still present, or that he was watching. He could tell Clarence whatever he wanted, she would deny it. She just couldn't remain in Travis's arms. Not and remain sane and sensible.

She looked up at Travis and felt like crying. God, she wanted him. There was no sense lying to herself about it. She wanted to lie next to him and feel his body wrap around hers again, feel his hands rove her flesh with that magical touch that carried her to another world. She wanted to feel him fill her again with his need, but she wanted him to love her, too. She wanted that above all else.

The thought surprised even her, though she knew, if she had truly examined her own heart, it shouldn't have. Hadn't she, while all the while denouncing him, secretly hoped that he would return to her? Hadn't she truly loved him all that time? Convinced herself all she wanted was revenge? She pushed the thoughts away. This wasn't the time to examine her emotions. She had to continue with her own plans, but at the same time she had to try to protect Travis. If he thought she wanted nothing to do with him, still blamed him for what had happened seven years ago, maybe he would stay away from her, and thus away from Clarence. Maybe that way he would remain out of danger. And oh, God, she didn't want him in danger.

Purposely turning her features cold, Suzanne glared up at Travis. "But I don't need you, Travis," she said softly, though her tone was hard, almost hateful. "I don't want you, and I don't need you."

Travis grabbed her arm and pulled her back against him. "You want me just as much as I want you, Suzanne, so don't lie about it." He voiced the angry words only loud enough for her to hear. "Why this damned hot and cold game? What's Lonchet holding over you, Suzanne? What?"

She threw a quick glance at Morgan. He was watching intently. She looked back at Travis. She was taking a risk, she knew, but she had to warn him. *He* might not love *her,* but she could no longer deny, even to herself, that she loved him. She touched a hand to his cheek, tenderly, so that Morgan would think she was doing what she was supposed to be doing, seducing Travis. "Stay out of this, Travis," she whispered hastily. "Please. For your own sake. Stay away from me, away from Clarence, and away from the KGC. You'll live longer."

"What's that supposed to mean? What are they making you do, Suzanne?"

"Hey, Braggette, I'd like to talk with you."

Travis turned to glare over his shoulder at the owner of the husky voice that had interrupted his conversation with Suzanne. His gaze came to rest on Ben Morgan. Rage burned within him. The huge man towered over both Travis and Suzanne. He glared down at Travis from beneath bushy dark-blond brows.

"I'm busy," Travis said curtly.

Morgan threw a glance at Suzanne. "The whore can find another customer and come back for you later."

A faint gasp of surprise at the crude words slipped from Suzanne's lips, but she had enough presence of mind to cling to Travis in an effort to keep him from lunging at Morgan.

Travis turned, fury churning in his chest. "Morgan, I don't know who in the hell you think you . . ."

Ben Morgan held up his thick hands. "I don't want no trouble, Braggette, but I have to talk with you. And I think you'll be pretty interested in what I've got to say."

"It's all right, Travis," Suzanne said, her voice barely audible. She looked at Travis and, fighting to hold back her tears, smiled. "I'll see you tomorrow." She hurried away before he had a chance to answer.

Travis whirled on Morgan. "I don't know what the hell you've got to say, Morgan, and frankly I'm not sure I care, but I do care what you call Suz— Miss Lindsay."

"Fine. I'll apologize later." He stepped up to the bar and called for Jed to bring him a whiskey. When he had it in hand, he turned back to look at Travis. "You're a Knight."

Travis looked up at the burly man. "Is that a question or an accusation?"

"Neither," Morgan said. "It's a statement of fact."

"And just how would you know that?"

"It's not important how I know. What *is* important is that I've got a deal for you, and as leader of the Knights here in Virginia City, you—"

"I'm not the leader of the Knights here," Travis said, cutting him off.

"That's not what I hear."

"Then you hear wrong."

"Doesn't matter," Morgan said. "You've got a lot of influence in this town, and that does matter."

"I'm not interested in a deal, Morgan, especially if it concerns the Knights."

Ben Morgan frowned. "Your father was a Knight, Braggette, and from what I hear—"

"My father was a no-good son of a bitch, and he's dead. As for the Knights, any organization that accepted my father is not one I want to belong to."

"You've got a lot of gold and silver in these mountains, Braggette," Morgan continued, as if he hadn't heard Travis's words. "The Knights figure, since you've also got a lot of Southern boys up here, that some of that wealth should be used to help the cause."

"Some of it *is* being used to help the cause," Travis retorted.

"Yeah, but maybe not enough. We figure we could get our boys a little better organized up here, you know? Especially behind you. And then maybe we'd get a bigger share of the ore that goes out of this town."

"How?"

Morgan shrugged. "That's what I wanted to talk to you about."

"I'm not interested," Travis said.

Ben Morgan gulped down his whiskey and then

stepped away from the bar. "Think about it, Braggette. I wouldn't be surprised if you changed your mind."

"Don't count on it."

Morgan laughed. "Hell, Braggette, I don't count on nothing."

Suzanne stood behind the curtained doorway that led from the saloon to the dressing rooms. She held one side of the curtain slightly away from the other, giving herself a view of the saloon, and Travis and Ben Morgan. The men conversed for ten minutes, Morgan looking jovial yet cunning, Travis looking merely angry.

She was about to do something she knew she might regret, something that could endanger her own plans, could endanger her brother Brett if he was still alive. It could even endanger her own life. But she couldn't live with herself if she didn't do it. If something happened to Travis now because of her lack of courage, because she didn't warn him, because she'd been stupid enough to come here in the first place, she could never forgive herself.

The moment Ben Morgan stepped past the swinging doors of the Mountain Queen and disappeared from sight, Suzanne hurried from behind the curtain and approached Travis.

She touched his arm with her hand, drawing his attention. "Be careful of him, Travis," she said, keeping her voice low. "Whatever he wants you to do, be wary. He's not what he pretends to be."

"Not a journalist from San Francisco?" Travis urged. He knew exactly what Ben Morgan was. The man *was* a journalist, and a good one, but he was also a high-ranking member of the Knights in San Francisco. And in New Orleans. That's where Travis had seen him before, but he hadn't remembered until his contact in San Francisco had wired him back that Ben Morgan was actually Benjamin Mordaine. His family's bloodlines were long, but their monies were gone. Benjamin Mordaine had fled New Orleans twelve years before after killing a man in a duel and then being accused of having fixed the other man's gun so that it wouldn't fire. Travis knew all of this now, but he wanted to know just how much Suzanne knew. How much she'd tell him.

"Yes, he's a journalist, and he does work for the *Bulletin*, but that's not all he does. And I'm sure that's not what he was discussing with you just now."

Travis's eyes narrowed. "What do you know, Suzanne?"

Suzanne shook her head. "I've already said more than I should have, Travis. I can't say any more. Please don't ask me to." She looked up at him, sadness glistening from her eyes and etched within every line of her face. Things could have been so different for them if only. . . . She sighed softly. But their time had passed long ago, and now they were both on a different course of life, a different path. She pulled her cloak tighter about her shoulders. "Just be careful of him, Travis. Please."

Chapter Twenty

Several days passed with nothing unusual happening in or around Virginia City. No further attempts were made to rob the ore wagons, Ben Morgan made a few subtle overtures toward Travis again and was instantly rebuffed each time, and Suzanne continued to play her game of flirting with Travis whenever Clarence Lonchet was around and remaining cool and aloof when the manager was absent. The others he could take or leave at will, but Suzanne was another matter. Thoughts of her would not leave his mind, day or night, no matter what he tried to do. But worse was the fact that every time she came near him, his body instantly betrayed all of his good intentions and vows to ignore her. His hunger to have her in his bed was almost all-consuming, her flirtatious teasing almost more than he could stand. He was getting damned tired of dousing himself with cold water to cool off.

No woman had ever affected him so, but Travis was certain he knew the cure for his ailment. One more time in her bed, one more night of running his hands over that lithe body, of tasting the pleasures of her lips, experiencing his body melding with hers, filling hers, would satisfy his hunger for her.

Even now, standing at the bar, watching her move around the stage, winking at the audience, laughing between choruses and flirting with the men, he felt himself grow hard with want, felt his blood burn within his veins.

Travis had tried to talk with her several times in the last few days, to get her to open up to him, but so far his efforts had proven useless. Suzanne always managed to either avoid him completely, or quickly terminate the conversation. He'd also sent several more wires to friends around the country inquiring about Clarence Lonchet, but had received no answers yet.

There were only a few more nights left on the contract for her performance at the Mountain Queen. This evening Travis stood at the bar and watched her move across the stage. He hadn't been able to get Suzanne off of his mind for more than a few minutes at a time, but there was something else that kept nagging at him, too: the conversation he'd overheard between her and Lonchet. Either something was going on right under his and everyone else's noses, or something would happen soon, if it was going to happen at all. Ever since Duncan Clyde's murder, the freight drivers had been carrying guns and riding two to a wagon. And many were still leery about being on the road after sunset or before dawn. Especially when going through Devil's Gate.

But Clarence Lonchet and Ben Morgan had something planned, Suzanne had as much as told him that with her warning. He just didn't know what it was, and with the lack of love between him and the sheriff, there wasn't much point in trying to tell Morrow anything.

"Something, isn't she?" Clarence Lonchet said, suddenly appearing beside Travis.

He looked down at the smaller man. "Yes, she is. The boys are going to miss her when she leaves."

Clarence puffed out his chest, pushed back the lapels of his coat and slipped his thumbs into the sleeve holes of his vest. He smiled widely, smugly. "They always do." One brow rose high over his spectacles. "I understand you and my little songbird have gotten very close, Mr. Braggette. You're not planning on trying to steal her away from me now, are you?" Clarence chuckled softly and poked Travis's ribs with his elbow.

Travis smothered the start of surprise he felt at the man's words, along with the spurt of anger that erupted within him at the nudge. "Suzanne and I have known each other for a long time, Mr. Lonchet, as I'm certain she's told you," he said, purposely keeping his response noncommittal. "And we're friends."

"Yes, so I understand." Clarence looked back at Suzanne. "But I fear she's getting tired of traveling from town to town. I think her taste for excitement has dwindled. Of course, if she chose to settle down with someone like you, well, you're a very successful man, Mr. Braggette, and I can't say that I'd blame her none."

The subtle hint was not lost on Travis. Lonchet was busy playing matchmaker again, something he'd been doing with increasing regularity lately, if not with outright words, then with suggestive looks and nods toward either Travis or Suzanne. Travis looked back up at Suzanne. She had just finished her last song and, with the help of one of the boys, was descending the stage.

"Well, I really must be going," Clarence said. "I promised to stop in at Millie's before I retired for the night." He tipped his bowler to Travis and smiled at Suzanne as she approached. "I was just telling Mr. Braggette that I must be going," he said to Suzanne. "You can get back to the hotel on your own?"

"Don't I always?" Suzanne said, invoking a lightness to the caustic words with a smile.

"Um . . . yes . . . well." Clarence nodded to them both again and said over his shoulder as he hurriedly left the saloon, "I meant with Mr. Braggette's escort, naturally.

"Naturally." Suzanne glanced over at Ben Morgan. His interest seemed riveted to the game of cards in which he was involved. She turned back to see that Clarence had left. She met Travis's gaze. "Excuse me, I think I'll just get my cape and call it a night. I'm tired."

"I'll walk you to the hotel," he offered, though he hadn't the faintest idea why he bothered. He'd been offering to escort her back every night for several nights now and she always said the same thing: no. So instead of accompanying her, he'd followed her, watched her enter the hotel, and then returned to the saloon with nothing to show for his efforts other than wet boots and a cold nose. A few times he'd tried following Lonchet. That had proven just as rewarding. Travis had come to the conclusion that the man had struck up an acquaintance with the owner of just about every crib on D Street, and he evidently called each one of them Millie. Just the other day Julia had informed him that the whores had given Lonchet a nickname: the tiny terror.

"No thank you," Suzanne said coolly. "I can walk with Addie."

"She left earlier with Hank. Going down to Cabor's for coffee, I think."

Suzanne shrugged, lifted her chin and turned away. "Then I'll go by myself. After all, the hotel is only down the street."

Travis watched her flounce her way back across the saloon and disappear behind the curtained doorway that led to her dressing room. He'd felt like grabbing her and pulling her into his arms, crushing her against him and kissing all that coolness from her lips, and heart. But he didn't. There were more important things he needed to keep his mind on than satisfying the hungers of his body. Though at the moment he was hard put to think of just what they were.

Several minutes passed, but Suzanne didn't reappear. Travis found himself getting edgy. How long did it take to retrieve a reticule and a cloak? He gulped down his drink, threw his half-smoked cheroot into a nearby spitoon and crossed the room to the curtained doorway, half expecting her to appear before he entered.

She didn't.

He glanced back in the saloon to make sure she hadn't come out of the dressing room while he wasn't looking and was talking with one of the patrons. But there were only three woman in the saloon: the two barmaids he employed and Julia Bulette, who had just entered. Travis threw back the curtain and walked down the hallway toward Suzanne's dressing room, listening for voices and hearing none. Lonchet was gone. So was her maid, Addie. Ben Morgan was out in the saloon playing cards. Lowry, Fairmount, and Nathram, Suzanne's most steady and ardent admirers, were also out in the saloon. What was she doing back here? He approached her door cautiously, still leery that someone else might be with her.

Suddenly, from farther down the hall he heard the shutting of a door and knew instantly why she hadn't reappeared in the saloon and wasn't in her dressing room.

"Son of a bitch," he cursed softly. For some reason, and he fully intended to find out what that reason was, Suzanne had gone out the back door.

Hurrying to the end of the hall and up the short flight of steps that led to the rear door, Travis opened it and slipped into the darkness of the night.

Travis stood still for several seconds, letting himself become accustomed to the darkness and silence of the evening. His eyes finally accepted the lack of illumination and the surrounding shapes began to come into focus. He looked around for Suzanne but didn't see her.

"Damn it all." Travis suddenly realized that he'd probably done more cursing and swearing since Suzanne Forteaux had walked back into his life than he'd done for all the years he'd been alive. He looked to the right. She would have had to pass the rear of four buildings and circumvent one five-foot wooden fence and two structures half built into the mountain in order to reach the street by going in that direction. He discounted that route and turned his gaze to the left. Only Ebenizer Cornnell's leather and rigging shop and the Black and Howell building stood between the back stoop of the Mountain Queen and Taylor Street.

Travis stepped from the stoop onto the uneven ground that sloped upward to the buildings on the hilly streets above, and finally to the crest of Sun Mountain. He made his way to the side street quickly enough, but if Suzanne had come this way she was already out of sight.

Another string of curses danced their way through his

head. What in the hell was he out here for anyway? Trying to protect a woman who didn't want his protection and a town in which at least half the population blamed him for the War Between the States? Travis didn't even try to answer the question. Instead, he hurried down to C Street. Directly across the narrow thoroughfare, a dark shadow passed before the lighted Taylor Street side window of Pollan's General Mercantile. A momentary glimpse of yellow satin protruding from below the hem of the figure's cape confirmed for Travis that it was Suzanne. Waiting until she had traversed several yards father down the block, he crossed the street and hurried after her, making certain to remain in the shadows. He expected her to continue on down Taylor, as she had that other time she'd come this way and met Hanson Jones. Travis decided that if she was meeting Jones again, it would be the mine superintendent he'd follow this time, and he would damned well find out what was going on.

But rather than continue on down Taylor, Suzanne abruptly turned north on E Street. One block farther, a man stood on the corner. Travis recognized him immediately. It would have been hard not to. John Sabot was the only man in town, other than Clarence Lonchet, who was shorter than most of the women. But Sabot had another distinctive feature that made it hard to overlook or mistake him: his legs were so bowed that when he stood with his feet together, it created an almost perfect circle from his ankles to his crotch. Sometimes the children in town threw bones through Sabot's legs just so they could watch their dogs chase after them. But more important at the moment was the fact that he was the night superintendent of the Chollar Mining Company.

Travis ducked into a darkened doorway and watched.

Suzanne paused before Sabot and, as she'd done several nights before with Hanson Jones, pulled an envelope from beneath her cape and handed it to him. Unlike Jones, Sabot didn't make a grab for Suzanne or try to say anything to her. He just took the envelope and nodded. She turned away immediately and walked hastily up Washington toward D Street.

Travis assumed she was on her way back to the Union Belle Hotel. He should follow her, make certain she got back safely, but if he left his hiding place now, Sabot would see him and know he'd been watching them. So he remained still and watched Sabot open the envelope and look at whatever was inside. He stood like that for several seconds, as if studying the envelope's contents, then reclosed it, slipped it into an inside breast pocket of his overcoat, turned and started to walk down F Street toward the mines.

Travis stepped from the doorway and began to follow Sabot, though making certain to stay far enough behind him so that the man didn't sense his presence.

But instead of continuing on to the Chollar Mine as Travis had expected, Sabot continued on past it. After following Sabot for what he guessed to be more than another mile, Travis began to wonder how much farther they were going to go.

Just as Travis was trying to decide if he wanted to keep tailing Sabot, the man suddenly ducked behind a small outcropping of earth. Travis inched his way forward slowly, not sure what to expect and taking great care to make no noise. He felt for his gun, and cocked the hammer. Better to be ready to draw and fire than dead on the ground. He moved cautiously around the small mound of dirt and boulders Sabot had disappeared behind and then stopped.

If Travis hadn't been suspicious all along that something was happening right under everyone's noses, he would have been even more shocked at the sight before him. A hundred yards away, settled within a small canyon, was a group of about half a dozen men. Each was hastily transferring chunks of mined ore from two freight wagons that bore the name Chollar Mining Company burned on its wooden side panel into leather pouches slung over the back of a pack mule. There were other pack mules standing nearby. The men were working hastily, wasting no time or movement. On a small knoll just beyond them, another man sat watching everything, a rifle settled comfortably across his lap. Sabot climbed up to talk with him. Travis watched for several more minutes, trying to get a glimpse of someone's face, but it was impossible. The only light in the area was that shining down from the moon, which was only enough to let the men see enough to complete their tasks. And each and every one of them wore a hat, further shading their face.

Travis inched himself back around the protrusion of earth and out of sight. There had been at least eighteen pack mules. The men worked for the next hour and a half. Finally, when the wagons were empty, four men mounted horses, took control of the pack mules who were tied one to the other in two long lines, and headed out. But they didn't take the main road to Gold Hill. Instead, they circled around and headed north.

Fuller's Ferry, Travis thought. They weren't heading

for Carson City, but north toward Fuller's Ferry, obviously in an attempt to skirt Devil's Gate where the sheriff had positioned a deputy to watch over the ore wagons.

The other men jumped onto the now-empty wagons and headed back toward the mines.

Travis walked slowly back to town. So what in the hell was Suzanne doing? He forced everything else from his mind. Clarence Lonchet was a Knight. Travis was fairly certain of that. Morgan, too. What about Suzanne? There were female members in the KGC. He thought about that long and hard, and finally decided against it. From the conversations he'd managed to overhear, it seemed certain that whatever Suzanne was doing, she wasn't doing it willingly. Clarence, or both men, had something Suzanne or her father wanted, that was obvious. And because of that, Clarence was forcing her to do his bidding, which in the words he'd overheard her say that night in the cafe, included spying, passing information, and seducing Travis.

He pushed the last thought from his mind as a seething fury took spark at it, then reconsidered. Why would they want her to seduce him? To get close, he answered himself. But why? Clarence had said Judge Terry didn't trust Travis, so whatever they were up to, the judge knew about it. But the judge was gone. Travis forced his mind back to Suzanne. Had she been passing money to Jones and Sabot? Were they being paid by the Knights to rob those shipments of ore?

Travis smiled to himself and stepped up onto the boardwalk before the Mountain Queen. That had to be it. Lonchet and Morgan were behind the robbery and murder of Duncan Clyde, but now robbing the freighters had gotten too dangerous. So now they were paying Jones and Sabot to arrange for the ore to be stolen and transported out of Virginia City on those pack mules. And, Travis suspected, they most likely took a pretty good cut of the proceeds for their own pockets before any of that money saw its way south to the Confederacy. If any did.

Addie paused before Walton's Cigar Shop and quickly flattened herself against its shuttered window, fearful that Travis would turn as he paused before the Mountain Queen and see her. It had been merely a stroke of luck that Tom Cabor had asked Hank to help him unload a shipment of supplies that had just arrived at the rear of the store at the same moment she'd seen Travis hurry across the street only seconds after having seen Suzanne do the same. The opportunity had proven a golden one. Addie had insisted that she could walk back to the hotel herself, and promised Hank that she would dine with him the next evening.

She'd watched Travis watch Suzanne deliver something to some short, squat man, and had then followed Travis when he'd taken off after the man rather than Suzanne. And finally she knew what was going on. She'd almost broken her neck out there when the heel of one of her shoes twisted beneath her step and she'd managed to rip the hem of her gown while trying to climb up a rocky slope while following Travis, but that didn't matter now. She had the information she needed. The KGC was robbing gold from the mines, but no one knew it. At least, no one except those men who had transferred the ore from the wagons to the mules. And now Travis Braggette. And her. But what was she going to do about it? That was the question. And how was she going to prove that Clarence Lonchet was behind the robberies?

Magnolia Rochelle stood to one side of the swinging doors of the Silver Lady. She had seen Travis walking down the street, had watched him step up onto the boardwalk and had been just about to call out to him when she'd spotted Addie behind him and recognized her as Suzanne's maid.

Handling Travis was one thing. She didn't want anything to happen to him, and even if he did find out what was going on, she felt certain he wouldn't say anything. After all, he was loyal to the Southern cause, she knew that. And he always enjoyed the times he spent in her bed. But the maid, that was different. The first thing she had to do, was send a telegram in the morning, because if her suspicions were correct, Addie Hays wasn't Addie Hays at all, and she certainly was not a maid.

Chapter Twenty-one

Travis wanted nothing more than to barge into Suzanne's hotel room and demand that she tell him what the hell was going on. Explain her involvement with Clarence Lonchet, Ben Morgan, and the Knights of the Golden Circle. But he knew he couldn't do that. Even if he did, he felt certain she would not tell him a thing.

And why should she? She'd probably hated his guts for seven years. Had probably been almost happy to come to Virginia City and tease him.

Nevertheless, even if she still hated him, she had managed to stir something within Travis that he'd thought long dead. Passion he'd always had, the need of a woman in his bed, but feelings for the woman, caring whether she wanted him and wanting to protect her, that was something he hadn't felt for a long time, and thought he would never feel again.

Now that he did, he wasn't sure he liked it. Seven years ago he'd made up his mind that he didn't need a wife. Didn't want one. His father had caused the only woman he'd loved to turn against him, had practically forced him to leave town when he started the rumor that Travis had impregnated Suzanne Forteaux. And now Suzanne was back in his life. Stirring up feelings he'd thought she couldn't stir. Had thought no one could stir ever again.

But was she helping the Knights to somehow get even with Travis? Were they planning on eventually making it appear that he had been the mastermind behind the ore thefts? Or was she merely an unwilling pawn? Might she end up also being framed?

Travis walked into the Mountain Queen and directly to the bar. Jed approached immediately.

"What's up, Boss? You look kinda angry."

"I am. Where's Hank?"

Jed nodded across the room.

Travis turned to see Hank sitting at a table with several miners. They were playing Seven-Up, and, judging from the pile of greenbacks before him on the table, Hank was winning. He walked to the table. "Hank, I need to talk with you."

The saloon manager instantly threw his cards in the center of the table. "Deal me out, boys," he said. He pushed away from the table, scraped the greenbacks into his hat, then plopped it onto his head and followed Travis back to the bar. "So, what's up, Boss? Trouble?"

"Why do you ask that?"

Hank shrugged. "Got that look in your eye."

Travis motioned for Hank to follow him to the end of the bar, well out of earshot of anyone in the saloon.

"I need you to help me keep an eye on a couple of people. Anybody you can trust to help us?"

"Jed," Hank said."

"Besides Jed. I don't want anyone to know about this.

Things have to appear normal around here and they wouldn't if Jed was missing too often."

"Pete."

"Okay. I need someone to watch John Sabot, the night superintendent down at the Chollar Mine."

"What for?" Hank asked.

Travis glanced around to make certain no one was near enough to hear, then spoke in a low voice. "He and a group of men are stealing from the mines."

"Yeah? You mean it was them robbed old Duncan Clyde and killed him?"

"I don't know about that, but I know they're stealing now, only they're not attacking the ore wagons. They're hauling it out into a ravine outside of town, then transferring the ore to pack mules and taking it out over the mountain. Toward Fuller's Ferry."

"And all you want us to do is watch?"

He couldn't tell him any more. If he did, he'd be forced to explain about Suzanne, and he didn't want to drag her into it, not if he didn't have to. She was being used, he felt certain, but the miners wouldn't understand that. All they'd care about was that she'd helped steal their ore, and because of that a man had died.

"No. I want you to alert me when it's about to happen again."

"And what are you gonna do?"

"Have a little talk with Mr. Sabot."

"Okay. You want me to go now?"

Travis shook his head. "No, nothing more is going to happen tonight."

"More? You mean they already stole some tonight."

"Yes. But keep that quiet for now, would you? At least until I figure out what's going on, and who's really behind it." He slapped Hank on the back and turned away from the bar. "I'm going upstairs now, Hank. I'm pretty well bushed."

"Sure thing, Boss. Jed and me will close up the place."

"So, *mon cher,*" Magnolia said, "you have forgotten all about me."

Travis turned from the bureau. He hadn't heard the door open, and had been alerted to her presence only when she'd spoken.

"Damn, Maggie," he said. "You're quieter than a cat."

Reddish brows arched slightly higher at the comment and she smiled, pushing back one side of her black cape, revealing that she had worn nothing beneath it other than her shoes. She settled a hand on her bare hip. "And I purr, too *chéri,* when I'm petted."

Travis smiled as his eyes swept over her. "Yes, you do, don't you?"

Without taking her eyes from him, and allowing a small, almost wicked smile to curve her lips, Magnolia slipped from her shoes and took a step into the room. Reaching to her throat with one hand, she released the single button that kept the cape secured about her. It fell to the carpeted floor to surround her bare feet in a circle of darkness.

Travis felt his body, already strained nearly past the point of tolerance with its hunger for Suzanne, harden at the vision of Magnolia's nakedness. His eyes devoured the sight. Her flesh took on the glow of the lamplight at Travis's back, turning the ivory skin of her petite but voluptuous body to a pale amber. The wild mane of red hair that surrounded her face turned to tangled strands of fire. They tumbled down her back and cascaded over her shoulders to curl teasingly about ivory breasts that were heavy and full, her dark, rosy nipples already taut with anticipation.

His arousal swelled as his gaze traveled down the curving length of her body, past the slight rise of her stomach, and to the triangle of short red curls nestled tantalizingly, invitingly, between the apex of her thighs.

He had lain with Magnolia almost weekly for the past eighteen months and found her an exciting and passionate lover, well versed in the ways of pleasing a man.

Crossing the room to her, his bare feet making no sound on the carpet, his long legs taking the distance in only three strides, Travis slid his hands around her waist and pulled her up against him, crushing her naked body against him. He captured her mouth hungrily, savagely, wasting no effort on gentleness or tender affectations of love. Magnolia had never asked for nor expected tenderness or gentleness from him, as if knowing he was not willing to give them. His tongue plunged into her mouth, filling it, ravaging every crevice and curve with its exploration, engaging in a frantic, desperate duel with hers.

Magnolia's arms wrapped around him and her fingers dug into his shoulders as she held him to her. She pressed her body to his, grinding her hips against him teasingly. Travis Braggette was hers. He belonged to her, body and soul, and she would do whatever it took to keep him that way. She felt the hardness of his need press against her stomach and, tearing her mouth from his and pushing against his chest with the flat of her hands, she twisted away from him.

"Ah, my tiger is especially hungry tonight, yes?" she said breathlessly, and laughed. Taking his hands, she steered him across the room until they stood beside his bed. His shirt hung unbuttoned, the black string tie he'd worn that night tangling loose. He had been in the process of undressing and preparing to retire when she'd entered his room. Magnolia slid her fingers beneath the silk shirt and grazed his flesh with her long nails.

A shudder of desire coursed through Travis at her teasing touch.

Magnolia's hands moved suggestively over the solid wall of muscle, slid upward, caressed the muscular length of his upper arms and then pushed the shirt over his shoulders and down his arms, her lips moving voraciously over his chest as she did. She pulled one nipple into her mouth, sucked it, then closed her teeth around it gently.

Travis groaned as a stab of desire hit him, but he remained still.

He felt his body quiver with anticipation, felt himself spiraling into a cavernous void of desire, of need and hunger. Her lips moved slowly over him, torturing him with the wickedness of their touch, deepening his need with teasing strokes.

And just when he thought he could stand no more, Magnolia's lips disappeared. She stood and pressed her naked body to his and, moving slightly, urged him to bed.

His arms wrapped around her fiercely, dragging her to the bed with him as his mouth closed over hers greedily, demanding that she give him everything she had to give, threatening to devour her if she resisted. It was a savage kiss, a hard, almost cruel kiss, filled with want and hunger, with desperate need.

Rising slightly, Travis moved toward her.

"Yes, *mon cher,* yes," Magnolia cried, tearing her lips from his. "More. More."

"Suzanne," he moaned softly against her ear, the name slipping unbidden from his lips.

Magnolia froze. Fury suddenly replaced passion. Bracing her hands against his shoulders, she pushed at him, while at the same time twisting her own body in an effort to get away from him.

Travis, jerked from the haze of passion that had engulfed him, stared at Magnolia.

"Get off me," she snarled, her eyes blazing with anger. "Get off."

"But, I . . ." He stared down at her in confusion.

"Get off me, Travis, before I kill you." All thought of saving their relationship had fled Magnolia's mind when, in his delirium of passion, he'd uttered Suzanne's name. In that instant, the love and passion she had felt for him, the dreams she had harbored for them, had abruptly died, murdered by that one word: Suzanne. All Magnolia could think of now, all she could feel, was hatred.

Travis rolled from atop her. He stared at her as the passion that had gripped him subsided. A frown pulled at his brow. It was Maggie in his bed, not Suzanne. It was Maggie whose arms had held him tight, whose tongue had dueled with his, whose body had moved to meet his. Not Suzanne's.

He wiped a hand over his eyes and looked back up at her again. Guilt swept over him. Never, not once in his life, had he made love to a woman while thinking of another. "Maggie, I'm sorry, I . . ."

Hair flying wildly about her face, fury etched in every line of her body, Maggie cocked her head haughtily. "Sorry? You're sorry?" She laughed sardonically. "I should say you will be, Travis Braggette." She bent and swooped her cape up from the floor, then turned back to him, ramming clenched fists onto her hips and thrusting her breasts toward him. "I would have given you everything, Travis," she said. "Everything. I would have done anything for you. And what can she give you, *chér?* What *will* she give you? If anything.

"Maggie, I . . ."

She swirled the cape around her shoulders. "Goodbye Travis." Turning abruptly, Maggie jerked open the door and, without a backward glance, swept through it, slamming it shut behind her with resounding finality.

Travis sat for several long minutes and stared at the door. His world was quickly spiraling toward disaster.

Chapter Twenty-two

Travis looked up at the black sky and was grateful that there was at least enough moon so that its light allowed him to see across the landscape fairly clearly, though a little warmth in the air would have made him even more grateful. He shifted his seat and cursed again as he felt a rock stab at his backside. He'd been sitting on the side of Sun Mountain, hidden within a small ravine which he'd further camouflaged with dry brush for over three hours waiting for something to happen. So far nothing had. No ore wagons, mules, or men had shown up in the small canyon where he'd spotted Sabot's men making the transfer several nights before. For all he knew, the only other living thing out here were the rattlers, scorpions, and tarantulas who called the landscape of Nevada Territory home, not to mention the coyotes, wolves, wildcats, and bears.

Hopefully none of those creatures were out seeking a warm body to curl up against for the night. He cupped his hands in front of his face and blew into them, then rubbed them together. Summer might just be around the corner, but you sure as hell couldn't tell it by the night weather on the mountain. The snow of winter was melting away under the daylight sun, only small patches of it left here and there. But at night, and especially up here on the mountain, it was still colder than a witch's caress.

This was the third night they'd staked out the spot where he'd seen Sabot and his men transfer the ore from wagons to mules. He, Hank, and Pete did a three-hour shift each night, with Jed holding down things at the Queen. But Travis was beginning to wonder if the theft had been a one-shot deal, though he found that hard to believe, since Lonchet and Morgan were still around. He had to figure that meant they weren't done. But had they turned their schemes in another direction?

He looked past the brush into the canyon below where Sabot and his men had transferred the ore. His shift was just a little more than half over. Peter would be coming to relieve him and take the middle shift in less than ninety minutes. Travis was just about to push to his feet and stretch his cramped limbs when a faint noise in the distance caused him to freeze in position. The sound of heavily laden wagons rolling over the rough, uneven terrain of the canyon was unmistakable. Travis crouched low again and watched as two wagons pulled into the ravine. Five minutes later, passing so close that he was forced to nearly hold his breath in fear of being heard, two other men appeared on horseback, each leading a pack-mule caravan. Travis recognized them immediately as miners who he knew were followers of Judge Terry, which meant they were members of the Knights. Five more men, three on foot, two on horseback, appeared out of the darkness from the opposite direction.

He watched for the next hour as the men transferred
the raw ore from the wagons to the pack mules, his
mind going over each possibility as to what was happening and who was behind it. Suzanne was involved somehow, he knew that, but what could he do to protect her?
If he went to the sheriff, how could he arrange things so
that she wasn't implicated? Or could he? Was it already
too late to protect her?

This was obviously an operation carried out under
the instructions of the Knights, and it was also obvious
that the raw silver was intended for the Confederacy.
But was it Judge Terry behind this scheme? Or someone
else?

And again, how was Suzanne involved? Was she just
a courier, or was she involved further? He felt his gut
twist in anxiety at the thought. How in the hell did a
woman he barely knew, a woman he had known briefly
years ago, a woman he had been betrothed to marry by
arrangement and walked out on by intent, waltz back
into his life and manage to turn his entire world upside
down? Damn it, she was making him feel things he
didn't want to feel. Passion was fine, but anything beyond that was unacceptable. He had made himself a
comfortable life in Virginia City, a good life, and had no
desire to change it.

As always happened when Travis thought of Suzanne, he felt a stirring of desire warm his blood.

One of the men transferring the raw silver dropped a
hunk while picking it up from the wagon. It thudded
loudly on the bottom of the planked bed and yanked
Travis's thoughts back to the present. He watched as another man mounted and grabbed the lead line of one of
the mule caravans. Nudging his heels to his horse's sides

and jerking on the rope, the man started out. He and the first few mules disappeared into the darkness as they moved over the hill. Another man mounted and took up a position just behind the last mule. Ten minutes later, two more men repeated the process.

Sabot handed each remaining man an envelope. Two of them climbed back up onto the wagons and pulled out. The remaining three began to walk back toward town.

Travis remained in his hiding place, thankful for the decent cast of moonlight as he watched Sabot. The man had settled down on a rock, lit a cheroot and then took something from the breast pocket of his jacket. Sabot flipped open a leather billfold, pulled a thick sheath of money from its pocket and began counting it. Travis felt his temper soar. So, it wasn't only loyalty to the cause and allegiance to a flag that drew Sabot's support of the Knights and the South. That at least he could understand. Travis, too, was loyal to the South and helped the cause in his own way, but he drew the line at thievery, sabotage, and murder. Obviously, the Knights did not. But that shouldn't have surprised him. After all, his own father had been a member. His eyes narrowed as his mood blackened.

Sabot suddenly stood, tossed the cheroot to the ground and pocketed the billfold full of money.

Travis tensed.

The mine superintendent turned away from where Travis knelt, waiting, and began to walk in the direction of the Chollar Mine.

"Oh, no you don't," Travis mumbled. John Sabot was going to tell him exactly what was going on and who was behind it, whether he liked it or not. But first

Travis had to make certain that it was only the two of them out there so he would not get caught in an ambush.

He crouched low and inched himself along the hillside, one hand resting, alert and ready, on his gun butt as he kept stride with Sabot. When they were barely a mile from the mines, and Travis was fairly certain no one else was about, he scooted his way quickly down the hillside, drew his gun and ran up behind Sabot.

"Hold on there, John," Travis said, keeping his voice low and hard. He grabbed Sabot's shoulder and pressed the end of his gun barrel into the man's spine. "We've got a little talking to do."

Sabot's hands flew up into the air. "I . . . I don't want no trouble."

"Good, that makes two of us." He shoved Sabot forward.

"You can have the money, just don't hurt me."

"I don't plan to," Travis said. "And I don't want the money. Now, turn around."

Sabot turned, his hands still held high in the air.

"And put your hands down," Travis growled, though he made no move to lower the gun he still held pointed at Sabot's stomach.

John Sabot's arms snapped down to his sides. He stared at Travis, his eyes large with fear.

"What the hell's going on, Sabot?" Travis demanded harshly.

"Going on? I don't know what you mean. I . . . I just went for a smoke, that's all, and was on my way back to work."

Travis glanced down at his gun for emphasis and then spoke again. "I think you know exactly what I mean, Sabot. You went for a smoke, but that's not all you did back there."

"No, no, that's all, really, I . . ."

"You've got men driving ore wagons into the canyon, Sabot, and men transferring that ore to pack mules and transporting it out of town. I want to know where it's going and who's behind this scheme."

Sabot shook his head vehemently. "I don't know what you're talking about, Braggette. Uh-uh, I don't. No, sir. I just went out there for a smoke."

Travis shoved the gun into Sabot's stomach, the tip of the barrel disappearing within a fold of loose shirt fabric. "The truth, Sabot, unless you think a hole in your gut might look good."

The man's hands shot up in the air over his head as his eyes glanced down at the gun barrel buried in his stomach. "You . . . you wouldn't dare."

Travis smiled, a cold, calculating curve of his lips that he hoped would leave little question as to whether or not he would actually pull the trigger. But just to make certain Sabot believed him, he said, "I've got two bartenders, a saloon manager, and two waitresses who will swear I never left the Mountain Queen tonight." The smile widened. "So, yes, Sabot, I would dare."

The man's pallor turned nearly as white as the snow on the nearby hillside, and his hands, held just above his head, began to tremble violently. "Okay, okay. I got men taking ore wagons to the canyons, and packing it over the mountain by mule."

"On whose orders?"

He shrugged. "I don't know."

Travis eyes darkened. "What in the hell do you mean, you don't know? Someone's giving you orders,

Sabot. You're not smart enough to do this on your own. Now talk!" Travis jabbed the gun deeper into the man's stomach.

"Okay!" Sabot's hands shot higher into the air. "It's that singer you brought in to the Mountain Queen. That Georgette Lindsay. She's the boss."

"Georgette Lindsay?" Travis kept pushing the gun deeper. "You're lying."

"I ain't lying, I ain't. It was her, I tell you, it was that Georgette Lindsay woman."

Travis shook his head. "She paid you, Sabot, but she didn't give you the orders about what to do, and that's who I want. Now, who told you what to do?"

"She did, Braggette, I swear. She gave me the money and the orders."

"How?"

"When she give me the money. There was a note with the money. In the envelope. Told me to hire some men I could trust and bring the wagons here. Said I'd be met. That's all. Just hire the men, fill up the wagons and bring them here."

"But what got you that far, Sabot?" The anger Travis felt resonated in his tone, instilling it with a chilling hardness. "Who made you the initial offer?"

"I don't know, honest. I don't know."

"How could you not know who hired you, Sabot?" Travis pulled back on the gun's hammer.

"It was by note," Sabot squealed. "By note. I swear, I swear. I got a note. Slipped under the pillow of my bed at the hotel. It had the seal of the Knights on it and said if I wanted to make some easy money and help the cause, I should be on that corner. So," he shrugged, "I was."

"And that's it?"

"Yeah. I went to the corner like I was told and that Georgette Lindsay come by and gave me an envelope."

"And," Travis urged.

"Yeah, well, I tried to ask her what I had to do for the money, but she just said to read the note that was inside the envelope."

"What did it say?"

"That I was getting paid to bring two fully loaded ore wagons over there to that ravine. I was warned to keep my eyes closed about what happened to the rock."

"And the rest of the men?"

Sabot shrugged. "I hired the drivers, like I was told to. Don't know about the ones who brought the pack mules, though. Never seen them before. Probably not from around here. Guess that Miss Lindsay hired them, too."

Travis felt like strangling the man. Their surveillance of him had been a waste of time. They didn't know anything more than before. Except that all fingers of guilt seemed to point to Suzanne.

"If I find out you've lied to me, Sabot," Travis said, and pushed the gun harder against the man's stomach until the barrel nearly disappeared, "I'll do more than just *push* this gun into your gut."

Sabot nodded vigorously. "I ain't lying, Braggette, honest I ain't. That singer of yours gave me the money and the orders, and I don't know where the first note come from. Probably from her, too, but I ain't sure. That's the truth, Braggette. I ain't lying."

"I hope not, for your sake, Sabot. And if I were you, I'd keep this little conversation to yourself. It didn't happen. Understand?"

"Sure, sure. Anything you say."

"When's the next time you're supposed to do this? Rob the freighters?"

"Next week. Not till next week. Wednesday."

"How do you know that?"

"It was in the note. I got dates, once a week, but not always on the same day."

"Okay. then do it, and forget you told me anything."

"You want me to keep robbing the Chollar?"

"Yes."

"But . . ."

"No buts, Sabot. Just keep on doing what you agreed to do and don't tell anyone you talked with me, or it could be the last conversation you ever have." Travis reholstered his gun and waved Sabot on his way.

The man needed no further encouragement. The moment he realized Travis meant for him to leave, he was gone, scrambling over the rock-strewn landscape, kicking up dirt and scurrying out of sight as fast as he could without one glance back.

Travis walked slowly back to town. He remained alert the entire distance, the heel of his hand resting on the butt of his gun. Sabot had appeared shaken, and agreeable, but there was always the chance it had been an act, and Travis would rather not find that out by getting a bullet in the back.

Fifteen minutes later, he was back in town. He walked past the Union Belle, past the Mountain Queen, and turned on Union Street. Lamplight glowed from the small window of the sheriff's office and town jail. Travis pushed open the plank door, stepped in and slammed it shut behind him. The town's deputy, Liam Dibbet, sat behind a desk facing the door. He was leaning back in his chair, booted feet crossed and propped upon the desktop. Liam looked up from beneath a moth-eaten slouch hat at Travis's entry but did not rise.

"Can I help you, Braggette?" he asked arrogantly, folding his hands together over his stomach and looking up at Travis from beneath the brim of the soiled hat. Since the sheriff made no secret of the fact he didn't like Travis, Liam had assumed the same posture.

"Where's Morrow?" Travis asked, referring to the sheriff.

"Sleeping in the back."

"Get him up."

Liam shook his head. "Can't do that. Sheriff told me not to bother him less'n it was a matter of life or death."

"It is," Travis growled.

Laim's eyes wided and his brows soared upward. "Yeah, whose?"

"Yours, if you don't get Morrow out here now," Travis threatened. He was in no mood to fool around. Something was going on in Virginia City and he knew damned well that if he didn't stop it, not only was Suzanne going to end up in trouble, but most likely he would, too.

Liam bolted from his chair and hustled himself through a rear door that led to the jail cells.

Travis turned and looked back out the window that had a view of the street. He thought he understood why the judge had kept after him for the past few months about attending the KGC meetings and publicly offered him the leadership of the Knights when he'd known damned well Travis would turn it down. It was all a plan to set up the robberies and skim off the profits.

He had it almost all figured out now. Clarence

Lonchet had contacted him about having "Georgette Lindsay" play the Mountain Queen. Managers don't usually do that. It looked obvious now that there was a connection between Lonchet and the judge, and Morgan, too. They were all Knights, but there was more to it than that. One of them, probably Judge Terry, had masterminded these robberies, and the other two men were probably his partners, and the ones sent to carry the scheme out.

Travis swore under his breath, cursing the day he'd ever decided to join the Knights. It had been a stupid, rebellious thing to do, and he'd learned that quickly enough. He'd stopped going to the meetings, but by that time the Knights had considered him a full member. And most likely some of them still did, though others, like the judge, evidently considered him an untrustworthy traitor.

Sheriff Morrow shuffled out from the rear of the jail, the part which housed the cells.

When Travis turned to face him, the sheriff glared at him. "This better be good, Braggette," he snarled, and rubbed at his eyes. "I ain't partial to being woke up for nothing."

"How about a robbery, Sheriff? Is that a good enough reason to interrupt your sleep?" Travis goaded.

Morrow looked at Liam and then back at Travis. "Robbery? What robbery? Something happen we don't know about?" He grabbed for his gun and holster which hung from a wooden peg on the wall.

"A couple of ore wagons have just been robbed."

"Anybody hurt?"

"No. And you can leave those guns there and relax.

We're not going anywhere." Travis pulled up a chair and sat down in front of Liam's desk.

"Not going anywhere?" The sheriff ignored Travis's comment about leaving his guns on the wall and buckled on his holster. "What in the hell do you mean? Trying to tell me my job again, Braggette?"

Travis smiled. "No, but I'll help you solve these robberies if you'll do it my way."

"When did they take place? And where?" He tied the holster to his thigh. "How come I ain't heard? Who got robbed?"

"The Chollar, but they don't know it yet."

"Don't know it yet? What're you saying, Braggette? How in blazes could you know about the Chollar being robbed if them mining officials don't even know about it unless . . ." his expression turned to one of suspicion and a crafty spark of pleasure lit his eyes, " . . . . unless you did it?"

Travis chuckled softly and shook his head. "Sorry to disappoint you, Sheriff. I know you'd like nothing better than to lock me up in one of your cells and throw away the key, but I'm not your thief. John Sabot, the Chollar's night superintendent is one of them, Hanson Jones, the night superintendent of the Savage is the other . . . although there are more. They've been sneaking ore wagons away from the mines and taking them to a canyon outside town. About a half dozen other men are involved. Some meet him there with a caravan of pack mules. They transfer the ore to the packs and carry it out. They stay away from the roads and travel over the mountain. The ore wagons are returned to the mine and no one knows anything was even taken. Except for those involved, of course."

"The night superintendents? Come on, Braggette," the sheriff sneered. "You expect me to believe this? What do you take me for anyway?"

"I'd rather not get into that, Sheriff," Travis said. "But if you don't follow this up and the robberies are discovered, and it comes out that I warned you about them, well . . ." He shrugged, letting the sheriff figure out for himself just how bad it would look.

"Okay, but what if I figure *you're* the one pulling these robberies, Braggette? Since you seem to know exactly how they're being done." The sheriff smiled shrewdly. "Maybe you're in cahoots with Sabot and he double-crossed you. Is that it, Braggette? Sabot double-crossed you so you're turning him in to take the blame alone?"

"You could figure it that way Sheriff, but you'd be wrong. And since election time is coming up in a few weeks, and with the way feelings are running in town about the war, splitting it down the middle and all, I'd say you could use a little help getting votes. Wouldn't you?"

"Yeah. So?"

"So you haven't got a thing on Sabot or Jones. I saw Sabot actually make the transfer, you didn't. Help me stake out the place and we'll catch one or both of them in the act, and maybe their accomplices, too."

"Yeah? Who are they?"

"I'm not sure yet, that's why I need your help."

The sheriff looked long and hard at Travis. Finally, he voiced what was so clearly on his mind. "How do I know I can trust you, Braggette? That this isn't some kind of double cross?"

"I don't have a reason to double-cross you, Sheriff."

"You're one of them Knights."

"I'm a Southerner," Travis corrected. "That's all. Not all Southerners are members of the KGC."

"Yeah, maybe," the sheriff drawled. "But you was a good friend of the judge."

"I thought so, too," Travis said. "But so was Julia, Tom Lowry, Bob Fairmount, and at least half the town. That doesn't mean we're all members of the KGC."

"Okay, okay, we'll do it your way for now." He leaned against the edge of Liam's desk and pushed his hat back off his forehead. "So, who do you figure is in on this thing? Who's giving the orders?"

"I figure it was the judge who cooked this whole thing up, though we'll never prove it, since he's gone. But I think I know who he left in charge."

"Yeah, who?"

"Clarence Lonchet," Travis said.

"The puny little guy who manages that songbird from your place?"

Travis nodded.

"And her? Is she in on this, too?" The sheriff grinned. "Maybe seducing some of these boys to do what Lonchet wants when they ain't already too keen on the idea?"

"No." The denial came out much as an abrupt crack of lightning, sharp and striking.

Morrow jerked in reaction. "Awful sure of that, ain't you, Braggette?"

Chapter Twenty-three

Travis positioned himself behind one of the empty freight wagons set off to one side of the entrance to the Savage Mine. No one had seemed to notice his approach, and he wanted to keep it that way. Pulling his hat lower onto his forehead and checking his gun for the umpteenth time by resting a hand on its butt, Travis hunkered down and waited for Hanson Jones to appear from within the mine. The man had to take a supper break, and Travis hoped that when he did, it was to get more than supper.

Half an hour later, Hanson Jones appeared at the mouth of the mine. He talked with several men, including one Travis recognized as the assistant night superintendent. They seemed to argue about something for a few minutes, then Jones nodded and turned toward town.

Travis followed stealthily, making certain to keep far enough back not to alert the man to his presence, yet close enough not to lose him in the shadows.

But if he was hoping that Jones would go immediately

to a ravine and be joined by fully loaded freight wagons and a caravan of pack mules, he was disappointed.

Travis muttered a string of curses under his breath. He leaned against the wall of Mallard's photography shop and watched as Jones entered Cabor's Restaurant. Now what the hell was he supposed to do? "Well, one thing's for certain," he muttered to himself. "It's too damned cold to stand out here."

Tossing the lucifer he'd been fingering onto the ground, Travis walked across the street and entered Cabor's. He joined a table already occupied by three other miners by the door. The men exchanged pleasantries and Travis waved for the waitress. "Coffee," he said when she approached.

Thirty minutes later, Jones was on the move again, and so was Travis. But he wasn't any happier about where they ended up than he'd been at seeing Jones enter Cabor's. And this time he couldn't follow the man inside.

Standing in the shadows of a building across the street, Travis watched as Hanson Jones entered a delapidated crib on the corner of D and Washington streets. He didn't know who it belonged to, but figured the whore who lived there couldn't be too successful at her profession. The place looked about ready to collapse. Pieces of scrap wood had been nailed over various spots in the walls to cover holes that needed patching. The place offered little protection from the wind. The shingles on the roof were half gone and the stovepipe had only one side left to it at the top. The front door was framed by a window on each side. One had glass, the other a piece of canvas nailed over it.

Travis decided Hanson Jones must be one tight son of

a bitch. He made good money at the Savage, but evidently picked the cheapest whore in town. He watched in amazement as one wall of the small cottage began to shake. Obviously, the woman's bed was up against that wall, and Hanson Jones was a very active man in bed. Travis chuckled to himself at the thought of the gruff-looking miner and an even gruffer-looking prostitute locking limbs.

Then he remembered that he was standing on a lonely street corner in the dead of night and cold as hell. His chuckling ceased immediately. Just as Travis was about to decide that Hanson Jones was going to spend the entire remainder of his supper break humping a prostitute, the front door of the crib opened and the man stepped out onto the street, still in the process of buttoning his trousers.

The mine superintendent walked back up to C Street, and Travis followed at a discreet distance, silently cursing each step that took them closer to the center of town. The sheriff had offered to have Liam follow Jones, but Travis had insisted he'd do it himself. He hadn't wanted to take a chance that Suzanne would meet the man again and that the deputy would see it. The sheriff's deputy was following Sabot. Travis figured if Suzanne was going to meet one of the men again, it would be Jones. Now he wished he'd taken Morris up on his offer. Obviously, Jones wasn't going to do anything tonight.

To his surprise, the miner walked directly into the Mountain Queen.

"Damnation," Travis muttered. "I spend the evening freezing my rump off following him and he leads me right back to my own place." He barged through the saloon's swinging doors. He walked to the end of the bar. "Jed, give me a bourbon," he yelled to the bartender. "In fact, give me the whole damned bottle."

"What's the matter, Boss?" Jed asked, sliding a shot glass toward Travis and filling it from Travis's special bourbon.

Travis downed his drink and slammed the glass back on the bar. "Where's Hank?" he growled, ignoring the bartender's question.

Jed nodded across the room and refilled Travis's glass. "Keeping an eye on that gambler fella who came into town last night. Couple of the boys been losing pretty steady to him and think he's been cheating at cards."

Travis took his drink and walked across the room to stand beside Hank. The saloon manager was leaning against the wall a good five feet from the gambler's table and watching the card game in progress.

"He cheating?" Travis asked softly.

Hank shrugged. "I ain't caught him at nothing, Boss, but if he's not backsliding cards outta some place or bottom dealing, he's sure packing a heavy load of luck. I ain't seen him lose but one hand in the last hour."

Travis raised his glass to his mouth and gulped down the bourbon. "Well, keep an eye on him, Hank. I don't want any trouble starting in here. The boys broke enough chairs and glasses the other night, and the new ones won't arrive from San Francisco until next week. To say nothing of my mirror."

"Sure thing, Boss."

"And if you do see him cheating, touch the back of his head with your iron and haul him on down to the jail."

Hank nodded. "You have any luck on your end, Boss?"

Travis jerked his head toward Hanson Jones, who was sitting at another table playing faro.

Seated at yet another table, Sheriff Morris leaned back in his chair and surveyed the room. He'd been watching Ben Morgan, as they'd planned. Another deputy was watching Clarence Lonchet. Travis approached.

"Nothing going on with him, either, I take it?" he said to the sheriff.

"No. You sure about this thing, Braggette?" The sheriff gave him a hard stare. "You wouldn't be setting me up here while you pull something of your own, would you?"

Travis sighed. There was no love lost between himself and Morrow. Never had been. Not that either of them really cared. "No, Sheriff, what I told you is the truth."

"Better be, Braggette, for your sake."

"Where's Lonchet?"

"Got a man on him, don't worry. He left a while ago."

Travis nodded and walked back to stand at the bar. Suzanne came out and began a song. Travis watched her with hungry eyes. What in the hell had she gotten herself into? And why?

The night wore on, and Travis began to wonder what was going on. Instead of returning to the mine, Hanson Jones remained in the Mountain Queen, cheering Suzanne's performance, gulping drinks, and betting heavily on faro. He laughed loud, cheered loud, and talked loud, drawing a lot of attention to himself, which he didn't seem to mind.

About two in the morning, Travis gave up. He turned

to Jed. "I'm calling it a night. I don't think anything's going to happen. Jones is too well ensconced here. Tell Hank to close up, would you?"

"You sure you want to do that, Boss?" Jed said. He nodded toward Hanson Jones.

The man had finally risen from his seat and was heading for the door.

"Damn," Travis muttered. Grabbing his hat from the end of the bar where he'd set it earlier, Travis sauntered casually through the swinging door and out onto the street. Hanson Jones was staggering his way down the boardwalk in the direction of the mines. Travis followed at a distance, wondering why he was bothering. The man was probably just going to his own shack. They reached Washington Street. Travis watched with a mingling of disbelief and suspicion. The man couldn't be going back to his shift at the mine, could he? He was so drunk he was probably nearly blind.

Jones crossed Flowery Street and continued on C Street. The sounds of the mines echoed in the night air as Jones and Travis neared them. Suddenly the sag of Jones's shoulders disappeared as he seemed to shake himself and straighten. The weaving walk of a drunk also disappeared.

"Well, I'll be damned," Travis muttered. Jones wasn't drunk at all.

But instead of going back to the mine, the superintendent continued on walking . . . right out of town. Finally, just before reaching the first dipping curve in the road that would lead them into Gold Hill, Jones veered off the trail and entered a small canyon.

Travis inched his way to the mouth of the canyon. It was completely dark except for a light at its very end, which appeared to be a goodly distance away. Hopefully, Jones had continued on and hadn't discovered he was being followed and lying in wait to ambush him. Travis pulled back the hammer of his gun, just in case, and entered the canyon. The nearer he got to the light, and what he figured must be the end of the canyon, the more sounds he heard: men talking, horses shuffling, and Hanson Jones giving orders. Travis moved up the side of the canyon, thankful that it was a mild slope and not a sheer cliff. When he reached its crest and moved to just above where the group of men were congregated, he saw exactly what he expected to see: a half dozen men removing junks of ore from two freight wagons and reloading them into leather packs slung over a caravan of mules.

As Sabot had done the night before, Hanson Jones remained behind as the four mounted men led the pack mules out of the canyon by ascending the southern slope and the two freight drivers headed their wagons toward the mouth of the canyon. Jones squatted down beside a single oil lamp on the ground and pulled a cheroot from his pocket.

"Don't you think you ought to be getting back to the mine so you can check out from your shift?" Travis asked.

As Hanson Jones jerked around, startled, his legs twisted and he collapsed to the ground. He stared up at Travis. "Hot damn, Braggette," he swore. "You nearly scared me half to death."

Travis struck a casual pose but kept the heel of his right hand settled indifferently atop the butt of his gun. "Last thing I want right now is you dead, Jones." He hunkered down in front of the man and, pulling a lucifer from his breast pocket of his jacket, scraped it against the heel of his boot. It erupted into flame and he held it out to Hanson Jones.

The man stared at the tiny spurt of dancing fire and then lifted his gaze to Travis.

"Go on, Jones, light your tobacco."

Jones stuck the cheroot into his mouth and, bending forward, touched its end to the lucifer Travis held, puffing quickly to draw the flame to the tobacco.

Travis extinguished the match with a flick of his wrist and tossed it away. "Now that you're comfortable, Jones, let's have ourselves a little talk."

"About what?" Jones grumbled, eyeing Travis suspiciously.

"Oh," Travis smiled, "about those freight wagons you and your men just unloaded, and the pack mules that are carrying that ore to. . . ." he shrugged. "To wherever."

"I don't know what you're talking about."

"Really? I was seeing things then?"

Jones took a long drag from the cheroot and exhaled it slowly, arrogantly. "Musta been."

Travis nodded. Then, with lightning speed, he latched both hands around the man's collar and hauled him from his crouched position onto his knees. The cheroot dropped to the ground.

"I don't conjure up things, Jones," Travis snapped, his eyes little more than a few inches from the other man's. "I saw your men, and I saw you, stealing that ore. Tell me what's going on here, Jones. Tell me who's behind all of this, or I swear I'll take you to the sheriff right now. And we both know how he makes a man talk, don't we?"

Sheriff Morrow had a reputation for beating a confession out of a man, whether he was guilty or not.

"The ore's going for the cause, Braggette, which I'd a'thought you shouldn't have any trouble with," Jones sneered. "And that's all I know."

"Who's behind this? Terry?"

"I don't know."

Travis had the sinking feeling that he was about to hear the same story Sabot had told him the night before. "What the hell does that mean?" he asked.

"Just what I said; I don't know. I got my orders from that dame that sings in your place, so I figured you and her was behind it."

Travis released him, and Jones busied himself rearranging his shirt collar and fumbling on the ground for his cigar.

"Georgette Lindsay brought you your orders?"

"That's what I said, ain't it?"

"And your money?"

"Yeah."

"But who contacted you to see if you were interested?" Travis persisted.

"Don't know. Got a note in my bed one night. Said if I wanted to make some money and help the cause to be by St. Paul's Church at midnight a couple of nights ago. I was interested, so I was there."

"And Georgette Lindsay met you?" It wasn't really a question, since Travis already knew the answer. He'd followed her, he knew they'd met, but he wanted to hear Jones say it.

"Yeah."

"So who hired the freight drivers?"

"Me."

"And the mule packers?"

"I don't know."

"You don't know much, do you, Jones?" Travis said.

"Maybe not, but I figure you're a dead man, Braggette. If you ain't behind this, then you're sticking your nose into something I'd bet is going to get you killed."

"I don't think so." Travis suddenly had what he considered a brilliant idea. "Listen, Jones, I'm a Brigadier General in the Knights of the Golden Circle. You're a member, I'm sure you know what that means."

Hanson Jones's eyes grew big as surprise swept over his face. "Brigadier General? You?"

"Yes."

"Then you're. . . ." He swallowed hard. "Then you're one of the top guys. Even bigger than Terry."

"Yes."

"But I thought Terry was in charge here."

"He was. But we've come to discover that was a mistake."

"Yeah? What'd he do?"

"Jones, I don't really have the time for all these questions. Now, do you want to cooperate with me," Travis snapped, acting as if his patience was wearing thin, which in fact it was, "or should I turn your name in as someone who can't be trusted any longer?"

"Hell, Braggette, I didn't know about you. Course I'll cooperate. Whatever you guys want me to do, I'll. . . ." His eyes turned suddenly leery, his tone skeptical and sneering. "Hey, wait a minute. If you're a top guy like you say, then how come you asked me all those questions? How come you didn't know what was going on here, and who ordered it?"

"Because some of our own have been, shall we say, using the Knights for their own cause."

"Yeah? Like who?"

"I don't think you need to know that, Jones." Travis rose to his feet and, as he did, shifted the weight of his gun belt, a move to emphasize the authority he'd just claimed, and make Hanson Jones a little more nervous.

The mining superintendent scrambled to rise.

Travis was satisfied to see the man's eyes dart from Travis's, to his gun belt, and back to meet his gaze again.

"We've been watching Georgette Lindsay."

"Yeah, me, too," Hanson Jones sneered, giving Travis a lewd wink and smile.

"But I doubt in the way I mean."

Jones sobered immediately.

"We believe that Miss Lindsay, the judge, and Clarence Lonchet are all members of the KGC. Unfortunately, it seems that the silver you are helping to smuggle from the Savage Mining Company is not going to the cause, as they've told you, but into their pockets."

"Why, those lousy traitors," Jones grumbled.

"Exactly," Travis said. "Though we believe Miss Lindsay is being forced to cooperate with them. Nevertheless, because of this scheme I need your cooperation. Or rather, speaking for the KGC, *we* do."

"Hell, you got it, Braggette," Jones said. "I may be out here in Nevada Territory, but I come from Virginia and I'm proud of it."

"I'm glad to hear that, Jones," Travis drawled lazily. He struck a casual pose, tugging the brim of his hat just a little bit lower onto his forehead. He dropped his voice to a conspiratorial tone. "Now, here's what I want you to do."

Chapter Twenty-four

The next evening Suzanne approached Travis immediately after her first performance. Lonchet was seated
at the corner table with Ben Morgan, so Travis wasn't
surprised. She was still playing her little game.

"Buy me a drink?" she asked coyly, pressing close to
him.

"You don't drink," Travis said, and smiled.

"So buy me a sarsaparilla."

Travis ordered Jed to bring Suzanne what she
wanted. He leaned against the bar and looked down at
her as she sipped the dark soda. "I'm assuming, Suzanne, that when Lonchet finally leaves to meet whomever he's going to see tonight, you'll have no further use
for my attentions."

Suzanne jerked around, startled by his question. She
recovered quickly and smiled up at him, a teasing glint
in her eyes. "Oh, Travis, whyever would you say that?"
she cooed. "I always enjoy your attentions."

"Right. Like a rattler's."

She laughed lightly. "Well, now that you mention it,

there is a distinct similarity." To soften her words, she placed a hand on his and began to caress his fingers.

Travis looked past her to make certain no one was close enough to hear what he had to say and effectively, though not obviously, pulled his hand from beneath hers. Her touch had immediately brought an ache of desire which he didn't need, not if he was going to find out what in the hell was going on and just how involved she was. If she'd gotten herself in too deep, it could turn out that he couldn't protect her at all, regardless of what he did.

"Suzanne, let's not pretend anymore." He had to be careful what he said, just in case he was wrong and she was much more involved than he'd figured. Or whatever they held over her was more valuable to her than a man's life . . . namely his. "I don't know exactly what you're up to, but I know it involves the Knights, and that means you're in over your head."

She stared up at him, unable to think of a thing to say. Her mind raced about in a panic, searching for a response, for some flirtatious, inane thing to say, and found nothing. Instead, it nearly drowned in a sea of questions. If he knew she was involved with the Knights, then how much else did he know? Did he know about Brett? She felt an almost irresistible urge to ask him, and then fought it back down before her better senses were overcome. She couldn't explain to him about Brett. She couldn't tell him anything. If she did and learned Travis knew nothing that could help her and Clarence found out what she'd done, it could mean Brett's life. And possibly her own and Travis's as well.

"Suzanne?" Travis said softly.

She glanced at Clarence, who was watching her intently, then back at Travis and forced a smile to her lips. "Why, Travis," she said loudly, her tone instilled with a false cheeriness, "what ever are you talking about?" She laughed and slipped an arm through his. "Let's dance."

He resisted her pull on his arm, but having also noticed Lonchet's eyes on them, and hearing the fear beneath the forced levity in Suzanne's voice, he smiled. "Let's not," he said softly. "I'd much rather feel your body pressed to mine." Telling himself that she was just a beautiful woman from his past who he wanted in his bed one more time, he steeled himself against her, against the emotions he knew would well up, hot and fiery, within him as her lithe length fitted against his.

She snuggled into his arms as if she belonged there. "We're good together, Travis," she said softly, suggestively.

"As good as you and Lonchet?" he asked in a loud tone.

He felt her stiffen, but she didn't pull herself from his embrace.

Out of the corner of his eye, Travis noticed Clarence Lonchet push away from the table. Evidently he was satisfied that Suzanne was doing what she was supposed to do. He tipped his hat to Ben Morgan and the others at the table and took his leave of the saloon.

And as Travis had expected, the moment Lonchet disappeared through the swinging doors that led to the street, Suzanne pulled away from Travis's embrace. She looked up at him and, for just the briefest of seconds, he saw longing spark from within her blue eyes. And then it was gone, replaced by cold, biting indifference. Or dislike. He wasn't sure which. "Well," she said coolly, "I'd better get to the dressing room and powder my face before my next performance."

He touched her arm as she made to turn away. Suzanne paused and looked back.

"Suzanne, is there something wrong? Are you in some kind of trouble?" he asked, keeping his voice purposely low so that only she could hear him. "Tell me," he said. "Trust me, and I promise I'll help you."

Again a flash of surprise flickered within the fathomless blue depths as they gazed up at him, but again it disappeared as quickly as it had come. She smiled. "Of course I'm not in any trouble, Travis. I'm fine. Really." With that, Suzanne picked up the front of her skirt, a voluminous cloud of midnight-blue gossamer satin that rustled softly when she walked, and hurried toward her dressing room.

For once Travis was glad that a beautiful lady was walking away from him. If he'd been forced to remain standing only inches from her for any longer, he knew the last semblance of self-control would have deserted him. During their entire conversation he had struggled desperately to keep his eyes from straying to the deeply plunging neckline of her gown with its white lace trim that fairly called the eye to the swell of the bosom revealed tantalizingly above it. Another minute, another second, and he would have lost all restraint, dragged her to him and told her to forget about her next performance.

Just before disappearing behind the curtained doorway that led to the dressing rooms, Suzanne paused and looked back again. To her dismay, she found Ben Morgan watching her. She looked back at Travis and, smiling widely, blew him a kiss, sending it on its way with a flirtatious wave of her hand and a wink of her eye.

He smiled back at her, having already noticed, by glancing in the huge mirror that hung over the back of the bar, that Ben Morgan had been watching them. Evidently Morgan was taking up where Lonchet had left off.

For the next fifteen minutes, Travis watched Suzanne's performance. There wasn't much else to do. Hank was watching Hanson Jones, making certain he didn't pull anything, and Liam was keeping an eye on John Sabot. Travis had no doubt that Clarence Lonchet was in one of the cribs on D Street, since Julia had told him that the little man spent almost every night at one crib or another. Julia should know, being a prostitute herself and a good friend to almost every girl down there.

And Ben Morgan was sitting at his usual table in the Mountain Queen.

Travis turned back to the bar and motioned for Jed. The barkeep finished pouring a drink for a gambler who'd just hit town a few hours earlier and then sauntered toward Travis. He wiped his hands on the white apron tied about his waist as he approached and grabbed Travis's special bottle of bourbon from beneath the bar.

"Yeah, Boss, what's up?"

Travis waved off the drink. "Nothing. Miss Lindsay's final performance for the evening is almost over, Jed. I've got to go upstairs and check on something, but when she comes out to leave, would you tell her I'll walk her back to the hotel?"

"Sure thing, Boss."

Travis crossed the room and, taking the stairs that led to the second floor, stepped into his room. His gun belt hung on a wooden hook near the door. He retrieved it and strapped it around his waist, letting it settle low over his hips. Raising a foot to a small stool before the bureau, Travis bent and tied the leather thong that hung from the holster's tip around his thigh. He straightened, shifted the holster slightly and, picking up a pitcher from atop the bureau, splashed its tepid water into a bowl. Soaking a washcloth in the water, Travis squeezed the excess back into the bowl and slapped the cloth onto his face. Its refreshing coolness swept away any weariness he felt. He tossed the cloth back into the bowl. Water sloshed onto the bureau top, but he ignored it. He ran a comb through his hair and, pausing at the door, grabbed his hat, settling it onto his head as he stepped onto the balcony and closed the door behind him.

Ben Morgan leaned back in his chair and watched as Suzanne stepped from the curtained doorway. His gaze didn't veer from her as she made her way through the saloon. He saw her pause at the end of the bar when the barkeep called out to her, saw her shake her head negatively, and then hurry though the swinging doors. The burning sensation in his crotch intensified. He'd been bedding whores ever since coming to this godforsaken hellhole of a town, and he was tired of it. At least in San Francisco there was more selection. Lonchet had promised him that he could have his way with the Lindsay woman after they were through with her, but he didn't much feel like waiting anymore. And he wasn't sure he trusted Lonchet anyway.

He swilled down the whiskey in his glass, the last of the bottle he'd ordered only an hour before, and his second of the night. He slammed the glass back down on the table. Rotgut, that's what they served in the Mountain Queen. Rotgut. Couldn't get drunk on it even if he tried. Pushing away from the table, Morgan stood, swayed slightly, and wheeled around toward the door.

Suzanne held her cape tucked at her neck and her head bowed against the wind. It had been an oversight that she hadn't bothered with the hood, and now it was too late. She wouldn't be able to drape it on her head without stopping and she had no intention of doing that. Her fingers tightened their hold on the front of the cape, pulling it tighter about her. She was already chilled to the bone and she had been outside less than two minutes.

Suddenly she had the distinct sensation that someone was behind her. No, not just behind her—following her. She started to glance over her shoulder and caught herself. It was most likely Travis. He'd wanted to walk her back to the hotel, had even instructed the barkeep to request her to wait. He was probably attempting to catch up with her now, angry that she hadn't agreed to his plan. She pulled the cape tighter to her throat and hurried her step. It wouldn't do any good to give in to the feelings she had for Travis, even though she desperately wanted to. She would play Clarence's game, pretending to flirt with Travis whenever Clarence was around, but that was all. It wasn't hard really, since she wasn't pretending, but she couldn't let it go any further than that again. Her heart couldn't stand it. She couldn't refuse to do what Clarence ordered, but she could at least try to protect herself, and that meant keeping Travis at arm's length.

She walked quickly. She had to think of her brother first. She had to find out what had happened to Brett, where he was. And only Clarence could give her the information she wanted. Her fingers tightened their grasp about the cloak as she thought of Clarence. He hadn't told her why they were in Virginia City, though it hadn't been too hard to guess, and now even if she wanted to, it was too late to do anything about it. They'd find a way to blame her. To say she was in on the robberies, and the murder. No, what she had to do now was go along with Clarence and try as best she could to protect Travis until Clarence told her what she needed to know about her brother.

Suzanne paused at the corner of Taylor and C streets. Music and a roar of cheers drifted to her ears from the Maguire Opera House up the hill to her right.

A gust of wind swept down the street and rustled her skirts. The cape billowed about her legs. Suzanne felt her limbs tremble as a shiver raced through her. She held on to a support pillar of the boardwalk's overhanging roof and began to step down to the ground so that she could cross the street. Suddenly someone grabbed her from behind, yanking her shoulder painfully and jerking her back across the boardwalk.

"Hey there, Suzie, where ya going so fast?" Ben Morgan asked. The whiskey he'd been consuming all evening caused his words to slur.

Suzanne stiffened as the huge man dragged her up against his chest and held her there. She tried to twist away but found the effort futile. "Let me go, Morgan," she snapped.

He laughed and lowered his head toward hers. She knew immediately he was going to try to kiss her. Horrified and repulsed, Suzanne jerked her face to one side. His lips pressed to the curve of her neck, just below her ear. A shudder of revulsion shook her body, blending with the fury that already gripped her. "Let me go, you big ox." Pulling back a leg, she rammed the point of her shoe into his shin.

Morgan flinched as her foot crashed against the leather top of his boot. He cussed solidly for a few seconds but didn't release his hold on her. "Calm down, missy," he snarled, his tone turning ugly. "You been sashaying yourself in front of all them men, teasing them and showing half of what you got tucked away under that dress, so don't go playing all innocent with me, 'cause I'm going to have me some." He tightened his grip on her.

Suzanne twisted frantically, but her arms were pinned at her sides beneath his, her hands dangling helplessly at her thighs. "You're not going to have anything, you moron," Suzanne retorted. Her heart thudded frantically as both her anger and panic began to rise. "Now let me go."

Morgan laughed and made another attempt to catch Suzanne's mouth with his. Again he missed, this time slapping his thick lips atop her cheek.

Suzanne felt the wiry hairs of his mustache against her cheek, his beard against the curve of her chin. She smelled the stale, rank odor of whiskey that emanated from his breath, and her stomach turned violently.

"C'mon, Suzie," Morgan said. "You been friendly

with ever'body else, including that good-for-nothing that walked out on you before. Now be friendly with me."

Suzanne stared up at him in shock. He knew about Travis?

She felt his lips on her neck again and almost gagged, then stiffened as one of his hands slipped beneath her cape. She tried to twist away from him again and then thought better of it. The man was obviously too strong for her physical protests to do any good, and her verbal ones had been ignored. She forced herself to relax and instilled a suggestive tone to her voice.

Travis stepped from the room just in time to see Suzanne disappear through the swinging doors that led to the street.

Anger and disappointment had swelled within him at her rejection of his offer to see her back to the hotel. A second later it was replaced by a sense of alarm as he watched an obviously drunk Ben Morgan shove away from his table, rise and, staggering, follow Suzanne outside.

Travis descended the stairs two at a time. He didn't know if Morgan was actually following Suzanne, or if it was just a coincidence that the man left only seconds after she had, but something told him to find out. He stopped at the end of the bar. Jed hurried over immediately.

"I told her, Boss," the barkeep said, "but she just stuck that pretty little nose of hers up in the air and said to tell you she didn't need an escort."

"Thanks, Jed. I'll be back shortly."

The barkeep nodded, his bald pate catching the light of the chandelier overhead and glistening.

Travis pushed through the swinging doors, nearly colliding with a customer about to enter. He apologized to the stranger, and stepped to the edge of the boardwalk. Except for the light reflecting onto the street from a few windows here and there, mostly saloons, it was dark.

And Suzanne, he assumed, was still wearing a dress of midnight blue, most likely covered by her black cape.

He squinted into the darkness, but all he saw was a few miners staggering drunkenly toward him. And then a prostitute he recognized as one who usually worked out of Maggie's saloon moved down the boardwalk across the street and in front of a lighted window. She waved to him. He waved back and began to walk toward the Union Belle Hotel. About to pass in front of the Black and Howell Building at the corner, Travis heard what sounded like a scuffle, followed by a woman's protests. He stopped and cocked an ear. A second later he heard Suzanne's voice.

"Well, I can't exactly be friendly with you, *Benny,*" she said, emphasis on his name, "unless you loosen up on your hug, now can I? I mean, you're so strong, *Benny.*"

Morgan laughed and relaxed his hold on her. "So now, give me a big kiss," he said.

Peeking around the corner, Travis nearly laughed aloud but caught himself.

"I'll give you something," Suzanne said, her voice instantly turning hard and angry, "but it won't be a kiss, you moron." His brain diluted with two bottles of whiskey, Morgan reacted slowly. Before he could figure out what she meant, Suzanne swung her leg back and, throwing it forward with as much force as she could, rammed the front of her foot against his crotch.

A loud *whoof* blew from Morgan's lips, his eyes turned as big and white as two china saucers, his cheeks puffed, and his entire face turned purple. Then, Ben Morgan sagged to the ground, holding his groin with both hands and wailing. He began to rock back and forth, tears streaming from his face and a series of whispered curses spouting from his lips.

"Next time, Mr. Morgan," Suzanne said, "pick on somebody your own size. Or at least somebody who wants your attentions. I don't!" With that, Suzanne whirled around and continued on her way to the hotel.

Travis, standing in the doorway of the Black and Howell Building and consumed by its dark shadows, smiled. Suzanne Forteaux definitely knew how to defend her honor.

Chapter Twenty-five

The next morning, Travis called at the hotel for Suzanne but was told by Mavis Beale that she had left earlier with her maid, Addie Hays, and wouldn't be back until late afternoon. Mavis didn't know where they'd gone. Travis smiled, thanked her, and left, swearing to himself. If keeping him running in circles was what her "orders" had been, she was doing a damned good job. Not only was he consumed with worry over her involvement with the Knights, but he had begun to think about what it would be like once she was gone from Virginia City. He didn't like the feeling of emptiness that suddenly loomed up before him.

"I'll be fine," he grumbled to himself as he stomped down the street. "I'll be fine." All he needed was to get her out of his system. He'd do his best to keep her out of trouble when the Knight-robbery mess exploded, and then he'd help her get back home to New Orleans. He felt confident it would be out of sight, out of mind.

Tomorrow night was the last night of her contracted performances at the Mountain Queen. If Lonchet and Morgan were going to pull anything further, it would have to be soon, unless they figured they'd done all they could without getting caught. Somehow he doubted that.

Suzanne was involved in the silver thefts somehow, even if she had been nothing more than a courier of payoffs and instructions, but he needed to talk with her about it before someone else figured out the same thing. And furthermore, Duncan Clyde's death had transformed the whole thing from mere robbery to murder, and she was immersed in this scheme right up to her pretty neck.

Travis's hands clenched into fists at his sides. She was playing a dangerous game, a damned deadly game, and he wanted to know why. What was so important to Suzanne that she would risk her own life? And that her father would let her? Even encourage her? Travis leaned against the pillar in front of the Mountain Queen and, pulling a cheroot from his vest pocket along with a lucifer, scraped the match on the pillar and, cupping it in his hands, lifted the tiny flame to the end of the rolled tobacco. He puffed several times, and then let his mind return to the thoughts it had been mulling over.

He hadn't sensed anything independent in Suzanne seven years ago. She'd been little more than a kid following her father's orders; no spark, no independence, and definitely no passion. *That's* why he'd run, along with the fact that he'd been in love with someone else, someone who had walked away from him. That and because of his father. Thomas Braggette had caused it all; the rumor that Suzanne Forteaux was heavy with Travis's child, the resulting rejection of Travis's fiancée, and, finally, his own need to get away from a father who used his power to control his wife and children. A man who

would rather destroy his sons than let them lead their
own lives. That had been when Travis had finally realized why his older brother Traxton had left home. He
knew he had to do the same in order to survive. If he
hadn't run, if he'd stayed, there was no doubt in his
mind that Thomas Braggette would have beat him
down eventually to his own will, and enjoyed every minute of it.

That thought brought other memories of his father to
mind. The man had been murdered, if not by Henri
Sorbonte, the father of the wives of his two brothers and
a high-ranking member of the KGC, then by some
other member of the Knights. Travis felt certain of that,
and since the murder was most likely due to some illegal
scheme or double cross by his father, he didn't care any
more today than he had nearly a year and a half ago
when it had happened. Unless Clarence Lonchet was
behind it somehow, and that suspicion wasn't as far-
fetched as he might have once thought.

He paused on the boardwalk in front of the Mountain
Queen and looked up and down the street in both directions. The miner's change of shifts had long passed.
Those coming off the night shift had already gone home
to get some sleep. A few drays were tied up to hitching
racks here and there along the thoroughfare as their
drivers unloaded their freight, and another, loaded with
what looked like sacks of flour, was just about to pass by
him. He recognized a few of the men and women making their way along the boardwalks, but it was still too
early and the air too brisk for many of the city's resi-
dents to be out and about. At least the wind had died
down and the sun was shining brightly.

Travis reached into his vest pocket and pulled out a

watch, flipping open its cover with his thumb. Nine o'clock. Where in the hell could Suzanne have gone so early in the morning?

From behind the large front window of the Silver Lady, hidden from view of those on the street by the shadows of the boardwalk's overhanging roof and the swirling gold lettering painted across the window proclaiming the saloon's name, Magnolia watched Travis.

She pulled the pale-ivory batiste of her nightgown's wrap tighter about her. Unlike the Mountain Queen, which stayed open twenty-four hours a day, Magnolia closed her Silver Lady at four o'clock every morning and didn't reopen until noon, claiming she couldn't sleep with the ruckus the miners caused when in the saloon.

Her eyes traveled to Travis's vest as he pulled out his watch, then moved back up to his face. He had been hers now for well over a year, totally hers, paying attention to none of the other girls in town, not even Miss High and Mighty Julia Bullette. Magnolia scoffed silently. Julia Bullette, queen of the Virginia City whores. All the men loved Julia, though Magnolia didn't understand why. The woman wasn't really pretty. Magnolia felt a gnawing ache of longing as she saw the sun reflect off Travis's dark hair. Julia might be able to claim every other man in town as a customer, but she couldn't claim Travis. The thought gave Magnolia a moment's satisfaction—until she remembered that Travis hadn't been with her lately, either. Not since Suzanne Forteaux had come to town and Travis had suddenly found no time for Magnolia. Jealousy burned hot within her breast.

But in a few more days, she wouldn't have to worry about Suzanne Forteaux anymore. Magnolia smiled and felt a delicious sense of anticipation and satisfaction. Soon there would no longer be a Suzanne Forteaux.

While Suzanne sauntered about Sarah Janeen's millinery shop, trying on hats and looking over various gloves, veils, and ribbons, Addie excused herself, saying she had spotted Hank and wanted to speak with him a moment. It was a lie, and a blatant one Suzanne could easily see through if she chanced a glance out the window, but she didn't. Suzanne wasn't really even paying attention to what her maid said, and Addie felt safe that Suzanne wouldn't notice Hank wasn't actually anywhere around. As she hurried down the street, Addie glanced back over her shoulder at the millinery and, satisfied that Suzanne wasn't watching her, hurried into the telegraph office.

Too many things were happening and she needed help. She couldn't follow everyone at the same time. She'd watched Suzanne pass a note to Hanson Jones of the Savage Mining Company, but she'd also noticed Travis Braggette watching Suzanne from a distance. Then she'd seen Suzanne pass something to John Sabot of the Chollar Mining Company, and again Travis had been watching, along with Clarence Lonchet. She had her own suspicions about Clarence, but what did Travis's presence mean? Was he watching to make certain Suzanne did as she was supposed to do? Or was he spying on her? Was he a government spy? And if so, for what side, Union or Confederate. If Union, then why didn't she know about it? And if Confederate, why would he be spying on Suzanne and Clarence?

Addie knew Travis's family was from Louisiana and that his brothers were all enlisted in the Confederacy, but there had been more than one instance of brother fighting against brother, one wearing blue, one gray.

Then last night she'd seen Ben Morgan attack Suzanne. But had it really been an attack? Or just a ruse to cover the transfer of paper? Or information?

And of course there was Clarence, that little weasel of a man. She hadn't really seen him do anything wrong, but she was convinced he was behind whatever was brewing. He seemed to be holding something over Suzanne, making her do what he ordered. The way he talked to her, the few times Addie had been able to hear, was more threatening than friendly. And he seemed to frequent Magnolia Rochelle's Silver Lady an awful lot, though he never went there until quite late. Sometimes just before her manager closed the doors for the night. And more times than not, when he went to the Silver Lady, he didn't return to the hotel that night at all. That in itself wouldn't have been suspect, since every man liked to take up with a whore now and again, except that Magnolia Rochelle wasn't a whore. She was a woman with a two-thousand-dollar reward on her head, posted by Missouri for kidnapping freedmen and transporting them to Mississippi to sell as slaves.

Abram Lyle looked up from his desk as Addie stepped into the room, bringing with her a swirl of crisp morning air through the doorway.

"Good morning," she said cheerfully. "I need to send a telegram."

"Yes, ma'am," Lyle responded, walking to the counter where Addie stood waiting. "You've come to the right place." He chuckled softly at his own comment and slid a piece of paper and writing quill across the counter to her. "You just put down whatever you want, ma'am, and I'll send it."

Addie took the paper and, addressing it quickly, wrote out her message:

Lincoln Hays
Philadelphia, Pennsylvania
Dear Linc,—Something soon—SF all right, I think—Any word on the family man?—How's David doing?—I might need company—can you come soon?—Addie.

Abram stared at the note, then looked back up at Addie. "Short and sweet, huh?" "Yes," she answered, wishing he'd just send it without comment. If she wasn't in such a hurry she might have considered waiting until night and breaking into the telegraph office to send the damned thing herself.

"Note to your family? Letting them know everything's all right here, huh?"

"Yes." She smiled sweetly. "They worry, you know, with the war and all."

Abram nodded and smiled, his wide mouth nearly splitting his face in two. "Can't say as how I blame them."

Addie felt like flicking his protruding Adam's apple with her finger to get him to shut up and just send the message.

"Folks can get crazy sometimes during a war, I guess. Even way up here."

"Can you send the telegram, Mr. Lyle," Addie finally said, hoping she didn't sound too annoyed. "I'm hoping for an immediate answer and I'm rather in a hurry."

"Oh, sure, but I don't know about getting an immediate answer. They'll have to deliver it on the other end, you know. Might take some time." He moved to his desk and, setting down the note, reached for his telegraph transmitter.

"My brother is expecting to hear from me today," Addie said, thankful they'd thought ahead to make up the excuse for an immediate answer, since her message would be transmitted directly to headquarters. "He'll be there to receive my message."

Abram merely nodded and began to tap out the message on his transmitter. Mere seconds after he finished, the machine began to tap out a reply. Addie held her breath, praying Abram Lyle wasn't suspicious. He wrote down the message and, rising, walked to the counter and handed it to her.

"Guess your family's all right, huh? Someone coming to Virginia City to visit with you."

Addie's eyes quickly skimmed the note.

Dear Addie—Family man fine though there are a few complications—David has gone south and settled in. Your brother will arrive in Virginia City tomorrow on stage from San Francisco—Stay well—Linc.

Addie breathed a sigh of relief at the last sentence. Duncan Clyde's murder had unnerved her, and Suzanne's involvement with Clarence, Ben Morgan, and the two mine superintendents, Hanson Jones and John Sabot, had upset her even further. She knew Suzanne was being blackmailed into doing what she was doing. Or at least, she believed so. She had no proof, and she couldn't ask Suzanne without revealing her true identify. But from everything she'd managed to see and overhear, she felt fairly certain that whatever Suzanne was doing, it wasn't because she wanted to.

Addie nearly sighed in relief at reading the note again. Now, at least, she'd have help. Another agent would arrive tomorrow. She had been afraid everything was going to blow up and she'd be the only one around to try and stop it. And she had no doubt that things were going to blow . . . soon.

Stuffing the envelope into her reticule, Addie paid the telegraph operator and hurried back up the street to the millinery. She was relieved to find that Suzanne was still busy trying on an array of hats, veils, and gloves.

"Oh, Addie," Suzanne said gaily, "I'm glad you're back. Come here and help me choose a bonnet."

"I think I like that one," Addie said, pointing to a hat on the table near Suzanne. It was made of dark-blue velvet and adorned with white silk ribbon and feathers. "The color accentuates your eyes."

"You think so?" Suzanne turned back to the mirror and, picking up the hat, settled it atop her head. She studied herself in the mirror for a few seconds and then looked up at Addie. "So, did you catch Hank and have your little talk?"

Addie felt a nervous shiver trip up her back. Why did she have the feeling that Suzanne knew exactly what she'd just done?

* * *

Hank Davis came around the corner just as Addie Hays stepped from the telegraph office. He'd been about to call out to her, then paused. What had she been doing there? He frowned. There was really no reason to suspect her of anything, yet Travis had told him to suspect everyone involved with Georgette Lindsay of *any*thing. He just hated to suspect Addie. He kind of liked her.

Pulling his slouch hat lower onto his forehead, Hank waited until Addie disappeared into the millinery shop up the street, then hurried into the telegraph office.

"Abram, you just send a message?" he asked.

The young clerk look up, puzzled at the question. "Well, yeah, I did. That's my job."

"For Addie Hays?" Hank persisted.

"Well, yeah."

"Let me see it."

Abram shook his head. "Can't do that, Hank. Against the rules, you know?"

"I don't give a damn about the rules, Abram," Hank growled. "Let me see the damned message."

Abram shook his head again. "I told you, Hank, I. . . ."

Hank barged through the waist-high swinging gates that separated the customer side of the counter from Abram's office and stomped to the clerk's desk. "Abram, nobody has to know you showed me that message except you and me. Now come on, it might be a matter of life or death. Show it to me."

"Life or death?" Abram echoed. He shuffled through a pile of papers on his desk. "It didn't seem like that to

me. I mean, such a simple note. But why didn't you say
so, Hank. I mean, maybe it's in code or something." He
found Addie's note and handed it to Hank.

Hank read it quickly, then looked back at the clerk.
"She get an answer?"

"Yeah." Abram plowed into the papers again, found
the answering message, and handed it to Hank. "Came
back almost immediately. She said her brother was waiting for her message and she knew he'd answer right
away, so she waited."

He read it, then, grabbing Addie's note again, stuffed
both pieces of paper into his pocket.

"Hey, you can't take those."

"You'll get them back," Hank said. "Later." He exited the telegraph office, leaving a still sputtering Abram
Lyle behind, and hurried toward the Mountain Queen.

Travis was helping Pete resettle the chairs onto the
floor after having set them on the tabletops so that the
day barkeep could wash the floor.

"Hey, Boss," Hank called. "Got something here you'd
best take a gander at."

Travis walked over to the end of the bar where Hank
had placed the two notes.

"Got these from Abram, the telegraph operator. Miss
Lindsay's maid, Addie, sent that one." He pointed to
Addie's message. "This here one," he pointed to the
other, "was her answer. And it came back real quick
like."

Travis read the notes, then looked at Hank. "I'm not
sure I understand them, Hank. Why is she wiring someone in Pennsylvania when she told me she was from
Virginia?"

Hank shrugged.

Travis looked back at the notes again. "Who's the family man?" he murmured, trying to decipher the note's meaning. "David gone south. Brother will arrive tomorrow from San Francisco." Travis looked at Hank. "Whose brother? Does Addie have a brother?"

Hank shrugged.

"And if she does, why did she wire someone in Pennsylvania asking about her brother, who obviously, from what this says, is in San Francisco?"

"You got me, Boss," Hank said. "We ain't talked about no family."

"Hank, I think there's more to Miss Addie Hays than we know. You've been seeing her, right?"

Hank nodded. "Kind of."

"So what does she need help for?"

Again Hank shrugged.

"See if you can find out, Hank. Find out whatever you can about Addie. Get into her room if you can, preferrably when she's not there." Travis smiled. "Go through her things. Maybe you'll find something that will tell us about what our little Miss Addie Hays is up to."

Chapter Twenty-six

That evening, while Suzanne was on stage and Hank was busy wooing Addie at Cabor's Restaurant, Travis approached Clarence Lonchet and Ben Morgan as the two men sat at the table Morgan had commandeered all week. Travis hadn't had a chance to talk privately with Suzanne yet, but he'd left instructions with Jed that if he was detained elsewhere, the bartender should not allow her to leave the saloon, no matter what. *Hogtie her in place if you have to,* Travis had ordered.

He glanced from Lonchet to Morgan, noting the contrast, not for the first time, in the physical appearance as well as the attire, between the two men. Where Lonchet was diminutive, Morgan was a burly giant of a man. Lonchet dressed impeccably in expensively tailored suits and crisp white shirts, while Morgan looked as if he'd slept in his clothes for the past week, and they hadn't been expensive or well fitting to begin with. Travis pulled a chair away from their table but remained standing. "Mind if I join you, gentlemen?"

The two men looked up at him, surprise and suspicion etched across their faces. Lonchet turned a quick

eye to Morgan, who met it and then, as if a silent message had been transmitted between the two, their gazes
swiveled back to meet Travis's again. Both men instantly
brandished crafty smiles.

"Hell, no, Braggette," Morgan said a little too jo-
vially. He motioned toward the chair Travis's hand
rested on. "Sit yourself down and join us in a drink." He
held his glass up and motioned for a waitress to bring
another for Travis. "I shoulda invited you a long time
ago anyway, hogging your table like this every night.
Come on. Sit down, sit down."

Travis didn't move. Instead, he looked at Clarence.
"Mr. Lonchet?"

"Oh, well, of course," Clarence said, removing his
spectacles and wiping a handkerchief quickly over the
lenses. "Of course, Mr. Braggette. I just assumed you'd
be waiting for . . . uh, *Miss Lindsay.*" He looked toward
Suzanne, who was in the process of descending the
stairs of the stage. She seemed to be singing to one
scruffy miner in particular. "Beautiful girl. Beautiful."
Clarence moved his gaze back to meet Travis's. "And,
well, I know she wouldn't like to hear me telling you
this, but she's very fond of you, Mr. Braggette."

"Good, because I'm very fond of her." He chuckled
derisively. Clarence Lonchet wanted him seduced by
Suzanne, so he'd play along with that for the time being, letting the man believe Suzanne was doing what she
was supposed to be doing. He suspected it might prove
dangerous to Suzanne to do otherwise. "I'm always fond
of a beautiful woman. Especially a . . ." he glanced toward Suzanne again and smiled, ". . . a passionate one."
Travis straightened in his chair and sobered his features.
"But I didn't come here to talk about Miss Lindsay, gen-

tlemen. I have a little business proposition I need to talk over before I can turn my mind to pleasures of . . ." He glanced over his shoulder at Suzanne again for emphasis. The red satin of her gown caught the light of an overhead chandelier and reflected it brilliantly. He felt a stab of desire and fought to quell it. "Well, of that kind," he finished finally, turning back to Morgan and Lonchet. "I'm sure you understand that."

Both remained silent, the words *business proposition* turning them instantly alert and on edge.

Travis settled into the chair and poured himself a drink from the whiskey bottle in the center of the table, then set the half-full shot glass down in front of him. Whiskey was not his drink. But he wanted amiability at this table, camaraderie, and sharing a drink usually helped evoke that feeling.

"Morgan," he began purposely dropping his voice to a conspiratorial tone that would be drowned out by Suzanne's singing and the accompanying piano before it could carry to anyone sitting at the other tables nearby. "Since we've talked, I assume everything between us is out in the open. I know you're a Knight and you know I'm a member."

Morgan nodded and sipped at his whiskey.

Clarence's head jerked around as he shot Ben Morgan a scathing look. "You admitted that?" he spat, looking as if he was gazing at a misbehaving child. "You admitted it?" His fingers gripped the arms of the chair and his face took on the color of a ripe tomato. He looked ready to explode. "You just out and out admitted you were a Knight?"

"Yeah, so?" Morgan challenged, glaring back at

Lonchet. "I figured we done enough pussyfooting around."

Travis expected Clarence Lonchet to back down from the challenge, but found himself surprised.

"Fools," Clarence mumbled. "That's what this country is made up of, fools. And you, my friend," he jabbed a forefinger into Morgan's chest, "are their king." He shook his head and turned away. "Fools," he muttered again. "Fools." Fury and outrage registered clearly on his squirrelly features.

Travis stared at Clarence, impressed in spite of himself. "Lonchet, I wasn't certain about you, but since you have been keeping close company with Mr. Morgan here, and Miss Lindsay, too, I'm pretty confident you're also a member, which means I should be able to trust you."

Clarence merely stared at him, refusing to respond to the statement one way or the other.

"Have it your way, Lonchet," Travis said. He chuckled again and leaned back in his chair, assuming a pose of confident casualness. "I wanted to get straight to business, but," he shrugged, "if this will make you feel better." He stared at Clarence for a long moment before speaking again. "Close . . ." he said, having decided that using one of the KGC's codes to identify one Knight to another would calm down the man and convince both Lonchet and Morgan of his sincerity when he finally sprung his plan on them. He only hoped the one he'd chosen wasn't outdated.

Clarence's eyes narrowed slightly. "The . . ." he said.

"Door . . ." Travis added, feeling a wave of relief.

"On . . ." Clarence snapped.

"Union . . ." Travis said.

"Tyranny," Clarence finished.

Travis smiled and extended his hand to Clarence. "I believe we can trust each other now?"

Clarence nodded and accepted Travis's hand.

"Morgan?" Travis said, turning to the burly blond man. "What about you?"

"Hell, Braggette, I never did have a problem with you. The judge said you were okay, and that was enough for me, so forget about spouting off another poem."

Travis felt a tickle of apprehension at Morgan's words. If the judge had said he was all right, he'd eat his damned hat. Morgan was lying. Knowing Judge David Terry, he had most likely said exactly the opposite, unless he hadn't said a thing and this scheme was indeed all Lonchet and Morgan's.

"So, Mr. Braggette," Clarence said, "what is this business you have to discuss with us?"

"Well, I'll come right to the point, Lonchet. I know what you two are up to." Travis said it calmly, confidently, then sat back, watched them, and waited for their reactions.

Two sets of eyebrows instantly soared skyward, paused, and quickly dropped back down. Each man made a visible effort not to look at the other. Lonchet began to fiddle with his spectacles again. Morgan downed another shot of whiskey.

Neither would make very good poker players, Travis thought. He nearly chuckled but maintained a stony face instead and continued to wait. He looked at the glass of whiskey in front of him but didn't reach for it.

"Really?" Clarence said finally. "You know what

we're up to. And just what would that be, Mr. Braggette, pray tell?"

"You're robbing silver from the mines and shipping it south, Lonchet. For the cause. You've been bribing the night superintendents of the Chollar and Savage mines and a couple of drivers to bring out some wagons of ore and transfer them onto pack mules. Then a few of your men take it over the mountains. I assume into California and then south somehow. Maybe the same way, maybe by ship. Am I right?" He smiled amiably.

"Let's say you are," Clarence said softly. He slipped the spectacles back onto his face, settling them on the bridge of his nose and staring back at Travis through the thick, polished glass. "So what?"

"Okay, let's say I'm right." Travis smiled. "I could turn you both in to the sheriff, who, in case you weren't aware, is one dyed-in-the-wool Union man. I'm sure once Sheriff Morrow has made it known what you two have been up to, which now includes murder since we all know Duncan Clyde didn't shoot himself, there are plenty of folks around here that would be just itching to get a rope around some good old Confederate necks. Especially one that belonged to someone who killed a freighter. I'm also sure our good sheriff would try his damndest to uphold his authority and prevent that. But he wouldn't succeed."

Clarence gulped and touched the gold silk cravat at his neck.

"Or I could offer you both a way to get rich." Travis felt a thrill of satisfaction at the gleam of greed he saw instantly spark within each man's eyes. "Without taking any more risk than you're taking now," he added.

Both sat up straight and leaned forward against the table.

"Rich?" Morgan echoed.

"How?" Clarence demanded.

Travis held up a hand. "Are you in?"

"Why do you need us?" Clarence asked instead of answering Travis's question. "Why not use some of your local boys? Your friends?"

Travis smiled shrewdly. "First of all, Lonchet, a smart man doesn't do this kind of business with his friends. If it goes sour, it's much easier to kill an enemy than a friend."

Clarence started, and his eyes widened.

"Secondly," Travis continued, "the Knights here in Virginia City are very loyal to the Confederacy. If the silver is going to go, then they want it to go to the cause. *I* want it to go into my pocket. I'm getting kind of tired of living up here on this mountain, you know? And there's another reason I figured we should join forces on this one."

"Yes," Clarence said. "And what is that?"

"I figure since you two are still in town, you're not done here. I also figure that you just might be planning on robbing another load."

Lonchet and Morgan looked at each other.

"And if that was the case, then we've got a problem. Or rather, *you've* got a problem."

"We do?" Clarence asked. "And what would that be?"

"Well, if you two are planning on robbing a load tomorrow night, then you'd be interfering with my plans, and I wouldn't like that. I'd probably have to kill you."

"We weren't planning another robbery," Morgan said.

Clarence shot him a scathing glower, then turned to Travis. "That is," he whispered, "if we had pulled a robbery in the first place." His eyes darted to the other tables to make certain no one was paying attention to their conversation.

"Good. So, are you in on this?" Travis asked, not believing Suzanne's shrimp of a manager for one second.

"If it's a plan I think will work," Clarence said, "then yes, we'll consider it. Except how do we know this isn't some kind of trap, Braggette? How do we know you're not a Union agent? Or even a spy for the Knights?"

Morgan nodded.

"You don't." Travis smiled. "But I don't think my family would be too pleased to hear that accusation. We've always taken great pride in being Southerners, and still do as far as I know. And anyway, Lonchet, aren't members of the KGC supposed to trust one another?"

Clarence, his lips pursed tightly, merely stared.

"Yeah, okay," Morgan said. "So we trust one another. Let's cut out all this gabbing about trust and loyalty and crap, okay? What's your plan, Braggette?"

"The Gould and Curry Mining Company is planning to ship out a double load tomorrow night headed for the Union government, and it's going out by way of the Gate."

"Son of a bitch," Clarence muttered.

"And the Knights of Virginia City are planning on robbing it for the Confederacy. Though only a few members are involved. Less than a handful, really."

"So how in the hell does that put money in my pocket?" Morgan demanded.

"I'm leading them, Morgan," Travis said, drawing out the words patiently. "They'll rob the freighters, then transport the ore to another place, just like you did." He chuckled. "We like your style, actually. Anyway, we'll transfer it, like you did, and my men will return to town. Later, we'll transfer it again. Only it won't all go in the same direction. The Confederacy will get half of the shipment, and we split the other half."

"How much is that?" Morgan asked. "Per man?"

Travis shrugged. "I figure probably a million dollars each, maybe more."

"Why?" Clarence snapped. His beady little eyes peered through his spectacles at Travis.

"Why?" Travis repeated.

"Yes," Clarence said. "Why do you want us in on this with you, Braggette? If you've got other men, other Knights, why do you need us?"

Travis sighed, as if impatient. "I told you. The Knights are doing this for the cause, Lonchet. We wouldn't be." He shrugged. "Well, not entirely." Travis glanced over his shoulder at Suzanne, who had returned to the stage, then turned back to Clarence Lonchet and smiled. "I should congratulate you, Lonchet. I never would have believed Suzanne Forteaux could hold a roomful of miners mesmerized. She was kind of skinny and plain the last time I saw her. And shy." He smiled, letting it sink in to the tiny man's consciousness that Travis was aware that Lonchet knew of Travis and Suzanne's previous relationship and that coming to the Mountain Queen had not been a coincidence. "But, getting back to business. I also know that in a few days you'll both be gone from Virginia City and I won't have to worry about getting a bullet in my back to keep me quiet."

"One of us could come back," Clarence suggested with a cunning sneer.

"You could," Travis agreed, "if you wanted to die."

Clarence stared long and hard at Travis before he finally spoke again. "So we do this, and then we part for good."

Travis nodded.

"Then we're understood," Clarence said.

"Good." Travis nodded.

"Good," Morgan echoed.

"We'll meet tomorrow night." Travis pushed back his chair and rose, the glass of whiskey before him still untouched. "Midnight. Precisely."

"Where?" Clarence asked.

"Here," Travis said. "At the Queen."

Clarence shook his head. "No. Olmer's General Store, at the southern end of town," he countered. "We'll meet there."

Travis shrugged. Where they met really didn't matter. "Whatever you say, Lonchet." Travis turned and walked back to the bar.

Ben Morgan poured himself another drink.

Clarence Lonchet quickly left the saloon.

Travis glanced at the sheriff who slowly rose from his seat and followed Clarence out the door.

Travis entered Suzanne's dressing room behind the stage of the Mountain Queen and sat down on the settee situated against one wall. Propping one arm up along the top of the back cushion, he absently fingered the rough, multicolored brocade covering. He could hear Suzanne singing her last number, and he sighed deeply. He'd thought about her most of last night, when he had lain in his bed futilely trying to sleep. To be truthful with himself, he had to admit he'd thought of her every night, and every day, since they'd made love. No, since the moment she'd stepped off the stagecoach. She was hardly ever out of his thoughts. Travis opened his eyes and stared up at the plain painted ceiling. A soft curse slipped from his lips and he damned his lack of self-control. Somehow, without his even being aware of it, he'd begun to care about Suzanne Forteaux, and that scared the hell out of him.

He didn't want to care for her. He didn't want to care for any woman, not as anything more than a friend. He'd tried that once and it hadn't worked. Love meant trust, but in the end Lisa hadn't trusted him. Instead, she'd believed the rumors. And Suzanne certainly didn't trust him; she'd already proven that by refusing to confide in him and tell him what Lonchet was holding over her. No, love wasn't for him.

But he couldn't just walk away from her, either. She was involved with Lonchet and Morgan, and with the Knights, and any way he looked at it, that meant she was in danger. He wanted to believe she was an innocent party to their schemings. He wanted that more than anything. But *was* she innocent? That was the question that kept gnawing at him. *Was* she innocent? Or was she a direct accomplice, a willing participant? Perhaps even an eager one? Travis found it hard to believe, hard even to contemplate, but he had to consider the possibility.

He sighed. For the past several days, he had forced himself to think as little as possible about Suzanne except for her involvement with the Knights. He'd tried to concentrate on Lonchet and Morgan, and on the silver thefts. The town was still divided into two factions, and those loyal to the Union seemed to be holding staunch to their belief that Travis was the new head of the Virginia City Knights. Thanks, he guessed, to Charlie Mellroy. Now that rumor possibly had played into his plans. It had helped him convince some of the boys to go along with this scheme. Now all he had to do was pray he was right about Lonchet and Morgan and that his plan worked.

He was suddenly aware that Suzanne's song had ended and the piano music had stopped. A second later, the men in the saloon erupted into a series of loud cheers, clapping, and foot stomps. They called for another song, goading, pleading, begging with her, and she complied, singing them "The Yellow Rose of Texas."

Travis thought the Queen's roof was going to come down. He'd never heard such noise. The men stomped the floor with their heavy boots, banged their whiskey and beer glasses on the table, and sang along with Suzanne at the top of their lungs. And when the song was done, they cheered her again.

But this time, even though they begged just as fervently, she didn't sing another number. Travis heard her footsteps as the cheering died down and she approached the door to her dressing room. He sat up and watched the door. It opened, and Suzanne stepped into the small room. Travis rose to his feet. Suzanne turned and almost walked straight into his arms.

"Suzanne," he said, her name rolling off of his tongue

in a deep, sensuous drawl. His hands moved to clasp her upper arms. The heat of longing filled him instantly, coiled deep within him, hungry, attempting to wipe every other thought and consideration from his consciousness but his desire to take her again.

Suzanne pulled away and, brushing past him, hurried toward her dressing table. She began to remove the large feather-and-jeweled brooch that was pinned to one side of her hair. "I'm sorry, Travis," she muttered. "I didn't know you were in here." At the mere touch of his hands on her bare arms, her heart had tripped into a thudding beat that left her nearly breathless. She wanted so desperately to be held by him, to feel his body press against hers again, to taste his lips as they claimed hers, but she couldn't let that happen. Maybe later she could come back, when this whole horrible mess was over, when Clarence told her where Brett was. When she found her brother and knew he was safe, then she could come back.

"Suzanne, I want you to stay on at the Mountain Queen," Travis said. He ached to reach out for her and pull her into his embrace. "Extend your engagement beyond tomorrow night."

She heard his words, and though she wanted to agree to his request more than anything, she remained silent, damning the trembling that had invaded her fingers. She fumbled with the hair pin and stared at her image in the mirror. What was she thinking about? Stay? That was impossible. Come back? Why? He didn't really want her, not in a permanent way, except maybe as a singer at his saloon. And perhaps a body in his bed. Hadn't he just said that? She was nothing more than a draw to bring the customers and their money into his establishment. That was what he truly wanted. Not her. He didn't want her. He'd made that clear seven years ago, and in case she'd forgotten, he had just made it clear again.

Suzanne suddenly felt like ramming a curled fist into the image staring back at her from the mirror. She had no more sense about life now than she'd had seven years ago. At least where Travis Braggette was concerned. He hadn't even told her he cared for her, and in spite of that she'd dropped into his bed like a swooning ninny and let him have his way with her. Even then, he still hadn't said he cared. And now he had the audacity to ask her to stay on and continue singing in his saloon. She'd come here because of Brett, and to seek revenge on Travis, and instead she'd yet to secure the information Clarence claimed he had about Brett's whereabouts, and she'd fallen in love with Travis all over again. She whirled around to face him, anger melding with sadness giving her a strength she hadn't been aware she possessed.

"Stay?" she said, smiling, though her tone seemed to drip ice.

"Yes, I want you to stay. Here. At the Mountain Queen." He hadn't intended to say it like that. His words sounded cold, impersonal, and stilted.

"Stay at the Mountain Queen?" she echoed. "As Georgette Lindsay?"

He was making a mess of this, he knew but he couldn't say the words he sensed she wanted to hear. "Suzanne, I . . ."

"Thank you, Travis," Suzanne said coldly, cutting him off, "but no, I think I'll be leaving on the stage the day after tomorrow, as I'd planned."

"To go where?"

Suzanne looked up at him, taken aback at his curt demand. She had no answer, since she didn't know yet what Clarence would tell her of Brett's whereabouts.

Surprising her further, Travis reached out and pulled her into his arms. "Suzanne, I know you're involved with the Knights."

She stiffened and turned her face away.

"Suzanne," Travis said, his tone hard and demanding. "Talk to me."

"I haven't done anything." She tried to twist away from him. "Let me go, Travis."

"I know you've been acting as a courier. You're in trouble, and I want to help."

Shocked at his words, she placed her hands on his arms and pulled back from him, but not out of his arms. She stared up at him. "How . . . how did you know?"

"I followed you." He smiled. "The first time was more by accident. The second time wasn't. I saw you meet Sabot and Jones and hand both of them an envelope, then I followed them and later had a talk with each man."

"But all I did was deliver the envelopes. That's all. I didn't do anything else."

"Maybe, but both men swear that you're the only contact they've had. They've been helping to steal silver, Suzanne, from the mines." He grasped her shoulders and looked intently into her eyes. "Don't you realize how much trouble you could be in? You're the person who brought them their orders and the money. You're the one the Knights implicated in all of this, purposely, and you're the one who will be blamed if it all comes to light."

Suzanne felt a chill of fear. "But I didn't have anything to do with the robberies."

"And murder," Travis said.

Suzanne gasped. "No."

"Suzanne . . ."

"I just delivered the envelopes." She tried to twist away from him again as tears filled her eyes, but he held her firm. "Just the envelopes, Travis, that's all. I didn't even know what was in them."

"Who gave them to you?"

"Clarence."

"Did anyone ever see him give them to you? Addie, your maid, did she ever see him hand you one of the envelopes?"

Suzanne shook her head. "No, Clarence was always cautious and made certain we were alone."

Travis sighed and released his hold on her. "The Knights are responsible for the robberies, Suzanne, and the murder of Duncan Clyde."

She nodded. "I had begun to suspect, but . . ." she shrugged her shoulders, "there was nothing I could do."

"They've put you in a position to take the blame if something goes wrong."

Suzanne shook her head. "But I only delivered the envelopes. They did everything else. I didn't even know what they were planning."

"There's nothing linking you to the Knights, Suzanne, except for your association with Lonchet and Morgan. Proving that they're Knights could be impossible. Believe me, I know. I also have a hunch they'd disappear very quickly and leave you for the authorities if things started to sour."

"But I could tell the authorities about them, about

Clarence. I could tell them they were Knights and that Clarence gave me the envelopes to deliver."

"Have you delivered envelopes in other towns, Suzanne?"

"Yes. Several."

"And Addie never saw any of this?"

"No. I told you, Clarence was very careful."

"And Morgan?"

"He usually shows up several days after we're already in town. I don't know what he does. I guess he's Clarence's partner. Maybe his bodyguard."

"His name isn't really Ben Morgan," Travis said.

Suzanne looked at him, puzzled.

"It's Ben Mordaine."

Her eyes widened. "Of the New Orleans Mordaines?"

Travis nodded.

"He's the older son who's wanted for murder?"

"Yes." Suddenly, another memory sprung to his mind, unbidden, and seemingly inconsequential until he dwelt on it for a moment. Ben Mordaine had been a good friend of Jay Peychaud's, and Jay had married Travis's little sister Teresa, and then disappeared on their wedding night. A frown tugged at his brow. And, almost two years later Jay Peychaud was still missing. Could there be a connection?

Suzanne stared up at him, terrified now at the picture he had painted of her situation.

He clasped her arms again and pulled her to him. "Tell me what they're holding over you, Suzanne, so I can help you. What are they using to make you do this?"

Chapter Twenty-seven

Tears suddenly filled Suzanne's eyes as she looked up at Travis. "I can't tell you," she said, her voice breaking on the words. The tears spilled over and ran down her cheeks, rivers of moisture that glistened silver in the glow of the room's lamp. She sobbed then and shook her head as he stared at her. "I can't, really, I can't."

"Damn you, Suzanne," he growled softly.

He stared down at her for what seemed endless minutes, a fleeting yet dragging span of time that encompassed both the moment and the eternity, pulling together their yesterdays, todays, and all their tomorrows. Travis felt the familiar burning ache inside that always came to him whenever he was near Suzanne, felt that overwhelming urge to pull her into his arms, against his body, and capture her lips with his. He was lost to her, he had known it, had sensed its inevitability, but hadn't wanted to admit it to himself. He had wanted to fight it, and couldn't. That denial was no longer an option to him.

His hands reached out for her, encircled her waist and pressed her against him. Steely arms tightened about her in a demanding embrace and crushed her body to the long length of his, fitting curve to plane, line to line. His lips caught hers in a hungry kiss, his tongue plunged into her mouth and filled it, purposely arousing her passion and mercilessly teasing her senses, each caress of his tongue, his hands, demanding she respond with the same compelling force, the same need and hunger, that threatened to devour him.

In the cold, stark light of reality, Suzanne could refuse him, could say no to him, even force herself to say good-bye to him, but not when he held her in his arms, not when his lips ravished hers and the touch of his body turned her own to an inferno of need. She could feel his arousal press against her skirts, against her stomach, and the ache of her own burning within her, responding to him, wanting him.

Travis knew what he was doing was wrong, for both of them, but he no longer had a choice. The emotional bent of his heart and body had overruled the logical force of his mind, and it refused to pay further heed. Suzanne wanted a normal life, he knew. She wanted, deserved, a house she could call home, a solid, upstanding husband who went off to a respectable job each morning and came home each evening for dinner. She deserved to have children, to live in a normal city, shop at all the best shops, and have a social life that included visits from all the right people.

His tongue plunged deeper into her mouth as his arms tightened about her, crushing her to him in an embrace that was filled with the fear of losing her.

Once he might have been able to give her all of that, if he had stayed in New Orleans, if he had married her seven years ago. But he hadn't, and he couldn't give her those things now, because they weren't what he wanted.

Beyond the passion that controlled him, Travis's mind spun with logic. He owned and operated a saloon in one of the rowdiest mining towns west of the Mississippi River. He was a gambler himself, by choice, a man who lived in a suite of rooms atop his own saloon, bedded the same whore every Friday night, drank a little too much liquor, smoked too many cheroots, and was deadly with a gun. He was not the same man who Suzanne had known seven years ago, not the same *boy* she had promised to marry. He couldn't give her the things she wanted from him, but neither could he deny himself tasting her passion one last time.

He let his lips travel down the long ivory column of her neck, press to the shallow valley at its base, and skim across the swelling mountain of flesh revealed above the plunging neckline of her gown. Logic and reason disappeared finally, consumed by his desire for Suzanne, his need to love and be loved, if only for a few moments.

Her arms slipped around his neck, holding him tight to her as she kissed him with all the fervor, all the passion with which he kissed her. She had come to Virginia City, to Travis, seeking vengeance, and instead been betrayed by her own heart. He was all she'd ever wanted.

Suzanne felt his fingers release the buttons at the back of her gown, felt his hands slide its sleeves from her shoulders, felt him unhook the waistband of the crinolines beneath her skirt. Satin, muslin, and lace, with small encouragement from his hands, fell to the floor to encircle her feet.

He wrapped her in his embrace again, his lips continuing their assault upon her. As he held her tightly pressed to him, Travis lowered them both to the carpeted floor. In spite of the urgency that gnawed at his body, he moved slowly, caressing and kissing her as he removed the last flimsy scraps of clothing that covered her and tossed them aside. Then, pushing himself up on one elbow, he stared down at her, his eyes raking over the lithe body that lay beside him. Her breasts were full, her nipples pebbled with passion into rosy peaks, and the tiny breadth of her waist was an enticement to his hands. His gaze dropped lower, to the ivory skin that stretched taut across her stomach, her hips, her thighs, and proved a tantalizing invitation, while the small triangle of dark hair between her thighs promised the eventual treasure.

He felt his own body tighten and grow almost unbearably hard with need. Bending forward, his mouth closed over one taut nipple. He laved it teasingly with is tongue, flicking, tasting, caressing it, while his other hand moved sensuously over the rest of her body, sliding over the curve of her hip, moving down the line of her thigh, up the inner thigh. His fingers slipped through the short dark curls of hair that made up that deliciously teasing triangle.

Suzanne gasped and clung to him, her body arching involuntarily upward toward his touch, silently begging for him to continue the sweet torment, pleading with him to take her, to join them together as he had before.

Travis pushed away from her.

Suzanne's eyes flew open, the sudden absence of his arms, his lips, instilling her with an instant ache of loss she found unable to endure.

Travis ripped off his jacket and flung it aside, then

unbuckled his holster and let it fall behind him. His fingers deftly unbuttoned his trousers.

Suzanne reached out for him. Her mouth sought his hungrily and, as her arms encircled his neck and pulled her to him, her fingers became lost within the dark curls of his head.

Travis felt a warmth of rapture invade his body, a beautiful, sensuous feeling like none he had ever experienced, a satisfying sense of right, of belonging, of having finally come home. Every other woman he had ever bedded, including Magnolia Rochelle, vanished from Travis's memory as he kissed Suzanne. None had ever touched him as deeply as she did, or invaded his every thought and desire. He lifted himself over her as his hand slid between her thighs.

Travis walked beside Suzanne toward the hotel. Both were silent, preoccupied with their individual thoughts, desires, and fears. He held her hand safely tucked within his as they moved down the boardwalk, crossed the street, and entered the hotel lobby. He held back at the bottom of the stairs. Suzanne, having already mounted the first step, felt his hesitation and turned. Her face was level with his.

"I have something I have to do," Travis said. His hands slipped beneath her cape. "Will you join me for breakfast?"

"Yes," she whispered, and brushed her lips across his.

He released her then, before the devastating hunger she always aroused in his body could overwhelm him once more. He had thought, perhaps hoped, that making love to her again would satiate that hunger permanently, but it hadn't. He wanted her just as badly now. Travis watched her walk up the stairs and disappear around the corner. It didn't really matter, though. It couldn't. Nothing was going to change the fact that he didn't want the same things out of life a woman like Suzanne Forteaux wanted. He wasn't husband or father material.

Pulling his watch from the pocket of his vest, a quick glance confirmed that it was later than he'd thought. Morrow might not even be in his office now, and if he was, he was probably asleep. But rather than a determent to his plans, that thought only reinforced and encouraged them. Travis smiled. If the good sheriff had already retired, he could just damned well get up.

Travis left the hotel and walked the few short blocks to the sheriff's office and jailhouse. He didn't bother to knock on the door. Instead, he swung it open and walked into the room. The sound of his boots on the wooden floor filled the small front office. He paused, hooked his thumbs over the gun holster that wrapped around his hips, and looked down at Liam. "Where's Morrow?" he asked, his tone harsh and demanding.

"Asleep," the young deputy answered, his tone surly. He didn't bother to move from his chair or lift the brim of his hat from over his face.

"Get him," Travis ordered curtly.

Liam suddenly stiffened. He reached up and pushed the hat back, then gulped loudly and stared wide-eyed up at Travis. "Sorry, Mr. Braggette, I didn't know it was you."

The deputy bolted to his feet, and the chair snapped back into place with a loud creak. Liam hurried across the room and opened the door that led to the jail cells at the rear of the building. "Hey, Sheriff," he called into the dark hall. "Mr. Braggette wants to see you again."

After a few seconds of rustling sounds, blended with a series of distinct grumbles and a cell door clanging shut, Kurt Morrow appeared at the door looking as if a freight train had run over him. His clothes were badly disheveled, his hair, what little there was of it, hung limp and uncombed, and the bags under his eyes had turned to loose pouches. He looked at Travis with bloodshot eyes.

"Did something happen?" Sheriff Morrow asked, sleep still heavy in his voice.

"I thought you were supposed to be watching Lonchet and Sabot," Travis said.

"Lonchet's bedding down at the Silver Lady. He went in about three and never came back out. Maggie's closed up now, so I figure he's in there till morning, but I got a man watching the place just in case."

"And Sabot?"

"He's on his shift, just like he's supposed to be. Got a man watching him, too."

"Good."

"So," the sheriff repeated, "did something happen?"

"Not yet," Travis said easily. He didn't know whether he felt more like laughing or swearing. The man was as poor a sight for a lawman as he'd ever seen. "But something is going to happen and I figure it'll be soon, so if you're not too busy, I thought we could discuss it and form ourselves a plan. Then maybe we'll catch these gentlemen in the act."

The sheriff turned to his deputy. "Liam, run on down to Cabor's and get us a pot of coffee. And tell Dolly to make sure it's strong, you hear? That stuff you brought back last time tasted more like dishwater than coffee."

The young deputy sped toward the door. "Sure thing, Sheriff. Right away."

"You've got him trained pretty well," Travis said. He took one of the chairs that faced the sheriff's desk.

"He wants my job," Morrow said. "Thinks being my lackey will help him get it. Fool. Ain't got the brains of a mule." He yanked his chair up to his desk.

Travis felt like saying that he didn't think the sheriff had any more brains than that, either, but he reconsidered. He might think the sheriff was a slob, that he was pretty lax about his duties and that he let some offenders go when he most likely shouldn't, but he wasn't stupid. Lazy, but not stupid.

"So, what's this about something going to happen, Braggette? What? And When?"

"The Chollar is moving a double load down the mountain tomorrow night."

"Since when do they move double loads?"

"Since I asked them to," Travis said.

"Yeah? How come?"

"I thought we'd set ourselves up a little trap."

Morrow smiled. "Good idea. So, what's going to happen?"

Travis pulled a cheroot from the inside breast pocket of his jacket, slipped it into his mouth, and lit it. "Well," he said, and puffed several times to draw the flame to the tobacco, "it's going to be robbed."

"Shit."

Travis chuckled. "Now, don't go getting yourself all riled up, Sheriff. You're going to be there to stop it."

The sheriff's brows rose and a look of pleasure lit his face. "Yeah?"

"Yes. I'm meeting Clarence Lonchet and Ben Morgan, along with several of their cohorts, I expect, at Olmer's General Store tomorrow night at midnight."

"Lonchet? The manager of that songbird you brought in?"

"Yes."

"And Morgan's that newspaper fella?"

Travis nodded.

"You sure they're behind the robberies? And Duncan's murder?"

"Yes, but there's no way to prove it, and the only way we're going to get them is to catch them in the act."

Morrow nodded. "Yeah, catch them in the act."

"Which means we set them up."

The sheriff smiled. "Sounds good to me."

"Good. Now, listen. The shipment pulls away from the Gould and Curry just a little after I meet Lonchet and Morgan at Olmer's. They think they're joining up with me and a couple of Virginia City Knights to rob the freighters and split the money."

"But they ain't?" the sheriff said, his eyes narrowing in suspicion.

"Of course not, because you and several deputized men are going to be hidden at Devil's Gate waiting for us. You stay well out of sight and back from the pass so that we can set up our ambush there. When the wagons show up, we'll come into view and order the drivers down. They've been filled in on what's happening, so they'll know to get out of sight fast. They won't put up a fight. When the drivers are out of the way, that's when you and your boys come in to make the arrest."

"There might be shooting," the sheriff said.

"Might be," Travis agreed. "That's why you wait until the drivers are out of the way. And if there *is* shooting," Travis leaned forward across the desk and looked pointedly into the sheriff's eyes, "you just make certain your aim is at them, Sheriff, not me."

Morrow smiled craftily.

"And in case you figure your aim might be a little shaky from all the excitement, I'd suggest you remember one thing, Sheriff.. . . ." Travis's features hardened. "I've taken a few precautions of my own, one being to alert some very important people as to what this plan is all about, what is supposed to happen. Me getting killed is not one of the planned events. Now," his stare was sharp and intent, "you do understand that, don't you?"

The sheriff remained silent, dislike for Travis gleaming in his eyes.

Chapter Twenty-eight

Travis walked into the sitting room that adjoined his bedroom and doubled as his office. He moved to stand at the window that offered him a view of C Street below, pulling aside the sheer lace panel but making certain to stand to one side of the window so that no one outside could see him. The stage was due any time now, bringing in whoever it was that was coming from San Francisco to meet Addie Hays, and he wanted to see just who that was.

No sooner had the thought entered his mind than the unmistakable rumblings of the arriving stagecoach met his ears. Travis realized instantly that, although he could see the stagecoach from this vantage point, he would not be able to see the debarking passengers because of the boardwalk's overhanging roof. Moving quickly, he left his rooms and ran downstairs and to the saloon's front window.

Addie was nowhere to be seen.

Two passengers debarked. The first Travis recognized as a vendor who came to Virginia City every three or four months. He carried his sample valise in one hand.

The other man Travis had never seen before. He was tall, well over six feet, and as lanky as a newly planted birch tree. His suit looked store bought and both the sleeves and the trouser legs were just a hair too short for his long limbs. Travis studied him with assessing eyes. The man had the face of a goat. A pair of thick spectacles rested on the hump of his nose, and a bowler sat propped stiffly on his head.

"If that's a government agent, then I'm Abraham Lincoln," Travis muttered to himself. Maybe the man really was Addie Hays's brother.

From across the street Magnolia Rochelle, standing beside the window of her saloon and sheathed by shadow, also watched the arrival of the stage. But, unlike Travis, she recognized the tall man who descended the coach.

"Zachary Kittle," she mumbled, and banged a curled fist against the wall beside the window. "Damn." She hit the wall again. "Damn, damn, damn. That's all we need here now, a damned Federal agent."

Suzanne's last night at the Mountain Queen brought out almost every Virginia City miner who'd seen her perform, and some who hadn't. They crowded into the saloon, happy to be there but grumbling at the prospect of losing the prettiest little songbird the mountain town had ever seen.

Travis stood at the end of the bar as usual. He felt the same as the crowd, only worse, and he didn't know what to do about it. She'd already turned down his request to extend her contract. He had tried again over breakfast that morning to convince her to stay, at least for a little while longer, but she'd said no, and he couldn't offer her anything more permanent than that.

He downed a shot of bourbon and silently ordered himself to shape up. There were other matters he had to see to tonight, and he'd best keep a clear head or he could end up not worrying about anything at all except what he was supposed to say when he got to the pearly gates. Assuming he'd go in that direction. Travis nearly laughed aloud. Hell, with his track record there it was probably better than even odds he'd go the other way.

Half an hour earlier he had noticed Lonchet and Morgan sitting at their usual corner table. Travis glanced again in that direction. The saloon was so crowded, with men standing about the bar near shoulder to shoulder, that he couldn't see across the room to the corner table.

Suzanne came out on stage to a round of thunderous applause and cheering. Travis looked about at the room's inhabitants and then glanced up at the ceiling. The crystal chandeliers were jiggling, their teardrop prisms vibrating as a result of the raucous shouts. Travis prayed the men would stop soon, before crystal prisms began to rain down on everyone in the room like glass arrows.

Hank shouldered his way through the crowd and toward Travis. "Hey, Boss!" he yelled.

"Yeah?" Travis glanced around until he saw Hank. "Anything wrong?"

"No." Hank moved up beside Travis. "I'm on my way out for a while. Told Addie I'd take her to dinner, if that's okay. You won't need me till later, right?"

Travis shook his head. "Just make sure you're there on time, Hank. Midnight."

"Sure thing, Boss. You can count on me." He started to turn away, then paused when Travis called him back.

"Anything on Addie, Hank?"

"Nah. I don't think she's anything other than what she says, Boss, a maid. She told me she grew up in Virginia. Her parents are sharecroppers. She went to work for Miss Lindsay about six months ago. Before that she worked for some family in Virginia named Dulcet. Ever heard of them?"

"No, but then I haven't exactly kept up on the social circles of the South. What about that guy who came in on the stage this afternoon?"

Hank shrugged. "He took a room over at the Union Belle. Registered as Zachary Kittle."

"So he's not Addie's brother?"

"Nope. Leastways it doesn't look like it, though I ain't asked her outright. Mavis said Kittle claims to be looking for a place to set up his business. Says he's a dentist."

Travis nodded. "Okay." He clapped Hank on the back. "See you later, but let me know if you find out anything else from her. Especially about this Kittle guy."

Magnolia Rochelle entered the Mountain Queen just as Hank was about to exit. She made her way through the crowd to Travis.

"I think you've stolen all the business tonight, *mon cher,*" she said, her tone suggestive. She pressed herself between Travis and another man at the bar, leaning toward Travis so that the plunging neckline of her emerald satin gown offered him a tempting view of her voluptuous assets.

Travis smiled and chucked a finger under her chin. "Ah, Maggie. I know you're flirting, but are you sulking, too?"

She gave him a sultry pout. "Perhaps *mon cher*, but not because of business."

He looked toward the stage, fully aware of both her meaning and her jealousy. "Things will get back to normal in a few days, Mag."

She turned to follow his gaze. Yes, she thought, things will definitely get back to normal in a few days, *mon chere*, but not for Miss Suzanne Forteaux. She will find her world very different. Magnolia smiled, but her eyes remained as cold as a winter gale as they settled on Suzanne. Very different indeed. She turned back to Travis, and her gaze instantly warmed. "Why don't you come to the Lady later, *chéri*? It has been too long, you know?"

Travis sighed. He wanted things to get back to the way they had been: simple and forthright, no commitments, no expectations. That's how he lived his life, how he wanted to live his life. He looked from Magnolia to Suzanne, and back to Magnolia. He feared going back to the way things had been just wasn't going to happen. He had no desire to share Magnolia's bed, or any other woman's for that matter, except Suzanne's.

He nearly cursed aloud, catching himself only a second before the words left his lips. After Suzanne was gone, after she left Virginia City and went to wherever it was she was going, he would forget about her, and the gnawing ache to hold her, to taste her kisses and her passion again would subside. Then things would go back to the way they had been. They would. He'd make them, damn it. He'd make them.

Travis was suddenly aware of Magnolia's hand sliding

over the front of his shirt in a seductive and flaunting caress. She was looking up at him from beneath a thick ruche of dark lashes, her eyes as caressing as her hand. He clasped her fingers and drew her hand from his chest. "It *has* been too long, Maggie," he said softly, "but I've got some things to do tonight. I'm sorry."

"Things?"

"Things," he confirmed. He leaned down and brushed his lips lightly across her cheek. It wasn't her fault things had changed between them. "Maybe tomorrow night, Maggie. We'll talk."

From her position on the stage, Suzanne smiled down at the audience, but her eyes watched Travis. She saw him bend down and kiss the woman standing before him. A pang of jealousy stabbed at her heart. She tried to concentrate on the song she was singing and flounced her way across the stage. Tom Lowry caught her eye and winked. She smiled back, wishing it was Travis who had just flirted with her. She turned to sashay back to the center of the stage, and as she did, her eyes strayed back to the end of the bar, but neither Travis nor the woman were there.

Suzanne continued on with the show because she had to, but her heart was in despair and her eyes just wouldn't quit veering to the end of the bar where Travis usually stood. Yet each time she looked over there, she found her sadness deepening. Finally, by the end of her first performance of the evening, her lips issuing the words to the songs automatically as her mind dwelt on Travis and her heart felt as if it were breaking, she found herself forced to confirm the accusation that had been swirling in the back of her mind for days: she had once again played the fool.

As the miners screamed cheers, Suzanne smiled and bowed, and then hurried off the stage before they could see the tears that had begun to fill her eyes. She stepped into her dressing room and hastily closed the door behind her.

Suddenly something flew into her face, momentarily plunging her into darkness and throwing her into an instant state of hysteria. She shrieked, clawed at the dark fabric and flung it aside.

"Hurry up and change into that riding habit," Clarence ordered. He settled himself on the settee and glared up at her. "Well," he snapped when she merely stood still, trying to calm her thudding heart and slow her breathing. "Hurry up."

Dumbfounded, Suzanne looked at the garment she'd just thrown to the floor. Her brown riding habit, along with a white blouse. Her boots stood next to the chair of her dressing table, her gloves lay on the table itself. She looked back at Clarence. "What are you talking about? I can't go riding, I have another show to do in an hour."

Clarence's eyes turned mean. "Get that damned riding habit on, Suzanne," he repeated. "Now."

She didn't move. "Why?"

Moving with lightning speed, he shot up off the settee and grabbed her arm, his fingers bearing down like steel claws upon her bare flesh.

She winced and tried to jerk away as his impeccably manicured nails dug into her skin.

His hold remained strong. "Change!" Clarence ordered. "Unless you want me to do it for you."

Suzanne glared at him, their eyes level. "Try it and you're dead."

Her challenge hung in the air between them. Finally, Clarence sat down. "Fine, don't change. Don't cooperate. It's up to you, really. But I thought you truly cared for your brother."

All resistance fled Suzanne at the mention of her brother, replaced by resignation at doing what Clarence ordered. She sighed. "Where are we going?"

"You don't need to know that," he snarled. Both his tone and his demeanor were uglier than ever, and rather than merely being repulsed by him, as she usually was, Suzanne felt a shiver of fear.

Ten minutes later, after she'd changed into the riding habit as he'd ordered, Clarence ushered her out the back door of the Mountain Queen. They moved quickly past the rear of the buildings until reaching Taylor Street, but rather than turn left to go toward the hotel, Clarence forced her in the opposite direction, toward the Mountain. Then at B Street, they turned again and headed south.

"Where are we going?" Suzanne asked again.

Clarence still had a firm hold on her arm. "To do a little last-minute business."

Suzanne felt her fear escalate. Was he involving her deeper into his schemes? "What kind of business?"

"Never mind. Just do as you're told, Suzanne. And just in case you have an urge not to, remember our deal."

She threw him a scathing glare, nearly tripped on the boardwalk, and turned back to pay attention to where she was stepping. "Where's Brett?" she asked.

"All in good time, my dear," Clarence answered. "All in good time." He steered her into the door of a general store.

Suzanne looked around, confused. Ben Morgan was slouched against the counter talking with a man who was either the owner of the store or a clerk. Hank Davis, Travis's saloon manager, was sitting in a chair by a metal stove. He was leaning back casually in the chair and had one foot propped up on a nearby crate of potatoes. She felt the waves of heat the stove sent throughout the small, crowded store. Two men she didn't recognize stood near an apple barrel in one corner. Another man, one she'd seen in the Queen several times but didn't know, stood near the window that looked out onto the street. She looked back at Clarence. "What's going on?"

"Never mind, Suzanne. All you have to know is that in order to find your brother, you'll do as I say." He half urged, half pushed her into the room, then released his grip on her arm. "Where's Braggette?" Clarence demanded of Hank.

The saloon manager remained seated, and silent, his only movement that of his half-smoked cigar shifting from one corner of his mouth to the other.

"Right here," Travis said from behind Clarence.

Both Suzanne and Clarence whirled around, each startled for different reasons. Suzanne hadn't expected to see Travis there, and Clarence didn't like his enemies coming up behind him.

Travis stood in the doorway, the blackness of night at his back, the soft glow of the room's lone lantern and the fire in the stove at his face. Suzanne's gaze roamed over him hungrily. He was dressed entirely in black— boots, trousers, jacket, and hat—except for his shirt, which was, as always, a pristine white. His trousers were pulled taut by leather *sous pieds*, the already snug fit revealing long, lean, yet muscular legs.

Suzanne shivered, remembering the feel of those legs entwined with her own.

The jacket was cut broad at the shoulders, tapered in over the chest, and in further to follow the narrow breadth of his waist. It flared again as it hung over his hips and ended midthigh. But it did not hang straight now, at least not on the right side where the front of the jacket had been pulled aside and draped behind the gun that was settled comfortably in its holster, giving Travis easy and quick access to the weapon.

Suzanne's eyes moved to his face. The lower portion was cast in the light of the lamp, while his eyes remained shrouded within the shadow created by the brim of the black hat that was pulled low onto his forehead. Small silver conchos decorated a thin strip of black leather that encompassed the hat's crown.

Travis stepped into the room and she felt his eyes on her. The air fairly bristled with tension.

"Is this everyone?" Clarence asked him.

Travis paused before Suzanne. Fury reflected from every line of his face, and his eyes, now that she could see them, had turned near black, cold and hard.

"What're you trying to pull, Lonchet?" he demanded of Clarence without taking his gaze from Suzanne. "What's she doing here?" His voice was harsh and demanding.

"She's a Knight," Ben Morgan said from the other side of the room. "And our partner."

Suzanne saw the small flicker of surprise that registered in Travis's eyes at the comment, but knew no one else had. It was a lie, of course. She wasn't and never had been a member of the Knights, or Morgan and Clarence's partner, but she couldn't explain that now. She turned her gaze away. Anyway, what did it matter whether she could explain or not, if Travis knew the truth or not? Nothing had changed between them, except that she had allowed him to make love to her . . . twice. Seven years ago he had been the first man she had ever kissed. Now he was the first who had seduced her. He was also, she knew now, the only man she would ever love.

"Since when is a woman Knight allowed to go on a mission like this one?" Travis asked. "Women are for spying and transporting information. Not for participating in robberies."

Any other time Travis's chauvinistic attitude would have brought about her own fury and indignation, but not now. This time Suzanne would have been more than willing to be relegated as unfit to participate with "the men." She practically held her breath and waited for Clarence to answer.

"Since I say so," Clarence said.

"Women mess things up," Travis retorted. He turned his stony gaze on Clarence.

"Sorry, Braggette, but on this one I have to insist, *if* we're going to go on with this. Suzanne is my partner, and Morgan's, of course. What we're involved in, she's involved in. That's it. If she doesn't go, neither do we."

Travis felt like reaching out and grabbing the man by the throat, circling his scrawny little neck with his fingers and squeezing the breath from him until he turned purple. Or his eyes bugged out. Or he popped. Or all three. But Clarence Lonchet was saved from annihilation, or at the least near suffocation, when Travis's attention was drawn from him as Jed walked through the entry door into the store.

"Got Pete minding the Queen," he said. His gaze went immediately to Suzanne, then back to Travis. He swore softly. "We're going to have trouble, Boss, if Miss Lindsay ain't there to sing her last act. The boys are all hepped up over hearing her one last time."

Travis threw Clarence a pointed, threatening look.

The man fiddled with his spectacles and turned away.

"Olmer," Travis said to the store clerk. "Get down to the Queen and tell my bartender to have Lottie go on stage and sing." He turned back to Clarence. "If my place gets damaged, Lonchet, because of your little shenanigan, I'll take the repair expenses out of your hide."

"Okay, so fine," Morgan bellowed from across the room, "let's get going, huh?"

"Yeah, I ain't got all night," one of the men piped up.

Travis looked at Charlie Mellroy and again the urge to strangle swept over him.

"What's your plan?" Clarence asked Travis, jerking his attentions back to the matter at hand.

"We're riding down to Devil's Gate. The ore wagons should come along just about one. We'll hide at the base of the pass, that way we're in the shadows and the drivers won't spot us until we step into the road. Suzanne, here," he glared at her, "can stand back in one of the canyons and mind our horses."

"You arrange for pack mules?" Clarence asked.

"Better," Travis said. "I've got several wagons waiting in Gold Hill and a stagecoach in Silver City. We'll drive the ore wagons to Gold Hill and transfer the rock there, then you three . . ." his gaze darted from Clarence to Suzanne to Morgan, "can unload your shares there and take the stage to wherever it is you want to go. I'm assuming one of you can drive a coach?"

"I can," Morgan said.

"Good, then we're set."

"And where will your men be?" Clarence asked. "If Morgan and I are at the base of the pass."

"On the top, covering you. Just in case any of the drivers decides he doesn't want to part with his wagon."

"And you?" Clarence said, clearly suspicious.

"Right beside you, my man," Travis answered, and smiled. "Right beside you."

"If there's shooting, you know we won't get those wagons away before someone comes to see what's going on," Clarence said.

"There won't be any shooting, Lonchet. At least not from my boys," Travis countered. He turned to look at Hank. "Show him," he ordered.

Rolling easily from his seat by the stove, Hank rose to his feet. At the same time, one hand reached into the top of his knee-high boots and pulled out a knife. Its highly polished silver blade gleamed wickedly against the light. Turning, Hank drew his arm back and, throwing it forward, released the knife. It zinged across the room quicker than anyone's eyes could follow it. The next thing they knew, it was protruding from the thin oak frame that encased a glass display on the counter behind Morgan. The knife was a mere two inches from Morgan's arm.

He jumped aside, his eyes wide, then looked at Hank. "You coulda killed me," he accused.

Hank smiled and walked across the room toward Morgan. He grabbed the knife's handle and pulled its metal tip from the wood. "Yeah, I could of, Morgan, if I'd wanted to."

"The point is," Travis interrupted as Hank and Morgan glared at each other, "if any of the drivers look like they're going to be trouble, Hank and Jed there can take them out with no one hearing."

"He's that good with a knife, too?" Morgan asked, turning to look at Jed.

Jed's hand moved slightly and a silver blade zipped through the air and struck the edge of the counter to Morgan's right, half an inch from his hip. At the thud it made upon impact, Morgan jumped aside again.

"Son of a bitch," he snarled.

"Answer your question?" Travis asked, smiling smugly.

Chapter Twenty-nine

"So what do you think they're doing?" Addie whispered.

Zachary Kittle dropped the tiny binoculars from his eyes and shook his head. "Well, Miss Hayley, I'd say they're planning something, but I can't really see much. Too dark."

"How many do you think are in there?"

"Well, there's your friend Miss Lindsay and her manager, and Mr. Braggette for sure. And that bartender fellow that just went in with Braggette." He lifted the binoculars to his eyes again. "From what I can see, which isn't much, I'd say there are at least four or five others in there with them." He began to lower the binoculars again then stopped. "Wait, I think they're leaving the back way."

"Our horses are tied up around the corner," Addie said. "Come on, we'd better hurry."

"No, wait," Zachary ordered. "We want to make certain they don't realize we're following them. Let them get mounted and on their way first. They can't travel too fast in this darkness." He looked up at the moon, only a sliver in the sky, as if to confirm his words.

Addie threw Kittle a disgusted look. The agency sends her on one of the most important assignments of her life and when she asks for help, who does she get? Zachary Kittle! She fumed. He was the best the agency had to offer. The best! Once this thing broke, no one would even know she'd been involved in the case. All they'd remember was that Zachary Kittle had been on it. Zachary Kittle had broken it.

"All right, come on," Zachary said, breaking into her musings. "We'll follow and watch, but that's all we can do tonight."

Addie felt a jolt of shock. "Watch?" She stared up at Zachary who had risen while she remained kneeling. "They're going to rob the ore wagons, and all you want to do is watch?" she whispered harshly.

He stared down at her as if looking at a small child whose brain had yet to develop any logic. "Yes," he said simply.

Addie scrambled to her feet. "Why? If they really are going to rob the ore wagons, why don't we arrest them after they do it? Or better yet, *while* they're doing it. Isn't that why were here? To prevent any more robberies? To stop the Confederacy from getting any more gold and silver?"

Zachary sighed, obviously not used to having to explain himself. "I don't want to get myself killed tonight, Miss Hayley, if that's all right with you." He glanced back at the general store, now empty. "There are at least half a dozen men involved in this, plus your Miss Lindsay. There are only two of us. I don't particularly like those odds."

Addie sniffed. "Well, I don't *particularly* relish watching a crime being committed while I sit by and do nothing about it."

"Miss Hayley . . ." Zachary started.

"Don't call me that. My name is supposed to be Hays," Addie snapped.

"Fine. Then, Miss Hays, will you please. . . ."

"Mr. Kittle," Addie rebuffed, "I don't know why you were sent here, but I was sent to not only watch over Miss Forteaux, or rather Miss Lindsay, but to check out Clarence Lonchet and Ben Morgan. They are suspected members of the KGC and very deadly. In fact, *in case you didn't know,"* she said sneeringly, "we believe them responsible for several events of sabotage against our government that have ended in numerous deaths. Not to mention quite a few gold and silver robberies in various mining towns across the West. They've also been involved with the passing of information that has resulted in two battles in which the Union has lost to the Confederacy, battles with extremely high casualties, I might add."

"I am quite aware of that, Miss *Hays.*"

"And you're going to just stand here and watch them pull off another robbery?"

"Those are my orders."

"Well, they're not mine." Addie turned and stalked toward their horses.

"Yes, they are," Zachary said, following her.

Addie whirled. "Says who?"

Zachary pulled a folded piece of paper from the inside breast pocket of his jacket and held it out to her. "Mr. Lincoln."

Addie stared up at him.

"Well, Miss *Hays*," he said finally, grabbing the reins of his horse. "Are you coming?"

"What for? The robbery will probably be over by the time we get there, and if we're not going to do anything about it, why go? I'd rather spend the night in a warm bed."

"My orders are to verify who is involved in these robberies, Miss Hays. *Who*. And I can't very well do that standing here arguing with you."

"I wasn't arguing."

"You could have fooled me."

"I doubt that's too hard to do," she shot back. Ohh, she'd taken such an instant dislike to Zachary Kittle that just talking to him made her want to scream.

He'd already mounted and now glared down at her. "If you'd rather not come and observe the proceedings, Miss Hays, that is perfectly all right. I'll just put in my report that you felt it unnecessary to accompany me in following the suspects and retired for the night instead."

Addie grabbed the reins of her horse and rammed a foot into the stirrup. "Oh, I'll just bet you'd love to do that, wouldn't you, Mr. Kittle?" She pushed off the ground and, throwing her leg over the horse's rump, settled into the saddle. Good thing it was dark so no one would see a "lady" riding astride. "All you men are the same," she grumbled. "Can't stand it when a woman proves she can do a job just as well your kind."

"Contrary to what it seems you believe, Miss Hays, I would not relish putting anything derogatory about you in my report. You seem to be an agent who shows considerable promise."

Her jerked around and she glared hatefully at him. "Promise? Promise? Why you pompous, overrated . . ."

She stopped before issuing the very unladylike curses that were prancing through her mind.

"Let us go, Miss Hays, please," Zacharay said, "before the robbery is thoroughly completed and we're able to witness nothing." He pulled his horse away from the hitching rack.

Addie stared at the rear end of Kittle's horse, fury heating her cheeks. If she'd had something to hit that horse's rump with, she would have, as hard as she could, and sent both the horse and the conceited Mr. Kittle dashing hell-bent for leather on their way back to Washington.

Kittle reined in and looked back at Addie. "Miss Hays?"

She smiled sweetly. "Coming, Mr. Kittle."

Travis urged Starhawk up beside Suzanne's mount and forced the animal to match his gait to that of her horse. "What in the hell are you doing here, Suzanne?" he whispered, anger steaming from each word. She was supposed to be back at the Mountain Queen giving the miners her last performance, safe and uninvolved in the robbery.

"I could ask you the same question," she retorted. "I must say, Travis, you had me fooled, with all that talk about me being a fool because of my involvement with the Knights. And here all the time you're their leader in Virginia City. Hah! And striking a deal with Lonchet and Morgan." She shook her head. "Lord, I really am a fool."

"Suzanne, stop that," Travis hissed. "It's not like that,

but I can't explain now. Turn your horse around and get back to town."

"I can't."

He looked at her through eyes narrowed with anger and suspicion. "What do you mean you can't? Just do it."

"Suzanne," Clarence said, riding up on the opposite side of her and using her real name in front of Travis for the first time, "when we get to the pass, I want you to stay with me."

"She'll stay with me, Lonchet," Travis growled, leaning forward to look past Suzanne.

"Well, I really don't think, under the circumstances, that's a very good idea, Mr. Braggette."

"She'll stay with me," Travis repeated.

"Oh? Well, certainly," Clarence said, then smiled and shrugged. "If you wish."

Travis didn't like what he was hearing. Why was Lonchet suddenly so agreeable? And why did he want Suzanne and Travis near each other? The answer came to him almost immediately. Because the man planned a double cross, that's why. A double cross that would leave no witnesses behind. Travis's right hand moved slowly from where it lay casually on his thigh to rest on the handle of the gun that sat snugly in its holster. His thumb instantly found the hammer as his fingers closed around the handle, and his index finger slipped to curl around the trigger. He pulled back the hammer.

"I just thought," Clarence continued, and smiled widely, "I'm used to protecting Suzanne and, well, this could be dangerous and you might have other things on your mind."

"You'd be surprised how many things my mind can

handle at the same time, Lonchet," Travis said. "You just make certain you take care of your part and do what you're supposed to do."

"Certainly, certainly." Clarence reached over and patted Suzanne's hand. "Just stay back, my dear, out of sight and everything will be fine."

"Why did you make me come, Clarence?" Suzanne asked, determined to ignore his false concern.

"Yes, Lonchet," Travis said, startled at her words. "Why did you bring her along? Feeling like a song?"

Clarence gave Suzanne a hard, long look before answering. "Because I thought it necessary," he said finally. Nudging his horse, he moved away from them.

"I don't like this," Travis said.

"That makes two of us," Suzanne said softly.

"Stay close to me, Suzanne."

"Why? What's going to happen?"

"Just stay close. Real close. Can you handle that horse if he spooks?"

"Travis, what's going—"

"Can you?" he demanded harshly.

"Yes."

"Good. Then stay close and stay ready."

"For what?"

Suzanne had no sooner said the words than Devil's Gate loomed up before them, its craggy rocks jutting high above the road on each side to create a wall through which the road passed. It was a natural ambush site if ever Travis had seen one, and it had been used for exactly that purpose numerous times already. In fact, it seemed surprising to Travis that the miners continued to travel through it, but then, what choice did they really have. It was the only road that led down to Gold Hill and Silver City, and then on to Carson City. The only other routes out of Virginia City were in the opposite directions, one north, one east. The road north was a winding, cliff-ridden road that led down to the tiny valley town of Fuller's Ferry. The road was dangerous enough in the daylight, but after dark its curves and twists were deadly, even with a full moon. The eastern road was Six Mile Canyon and took a traveler miles out of his way into the desert if Carson City was his destination.

Travis chanced a quick glance toward the top of the pass, and then to each side. If Morrow and his men were there, they'd hidden themselves well. If they weren't there, the sheriff had better be long gone from Virginia City or Travis would see him locked in his own jail cell, permanently. He swung around and looked back at Hank.

The saloon manager nodded that he was ready.

Travis glanced at Jed, riding on the other side of Suzanne.

Jed felt Travis's gaze, returned it, and cocked his head slightly, indicating that he, too, was ready.

Travis nudged Starhawk and the horse bolted forward.

Suzanne followed Travis's motions.

They reined up beside Clarence. "Okay, you take your men and position yourselves over there. And there." Travis pointed to each side of the pass. "Stay well back in the shadows where you can't be seen until the wagons are nearly at the pass, then ride out in front of them so they'll stop."

"And where will *you* be?" Clarence asked.

He pointed back to an area they'd just ridden past.

"My boys and I will hide in the curves of land over there. The wagons will roll right past us and then we'll ride out behind them. That way, they're pinned in. You and your men in front, us in back."

"No."

Travis looked at Lonchet. "No?"

"No. I want you and Suzanne by me."

"Look, Lonchet, if you had a problem with this plan, you should have—"

"I would have," Clarence interrupted, "if you had told me the details of our attack before. You two stay up here in the shadows with me, or no deal. My men and I, and Suzanne, of course, will just ride on out."

Travis sighed. Lonchet was throwing him a curve, but there wasn't much he could do about it now except hope that Morrow and his men could tell the difference between him and Suzanne and Clarence and his men if any shooting started. "All right, we'll stay with you."

Clarence smiled. "Good." He wheeled his horse around and headed for the spot Travis had indicated.

"Travis," Suzanne whispered, leaning toward him, "do you have a plan to get us out of this?"

"I certainly hope so. But I'd still like to know what the hell you're doing here."

Suzanne closed her eyes for a long second, and then, taking a deep breath as if to summon the courage to go on, turned to Travis. "When the war broke out, my brother Brett joined the army."

"Suzanne!" Clarence yelled. "Get over here!"

She looked quickly at Clarence then back at Travis. "He left the Army a little over a year ago and joined the Knights. For a while he only did local things for them. Then, nearly ten months ago, they sent him on some kind of secret mission and we haven't heard from him since. Nothing. Not even a letter. Clarence told me if I—"

"Boss," Hank said, moving up beside them and interrupting Suzanne, "I hear the wagons coming."

Travis looked back at Suzanne and reached out to squeeze her hand. "Stay close to me," he said.

She nodded.

"Take your positions," Travis whispered harshly to the others. "The wagons are coming."

Everyone scurried to take their assigned posts.

Travis positioned Suzanne between himself and the rocks of the cliff, both remaining mounted, as did the others.

Clarence pulled a small handgun from beneath his vest.

Only a weak cast of moonlight lit the road, but it was enough to discern the ore wagons from the surrounding blackness as they followed the winding trail and neared the pass. It also helped that the driver of the first wagon, following Travis's instructions, had a lit cigar in his mouth. Its burning tip was like a tiny beacon of orange fire piercing the night.

"Remember, Lonchet," Travis whispered. "No shooting unless they start it."

"Hold it right there!" Clarence called out. He nudged his horse, and the animal walked into the road, blocking the wagon's path. Olmer Clancy moved into the open beside Clarence.

"Stop the wagon!" Ben Morgan bellowed. He and Charlie Mellroy moved from the shadows of the other side of the pass and into the road.

The driver of the first wagon pulled on the reins and

the mules halted. "This a robbery?" he asked, and threw the cigar down to the ground. That was the sign for Morrow. The wagon drivers immediately jumped down and scurried to hide under their wagons.

"All right, Lonchet, Morgan!" Sheriff Morrow yelled from his position high atop the rocky cliff of the pass. "Throw your guns down. You're under arrest."

For one brief, all too short second, no one moved. Silence hung heavy in the air, tension high. Then suddenly, with a low hissing curse, Lonchet whirled around in his saddle to face Travis and Suzanne. "You did this," he accused Travis. "You double-crossed me." He pointed the gun at Travis's heart.

"No," Suzanne screamed, and lunged forward.

Clarence pulled back on the trigger.

Chapter Thirty

Travis grabbed Suzanne's arm and jerked her toward him, and down. She felt her shoulder ram violently into the horn of the saddle and her hip slam against its crest. The pain barely registered in her mind, but the bullet whizzing past and slamming into the cliff behind her clearly did.

She screamed.

Suddenly, gunfire erupted all around them.

Travis pulled his own gun, but when he rose in his saddle and looked up, Clarence Lonchet was nowhere to be seen. He turned to Suzanne. "We've got to get out of here!" he yelled. "Get to cover."

Suzanne nodded, pain and fear having stolen her voice.

Travis grabbed the reins of her horse and, with a well-placed and sharp kick to Starhawk's ribs, urged the horse to bolt forward. The animal obeyed instantly.

Clarence rose from behind a large rock. As Travis and Suzanne passed, he lifted the rifle in his arms and took aim at Suzanne's back, then, his hatred nearly overwhelming him, switched his sights to Travis.

A bullet struck the rocks behind him, sending small shards of grit spraying out around him, but Clarence ignored it.

"Stay down, Suzanne!" Travis yelled.

Suzanne hunched forward over the saddle, hugging the horn and hanging on to it for dear life.

"Suzanne! Hurry!" Addie jerked her own weapon up from the concealment of her riding skirt and took quick aim.

Zachary Kittle, with a reputation for being cool under fire and always in control, looked at Addie in speechless shock. "A Savage .36 Navy revolver with a shoulder stock and long-range sight," he whispered to himself in surprise.

Addie pulled the trigger, and a roar from the gun filled the air around her and Kittle just as Clarence began to squeeze the trigger on his gun.

Suddenly, something slammed into his chest. His finger snapped down on the trigger of the rifle, but the shot went wild as the weapon jerked upward and flew from his hand. He crashed against the rock wall at his back. Pain, blinding, piercing, all-consuming, filled his chest, his arms, his entire body. He clutched at his shirtfront and felt wetness, then slouched forward and fell onto the rock he had been hiding behind, his right cheek smashing down upon the rough surface. The pain lessened, replaced by a numbing coldness that moved over him steadily, rapidly, followed by a creeping blackness. It began to well up from the outer reaches of his mind and sweep through his consciousness.

"Damn you, Travis Braggette," Clarence whispered raggedly as he felt his life slipping away.

Within minutes, Sheriff Morrow and his men, along

with Hank and Jed, had overpowered Ben Morgan, Charlie Mellroy, and two others Charlie had brought to help in the robbery. Silence hung heavy over Devil's Gate again.

"Okay to go on now, Sheriff?" the driver of the first freight wagon asked. He and the other drivers had returned the moment the shooting had ceased.

"Sure, go ahead," Morrow answered. "Couple of my deputies will see you on down to Carson, but you shouldn't have any more trouble tonight."

"Don't expect so," the driver said. He climbed up onto his wagon and waved for the others to follow suit.

"Okay, let's get these boys back to town and bed 'em down in a cell," the sheriff said. He glanced toward Clarence's body. "Guess this one can go in a box."

"Well, that's just great," Zachary Kittle snipped, looking down at Addie. "You've just killed the one and only person we might have been able to get enough information from to infiltrate the KGC."

Addie stared up at him angrily. "What would you rather have had me do, Kittle? Let him shoot Suzanne Forteaux or Travis Braggette in the back?" She stood, momentarily putting herself above Kittle as he remained hunched down.

"It wouldn't have been as big a loss."

"Oh!" She glared at him in disgust.

"Ah, hell, I didn't mean that," Zachary said. His mouth drooped with guilt. "It's just that I've been trying to find a way into the KGC for two years now, and I thought this was going to be our break."

"You've still got Ben Morgan."

Zachary shook his head. "Morgan was muscle, not brains."

Addie looked down at him. The man was uglier than a turkey vulture and his tactics definitely weren't to her taste, but he was a good agent, reputedly one of the best, and maybe not quite as horrible a human being as she'd thought. Though she wasn't willing to bet any money on that just yet.

Then she remembered Hank. Her eyes darted down to the road below and, squinting hard to make him out in the faint moonlight, was finally able to breathe a sigh of relief to see him standing and unhurt. She hurried down the hillside toward him.

"Addie?" Hank said, shocked to see her there. Then he noticed the gun still clutched in her right hand.

Her eyes followed his and she suddenly realized she was still holding her weapon.

"What the hell's that thing?" Hank asked. He looked back up at her. "And just who are you anyway?"

Addie smiled sheepishly.

"Don't answer that," Zachary Kittle said, moving up to stand behind her.

"And just who the hell are you?" Hank growled.

Addie moved quickly, slipping her free arm around Hank's and steering him over to the side of the road. "Hank," she said softly, "I think we need to talk."

"Are you all right?" Travis said anxiously, helping Suzanne down from her mount. "You're not hurt?" His insides had been in a turmoil ever since he'd walked into Olmer's General Store and saw her there. He'd been terrified she'd be hurt, caught in the middle if the shooting started, and that's exactly what had happened. But then, he had a sneaky suspicion that's exactly what Clarence Lonchet had planned. His eyes traveled over her quickly, examining every inch of her body, looking for anything out of the ordinary—torn fabric, a wound, a bloodstain.

"I'm fine," Suzanne said, sliding down the saddle and to the ground.

As Travis realized that she was, indeed, unscathed, relief swept through him, followed instantly by a wave of outrage that she'd been there in the first place. "All right, good." He released her and, jamming clenched fists onto his hips, glared down at her. "Now, tell me, just what in the damn Sam Hill were you doing, going with Lochet out there?"

Pete stepped through the swinging doors of the Mountain Queen. "Everything go okay, Boss?"

"Yes," Travis snapped. He kept his eyes pinned on Suzanne, not even bothering to glance toward Pete.

"Well, okay, good," the bartender mumbled, looking uncertainly from Travis to Suzanne and back to Travis. "I guess." He turned around and disappeared back into the saloon.

"I asked you the same question, Travis, if you'll be so kind as to remember," Suzanne snapped back, her nerves so frayed and frazzled she was beyond being scared, relieved, or thankful. "And I don't recall *you* answering me."

He glared down at her for several long seconds, then, with a moan deep from within his throat, his arms slipped around her waist and he yanked her roughly to him. "You little fool," he whispered into her hair. "Do you know how frightened I was for you? That you'd be hurt?"

Suzanne clung to him, wanting nothing more than to remain in his arms for the rest of her life. "Oh, Travis," she said. "Oh, God, Travis, I was so scared."

His hands grasped her upper arms tightly and he pulled away from her again, his eyes having resumed some of their hardness. He didn't want to talk. He wanted to hold her, kiss her, make love to her, but things weren't over yet, not until he knew the truth. All of it. "Damn it, Suzanne, you could have gotten yourself killed by going with Lonchet. You could have gotten us both killed."

"But, Clarence—"

"Suzanne," Travis said, holding a tight rein on his patience. "Tell me what's going on. Tell me the real reason you came to Virginia City, the reason you were with Clarence Lonchet, and why you're singing in saloons in the first place. I want to help you, Suzanne. I *will* help you, but you have to tell me everything, all of it, from the beginning."

She shook her head, and he saw the tears that filled her eyes. "I can't. If I do . . ."

"Clarence is dead, Suzanne. He can't hurt you any more."

"But there are others. There's . . ."

"Trust me, Suzanne," he said softly, moving a hand to her cheek, "Tell me, and we'll face whatever it is together. I promise."

She looked up at him, past the tears, past the darkness of night, past all the hurt and anguish of the last seven years, to see the only man she had ever truly loved, the only man she knew she would ever love. She had tried so hard to forget him, to hate him for leaving her, but she had never quite succeeded.

She nodded. "All right."

Travis took her hand and led her to the edge of the boardwalk. Rather than enter the saloon, they sat down together on its street steps, side by side, the fingers of her right hand entwined about the fingers of his left.

"Now, tell me," he said softly. "All of it."

Suzanne took a deep breath. "When the war started, my brother, Brett, joined the army, but it didn't last long. My father convinced him to leave and join the Knights of the Golden Circle. My father is a member and convinced Brett that he could do more good for the cause through the Knights than with the Army. I think he was just afraid my brother would be killed in battle."

Travis nodded. He wasn't unfamiliar with the reasoning. Thomas Braggette had been dead by the time the war had officially started so that rationale hadn't been used on any of the Braggette siblings, not that they would have listened to a word their father had to say anyway. But, when he'd been in New Orleans for his brothers' weddings and the war had broken out, he'd heard that same type of reasoning used, sometimes successfully, on a few of his friends and acquaintances. And maybe in some cases it was true that the men could further the cause, help the Confederacy more by being involved with the Knights, or one of the other organizations like it, than the Army. But surely not in all cases. Travis knew that only too well. Most of the members of the Knights were good men, honest men, but there were some, like the late Thomas Braggette, who saw membership only as a way to accomplish their own wants and needs. A means to profit off of the misery or loss of others.

"I've heard that reasoning," Travis gave voice to his musings.

"Yes, well, Brett joined the Knights. Father thought they'd give him some simple tasks to start off with, around New Orleans."

"But they didn't." It was more a confirmation to her statement rather than a question.

"No. I mean, yes, I mean, well, we're not sure." She closed her eyes and remained silent for a second, then, taking a deep breath, opened her eyes and began again. "He did do a few things around home, though he wouldn't say exactly what they were. Not even to Father. But if he was gone on a mission, it was only over-night, so we didn't worry all that much."

"And then he left and didn't come back?" Travis said.

"Yes."

He heard her rasping intake of breath and knew she was fighting not to break down into tears.

"He came home one afternoon very excited and said he'd been given an important assignment and would be gone for a while. That's all he would say. Father tried to reason with him, get him to at least tell us where he could contact him if an emergency arose, but he wouldn't say. Brett swore that his mission was top secret and he just couldn't tell us anything."

"How long ago was that?"

"Ten months."

"And you haven't heard from him since?"

"No. We assumed he'd be gone for a few weeks. When that time passed and he didn't return, Father said maybe the assignment the Knights had given Brett was more important than he'd thought and thus it would take more time. Several months passed, and still he didn't return." Suzanne turned to Travis. "And he didn't even write, Travis. Not one letter in all this time. We don't even know if he's alive." She nervously fingered the ruby ring Brett had given her so long ago.

"Do you have any real reason to suspect he isn't?" Travis asked. "Other than the fact that you haven't heard from him?"

"Well, no, but not even a letter, Travis, to let us know he's all right. That's not like Brett." A tear fell from her left eye and snaked its way downward over her cheek.

"And that's what you're doing now? Trying to find him?"

"Yes. My mother and father are panicked. In fact, in the last few months my father has. . . ." Her voice broke and she paused. "Oh, Travis, I know you hate him because he conspired with your father to force us to marry, but. . . ."

Travis squeezed her hand gently to encourage her to continue. "That's in the past," he said gently. "Go on."

She took a deep breath and went on. "Father's health has declined terribly. He's convinced Brett is dead and that it's his fault. Father has nearly fallen apart."

"*Your* father?" Travis exclaimed, unable to believe what she'd just said. Landon Forteaux had always been a man of strength, both physical and mental. Trying to picture him as anything else seemed to Travis nearly impossible.

"Yes. I haven't seen him in several months, but he was terribly underweight when I left and Mother's letters say he's getting more debilitated." She looked at Travis, her eyes imploring him to understand. "He's so worried about Brett that he hardly ever eats. He picks at his food, stays up most of the night wandering the halls, or sitting in his study smoking and staring out into the darkness." She shook her head. "He went to everyone he could, men who were top officials in the KGC, and no one would tell him anything. That's when he became convinced Brett was dead. He's handed the running of the plantation to our overseer, and Mother has been forced to handle the accounts because Father just let them pile up and ignored them."

"That doesn't sound like your father."

"It's not, but he's just sick with worry over Brett, and he blames himself for talking Brett into joining the Knights." Suzanne wiped a new onslaught of tears from her cheeks. "I had to do something, Travis. I just couldn't sit by and watch him fall apart like that. Or let my brother disappear without a trace."

Travis held both her hands tightly within his. "So how did you get involved with Lonchet?"

She sighed. "I knew several gentlemen in New Orleans who were members of the KGC. I spoke with them, but they offered no clues. Then Clarence contacted me. I didn't know him, had never heard of him, but he said that the situation had been brought to his attention. He said the Knights had discussed it and decided that if I would do a few things for them, they would bend their rules and see that we received information about my brother."

"And what were those few things?"

Suzanne shrugged. "Singing in these saloons. And passing those envelopes."

"That's it?"

"That's it."

"Except that all the while you were innocently passing those envelopes, they were making certain that if anything went wrong you were the one the authorities would be led to."

Suzanne remained quiet.

"Has Ben Morgan ever shown up before?" Travis asked. "At any of the other towns?"

"Yes, a couple of times. And if it wasn't him, then it was someone else. Clarence always met with someone."

"And in each town you've sung in the saloons and passed notes to other men?"

"Yes."

"And these towns, they were all mining towns?"

"Yes," Suzanne said again.

"And when you were there, singing, there were robberies? Of their ore wagons?"

"Yes," she said softly. She stiffened in realization. "I suspected what Clarence was doing." She shook her head then. "No, I knew. I just didn't want to admit it to myself. All I wanted was for Clarence to tell me where my brother was. I didn't want to know what he was doing, or what I was doing. But each time we were ready to leave a town and I asked about Brett, Clarence always said that I wasn't done yet, that I had one more town to go to, one more 'mission' to finish first."

Travis nodded.

"And I couldn't refuse, Travis. I couldn't, not without getting the information about Brett."

"What was tonight, Suzanne?" Travis asked. "Why were you there tonight?"

"Clarence came to my dressing room at the Queen after my first show and said I had to go with him. But he wouldn't tell me where. When I asked, he refused to say, and when I objected, he threatened not to tell me anything about Brett."

Travis sighed. The odds were good that Brett Forteaux was dead and Clarence had been using Suzanne's desperation to find her brother as leverage to get her to do his bidding. But he couldn't say that to Suzanne, not without knowing for certain that he was right.

Suzanne turned her gaze toward the night sky. "I've been such a fool," she said softly. She turned to look at him. "I'm sorry, Travis."

The catch in his throat as his gaze met hers prevented him from answering immediately. For days he had been denying what his heart had been trying to tell him, but he couldn't, didn't want to, deny it any longer. He had turned away from her love once, but fate had given him another chance, Suzanne had given him another chance. She was his world, his home, and if he hadn't known it before, he knew it now, with more certainty than he'd ever known anything.

"No, *I* was the fool," he said, his voice as soft and soothing to her frayed nerves as a caress of rich, warm velvet across chafed flesh. His arms wrapped around her and pulled her into their embrace. "For not realizing earlier what you mean to me."

Suzanne looked up at him, her face a conflict of emotion. Fear for her brother, his safety, glistened in her tears, while the hope of a life of love and happiness with Travis shone in her eyes.

He touched his lips to each of her cheeks, wiping away her tears with his kisses, then brushed his lips across hers in a light touch that left her aching for more.

"I never thought this would happen to me, Suzanne,"

he said, his deep voice husky and raw as it filled with emotion.

She remained silent, sensing it was the time to listen, not talk.

"I love you, Suzanne. I love you more than anything in the world, more than life. I should never have left you, but I was young then, angry with the world, with my father, and all I wanted was to get away." He brushed his lips across hers again. "Forgive me, Suzanne."

At his words her heart felt as if it suddenly had wings, as if all burden, all sorrow and unhappiness had just been lifted from her shoulders. She wanted to laugh, to cry, to snuggle within his arms and stay there forever . . . but she couldn't. She'd wanted to hear his words for so long. She'd dreamed them hundreds of times, prayed to hear them, and now that she had . . . Tears filled her eyes again.

"I want you to stay here with me, Suzanne," Travis continued. "I want you to marry me, and live here with me in Virginia City." Not until he actually said the words did he realize how desperately he did want that. "I know it's not New Orleans, Suzanne, but . . ."

"I . . . I can't, Travis," she whispered finally, both her voice and her heart breaking on the words.

Pulling away from her only far enough so that he could look down into her face, Travis frowned. "Can't?" he asked, his voice suddenly hard and edged with suspicion. "Or won't?"

A fresh onslaught of tears filled her eyes, fell over her lids and streamed down her cheeks. "I love you, Travis," she said softly. "I've always loved you, but I can't stay here." She pulled away from him and rose to her feet, turning her back to him and crossing her arms tightly over her breast. "I came here in search of my brother." She put a hand to her mouth, covering it, to prevent the escape of a sob that filled her throat, then, swallowing hard, she forced herself to continue. "I can't give up on him, Travis. I have to keep going. Until I find out . . ." her voice broke again, "one way or the other."

Travis stood and moved to her, pulling her into his arms. They remained there, on the boardwalk before the Mountain Queen, for a long time, one holding to the other, each consumed by their own thoughts and desires, their own hopes, unknowing that they were one and the same.

Travis closed his eyes against the moonlight, against the reality of the world, against the tears that threatened to spill over his lids and stream down his cheeks. Seven years ago he had defied his father and run away, rejecting Suzanne in the process. Now she had proved to be the one woman he could love, truly love. He had a second chance with her, and damn it, he wasn't going to lose it, not for anything.

Magnolia stood behind the lace curtain of her bedroom window and looked down at Travis and Suzanne. She watched them kiss, then embrace, and as they did, her hands clenched into tight fists. Her long nails pressed viciously against the tender flesh of her palms, every muscle in her body taut with fury, every cell instilled with the fire of rage and jealousy.

Her eyes bore into Travis, as if willing him, ordering

him, to turn and see her behind the French lace, but he did not, and her wrath deepened.

He had ruined everything. Everything! They could have had it all, she and Travis, but he had rejected her for Suzanne Forteaux. Hatred glistened, hard and cold, from Magnolia's eyes. It had been a mistake to bring Lonchet here, with his little protegée. She could see that now, but how was she to have known that rather than seeking revenge against Travis, the girl still loved him. And, obviously, he loved her. Magnolia fumed. Her plan had been perfect, except for that unknown but important fact. All the girl was supposed to have done was keep Travis preoccupied and make certain he was at least loyal enough to the South that he wouldn't get in the way of an operation by the Knights that was supposedly to help the cause. That was all. Magnolia had specifically chosen Suzanne because of what had happened between her and Travis in the past, because she felt confident that Suzanne would not try to take Travis away from her. She was supposed to play with him, that was all. Not fall in love with him again.

Magnolia felt an urge to kill them both. She eyed the small derringer on the dressing table next to the window. Beside the gun lay her card. A small white calling card with a gold circle engraved in its center. Yes, she could do it, and they'd find a way to protect her, she knew they would.

She smiled. If she killed Suzanne, Travis would come back to her. She turned back to the window, but Travis and Suzanne were no longer on the boardwalk.

Magnolia began to pace the room. Once her plans for disposing of Suzanne were complete in her mind, her thoughts returned to the other events that had shaped the evening and ruined all of her plans. Everything had gone so smoothly, why did it have to turn wrong now? Duncan Clyde had recognized her that first night they'd robbed him. He'd looked up at her on the hill where she'd sat, mounted on her horse and watching everything, and even though it had been dark, she'd known he recognized her. So she'd ordered him killed, and thought that was the end of it. They had changed their mode of operation, but then Clarence had gotten greedy. The fool. She might love Travis, but thankfully she hadn't trusted him. She had only narrowly escaped capture by the sheriff's men at the pass, but at least Lonchet was dead, and he was the only one who could connect her with the robberies. He was the only one who knew she was a member of the KGC, the only one who actually got his orders from her.

Magnolia smiled. Everything was going to turn out just fine after all.

Chapter Thirty-one

The sun was barely peeking over the horizon when Travis walked into the sheriff's office. He'd left a still upset but completely exhausted Suzanne at the hotel, fast asleep. "Mrs. Beale said you had Liam clean out Clarence Lonchet's room last night, along with Ben Morgan's."

"That's right," Sheriff Morrow said, looking up at Travis from behind his desk.

"I want to have a go through Lonchet's stuff."

"I already have. Ain't nothing there I can see that any relatives would even want. Some clothes, a watch worth maybe a five piece, and his spectacles."

"Where is it all?"

"You looking for something specific?" Morrow asked, eyeing Travis suspiciously. "Like maybe something you wouldn't want me to see? Something that might tie you in with Lonchet?"

Travis sighed in disgust. "Sheriff, you ever heard the expression 'about as useful as a four-card flush'?"

"I ain't a gambling man."

"Well, think about it, and how it applies to you,"

Travis said. He was tired and he was desperate, and he had no patience left to deal with Kurt Morrow. "Now, damn it," he growled, "where's Lonchet's stuff?"

"Over there." The sheriff pointed to a table in the corner of the room.

Travis immediately moved to the table and began sifting through the things piled there. Saddlebags. He tipped them upside down. Empty. A small brocade satchel had been packed with a pocket watch, shirt studs, and several pairs of spectacles, along with the man's underwear. Travis opened a larger satchel and dumped its contents onto the table. Several shirts, another suit, four cravats, and a pair of highly polished shoes. But an inside pocket revealed more. He pulled out a billfold and opened it.

"Well, well, well," Travis murmured.

Sheriff Morrow, lounging in a chair at his desk, suddenly became alert. He jumped up and walked to stand beside Travis. "What? You find something?"

Travis held up a card he had pulled from Clarence's billfold. "Recognize this, Sheriff?" he asked.

Morrow looked at the card and frowned. "No, not really." He scratched the back of his head, causing his hat to slip lower down on his forehead. "Should I?"

Travis looked at the card again and smiled. It was white, with a golden circle engraved in its center. That was all. No words, no numbers. Nothing. Just the gold circle. "Care to guess?" he asked the sheriff.

"What the hell is it, Braggette?" Morrow thundered, losing what little tolerance he possessed.

"It's the calling card of a Knight."

"The KGC?"

"Yes, but not just any Knight. Only officers are issued these cards."

Travis pulled out several more cards that had been in the billfold, looked at each and then tossed them onto the table. Finally, he came up with a very thin notebook. "Ah, what do we have here?" he muttered.

Travis looked at the pages in the notebook, scanning them slowly. The scribbles were messy, obviously written in a hurry, or by a man whose handwriting was the worst he'd ever seen. And it was code. Travis was certain of that. "Sheriff, you got a piece of paper and a quill?"

"Yeah, in Liam's desk drawer. Why? What're you doing?"

"I just want to write down a few things." Travis retrieved the paper and quill and then settled himself at the absent deputy's desk. Ten minutes later, he'd figured it out. Lonchet's code hadn't really been that difficult to decipher, but then, Travis had also been a member of the Knights and had been familiar with most of the codes they'd used. Necessity had kept them simple. It had merely been a matter of figuring out which one it was Lonchet was using to chronicle and keep a record of his activities and missions.

Travis sat back in the chair and stared down at Lonchet's small journal. At least he could tell Suzanne where Brett had gone. That lifted his spirits and his hopes, but a more recent entry deeply disturbed him. He rose to his feet and turned to the sheriff.

"You ready to do your duty again and finish this thing?"

Sheriff Morrow looked up at him, clearly puzzled. "Finish? I thought it was finished."

Travis shook his head. "There's one more person out there you need to put in your jail."

"Yeah? That little book told you that?"

"Yes."

"Who is it?"

"The one who was in charge of this whole damned robbery attempt. The one who really took over the Knights here when Judge Terry left."

"Not you?"

Travis frowned. "No. Sorry to disappoint you again."

"Who then?"

Travis turned toward the door. "Magnolia Rochelle," he said over his shoulder.

Travis walked across the lobby of the Union Belle Hotel. He nodded to Mavis Beale, wished her a wonderful day, and took the stairs to the second floor two at a time. Several long strides brought him down the hallway where he paused before Suzanne's door. He knocked, then held his breath, praying that she was there.

The door opened almost immediately and Suzanne stared up at him. She had on a traveling suit.

Travis looked over her shoulder and past her into the room. Her satchels were packed and placed on the floor near the bed, waiting to be taken downstairs.

"Travis, I was . . ." She had to stop for fear of breaking down.

"Leaving?" he supplied.

She nodded.

"To continue looking for Brett?"

She looked back up at him, tears glistening in her eyes, and nodded again. "I have to."

He clasped her shoulders and gently urged her back into the room. With a backward thrust of his foot, he closed the door. "Suzanne, leaving you was one of the most foolish things I have ever have done, something I'll regret for the rest of my life. I didn't know then how much I could love you."

"Travis, please," Suzanne said. "It's no good, not now. I have to find—"

"No, Suzanne, listen to me, then if you still want to go, I won't stop you."

She nodded, though listening to him was tearing her apart. She wanted nothing more than to stay with him, to walk by his side for the rest of her life, feel his arms around her every night. She wanted to be his wife, to bear his children, to grow old with him, and die with him. But she couldn't stay. She'd made a promise to her father and mother, a promise to herself, that she would do everything in her power to find Brett, and she had to keep that promise, no matter what. She couldn't live with herself if she didn't.

"Suzanne, I love you. Nothing means anything to me if I don't have you to share it with. You have my heart. Maybe that's why I never fell in love with anyone after leaving New Orleans, maybe I always loved you and I just didn't know it. But I know it now, Suzanne, and I'm not taking no for an answer. I need you, Suzanne. I love you, and I want you to marry me."

"Oh, Travis . . ."

He silenced her with a finger pressed gently to her lips. "I said I wouldn't stop you from going." He smiled. "I lied." He pulled the notebook from his pocket. "Clarence had this in one of his satchels."

Suzanne frowned, not understanding.

"It's a journal of his missions with the Knights, of all his activities."

He flipped it open to August 20, 1861, and turned it so that Suzanne could see the page. She frowned.

"I know you can't read it, Suzanne, because it's in code, but I can."

She stared down at the unintelligible scribblings, suddenly afraid. "What does it say?" she whispered.

"It says that on August 20, 1861, Clarence met Brett Forteaux in San Francisco. That he handed Brett an envelope he had been handed by another Knight, higher up than himself, and instructed Brett to deliver it to the Confederate Ambassador to England."

"Brett's in England?" Suzanne said, gasping with surprise. She looked up at Travis with eyes filled with hope.

"It would seem so."

"Oh." Suzanne threw her arms around Travis's neck and hugged him to her, then just as promptly released him and stepped back. A wide smile curved her lips and fresh tears glistened in her eyes. "Ask me again, Travis," she whispered. "Please."

"Marry me, Suzanne," Travis said, taking one of her hands in his. "Marry me, and I swear I'll help you find Brett and make certain he's safe."

Suzanne pulled her hand free of Travis's and, pressing her body to his, wrapped her arms around his neck again. "I love you, Travis Braggette," she whispered softly, looking up into his gray eyes. "I have always loved you and yes, I will marry you." She stood on tiptoe and brushed her lips across his. "But this time you'd better show up at the altar."

Turn the page for a sneak preview
of the third book about the
Braggette family,

HEARTS DEFIANT
by Cheryl Biggs,

an August 1995 release.

Chapter One

Late June, 1863

"Who are you?"

Startled, Traynor spun around at hearing a female voice. The commandeered map he held in his hands, showing a detailed sketch of the Mississippi river with its marked sankbanks, fallen trees and low water points, was momentarily forgotten. His eyes widened in further shock at the sight before him. She was no more than five-foot-three, with a mane of fiery red hair that cascaded down over her shoulders like a veil of crimson silk. Green eyes that could rival any emerald stared at him contemptuously.

Traynor stiffened at the haughty question, to say nothing of her presence. Judging from that, the clenched fists she'd propped on her hips, and the frown that creased her brow and pulled delicately arched red brows together she was obviously very upset.

But then, so was he. Traynor's dark brows delved into a slashing V across a forehead marred by his impatience. "Me?" he managed finally. His voice took on a more authoritive, commanding tone. "Who the hell are you?"

"I asked you first." She crossed her arms tightly across her breasts and glared at him. Moonlight shone at her back, sprinkling the wavy strands of her long red hair with sparks of gold while the lamplight of the pilot house fell on her face. Its soft glow lent a golden cast to her ivory skin.

The combination of her beauty with the oil and moonlight gave her an almost ethereal quality and forced Traynor to blink, hard, to make certain he wasn't seeing things. He didn't need this. He really didn't. Not now.

"Answer me," she demanded when he didn't respond, and she stamped one foot on the floor.

Traynor's temper, which had been simmering for the past few days, flared instantly at her tart words and sassy gesture. Ever since he'd received his mother's note, he'd found controlling his temper harder and harder to do. He had no time to fool around with word games or tempermental females, no matter whether they were beautiful vixens or ugly old crones. And this one was definitely not an ugly old crone.

He crumpled the map in his hand and thrust it at Brett Forteaux, who stood just behind him in the small pilot house. Swiping a hand through the ragged locks of his black hair, Traynor turned an impatient eye back to the woman. "I am General Traynor Braggette of the United States Army, and commander of this gunboat. Now, I don't know who you are, Miss, or how you got on board, but. . . ."

"You are not the commander of this gunboat."

"Oh-oh," Brett muttered under his breath.

Traynor ignored his best friend's soft exclamation. The woman confronting them might not look like a crone, but she definitely had the barbed tongue of a snake. And Traynor was of the opinion she had a personality to match. He decided to try and remain calm and use reason. "Look, miss, I really don't have time for this nonsensical chatter. My crew and I are on an important mission."

Her eyes narrowed. "How did you get on this boat?"

Traynor ignored her outburst. "Now, I don't know who you are or how you came to be onboard the Bayou Queen. . . ."

"*I* belong here."

His fingers itched to circle her pretty neck. "As I was about to say," Traynor growled through nearly clenched teeth, "I'm going to have to put you off at the next port. I can't be responsible for your safety, and you're certainly not safe with. . . ."

"I've never heard of a General Traynor Braggette," she interrupted. "Where was your last port, sir?"

Green eyes glared into gray, cool emerald defiance meeting hot volcanic mist.

"Who do you report to, General Braggette?" She thrust forward her chin. "Who's your superior officer?"

Traynor could feel the tight rein he had on his temper slipping further. He did not like snippy women. He especially did not like snippy women when they stood in his way. And when that way was trying to save his older brother Traxton from a hangman's noose, he *really* didn't like snippy women. Even if they were beautiful. And even if he hadn't been with a woman in so long his body was turning into a raging inferno just at her nearness. Lord knows, his physical needs had to be worse than he thought if his traitorous body was beginning to crave this little shrew-tongued harridan. "I really don't have time for this, Miss. . . ."

"Colderaine," she snapped haughtily. "Miss Marci-lynne Colderaine. But you can call me Miss Colder-aine."

Traynor reached out to take her arm, intending to steer her out of the pilot house. "Fine, *Miss Colderaine.* At the next port we come to we'll. . . ."

Marci whipped her arm away from his grasp. "Keep your hands off of me, Mr. Whoever you are." She grabbed onto the doorjamb and dug her heels into the floor. "Now, I demand an answer, and I'm not moving until I get one. Who are you, sir, and what are you doing on my brother's boat?"

"Your brother's bo. . . .?" Traynor nearly choked on the words and felt an instant sinking sensation in the pit of his stomach.

Before he could reply, he was interrupted by Brett fighting to keep his attention on maneuvering the steamboat around the curve of the river. He uncapped the exchange pipe and, cupping one hand around its end, bent forward until his lips were only a hairsbreadth from the pipe. "Give us more coal, Charley," he yelled into the metal tube as the river straightened out before them. Brett gave the huge mahogany wheel a quarter turn and the Bayou Queen maneuvered deftly around a partially hidden sandbar. "Damn, that was close," he mumbled, then yelled into the exchange pipe again, "More coal, Charley. We need more speed."

"Where's my brother?" Marci demanded, not having taken her eyes from Traynor at Brett's interruption. "What have you done with him? And his crew?"

Traynor tried to hedge. "Ma'am, really, I don't know what. . . ."

She cut him off. "Where are they? Where's my brother? I didn't see anyone onboard I recognized when I came up here." Marci peered past Traynor's shoulder. "And who's that man steering the boat? That's not Lieutenant Ephraim."

Traynor felt a moment's panic. Their plan had seemed so simple when they'd decided on it, so workable; pretend to be Union officers and crew on a special, highly secret mission for Lincoln. Commandeer one of the Yankee gunboats moored around Memphis, go downriver to the Yankee's camp near Bridgeport, Mississippi and save his brother Traxton's damned neck. Simple. Until now.

The one thing he hadn't counted on was running headlong into a fire breathing, red headed, Yankee dragon lady. He took a deep breath in an effort to calm himself. He couldn't let anything go wrong. It was up to him to save Traxton. Trace was off somewhere on a mission for Jefferson Davis, and they couldn't be certain the message their mother had sent had even reached him. Travis was in Nevada and would never get to Traxton in time. Traynor fought to remain calm. "Miss Colderaine, as I was saying; my crew and I are on a very special, very dangerous mission. We commandeered your brother's ship. . . ."

"Boat," Marci corrected haughtily.

"Boat," Traynor repeated, grinding out the word. A string of curses unfit for even the coarsest ear danced through his head. He could almost feel the note he'd received from his mother several days before burning a hole through his inside breast pocket and searing his chest. It had taken several days for the letter to get from New Orleans to Fort Fisher, where it had sat several more days waiting for his blockade runner to arrive from Bermuda with his load of supplies. Another day had passed as Traynor arranged everything and two more were spent getting from Fort Fisher to Memphis. They were getting closer, but not close enough. Time was running out, and so was his patience. According to his mother's note, they'd received word that when Vicksburg fell to the Yankees, his brother, Traxton, would be hanged. From all accounts of the way Grant was pounding on the city from both land and river, the city's defeat could occur at any moment.

Her eyes remained piercing, lips tight, hands balled into fists.

"I commandeered your brother's *boat,* Miss Colderaine, because it was my prerogative and authority to do so." The words snapped from his tongue like the flick of an overseer's whip. "As I have been explaining to you, my men and I need to get to Bridgeport as soon as possible, and the Bayou Queen happened to be in the right place at the right time." Which is more than he could say for her.

"So where's my brother?"

"The Queen's commander and his men debarked in Lockspur, a few miles upriver from Memphis."

"I know where Lockspur is." She stamped her foot angrily on the planked floor. "Why didn't someone wake me up? All I wanted was a ride to Memphis to visit Salle May Rhinehart, so if we were there, why didn't anyone wake me?"

Traynor glared at Brett, noticing the smile he tried to hide, and then looked back at the minx who was

handing him an unexpected dollop of trouble. He had
the momentary thought that perhaps Commander
Colderaine had known all along that he and his men
were Southerners masquerading as Union men and had
purposely left his sister on board. A new kind of enemy
punishment, perhaps. "I'm sorry for the inconvenience,
Miss Colderaine," Traynor said. "Truly. I believe your
brother had just put in to dock when my men and I arrived and handed him the orders to relinquish his vessel.
Perhaps he hadn't time to wake you, and in the
hastiness of transferring the boat to me, he simply forgot
about you." Traynor made a mental note to track down
the man and bury his fist in his face once they'd saved
Traxton. Maybe the blow would enhance his memory
and save some other poor soul from an encounter with
Miss Colderaine.

"Well, if he did forget about me, I can assure you it
will never happen again."

"I'm sure," Traynor said.

"Oh, yeah," Brett whispered behind him.

"Be that as it may," Marci quipped, "you'll just have
to turn the Queen around and take me back to Memphis. I'm already overdue at Salle May's as it is."

"Much as I wish we could take you back, Miss
Colderaine," and Lord knew, that was true, "I'm afraid
it's just not possible."

Marci's eyes suddenly blazed with renewed fury and
indignation. "Do you know, General Braggette, if you
really are a general, that I am a second cousin of Mary
Todd Lincoln's? You have heard of Mary Todd Lincoln,
haven't you?" she challenged arrogantly. "The President's wife? Mrs. Abraham Lincoln—the First Lady?"

"Miss Colderaine, I said I was sorry," Traynor practically thundered, the rein on his temper snapping soundly. And he was sorry—sorry he hadn't picked another boat to commandeer, sorry he wasn't the kind of man who would pick her up and toss her overboard.

"I could have your rank for this, sir," Marci retorted. "One word to my cousin, just one word, and. . . ." she snapped her fingers in his face, "just like that, you could be a foot soldier again."

"I never was a foot soldier," he growled softly.

"Then you could have a new experience."

A vein on Traynor's temple began to swell slightly. "We cannot turn around, Miss Colderaine, and unfortunately, we cannot stop to let you debark elsewhere, though believe me, I wish we could." The words were rapier sharp, cutting, and cold. "Now, if you will please excuse yourself and return to your cabin. . . ."

"Wonderful. You're sorry, and I'm stuck on a boat going on a secret mission. Most likely to some little hole—in—the—wall town no one's ever heard of and no one cares about. Just what I've always wanted to do." Slivers of gold color flashed in her eyes like sparks of fire. Lifting her chin insolently she looked down her nose at him, as much as she could considering he towered at least nine inches above her. "But I still don't know who you really are, sir?"

Traynor cursed silently. It would be such a simple thing to just drop her over the side of the boat. But with his luck she'd probably float and be waiting downriver with a patrol unit to overtake them. He hadn't been so vexed since . . . since . . . Oh hell, he didn't know when he'd been so put out at a woman. He forced a pleasantness back into his voice that he was far from feeling. "I told you, Miss Colderaine, I am General Traynor Braggette."

"And who do you report to, General Traynor Braggette?" Marci asked, her tone one of thorough disdain. "Who is your commanding officer? Your *direct* commanding officer?"

"I report directly to the president, Miss Colderaine," Traynor said, figuring that was the safest thing to say. He was a blockade runner, not a soldier, and as such he didn't have the faintest idea of who commanded who or what on land. Especially in the damned Yankee army. But obviously she did.

"The president?" Marci echoed and smiled slyly. "Really? How very unusual."

Traynor suddenly remembered that she'd just said President Lincoln's wife was her cousin. He saw the sly little smile that pulled the corners of her lips upward and knew instantly that his claim had been a mistake.

The smile widened. "You're lying, General. Or is it really General? Are you a Confederate spy, Mr. Braggette? Is that even really your name? Maybe its really Stuart." She laughed softly. "Are you the famous Jeb Stuart, sir? Or the devil himself, Forrest? Or maybe you're really that bothersome raider, John Hunt Morgan?"

Traynor cleared his throat. "Miss Colderaine. . . ."

"As the sister of one of the Union's top gunboat commanders, for whom I act as hostess, and since I am a resident of Washington, I believe I have met just about every high ranking officer the United States Army has to offer." Her eyes raked up and down him insolently. "And I can assure you, sir, that you are not one of them."

Author's Note

Virginia City, Nevada, during my growing-up years was like a second home to me, as it was the one place my parents insisted on spending at least part of their yearly vacation. And I loved it. I have seen some changes over the years with each of my returns, some good, some I'd rather not see, but the small mining city that sits perched on the side of Sun Mountain always retains her charm and spirit of the past.

Unfortunately, in 1875 a fire destroyed nearly the entire town of Virginia City. Although it was quickly rebuilt, grander and more elaborate than before, almost all of the records and pictures of what the town looked like before the fire were either destroyed or have disappeared, and only a few buildings survived that disaster. I have used as many of those surviving buildings, and some that didn't survive, in this story as possible. Also, the mines I have referred to in this book are authentic to that time, as well as the trails called Six Mile Canyon and a pass named Devil's Gate, and the U.S. Army outpost, Fort Churchill. The street names, too, are as authentic as research allows to that time, as is the locations of the red-light district and Nellie Sayers's saloon, reputed to be one of the worst dives in the city.

Any other structures referred to in *Hearts Denied*—the Union Belle Hotel, The Diamond House, the Mountain Queen, and Silver Lady—are of my imagination, although I hope I have managed to inject them with the flavor of the time.

Some of my characters were alive in Virginia City during the 1860's: Judge David Terry did reside for a while in Virginia City. He was deeply involved with the Southern cause and reputedly was Confederate President Jefferson Davis's choice of a governor for Nevada if the South won the war. In the early years of the war, Virginia City had a strong populace of Southern men and Southern sympathizers (as did California) and most rallied behind David Terry's plan to conquer Virginia City and use its wealth for the Confederacy. His involvement with the Knights of the Golden Circle is factual, as is their plans to take over Virginia City, and California. But the scheme in my book in which he partakes is strictly fictional and of my imagination. Judge Terry left Nevada in 1862 after it became obvious his plans would not work there, and traveled to Texas where his brothers resided, so that he could partake more strenuously in the Southern cause.

Julia Bullette was indeed a prostitute in Virginia City, though the date of her arrival in that city is in question. Julia was what they called a middle ranking prostitute, one step below the elite, which mainly consisted of high-class actresses and singers. She had her own "crib" (cottage) in the red light district at D and Union streets, just below the saloons, and was one of the most loved, and still celebrated, personalities of the town, due to her generous and kind nature and many charitable donations. She was made an honorary member of the VC Fire Company for both her donations and endless help at fires and her clients, and friends, numbered some of the most important men of the time. She was brutally murdered in 1867 by a French transient. Julia's funeral was one of the grandest and most well-attended Virginia City ever saw, though because of her profession her body was not allowed to be interred in the VC Cemetery. It rests on a small hillside below the town, surrounded by a white picket fence which is still maintained to this day.

As for the Knights of the Golden Circle, they did indeed exist, and were quite active in trying to help the Confederacy, including an attempt at smuggling silver and gold from Virginia City. The Knights were a secret society of men, and a few women, formed long before the Civil War as a group in support of annexing Mexico into the United States. With the outbreak of the Civil War, the Knights gave their allegiance and support to the Confederate cause. Many acts of sabotage and spying during the war were attributed to members of the KGC, but, to the best of my research, never proven. Betrayal of the Knights by a member, or revealing the identities of any of its members or its dealings or plans, meant a conviction of death from the KGC.

Ken and Stacy Ferguson did not own the Ophir Mine, thankfully, for they are my sons, and Tony Brassea did not live in Virginia City in 1862, again thankfully, since he is my father, and Johnny Dellos lives right here in California with me, as John D. Biggs, my wonderful husband. Their names were used as a bit of my whimsical fantasy.

I hope you enjoyed *Hearts Denied*, (the story of the Braggettes started in *Hearts Deceived* with Traxton and Trace's story, and the beginning of our mysteries) and that you will continue reading the story of the Braggettes with Traynor's story, *Hearts Defiant*, due for release in August of 1995, and Teresa's story, as well as the conclusion of the saga and reuniting of the family, in *Hearts Divided*, due for release in April, 1996. My previous releases include *Mississippi Flame* and *Across a Rebel Sea*.

Also, I have begun writing for Pinnacle using the pseudonym *Cheryln Jac*. My first release under that name was *Shadows In Time*, a time travel, in April of 1994. My second was *Night's Immortal Kiss*, a paranormal romance, in August of 1994.

And to all my readers: I love to hear from each and every one of you. I will send you whatever promotional materials I have, and put you on my mailing list, if you write to me and enclose an SASE at: P.O.B. 6557, Concord, CA 94520.